The Wings of the Wind

by Shaun Lewis

"He parted the heavens and came down; a dark cloud beneath his feet.
He rode on a cherub and flew; soaring on the wings of the wind."

Psalm 18, verses 9 and 10

Published by Hilary Clare Publishing
First published in 2020

OTHER BOOKS BY SHAUN LEWIS

They Have No Graves as Yet

and

The *For Those in Peril* series comprising:

The Custom of the Trade (For Those in Peril #1)

Now the Darkness Gathers (For Those in Peril #2)

Where the Baltic Ice is Thin (For Those in Peril #4)

In memory of Moira Eileen Lewis, who died in June 2019. An indomitable mother.

Chapter One
April 1912

The Norton 3½ had been built in 1911 and was so named because its engine offered 3.5 brake horsepower. This engine had a cubic capacity of 490 centimetres, giving the motorcycle a top speed of 68 miles per hour. Unlike its competitor manufactured by Bradley, this particular motorcycle did not incorporate Sturmey-Archer's newly-released three-speed gearbox. Such technical details are of no interest to most people, except the aficionado, but they mattered to Paul Miller very greatly. Before he leaned into the right-hand bend, he looked over his shoulder and noted with relief that he was opening a lead on his pursuer.

As he straightened the machine out of the bend, he opened the throttle and leaned over the handlebars to reduce the wind resistance. He remembered, too, to tuck in his elbows and knees. It was a spring day with busy birds chirping away, but all Paul could hear was the hum of his machine and the wind ruffling his cap and hair. He glanced down to the speedometer. Now he was on the straight again, he was accelerating. 50 miles per hour… 55… 58… time to brake and line up for the next bend. Better not be too hard on the brakes here, he thought. There's some mud on the road and I daren't risk a skid. He braked gently and lifted himself in the saddle to use his chest as a brake.

That was smooth, he thought with satisfaction. Full throttle again, head down, tucked up nicely. He wiped from his goggles some dead insects that seconds before had been flying as a cloud between the hedgerows. 'Don't look back again, Paul,' he muttered to himself. 'Darley Bridge is ahead and you need to concentrate. He won't be keeping up with you on these bends.'

As he approached the left-hand bend, Paul leaned to his left and grimaced with pain. He had taken the bend too tightly and caught his elbow in the blackthorn hedge. A flap of cloth from his tweed jacket flapped in the wind. *Mutti*'s going to give me hell for that, he thought.

Right, let's take this right-hander of the S-bend a little better. Lean over now, put out your right knee to take you round. Whoa! The bike's not taking the turn. She's under-steering and I'll be in the opposite hedge if I'm not careful. Ease the throttle a little. That's better. She's turning now. Perhaps I should have braked. Fine as you are now. Darley Bridge coming up. I daren't jump this one. I'll ruin my suspension. Here we go. Cut the power, brake hard, lean forward in the saddle and back down as we go over. Nicely done. Now open her up for the straight.

The speedometer needle quickly rotated clock-wise as the speed passed 50 miles per hour again. At 55 miles per hour the handlebars began to vibrate a little, but she was gaining speed. Paul risked a look over his shoulder and, as he had suspected, there was no sign of the other motorcyclist. He began to relax. He need not have worried. He was going to win this race, after all.

Half an hour earlier, he had not been as sanguine. Rashly, he had allowed himself to be pressured into a wager that his Norton could outpace the other rider's 1911 Humber on a circuit of the Lancashire Fells. Twenty pounds was not a sum he could afford to lose, despite Pops's generous termly allowance for his studies at Cambridge, but D'Arcy Crichton, second son of Lord Sedburn, the proprietor of *The Northern Messenger*, was such a swank and had goaded him into it. Crichton's machine was capable of a maximum speed of 70 miles per hour. A similar motorcycle had been used to win the Isle of Man Junior TT race the summer before. However, Paul had grown up at the nearby Marton Hall and knew the roads of the Forest of Bowland like the back of his hand. Moreover, he was confident he was the better rider.

Even so, he knew he should not have taken the bet. He was already in hock for half the coming Easter term's allowance. Modifications to his new motorcycle had cost more than he had anticipated and his wine bill had not helped. Paul felt his face flush, despite the 60-mile-per-hour wind, at the memory of the fearful row he had had with Pops over his first Michaelmas term's wine bill. Pops would skin him alive if he was to learn of his present impecunious state.

He couldn't see beyond the crest of the road ahead, but he knew he was near Howard's Ark. The road curved to the right immediately afterwards. No need to close the throttle, he thought. Just get as close to the edge as possible. If you're in the right place, the camber will take you round.

How he loved the thrill of motorcycles. That feeling of freedom and, above all, speed. There was danger, of course, and *Mutti* worried about him, but he knew he was good. It was an edge he had over his two elder brothers, not that his eldest brother, Richard, rode motorcycles. He was too pious for such fun. That said, Richard shared his bent for all things mechanical and Paul respected his courage for serving in submarines. In fact, although far too righteous, Richard wasn't a bad chap. He'd been quite helpful with modifying the motorcycle for racing, actually. Peter, just four years older, was more of a rival. Paul resented being called the runt of the litter by him. Admittedly, he had not inherited Pops's great height and was shorter than his two elder brothers, but at five feet nine inches he was hardly a pygmy.

Whoops. Concentrate on the road, Paul. You should have missed that drain cover. It nearly had you off the machine. Hang on a minute. She's losing speed. There must be something wrong with the fuel supply.

Paul coasted to the gateway of a field ignominiously and the engine cut out. He knew the defect could be any one of a number of things and he would have to trace and fix it as quickly as possible if he was to maintain his lead. Already he heard the drone of another motorcycle in the distance. It could only be D'Arcy.

Within two minutes, he had stripped down the throttle cable, just as D'Arcy Crichton hove into view. The other motorcyclist slowed down to a stop beside him.

'Having a spot of trouble are we, Miller?' Crichton asked with a smirk. 'You should employ a proper mechanic, you oily lout. That'll teach you. Just make sure you have my twenty pounds ready. I'll see you back at the pub.' Crichton didn't bother to await an answer and sped off into the distance.

'Pompous ass!' Paul shouted after the retreating Crichton's back. He realised it was a futile gesture and a waste of time. More happily, he had been right first time in his diagnosis of the fault. The throttle cable had kinked. It was a common enough problem on these winding roads, but why choose now to happen, he wondered ruefully. He quickly untwisted the cable and rummaged in his saddle bag for the tin of grease he always kept there. It could have been worse, he thought, but time was running out, nonetheless. Swiftly, thanks to much practice, but carefully, he re-greased and re-connected the throttle cable. Let's hope that's done the trick, he thought. He ran alongside his machine as he pushed it for a few yards, dropped the valve lifter and jumped into the saddle. Luckily, the engine came to life again immediately. This time, the throttle behaved itself and, after opening and closing it a few times, Paul was satisfied that his hasty repair had been successful. However, unless some calamity was to befall D'Arcy or his machine now, he would be a couple of miles ahead by now and sure to win… unless?

Paul turned his Norton around and headed back down the road he had just come. This side of Howard's Ark was a bridge across the River Hodder. The road on which he and D'Arcy were travelling followed the river, but the Hodder curved in two long loops. The track on the other side of the river, however, ran straighter, but it was not macadamised. It would save about three miles and that might just be enough to get ahead of the Humber.

Paul turned left across the bridge and, almost immediately, left again onto the track through the woods. The surface was rough and jolted him fiercely. Paul rode the Norton like a horse, using his arms and legs as his suspension, but even so, neither his body nor motorcycle could withstand a speed of much more than thirty miles per hour. It was going to be nip and tuck.

Five minutes later, he came out of the trees and caught sight of the Hodder again. To his amazement, he also saw a lone motorcyclist, on the opposite side and going in the same direction. From the distinctive yellow tank and the rider's black leather coat, it was obviously D'Arcy. He must have been coasting, thinking the race was already won. If D'Arcy didn't spot him, there might just be a chance of sneaking ahead of him at the junction the other side of the river. It was then barely two miles to the finish point at the Inn of Bowland. The track became smoother and Paul opened the throttle.

D'Arcy must have seen him in his peripheral vision as he suddenly accelerated and began to draw ahead. Paul opened the throttle further and felt he would be shaken off the machine if he was not careful, but his speed was still less than forty miles per hour. He didn't even look for D'Arcy as he leant into the left-hand bend to join the road across the bridge. Thinking only of avoiding an unpleasant encounter with Pops, he accelerated further on the approach to the bridge. He could see the junction on the other side and it was now neck and neck as to who would make it first. Now wasn't the time for caution. Without braking or any deceleration of speed, he hit the upward slope of the bridge and jumped it. Time seemed to stand still as man and machine hung in the air. Paul stretched upwards and braced himself for the fall to Earth. Within a split second, he was back on *terra firma* with a bone-shattering jar, but he let his knees and elbows go loose to absorb some of the shock and managed to keep his balance.

Immediately, he judged he had just about done enough. D'Arcy's relative bearing had drawn left and that meant Paul was going to reach the junction first. It would mean a sharp turn to the right, but he would be ahead of D'Arcy, now only yards away to his left. He positioned the Norton as close to the left-hand edge of the road as he dared and, in one movement, eased back the throttle and leaned far over to his right, almost grazing the road surface with his knee. His motorcycle drifted across the road into the junction, he saw a fleeting glimpse of D'Arcy flashing past just feet away and he was round.

There was no time for triumph, however. Just as he tucked himself in for the run home, he heard an ear-splitting scream and a terrific crash. His blood ran cold. It could only mean one thing and he braked heavily. Sure enough, looking back down the road, he saw that D'Arcy had come off the road and was lying near the bank of the river underneath his Humber, the engine still running and the rear wheel turning. D'Arcy needed help urgently.

*****

'Where's my son? I demand to see my son.' The burly, red-faced man towered above the petite sister on duty at the Preston Royal Infirmary.

'And who might you be, sir?'

'I'm his father, of course.'

'Yes, sir. I'd worked that out. Let's try again, sir. Who are you here to see?'

'My son. I've told you already. Come on woman. Don't dilly-dally further… Ah, I see what you mean. I am Lord Sedburn and I'm here to see my son, D'Arcy. I understand he is in a private room.'

The sister checked her list. 'Oh, yes. You must mean Mister D'Arcy Crichton. You're quite right. He's in a private room. His mother's with him now. Come this way, sir.'

Sedburn had barely had time to set eyes on the prone figure in the bed before his wife wrapped her arms around him. 'Oh, Archie. Thank goodness you're here. It's utterly dreadful.' Lady Sedburn burst into tears and buried her head into Sedburn's chest, but he cast her aside and knelt beside the bed. He was shocked by the paleness of his conscious son's face.

'D'Arcy my boy,' he took his son's right hand gently. 'Are you all right?'

D'Arcy smiled weakly and raised his head a little before speaking. 'I think so, Father. The surgeon seemed satisfied with the operation, leastways.'

'Operation?' Sedburn leaped to his feet and turned to the sister witnessing the tender family scene. 'What operation? How bad is it?'

'Your son has suffered a ruptured spleen, my lord. Mister Davies, the surgeon, is completely satisfied that there are no complications and your son will be well again in a few weeks. Your son was very lucky to have received prompt attention. There's nothing to worry about, sir.'

Sedburn relaxed visibly and turned again to his son. 'Thank God for that. But just what tomfoolery were you up to on that new motorcycle of yours?'

D'Arcy told the story of the wager and race, but not without several interruptions. He finished the tale with a request of his father. 'There is one thing you could do for me, Father. As I'm going to be laid up here for a few weeks, I'd like you to see that Miller receives the twenty pounds I owe him.'

A quarter of the Royal Infirmary heard Lord Sedburn's outburst and no doubt a few of the neighbours, too. 'Never! I swear it, never!' He spluttered with anger and began to choke. Lady Sedburn suddenly became more concerned for the puce colour of her husband's face than the state of her son's spleen.

D'Arcy took advantage of his father's temporary incapacitation to continue. 'Father, I lost that race fair and square…'

'Fair and square be damned! He caused your accident through his recklessness. And more than likely he cheated, too. He clearly took a short cut.'

'No, father. I was just as reckless in not giving way until the last second. And we never agreed a fixed route.'

'I won't hear of it, I say. It's sharp practice in my book. The fellow's obviously a cad. There's no question of settling the wager. Indeed, I've a mind to send the bill for your medical expenses to his people.'

Sedburn walked over to the window and clenched and unclenched his fists repeatedly. He turned around to face his son again. 'I'll tell you this for free, my boy. That Miller fellow has made a powerful enemy. I'll be finding out more of this young scoundrel and then I'm going to break him.'

Chapter 2
May 1912

Captain Ernest Grafton, the captain of HMS *Hibernia*, checked the wind speed and direction once again. His ship was a *King Edward VII*-class battleship, but since early 1912, she had looked like no other battleship afloat. On her foredeck, extending from atop the forward turret right up to the bows, had been built a strange-looking wooden ramp, fitted with rails. It had been transferred in April from the battleship HMS *Africa*, along with other aircraft take-off gear, for the structure was in fact a runway. With this extra equipment *Hibernia* had been transformed into an aviation trials ship and was about to rehearse an operation to be performed the following week in front of the King at the Naval Review on 9 May 1912. Also, on board for the trial were several members of the Press and a number of senior officers from the Admiralty.

The wind was only a light breeze and the slight waves, disturbing the blue-green sea, showed it to be blowing from west by north at about Force Two in strength. Grafton turned to one of his guests waiting patiently at the back of the bridge. 'Will that do for you, Sueter?'

Captain Murray Sueter, the newly appointed Director of the navy's new Air Department or DAD, following his experience with the development of airships, nodded.

'Very well,' Grafton replied and, turning to the lieutenant on his left, ordered, 'Officer of the Watch, I'm bringing her into the wind. Come right onto a course of zero-five-six and order revolutions for five knots.'

Sueter turned to his colleague representing the War Staff, Captain William Miller VC. Of all those on board the *Hibernia*, only Sueter would have known that Miller was in fact the Deputy Director of the Naval Intelligence Directorate. Sueter had once worked for him. At six feet four inches in height and with a powerful-looking physique, Miller stood out in a crowd. Although still dark-haired, his greying temples betrayed his age as being in his mid-fifties, a late age for a naval captain. His most striking feature, however, was his eyes. Deep set and almost black, those who met them often thought them hypnotic.

'That should give us a headwind of about ten knots for the launch, William. Ample enough for our purposes,' Sueter said quietly to Miller.

'So, you intend sticking to the term "launch" then, Sue, and not "take-off", like our army colleagues?' Miller replied.

'Naturally, we will,' growled Grafton in return. 'I fail to see why we should treat the damned things any differently from boats. The terms "launch" and "recovery" have served the navy very well for centuries.'

The Midshipman of the Watch, Kenny, noted in the bridge log the change of course as taking place at 16.30. Once the 17,000-tonne battleship settled on her new course, he took a fix using the bearings of the conspicuous landmarks of Portland to port on the Dorset coast. Kenny could not wait for the First Dog Watch to end at 18.00. He was under pressure. If he didn't complete his journal and submit it to the First Lieutenant before supper, then his leave would be stopped for a week on the ship's return to harbour.

Grafton checked that his ship had settled on the correct course, before handing over the responsibility for the bridge to the Officer of the Watch. 'Gentlemen, shall we go forward to see how arrangements are progressing for the launch?' He gestured for his fellow captains to precede him down the ladder from the starboard bridge wing.

'So, Grafton,' Miller asked. 'What's your view of this trial?'

'I'm glad my Executive Officer is not here to answer that, Miller. Like me, he's a gunnery officer and doesn't like to see the operation of the forward gun turret impeded by the ramp. Moreover, these aviation operations disrupt the ship's routine too much.'

'And how is that so?' Miller asked with interest.

'It's not the trials that grate. We're all used to the disruption they cause… and there have, naturally, been several delays to this launch caused by technical difficulties with the hydroaeroplane. It's the time it takes to range the machine and to hoist it outboard and back inboard.'

'The other factor,' Sueter cut in, 'is that the recovery of the machine can only be done when the ship is hove-to in a calm sea.'

'I see.' Miller was silent for a short while. Grafton interrupted his reflections.

'Don't misunderstand me. I'm in favour of this trial launch. It goes against the grain for our junior cousins, the United States Navy, to steal a march on the Royal Navy.'

In November 1910, the first launch of an aircraft from a ship had taken place when Eugene Ely, a professional test pilot for Curtiss, had taken off from the USS *Birmingham* at anchor off the Hampton Roads, Virginia. The feat had since been repeated from the *Africa*, but now it was hoped that the *Hibernia* would be the first ship to launch an aircraft from sea whilst underway.

'I will add, Sueter,' Grafton continued, 'I'm very impressed with your pilot for this trial. He even persuaded me to take a short flight in his machine.'

'Really?' Miller was all ears. 'That is interesting. And, as a gunnery officer, what were your impressions from this experience?'

'I was most impressed, I can tell you. The enhanced vision the aeroplane's height offers the pilot is amazing. The potential for reconnaissance is obvious and, as a gunnery officer, I can see a place for naval aviation in spotting for our gunfire. But you should listen to your young pilot's ideas for other uses, Sueter. He's full of them and has obviously given the matter considerable thought. They could be a godsend for hunting submarines.'

'I'm not sure Captain Miller wants to know that, Grafton. His eldest son is serving in the submarine flotilla.'

'No, Sue. I do. Please go on, Grafton.'

'Very well, Miller. I had not previously appreciated that from the air, although admittedly only in low sea states, the periscope of a submarine at periscope depth leaves a very obvious V-shaped wake or feather. These hydroaeroplanes can also spot mines in shallow waters. I still think I'd like them to operate from shore, though, and leave me free to fire my guns in peace.'

The three captains were now standing aft of the forward gun turret, from where they observed the men of the Air Department, all volunteers, ranging the specially-modified Short S.38 hydroaeroplane, designated T2, for launching. In fewer than two weeks these men would be members of the newly-constituted Naval Wing of the Royal Flying Corps. Only a year earlier, the maintainers had mostly been Engine Room Artificers or ERAs, but they had since undergone courses in aircraft design and servicing from Shorts, the aircraft manufacturers run by the three Short brothers.

The watching captains learned of a delay in preparing the aircraft so Grafton sent a message up to the bridge to stop the ship and allow her to drift in the calm sea. They were joined by a tall, dark, young officer with a fiercely-pointed beard.

'Ah, there you are, Samson,' Sueter called. Allow me to introduce you to Captain Miller from the War Staff.'

Charles Samson was to be the pilot for the trial. He had been serving in the Persian Gulf, hunting down pirates, before returning to England to commence flying training. He still retained his dark skin and Miller thought he looked much like a pirate himself. However, it sounded as if there was nothing swash-buckling about his approach to aviation.

'Good afternoon, sir. Flight Lieutenant… I mean, Acting Wing Commander… Charles Samson. How do you do, sir.'

'Samson has just been promoted and is to take command of the new Naval Wing a week on Monday,' Sueter added helpfully. He turned back to Samson. 'So, what's the delay?'

'Oh, just some rigging that needs replacement. It shouldn't take long. Perhaps half an hour.'

'Does it need your attention, Commander?' Miller asked.

'No, not at all, sir. The riggers are on top of the job. I'll just check over the repair before attempting the launch.'

'In which case, might you spare me a few minutes? I detect a fellow Lancashire accent. Where are you from?'

'Crumpsall, sir. It's part of Manchester now. Do you know the town, sir?'

'Sadly not. I come from nearer Lancaster. But perhaps we could take a turn about the deck. I would be interested to hear your plans for the development of the Naval Wing.'

Samson seemed flattered by the interest from a senior officer of the War Staff and readily agreed to walk with the captains around the upper deck of *Hibernia*.

'Just tell Captain Miller how you think the navy could use hydroaeroplanes as a new weapon system, Samson. You know – the sort of thing you've been banging on about since you gained your ticket.' Sueter patted Samson on the shoulder in a friendly manner.

'Very well, sir. I just hope I don't bore you. As I and a few of the other pilots see it, hydroaeroplanes are the perfect unit for reconnaissance. They can operate over the horizon to seek out the enemy or fly over a blockaded port to identify the enemy ships in harbour. Indeed, if we could devise a method for carrying and releasing bombs, we might even bomb the ships in harbour or their installations.'

'Do you think such flimsy machines could carry the weight of a bomb heavy enough to do any damage, Samson?' Miller interrupted.

'Well, maybe not just yet, sir. But, perhaps with a more powerful engine? Who knows? That's something I hope to work on later this year, by the way. For now, though, in talking to my fellow officers, it seems the main thing that is preoccupying them is the threat posed by submarines to our battleships and cruisers. Naturally, aircraft have immense advantages in searching out submarines both surface and dived. A submariner pal of mind has come up with an idea to attack the submarine, too.'

'Really? Captain Grafton mentioned how you might hunt submarines, but nothing about attacking them. My son who is serving in submarines will be mightily distressed to hear the devious way your mind is working. Young Richard and his colleagues seem to think the only things their blessed submarines have to fear are shelling and ramming on the surface, and mines beneath. Tell me how I am to shatter my son's complacency the next time I see him.'

Sueter turned to Grafton and added for his benefit, 'Captain Miller has two sons in blue. His eldest and youngest – now a cadet at Dartmouth. Do continue, Samson.'

'Very good, sir. This fellow, Williamson, reckons that if we could develop a fifty-pound bomb with a fuse designed to detonate twenty feet beneath the surface, then it would cause untold damage to a submarine. He calls such a bomb a depth charge.'

'I can imagine it would be a useful addition to the navy's armoury – if we could design an aircraft to carry it… And what is the purpose of today's trial, Sue?'

'The Air Department hopes that if we can prove it possible to launch hydroaeroplanes from the deck of suitably modified ships, then we can work on ideas to integrate aviation with the Fleet. Hydroaeroplanes embarked with the Fleet could be tasked by the admiral to provide a screen against mines, submarines or torpedo boats. The pilots could also serve as spotters to direct gunfire ashore. Samson even has the idea that, if fitted with a machine gun, his aeroplanes might attack enemy *Zeppelins* reporting the Fleet's position and manoeuvres.'

'My Lord. You chaps are imaginative. But how will you communicate with the commander at sea in real time,' Miller asked.

Samson answered. 'We can drop weighted messages onto the deck of a ship or communicate by aldis, but I grant that means the pilot must return to overfly the ship to make his report. As soon as the scientists can come up with a reliable and light-weight wireless telegraphy set we'll trial it. I've discussed it with the army already and will not rest until we've devised something suitable. If you're interested, sir, I'd be delighted to take you up one day to see for yourself the potential of aviation.'

'Umm – it's very good of you, I'm sure, but I'd rather not. I suspect I might suffer horribly from vertigo, so I'll decline your kind offer. But it sounds as if you have your hands full, Samson. Are you getting enough support from the Admiralty? I mean quite apart from Captain Sueter's Air Department. I don't mean to cause offence, Sue. I just know the difficulties.'

'None taken, dear chap. It's a good question. After the *Mayfly* disaster, my department was all but shut down. It's only thanks to the munificence of private donors that we still have an Air Department.'

'What do you mean by private donors? Surely the Admiralty still funds you, Sue?' Miller stopped still.

'Well, yes and no. We've now squeezed out enough funding for more machines and training of pilots. We've even managed to gain approval to rent ten acres at Eastchurch for use as an air station. Later in the year, I hope to gain approval for a site on the Isle of Grain from which to conduct trials on hydroaeroplanes. Bear in mind we had nothing to start, we're doing quite well, but we have relied overmuch on the generosity of outside parties. It was the Royal Aero Club at Eastchurch that got us off the ground.' Grafton and Miller groaned at the unintended pun. Miller recommenced his perambulation and the other officers followed.

'How was that? I mean the involvement of the Aero Club.' Grafton asked.

'One of the members, Mister Francis McLean, lent us two of his machines for training and his friend, George Cockburn, acted for free to instruct the first batch of naval pilots. We're now grateful to the Short brothers for their technical advice and assistance, and Horace has taken over the training programme. Do you know my assistant, Wing Commander Schwann, William?'

'I think I might have met him, but I cannot recall,' Miller answered.

'Well, believe it or not, he has even had to use his own aeroplane for trials with floats on water. The problem, William, is that there is no budget for experimental flying. Samson has been a marvel at persuading several enthusiastic officers to chip in funds from their own pockets, but frankly we are running on a shoe string.'

'My Lord. I thought the mandarins at the Foreign Office were stingy with my department, but this is far worse. Perhaps I might make a suggestion, Samson?'

'Certainly, sir. I've almost reached the stage whereby my chums avoid me. They're so used to me pushing around the hat.'

'I was discussing developments in aviation with Mister Churchill, our noble First Lord, a couple of months ago and he seemed quite taken with the project. You could do no better than inviting him to fly in one of your machines. He's a great enthusiast of new technology. I'd be happy to set up a meeting. I would also be prepared to offer some of my own funds to help you.'

'Why thank you, sir. That's remarkably generous…'

'So here you are, Samson.' The conversation was interrupted by the presence of the ship's Commander. He seemed quite irate. 'I've been looking for you for the past ten minutes, Samson. One of your artificers tells me that they've just about finished the repair and want you to check it over. Time is running on. With the weather forecast as it is, we must get you launched tonight. Otherwise there might not be another opportunity before the Fleet Review.' He turned to Grafton. 'Sorry to interrupt, sir, but I think you need to return to the bridge.'

'Thank you, Taylor,' Grafton replied and turned to Sueter and Miller. 'It looks like we'll have to break up the party. Please excuse me. It was a pleasure meeting you, Miller.'

'No problem at all, old chap,' Sueter replied affably on Miller's behalf. 'Charles here is, after all, the man of the moment and we should detain him no longer. Good luck, Samson.'

*****

Thirty minutes later, the engine of Samson's Short aeroplane initially coughed and then spluttered into life with a whiff of aviation spirit and castor oil. The ratings crouched alongside the machine on the ramp, struggling to retain their balance against the combined forces of the propeller's down wash and the ship's headwind. After less than a minute, Samson opened the throttle fully and almost immediately shouted against the wind, 'Let go all.'

As soon as the ratings released the aircraft's lashings, it surged forward like a dog let off the leash in pursuit of its quarry. The flimsy canvas and wooden structure shot down the sloping rails until they ran out over the bows of the *Hibernia*. There was a gasp from the members of the Press and ship's company alike as the aeroplane suddenly dipped a few feet below the bows and then gently rose into the air like some graceful winged creature. Great cheers then erupted from all hands, officers and visitors alike around the *Hibernia*. They knew they had just witnessed a momentous step in the development of naval aviation and warfare. Midshipman Kenny, however, had less interest in the historical significance of the event. He had just been relieved of his watch on the bridge and was in a panic to complete his journal. Before leaving the bridge to go below, he hurriedly scrawled in the log, '*1755, Aeroplane T2 left ship, Commander Samson as pilot, and flew to Lodmoor.*'

Chapter 3
June 1913

As the two Cambridge students ate their breakfast in the dining room of the Bluebird Hotel near Weybridge in Surrey, they anxiously surveyed the weather. Although the morning of 16 June 1913 was dry, it was overcast and the weak sun was struggling to penetrate the grey sky.

'I'm sure the clouds will clear in time, Paul,' Harold Stone opined to his friend and house mate, Paul Miller, before buttering another slice of toast.

'When I spoke to Tom last night, on the telephone, he seemed quite confident in the met' forecast. He was more concerned about the wind speed, but that looks to be fine from here.'

'I hope you're right, Harold. Easter was such a disappointment. I think I can see a spot of blue sky over there, though, so it might yet work out all right.'

The two friends had just completed the Easter term of their second year at the University of Cambridge. Stone was studying Law and Paul, Chinese. They had travelled down the day before on their motorcycles to the home of the Brooklands race track in the hope of witnessing a very special aviation feat. Harold and his two older brothers were all keen on the new craze for aviation. Unfortunately, the flight over the Easter weekend had been cancelled owing to the ferocious winds and exceptional rain and there had been further delays since, due to mechanical difficulties.

'Harold, are you going to sit there all day stuffing yourself with toast and marmalade? Shouldn't we push off over to the aerodrome soon? I'm keen to have a good look around.'

'Don't be impatient, Paul. It's only my second slice and nothing's going to happen until this cloud breaks up. Have another cup of tea and then we'll motor across.'

*****

An hour later, as the two friends parked their motorcycles outside a wooden shed of the Sopwith Aviation Company, the sun was winning its war with the clouds and almost half the sky was now an azure blue. Even so, it was still very cold. The flags around the race track indicated a steady, but light wind across the airstrip. In front of the shed doors a number of mechanics were clambering over the flimsy form of Thomas Sopwith's latest design, the Tractor Biplane. Stone took Paul over to meet a dark-haired, young man standing on one of the lower wings and talking to another seated at the controls of the machine.

'Hello, Tommy,' Stone hailed the man on the wing. 'Is she going to be able to fly today then?'

'Oh, hello there, Harold. I'm glad you could make it down again. I saw your brothers earlier. I reckon we're on today. It's going to be hellish cold up there for young Harry here, but otherwise no problems with the weather. Are you going to introduce me to your pal?'

'Of course, I was going to,' Stone replied curtly. 'Paul this is Tommy Sopwith, the designer of this collection of wood and canvas. Tommy, this is my good friend, Paul Miller.'

Sopwith jumped down to the ground to shake Paul's outstretched hand.

'Delighted to meet you, Miller. That's Harry Hawker up there. He's taking her up today. Say hello, Harry.'

'G'day, mate.'

Hawker leant over the side of the aircraft and waved to Paul. 'Are you a member of the Aero Club then?' Hawker drawled. Hawker was an Australian from Melbourne and had come across to England the year before. After a short while, he had ended up working for Sopwith and was rapidly becoming his chief test pilot. Paul was astonished at the youth of both Sopwith and Hawker. Despite being one of Britain's foremost aircraft designers and manufacturers, Thomas Octave Murdoch Sopwith was only twenty-five years of age, just five years older than Paul. Hawker was a year younger still.

'Er – no,' Paul replied shyly. 'I'm just down to see you make the record attempt. Sailing and motorcycling are more my line.'

'Ah well, there's plenty of time yet, mate. Take a good look around and get yourself a ride with somebody. It's great fun and I promise you there's nothing like it.' Hawker returned to testing the controls of the biplane.

'Harold has told me you speak Chinese, Miller. Is that right?' Sopwith asked. 'It sounds awfully impressive to me.'

'Er, yes. I've just finished my second year of study. It's not easy, but I dare say it's easier than learning to fly an aeroplane.'

'Rubbish,' Sopwith retorted. 'If you can handle a motorcycle, you can learn to fly. Take Harry's advice and get yourself into the air whilst you're here. Would you like me to show you around the machine?'

'Yes, please,' Paul replied enthusiastically, but then suspiciously. 'It looks so flimsy, though.'

'It has to be. We only have an eighty-horsepower engine and this baby is designed to carry three men. By the way, I hear from Harold that your father is a senior figure in the Admiralty.'

'Well, he's not that senior. He's a captain, but I'm not sure quite where he works in the Admiralty. However, I do know that he's interested in naval aviation.'

'That's good to hear,' Sopwith replied encouragingly. 'He might know a navy fellow coming down here today, Commander Charles Samson. He's a real pioneer in naval aviation over at Eastchurch. I'll introduce you if we bump into him. He's an amazing chap. Pass me that wrench, will you, Harry?'

'What's so amazing about this navy flier then, Tom?' Stone joined the conversation.

'Only that I think he was one of the first naval members of the Aero Club and since then, has virtually single-handedly persuaded the Admiralty to take aviation seriously. He even had them convert one of their cruisers to carry a hydroaeroplane. I'm rather hoping he can also persuade them to buy this little beauty. They've already ordered two and Samson reckons they might consider a contract for a third.'

*****

Back at the hotel as Paul lay in bed that evening, he could not get himself off to sleep, despite the effects of the copious amounts of champagne he had consumed earlier. His mind was far too alert and he was, also, more than a little anxious about the following morning. He reflected on a fascinating day. A whole new world had just been opened to him. He had witnessed history in the making as Hawker had set the British altitude record with one passenger and then gone on to set another with two passengers. Paul had also met an extraordinary bunch of people. To celebrate his and Hawker's success, Sopwith had thrown a party in the Royal Aero Clubhouse. There, Paul had been impressed by the camaraderie amongst the Club members. At Cambridge his fellow students were fiercely competitive and jealous of the success of others. At Brooklands on the other hand, aviators lauded and admired each other's successes in their common aim to extend the boundaries of aviation. There was a special bond between these men, almost a spirit of brotherhood. Aviators were romantic, daring, care-free and enterprising. One had to admire them.

As Sopwith had suggested might happen, they had met Charles Samson. Although not yet thirty years of age, he was already the navy's foremost expert on aviation and Sopwith had regaled Paul with tales of Samson's experiments on how aeroplanes might drop bombs and torpedoes, communicate with the ground or ships and, alarmingly, fly at night. It was during one of his conversations with Samson or Sopwith, he couldn't remember with whom, that he had rashly agreed to take a flying lesson with Samson the following day. He knew he had been enthused by the occasion and atmosphere, and perhaps, influenced by the champagne, but now all he could think about were the risks involved in pioneering aviation. He had heard of the frequent mechanical failures and the ensuing terrible accidents, often fatal. It struck him that his mother would not approve of this adventure, but he could hardly back out now without appearing a coward. He imagined falling out of the aeroplane and wondered how long it would take him to hit the ground. What would be his final thoughts? Supposing the machine crashed on landing and caught fire? How would it feel to be engulfed by the flames with no escape? He saw himself screaming as the flames started burning his clothing and…

With such thoughts he drifted off to sleep.

*****

The following day, as the two students checked out of the hotel, Paul was secretly disappointed that it was such a fine day. It looked perfect for flying. Unusually, he derived no pleasure or exhilaration from the short motorcycle journey to the Brooklands race circuit and aerodrome. Indeed, it just reminded him of how much his Swiss mother, *Mutti*, disapproved of motorcycles. She regarded them as extremely unsafe. What would she say or think if he had a flying accident, he thought miserably. Was it fair to put her through such pain for the sake of his dignity? He parked his Norton motorcycle once more at the airfield sheds and noted gloomily that Samson and a mechanic were already at work checking over a Grahame-White 'box kite'. A wave of terror overcame him as he saw the construction of the aeroplane. As only the wings were covered in fabric, the frail skeleton-construction of the remaining structure was plainly on view. Whereas the Sopwith biplane the day before had included a nacelle for the pilot and passengers, the box kite only offered two seats, both fully exposed to the elements. He was again tempted to back out of his adventure, but was more afraid of showing his fear to his friend, Stone. However, before he could deliberate the point further, Samson spotted the two friends.

'Morning, Miller, Stone. I've borrowed the services of Fred here to help start her up.' Fred Sigrist was one of the Sopwith mechanics they had met the day before.

'It's a fine day for a spin.' That was not what Paul wanted to hear. 'Can I interest you in a turn of the aerodrome, too, Stone?'

'No, thank you, Commander. I'll leave the heroics to Paul. He's more the daring type.'

'Fair enough, then. We'll meet you back in the Clubhouse afterwards. We shouldn't be long.'

Sigrist and Samson continued their checks of the box kite. Paul examined its flimsy frame carefully, too, and wondered at how it would take the weight of two men. His mournful thoughts were interrupted by Samson clapping him on the shoulder.

'Right, Miller, I'll guide you into your seat. Careful now! Just put your feet where I tell you. Although easily patched up, these are delicate machines.'

Paul's stomach heaved once again.

'Now you'll be up front here and I'll be right behind you. No straps I'm afraid, in case you have to jump out quickly, so be careful you don't fall out.'

Paul thought it too much. He felt his legs turn to jelly and he could barely climb up the aircraft rigging. As he sat gingerly in the front seat, he feared the flimsy structure would not support his weight on the ground, let alone in the air. He was seated right in the nose of the aircraft with only the control stick in front of him. To his left and right only a diagonal wooden spar prevented him from falling out. He felt as if he was sitting on the end of a see-saw facing the wrong way with nothing on which to hold.

'Tell me, Miller. Do you have a brother in submarines?'

'Why, yes. My brother, Richard. What of it?'

'I thought so. I recognised the name, but wasn't sure I had you placed correctly. I know your father.'

'Gosh! It's a small world.' Paul wondered if now was the right time for family introductions. He was anxious for his impending ordeal to be over.

'Good chap, your father. I owe him one. He has twice sent me fifty pounds to help fund my experiments and, moreover, set me up to teach Mister Churchill to fly. I'd better take care to bring you back in one piece, so pay attention. Once we start the engine, it will be very noisy, so I'll run through the controls with you. Now gently hold the stick between your fingers and thumb like this.'

*****

Thirty minutes later, Paul was in the air for the first time in his life. Samson took them up to 300 feet and then bawled in Paul's ear for him to take control of the aircraft. He encouraged Paul to make a few gentle turns to port and starboard, as well as to fly the machine in level flight. Paul was pleasantly surprised to discover how it was stable enough to fly a long way without any need to adjust the controls. Samson then cut the engine to demonstrate how well the aeroplane volplaned.

Within ten minutes, Paul was surprised to discover that he had completely overcome his earlier fears. He was enthralled by it. There was a tremendous sense of freedom up in the sky with the birds and the clouds. Looking down on the minute figures of people and animals on the ground, the world seemed insignificant and he felt sorry for those who had only experienced it in two dimensions. Above all, despite the noise of the engine and the wind in his ears, he felt a tremendous feeling of peace. In an aeroplane he could go anywhere. He was unfettered by the restrictions of travel along roads. It was even better than motorcycle racing. Why had he never done this before?

With huge disappointment and all too soon, he handed the controls back to Samson to return to the Brooklands aerodrome. It didn't matter, though. Those twenty minutes in the air had changed his life irrevocably. He knew he was hooked on flying for life and he resolved to become an aviator. He would follow in the footsteps of heroes such as Samson and the other intrepid pilots he had so recently met. His days at Cambridge were now behind him. They had been fun, but aviation offered so much more, and student life and acadaemia now seemed so trivial. The only difficulty he foresaw was how to break the news to Pops and, more alarmingly, what would *Mutti* say?

Chapter 4
August 1913

It being a Sunday, one of the navy's latest crop of midshipmen was pleased to find he had the compartment of the Great Western Railway train from Paddington to Weymouth to himself. The short, blond-haired seventeen-year-old had a cheerful countenance and seemed very excited. Indeed, John Miller was enthused by the prospect of joining his first ship after Dartmouth. Since passing out of Britannia Naval College at the end of July 1913, he had spent the intervening two weeks on leave with his parents in London. He was, of course, disappointed that he could not have gone on to join them at the family estate in Lancashire, at Marton Hall. Since his return from his duties as the Naval Attaché in Berlin, Papa had always arranged to spend the month of August in Lancashire. But the exigencies of the Service came first. John knew that time and tide wait for no man and his new ship was about to deploy to the Mediterranean, so his leave was of only secondary importance. In any case, life was a bit sticky at home at present.

It was all Paul's fault. Ever since he had announced he was chucking Cambridge to join the Flying Corps, relations between *Mutti* and Papa had been fraught. There had been a terrific row at home about it. *Mutti* had not yet forgiven Paul for giving up his prospects for a degree and a career at the Foreign Office. Worse still, she blamed Papa. Poor old Papa. *Mutti* suspected that he had had a hand in assisting Paul's fast-track entry into the Air Service, but according to Paul, Papa was in fact entirely innocent. Apparently, it was all down to his connections with a Commander Samson. Paul had told him confidentially that when he had discussed the matter with Papa in June, Papa had taken it rather well, but had by no means encouraged him to join up. Indeed, he had insisted that Paul first take a course of lessons at Hendon and obtain his Royal Aero Club Certificate before taking his application to the Admiralty further.

Unfortunately, the dispute at home had rather blighted the news of Papa's overdue promotion to Rear Admiral. Papa was in fact seeing the latest First Sea Lord, Prince Louis Battenburg, the following day to learn his new appointment. Was it selfish to hope that this might be a seagoing command in the Mediterranean? It would be no bad thing to have Papa on station to guide his future prospects.

He felt a little jealous of Paul. There was something quite dashing and adventurous in the idea of flying. Moreover, whilst he was immensely proud of his new rank of Midshipman, Paul had been accepted immediately with the rank of Probationary Flight Sub Lieutenant, technically a rank above him. And he hadn't had to endure life as a cadet at Dartmouth for four years. Nor would he face two years at sea as a 'snottie' in the Fleet.

Even so, he was on the way to the Mediterranean, it was a glorious August day and so the prospects were good for a calm boat transfer to HMS *Warrior* at a buoy in Portland Harbour. *Warrior* was a *Duke of Edinburgh*-class armoured cruiser of the newly-named First Battle Cruiser Squadron. Although he would admit it to no one, he was disappointed by his first appointment. He had rather hoped to be sent to a *Dreadnought*-class battleship or a fast battle cruiser. *Warrior* was already almost eight years old. However, Papa had taught him that all appointments presented opportunity and it was down to him to make the best of things.

Thirty minutes later, the train arrived in Weymouth. As he alighted, he noted that the platform was thronged with a mixture of holidaymakers, sailors and a large group of wealthy yachtsmen and their ladies. He retrieved his sea chest from the guard's van and then realised, with dismay, that the yachtsmen seemed to have monopolised the available porters and luggage carts. He was clearly in for a long wait before some assistance would be available.

'Would you like some help with that, sir?'

John turned around to find himself addressed by a short, red-haired, young seaman whose curly locks were barely contained beneath his cap bearing, in gold lettering on the black ribbon, the name, *Vivid,* the navy's training cruiser at Devonport.

'That's jolly decent of you, but are you not already encumbered by your kit bag?' John replied to his would-be helper, who, judging by his accent, was clearly a Welshman.

'Oh, you needn't worry about that, sir. If I just sling it over my shoulder like this, that gives me a hand free now, you see. So, if you'd be kind enough to take the other end, we'll manage along just fine.'

Together the two young men carried the sea chest to the station entrance where a Petty Officer was organising the sailors into an orderly group to await the next tender to the ships in Portland Harbour.

John was uncertain what to do next. He turned to his helper and asked, 'I presume you're bound for a ship, too. Any idea where we should go?'

'If you just wait here, sir, I'll ask the PO. Which ship are you joining, sir?'

'The *Warrior*. You've probably guessed… it's my first ship. How about you?'

'Well, I'm blowed! So am I. I'm Boy Seaman… First Class mind… Evans, sir, just passed out of *Vivid*. My father was a seaman, but on the colliers. We're from Swansea you see, but I fancied a life in the Royal Navy would offer more variety and excitement than colliers. Oh dear. There's me going on too much. My Ma'am is always telling me I talk too much. I'm sorry about that, sir.'

'Well, that's capital.' John responded gleefully. 'I'm Midshipman Miller. We'll join the ship together. Besides, I'll need a hand with the chest at the other end, if you wouldn't mind?'

Evans disappeared and returned a few minutes later.

'It's all right, sir. We just need to join that queue there, sir. There'll be a boat along in only a few minutes. Now let me help you with your chest.'

They made their way through the throng of sailors waiting for the Admiralty Yard boats to ferry their passengers out to the ships moored in the harbour. Despite their earlier chatty exchange of introductions, they now became separated by the conventions of the Service as they boarded the ferry boat, both to enter their separate worlds on board the same ship. Evans joined the other sailors in the forward section of the boat whilst John waited on the jetty with two young lieutenants. It was the custom of the Service that officers boarded boats last. Meanwhile, John's baggage was stowed on board by the boat's crew and, once they were ready to slip the jetty, the three officers stepped on board and proceeded to the after section of the boat's deck, the province of officers only. Neither member of this small party exchanged a word.

As the Admiralty Yard boat steamed out to the ships in the harbour, John was able to appreciate the magnificence of the four armoured cruisers lying at their moorings. The four-funnelled cruisers, including HMS *Warrior*, under the command of Rear Admiral Ernest Troubridge in his flagship HMS *Defence*, were being transferred to the Mediterranean station. Troubridge had taken command of the squadron in January after serving as the first Chief of the newly created Naval War Staff, a pet project of the First Lord of the Admiralty, Mister Winston Churchill. In John's joining instructions, Captain James Fergusson had informed him that just a few days before his joining, a new captain would have taken command of *Warrior*, so he wouldn't be the only new boy. John liked that, but of course, he recognised that there was a huge gulf between a new midshipman and the captain of a cruiser. Captain George Holmes Borrett had served under Papa in China and, according to him, was a highly intelligent, competent and decent officer.

The admiralty boat approached the flagship first to disembark its passengers. From his first view close up of a *Duke of Edinburgh*-class cruiser, John thought it resembled a pin cushion, with its two vertical masts, four funnels and horizontally, the ten barrels of its nine-point-two-inch and seven-point-five-inch guns. Six of these guns were trained fore and aft and the remaining four athwartships. The pin cushion effect was heightened further by the twenty-six three-pounder, quick-firing guns dotted about the upper decks and turret roofs. Hidden beneath the waterline lurked three eighteen-inch torpedo tubes. These ships were certainly well armed, but much less so than the thirteen-point-five-inch gun-carrying *Dreadnoughts*. It was rumoured that HMS *Queen Elizabeth*, currently under construction in Portsmouth, would boast fifteen-inch guns. The merit of the armoured cruiser was its speed rather than firepower. HMS *Warrior* was capable of twenty-three knots thanks to her four-cylinder triple-expansion steam engines.

Finally, the boat approached the accommodation ladder of *Warrior* and her returning sailors and new members alike deferentially waited for the officers to disembark first. John followed the lieutenants and, reaching the top of the ladder, saluted the quarterdeck and then introduced himself to the Officer of the Watch in charge of the side party. The Midshipman of the Watch, Nigel Faraday, took charge of bringing John's sea chest on board.

Faraday appeared to be a friendly sort of chap and, after introducing himself, quickly offered to show him to his cabin in the 'Grot' as the midshipmen's quarters was known.

Faraday led John aft and down several ladders. John was completely disorientated and felt sure he must be five decks down and well below the water line. At last, Faraday showed him to a large cabin, perhaps destined to be his new home for the next two years.

'Here you are, chum. You're in the twelve-berth with this bunch of scallywags. "Steerage" as we call it. Keep your nose clean and you might, in time, be elevated to the more refined quarters of our six-berth, rather than with this riff-raff.'

Faraday was suddenly pelted by a barrage of plimsolls and rolled up socks and quickly took cover behind the open door.

'I'll leave you to make your own introductions, what? I must return to the gangway.'

With the sudden and hurried departure of his guide, John immediately felt as the early Christians must have felt on entering the gladiatorial ring. Slung from the deckhead of the tiny cabin were about six hammocks from which a number of bodies in mixed attires of uniform, sporting clothes and even pyjamas, were emerging to peer at the new species to enter the grot. Considering that another six hammocks had still to be slung, including his own, the space was tiny. Moreover, he could not help but notice the acrid smell of stale sweat, oil and something his olfactory senses could not yet identify. Sitting at a fold-up desk, a tall, fair-haired young man rose to greet him.

'I say, old chap. Don't pay attention to Faraday. He's only been on board a year, but likes to play the swank. My name's Joynson. I'm supposed to be in charge of this rabble. You're Miller, I presume?'

John's nerves were calmed by the friendly greeting and, as he shook hands with Joynson, he thought he detected a more convivial air amongst his new cabin mates. Without introducing himself, one of the midshipmen still lying prostrate in his hammock called out, 'I don't suppose you have the latest Surrey score do you?'

'Ah, but I do, as it happens. Kent were forced to follow on and lost by an innings and forty runs. I was at the Oval to witness the result. I have the newspaper report here if you're interested.'

'I'll say I am.' Within a split second, his interlocutor was on his feet and bearing down on him with an outstretched hand and broad smile. 'Tell me, old man, are you by chance a Surrey, fan too? Cartwright's the name. How d'you do?'

John was a little taken aback, but replied as calmly and politely as he could.

'Actually, I tend to favour Lancashire, but when in London I often accompany one of my brothers or my father to the Oval,' he quickly added. 'I'm jolly keen on the game, in fact.'

'That's splendid. It's nice to be joined by some intelligent company at last. Tell you what, Joynson. Why don't you complete the introductions and we'll take Miller up to tea in the Gunroom, hey?'

It was all that was needed to make John feel completely at home amongst his new companions and, as he was introduced to them all, he became convinced that the lions might prove to be pussy cats after all.

Chapter 5
April 1914

The journey down to Eastchurch promised to be routine. It was 09.00 and the weather was set fair for the entire journey. The pre-flight checks had shown everything in perfect working order, although as the machine was brand new, anything was possible. Accordingly, one of the Naval Wing of the RFC's lately-qualified pilots, Flight Sub Lieutenant Paul Miller, took the precaution of asking several mechanics to hold the aircraft back whilst he ran the engine for a minute at full throttle. Satisfied that all was in order, he signalled to the handlers to release the aircraft and set off into the air. He climbed to 4,000 feet and headed south-east for Kent.

The sun was well up to his left on what promised to be a lovely spring day. The beautiful dales of Yorkshire were spread out below Paul and the combination of weather and landscape gave him a sense of calm and contentment. He had been sent by his CO to collect this new Avro 504 from the A.V. Roe and Company Limited aviation works in Manchester. Samson was a good sort and, knowing that Paul lived in Lancashire, had selected him for the ferry task. Paul had spent a very convivial evening with Grandmama and his older brother, Richard, at Marton Hall. It was a shame that his parents could not have been there, but they were in their London home in Cumberland Terrace. In fact, Paul had been lucky to have been spared for this ferry run. The CO was working the squadron hard and had been reluctant to release a more experienced pilot. He was convinced that war with Germany was inevitable and possibly only a year off. He had, accordingly, upped the tempo for bombing range training. Most of the squadron thought the CO dotty over this fixation, but Pops had suggested the CO was a forward-thinking officer.

For the first hour, all went smoothly. The Avro was a state-of-the-art, twin-seat bomber and had only just entered service with either wing of the RFC. However, trouble soon arrived in a threesome. First the air-speed indicator failed. This did not worry Paul unduly as the visibility was good and, although it affected his dead reckoning calculations for navigation, identifying navigation marks on the ground was not difficult. The French-designed, air-cooled, seven-cylinder rotary engine was still humming along nicely.

Unfortunately, thirty minutes later the compass failed. This made navigation yet trickier, but the sun was clearly visible and Paul was able to use it to estimate his heading. Then, forty minutes later, the engine revolutions suddenly dropped and the engine started to misfire badly. Paul shut off the petrol to the engine and started to volplane. He estimated that from his original height, he had four to five minutes to find a suitable landing field, so he need not panic. Engine failure was a frequent bugbear for an aviator in 1914.

Fortunately, he was now gliding over the rural landscape of Cambridgeshire and the countryside offered a plethora of choices for a suitable landing spot. He selected a field of pasture and gently guided his aircraft to land safely in a field of startled cattle. On his approach he had spotted two farmhands and their team of horses ploughing a nearby field, so he was sure that somebody would turn up shortly.

He switched off the fuel supply and climbed stiffly from the cockpit onto the wing and down to the ground. Remembering that he had not eaten since breakfast time, he sat against the starboard wheel and tucked into his packed lunch whilst he waited for assistance. Presently, a young farmhand appeared riding on the back of one of the plough horses. The lad was slight of build and fresh-faced with a mop of thick, brown hair covered in a baggy cap. He was wearing riding breeches with calf-length boots, a short, thick jacket and a dark-blue neckerchief. Paul put his lunch to one side, stood up and strode out to meet the lad.

'Good afternoon. I've had a spot of engine trouble and wonder if there's a garage and telephone near here. Can you help?'

The lad studied him inquisitively for a moment before answering. To Paul's amazement it was not a lad after all, but plainly a young woman who spoke, and a pretty one, too.

'There's a telephone up at the main house, about two miles away. However, the nearest garage is at Potton, about six miles away. We're a bit remote from modern conveniences round here. Can I offer you a ride up to the house?'

Paul could see that the ride intended was clearly on the back of the shire horse, behind the girl. He was unsure about the propriety of accepting such an offer and chose an easy way out.

'That's very kind of you, but I need to stay with my aircraft. Would you mind telephoning the local police station and asking them to send somebody to watch over my machine? Could you, also, ring my base to tell them what has happened? I can give you the telephone number and a message.'

'Oh, don't worry about that. I've already arranged for Frank, one of the farmhands, to ride down to the village to fetch the local constable. He shouldn't be long. I've also asked Frank to ring the house and send the Rolls down to us. If it will wait a while, we could travel up to the house together and you could ring the navy yourself. My name's Catherine by the way. Catherine Edgar.' She extended her hand confidently. 'This is my father's field you're standing in.'

Paul shook the proffered hand and noted a firm handgrip. 'Forgive me. I'm Paul Miller. You seem to have everything organised. I'm quite happy to wait until the constable arrives. My colleagues will not think me overdue until this evening, anyway… I hope you don't mind me saying, but you seem unusually dressed for a young lady.'

'I can thank my father for that. He's the Honorary Colonel of the local Territorial battalion and has enlisted all the fit, young men. They're off on a recruiting drive this week and we're a bit shorthanded, but the farm still has to be worked and managed. Daddy's convinced there will be a war before the year's out…'

'That's odd. So does our CO, but we think he's too pessimistic about it.'

'I'm not sure I can believe it either. We're surely too closely linked to Germany culturally. After all, they did produce Bach, Beethoven and Schubert. Anyway, it's all boys' business as far as I'm concerned. Daddy has told me that if we go to war, I'll have to manage the farms, so I was just getting some ploughing instruction when you dropped in on us.'

'Do you not have a brother to do it for you, then?'

'I have two as a matter of fact, but they're both in uniform already. Dick is a captain in the Royal Horse Artillery and Tom is an airman like you, but he's a lieutenant in the Royal Flying Corps.'

'Oh, so that explains why you seem so well organised in accommodating the needs of stranded flyers, then.' Paul laughed. 'I was impressed that you recognised my kite as belonging to the navy and not the army, too.'

'You mean the red-rimmed circle in place of the union flag? The colour of the uniform gives it away a little, too, don't you think?'

'How very observant. What does your brother fly?'

'BE2s. I believe they are reconnaissance aeroplanes.'

'You astonish me, Miss Edgar. You are truly very well informed on aviation matters.'

'I dare say you mean, for a woman.' Catherine responded angrily and her face flushed. Paul thought the colouring and flash in her brown eyes quite attractive. 'A woman is just as capable of reading the newspapers as men. Clearly you do not have sisters, Mister Miller, or do they just read the fashion pages?'

Paul blushed with embarrassment at his lack of tact. 'I'm sorry Miss Edgar. I meant no insult to you or your sex. As it happens, I don't have any sisters, but that is no excuse for my blunder. I apologise unreservedly.'

After several seconds of uncomfortable silence between them, Catherine laughed. 'Stop worrying. I'm sorry for appearing over sensitive. I have two older brothers who love nothing better than to put me down. All they and Daddy talk about is a coming war and how we should be making better preparations. I have no choice but to take an interest. Daddy retired from the army as a major-general seven years ago and is itching to come out of retirement. When not talking of war, Tom never shuts up about aviation either.

'Oh, look. Here comes Constable Baines and one of his special constables. That didn't take long. Good afternoon, Constable Baines. May I introduce you to… Oh, I'm sorry. I've forgotten your rank, Mister Miller.'

'Hello, Constable. I'm Flight Sub Lieutenant Miller of the Air Service. Thank you for coming so promptly. I wonder if you would mind ensuring no harm comes to my aeroplane whilst I go to telephone the nearest garage.'

PC Baines and his assistant, Special Constable Smith, dismounted from their bicycles. 'No problem, sir. We're used to that round here. Mister Edgar and his flying types are always dropping by and getting stuck. Honestly, I reckon these flying machines are more trouble than they're worth. Anyways, I called in on Fred Wilkes, the blacksmith, on my ways 'ere. He says he'll be along as soon as he's finished shoein' a 'orse. There's no need to call a garage.'

'That was good of you, Constable, but it's a mechanic I need and not a blacksmith.'

'I reckons I knows that, sir. Fred is a mechanic. He's mad about motorcycles and many's the time 'e's fixed up Lieutenant Edgar's machine. Like I said, sir, these flying machines break down regular.'

'I'm sorry for doubting you, Constable.' Paul was embarrassed for the second time in ten minutes. 'It seems you really do have everything under control. Thank you.'

Paul's blushes were spared further by the near-silent arrival of a navy-blue and gold liveried 1911 Rolls Royce motor car, driven by an elderly gentleman. Judging by his shooting tweeds and deerstalker, from which sprouted a wild head of hair in a shade of grey matching the impressive whiskers, he had all the appearance of the local squire. However, Paul guessed correctly that this was General Edgar. Despite the thickened waistline, he still retained his military bearing.

'Good afternoon, gentlemen, Kate,' he called affably. 'Looks like you have a spot of bother.'

'Good day to you, my lord,' replied the two constables in near unison. Baines went on to say, 'It's all under control. Wilkes will be along shortly.'

'Hello, Daddy. I thought you were off on manoeuvres or something.'

'Recruiting, dear. Our next camp's not until July. No, I'd just popped home to change – I'm taking tea with the Bishop at Ely, don't you know – when I heard the news of your visitor from the heavens. Thought it might have been young Tom.'

'I'm sorry to disappoint, but thanks for coming anyway, Daddy. May I introduce you to Lieutenant Miller of His Britannic Majesty's Naval Air Service?'

'Good afternoon, my lord,' Paul replied, taking his cue from the policemen. 'I'm afraid I am actually only a Flight Sub Lieutenant. I'm very grateful for the help I'm receiving. Your daughter, Constable Baines and his assistant here seem to have everything very well organised. Indeed, I may very well suggest to the Admiralty they designate this area as an official emergency landing ground.'

'I shouldn't do that, Miller,' the general chuckled. 'This field gets hellish boggy after the first frosts, but I'm delighted to meet you. My youngest son is an airman with the Military Wing of the Flying Corps, so I've come prepared. It must be cold up there today, so I arranged with Cook to bring you something. Thought it might come in handy. It's a hot game pie and a flask of tea. Shot the rabbits and the pigeons myself early in the week.' General Edgar winked conspiratorially at his daughter.

'Why thank you, sir… my lord. That's an inspired idea. I really am most hungry. I was just having a spot of lunch when everyone arrived as it happens. Would anyone care to join me?'

'Baines, how about you chaps keep an eye on this machine whilst I take young Miller here up to the house, eh? I assume you've arranged for Wilkes to come over to see what's wrong with the damned thing?'

'We have indeed, my lord. Just as soon as he's free.'

'Well, that's settled then. Tell him to come up to the house once he's finished and he can give this young fellow his report on what's to be done. Miller, I suggest you come with me and telephone to your unit. They'll be worrying about you soon, no doubt. That all right with you, Kate?'

'That would be fine, Daddy. Just let me take Pestle here back to Thompson in the seven-acre and you can give me a lift home.'

'Good. Now, Miller. Forget this, "my lord" business will you. It's too feudal. "General" will do just fine.'

*****

Langford Hall, the home of the Edgars, was an imposing early-Georgian house, at the end of a long drive through beautiful parkland. Since it had been built for the first Baron of Langford, the only additions to the house had been extensions of equal proportions on either side and another to the rear. The house, thus, still retained its original symmetry. The other side of the ha-ha the grass gave way to two well-stocked trout lakes and woodland.

Paul rang the station at Eastchurch and informed the duty officer that he would report again when he had received an assessment of the cause of his engine failure. Lord Edgar was not yet back from Ely and Catherine had gone to change, so Paul was left to his own devices in the library. He was engrossed in an article in the latest copy of *The Illustrated News* when the butler informed him that Wilkes, the blacksmith. was waiting to see him.

Wilkes was rather self-conscious and uneasy as he was shown into the library to make his report. The news was bad. The engine had 'thrown a rod'. The connecting rod in one of the engine's seven cylinders had snapped. Unfortunately, it had penetrated the crank case and wrecked the engine. A completely new engine was required and this was beyond the capability of Wilkes to remedy. Wilkes had just delivered this bombshell when Catherine reappeared.

Paul was stunned by the transformation. Catherine was about five foot six inches in height with long, brown hair beyond her shoulders. She was wearing a plain, mustard-coloured, full-length crinoline skirt and a shaped, pleat-fronted, white blouse. Both garments highlighted her slim waist and a full bosom to perfection. Without the earlier neckerchief, Paul could admire the pale and slim neck on which her beautiful head sat perfectly. He was captivated and gazed at her in rapture.

'Really, Lieutenant. You sailors. Have you never seen a woman before?' Catherine addressed him coyly.

Paul blushed with embarrassment and immediately looked away. Catherine turned to the blacksmith.

'Oh, Wilkes. Thank you for coming. What's the news? Will the gallant naval airman soon be on his way back to his squadron?'

'I reckons not Ma'am. The aeroplane needs a new engine and that's not something I can provide nor fit. It's up to the navy now.'

'What a pity. Well, thank you, Wilkes. We'd better let you get back to your smithy. If you pop by the kitchen, I think Cook has a few things for you to take home to your mother.'

'Yes, thank you, Wilkes. I'm very grateful for your time. If you would send me an invoice to this address, I'll see you are suitably recompensed.' Paul found his voice at last and handed over one of his cards.

After Wilkes had left the room, Catherine turned to Paul and said, 'You'd better let your squadron know. It would appear you are stuck here until they can send a new engine, so you are welcome to stay here until then. I'm sure neither Daddy nor Mummy would mind.'

It was odd, Paul thought, that until then he had never given any thought to the mistress of the house.

Chapter 6

Paul felt embarrassed to sit down to dinner in such a stately surrounding, dressed only in his reefer jacket. Given his absence of evening clothes, the Edgars had tried to make him feel more comfortable by not dressing for dinner themselves, but he had at least been able to root out a clean shirt and wing collar from his limited overnight baggage. However, it was obvious that Catherine had gone to some trouble with her appearance. If anything, she was even more attractive than when she had entered the library earlier. He was seated to Lady Edgar's left, opposite Catherine and, thus, could not help admiring her beauty. He had telephoned the duty officer at Eastchurch to explain the position with the engine. Just after six o'clock, he had received instructions to await the arrival of a lorry from A.V. Roe the following afternoon. He was to hand over the aircraft to the manufacturer and then make his way down to Kent by rail as soon as he could. A call to the local police station had confirmed that PC Baines and his 'specials' would take care of the security of his machine in the meantime. There was nothing more for him to do but wait and he had gratefully accepted Lord Edgar's offer of hospitality overnight.

'Forgive me, Lieutenant, but I note that whilst my son has cloth wings sewn onto the breast of his tunic, you navy flyers seem to have a rather charming brooch on your sleeve instead,' Lady Edgar commented to Paul.

Paul looked at the gold insignia above the still-shiny, single, wavy stripe on the left sleeve of his reefer jacket. He was rather proud of his pilot's brevet, introduced to the RNAS only the December before. He considered it marked him out as being special amongst other naval officers, but, nonetheless, he had not copied some of his contemporaries in replacing his cap badge with the version that substituted the anchor beneath the crown with a smaller version of the eagle brevet.

'Indeed, ma'am, we have Mrs Sueter to thank for that.' He responded to the quizzical look of his hostess by continuing. 'Mrs Sueter is the wife of the Director of the Air Department. We call him "Dad", so I suppose that makes her "Mum".'

His hosts seemed to like the joke and laughed naturally before he went on, 'She purchased the original brooch in Paris and was so taken with it that she persuaded her husband to adopt it across the Service. I'm rather glad the Lord Commissioners accepted the idea.'

'It's absolutely charming. I do so love the combination of the blue and gold of the navy uniforms. Khaki seems so drab by comparison.'

'Drab it might be, my darling, but khaki's a ruddy sight safer than the blues and scarlet on the field of battle,' the general interjected.

'I believe, general, we have to thank one of Charles the Second's ladies at court for the uniform, sir. I understand she always wore blue and gold and the dear old king, who was randy for her, thought he would…'

The general spluttered in astonishment at Paul's words and Catherine froze in embarrassment. Paul looked at Lady Edgar and she, too, seemed shocked, but she recovered herself quickly and chuckled a little artificially.

'What a charming story. I hope it to be true. But then I think your naval uniforms are outshone by those of the regiments at a mess ball.'

Paul thought it might be prudent to concentrate on his dessert than risk a further gaffe. He was finding Lady Edgar a *charming* hostess. Despite bearing five children and her age of fifty something, she had retained her slim figure and was most attractive. She put this down to her passion for horses and hunting. Her absence from the afternoon's excitement had been due to attending a charity committee. Over the course of the evening, Paul had learned that Catherine was Lady Edgar's fourth child. As well as two brothers, Catherine had two sisters. The eldest, aged twenty-eight, was married and living in London. The youngest, aged fifteen, three years younger than Catherine, was currently boarding at a school in Buckinghamshire.

Catherine came to his rescue by changing the topic of conversation. 'Have you heard the news, Lieutenant, that Sir Ernest Shackleton is planning another expedition to the Antarctic?'

'I had. I am surprised he has not had his fill of polar exploration after his last adventure. Moreover, the prize of being the first to reach the Pole has already been won by others.'

'Ah, but this time he aspires to be the first to cross the Antarctic continent. I believe…'

'Are you interested in polar exploration, Lieutenant?' Lady Edgar interrupted.

In Paul's peripheral vision he noted Catherine give him a barely perceptible nod and he took his cue accordingly. 'I confess I have not studied the topic greatly, but I did admire the late Captain Scott.'

'Then I'm sure you will have heard of Mister Cherry Apsley-Garrard, lately returned from the *Terra Nova* expedition and the nephew of my great friend, Agatha.'

Paul had not heard of the man, but thought it tactful not to admit his ignorance. 'Of course, ma'am, all the polar adventurers are to be admired.'

Lady Edgar then went on to describe in great detail the difficulties Apsley-Garrard was having in persuading the Natural History Museum to accept three Emperor penguin eggs. Paul took the opportunity to examine his surroundings and to steal surreptitious glances at Catherine. He had noted that one of the fastenings of her blouse had become undone. Whenever she stretched for her wine, she betrayed a glimpse of the upper half of one of her shapely breasts. He tried hard not to stare, but found the sight sexually arousing.

At length, Lady Edgar and her daughter withdrew from the dining room to leave the men to their port. Paul moved his chair closer to that of the general to ease conversation.

General Edgar, the Eighth Baron of Langford, was, at 57, younger than his grey shock of hair and whiskers suggested. Since taking early retirement following his service as Commandant of the Royal Military Academy at Sandhurst, he had been very content to immerse himself in his estate and life in the country.

'So, what sort of machines do you normally fly, Miller?' Lord Edgar filled Paul's glass with port as he spoke.

'Mainly the Avro, sir. I'm still a relatively new pilot, so my experience is limited.'

'That's the same type of aircraft you arrived in earlier today, ain't it?'

'Indeed, sir. Are you well acquainted with aeroplanes, sir?'

'Tolerably. You know my youngest son is in the RFC, of course? What about these hydroaeroplanes? Any experience of flying them?'

'None at all, sir. That's all done on the south coast. We call them seaplanes now, sir.'

'Really. Everything's damn well changing these days. So, you're a bomber pilot then, my lad?'

'Not entirely, my lord. I am training to drop bombs, but my experience to date has been more to do with reconnaissance and spotting.'

'So, what's the navy's opinion on the likelihood of war with Germany?'

Paul was a little discomforted by the question, but answered honestly. 'I cannot really say, sir. It's not something to which I have given much thought. The CO seems to be pushing us quite hard, though, so perhaps he has wind of something. But then he seems to be a workaholic. What do you think, sir?'

'Ruddy certainty, I'd say. Just a question of when. The frogs are itching for it.'

'Surely not, sir?'

'You can be damned sure they are. They want Alsace-Lorraine back. Mind you, they shouldn't have lost it way back in 1870. Serves 'em right.'

Paul was aware that Pops seemed equally certain that war was inevitable, but relations between them had never been of a nature whereby they discussed much apart from his supposed misdemeanours. He thought it better to let the general lead the discussion.

'You say your CO is pushing you hard? Must mean something.' Edgar helped himself to another glass of port. 'Want a top up, young fellow?'

'Thank you, General. I will.'

'My son, Tom, tells me he's just had his summer leave cancelled. It seems the entire RFC is taking part in some manoeuvres in June. They call it a "Concentration Camp" to test their readiness to mobilise. Nothing in the wind in your service, is there?'

'I don't rightly know, sir. I think my leave in August is still on. My mother likes all the family to join her and my father up in Lancashire in August.'

'Well, for your sake, young man, let's hope the Hun doesn't interrupt those plans. Now I think we ought to join the ladies.'

*****

A few hours later, after the household had retired for the night, Paul opened the windows, looked down outside and grunted with satisfaction. Quickly and nimbly, he stepped through the windows and his bare feet found security on the narrow ledge beneath and running along the wall of the house. There was no ivy this side of the house, but he, nonetheless, managed to find enough finger-tip holds to make progress, aided by the light of the moon. His quarry was four windows along. He had discovered the location of Catherine's room when he had escorted her there after dinner. She had not invited him in, but had allowed him to offer her a kiss on a cheek.

Most people would not have considered it sensible to climb along a six-inch-wide ledge on the exterior of the second floor of a tall house with no hand-holds, but Paul had spent many a night at Cambridge climbing the roofs of various colleges with a couple of like-minded pals. He had learned from experience that success lay in good balance, boldness and ignorance of the consequences of a potential fall.

Painstakingly, he made his way past the first two windows. Only the second showed a light peeping from behind the drapes. Paul suspected this might be from the general's dressing room, so he took especial care to avoid unnecessary noise. Clad in only his shirt above the waist, he began to feel the chill of the April night. His hands were cold, but he had not lost any feeling in his fingertips.

At last, he arrived outside the fourth window. The drapes were drawn and there was no light showing from within. Gently, he tapped on the glass and listened intently. He heard nothing and rapped the window more loudly. This time he was rewarded by the sight of a glimmer of light at the edges of the window. He tapped the glass again and, very soon afterwards, one of the drapes was partially withdrawn and he saw Catherine outlined by the lamp she was holding.

He called out quietly, '*But, soft! What light through yonder window breaks? It is the east and Catherine is the sun!*'

It was a passage he had learned at Cambridge to woo the fairer sex. To his satisfaction, he saw Catherine's shocked expression. She had seen and heard him.

'*Arise, fair sun, and kill the envious moon, who is already sick and pale with grief, that thou her maid art far more fair than she.*'

Catherine opened the right-hand section of the window and replied in a hushed voice, 'What are you doing, you chump?'

Paul ignored her. '*Be not her maid, since she is envious; her vestal livery is but sick and green, and none but fools do wear it. Cast it off. It is my lady, O, it is my love!*'

Catherine burst out laughing before replying, '*Oh Romeo, Romeo! Wherefore art thou, Romeo? …* Paul, you're an idiot. What are you doing?'

'I'm catching my death of cold. May I come in?'

'No, you may not. My parents are only down the corridor.'

Paul immediately burst into song with a soft tenor tone. '*Did you not hear my lady go down the garden singing? Blackbird and thrush were…*'

'Come in! Come in. You'll wake the dead,' Catherine implored. Paul wasted no time and was through the open window in a flash.

He kneeled on one knee with his right hand to his breast and continued to sing, '*Blackbird and thrush were silent to hear the alleys ringing. Oh, saw you not my lady out in the garden there? Shaming the rose and lily, for she is twice as fair. Though I am nothing to her, though she must rarely look at me. And though I could never woo her, I love her 'til I die.*'

Paul bowed extravagantly and looked pleased with himself. Catherine applauded softly. 'Bravo, my love-struck troubadour. But you are a goose, Paul. What's this all about? You might have broken your neck out there.'

'Ah, but lovely Catherine. It was worth the effort to see you in your nightdress.' Catherine responded by pulling her shawl tighter around her neck and shoulders. 'I could not sleep until I had received just one more kiss from you.'

Catherine trembled slightly and Paul could tell his arrow had gone home. 'Promise me just one more kiss and I will return to my room a contented man.'

'Very well. It behoves me to reward my gallant troubadour. Arise noble minstrel.'

Paul rose and took Catherine in his arms and kissed her passionately on the lips. At first, she resisted, but then she began to respond. As she did so, Paul held her tighter and his right hand reached down to caress her bottom. Catherine pulled her face away immediately. 'No, Paul. I'm not that kind of girl.'

Paul still held her in his arms. 'Of course, you're not what you imply. I have nothing but the fondest regard for you.' He tried kissing her again, but she turned her head.

'No, Paul.' She broke away from his embrace. 'I suggest you return to your room now.'

'But Catherine, I want to make a woman of you. I promise to be gentle and...'

'No, Paul,' Catherine retreated to the door. 'Go now and we part as friends or I will raise the household. My father has old-fashioned notions about these sort of things... and if he finds you here, is likely to have you horse-whipped.'

'Very well, my lady. I will retreat to leave your honour intact. I would value your friendship and shall now sleep with nothing but the most pleasant of dreams.'

He made for the window, but Catherine called after him. 'No, wait.' She opened the door and peered outside. 'Come this way and be quick about it. The coast's clear.'

Paul bounded across the room, but as he made to leave, she barred his exit. 'I promise we part in friendship and with this I seal it.' She leaned up, pulled his head towards her, quickly kissed him on the lips and released him. '*I would not for the world they saw thee here. Now go.*'

Chapter 7
June 1914

The hammering of the keys of the Petty Officer Writer's typewriter and the regular *ding* as he hit the carriage return lever were jangling on Paul's nerves. He had been ordered by his flight commander to report to the CO's office and that probably spelled trouble. Paul wondered if it was related to the incident in the mess the evening before. He and a couple of other members of the flight had rigged some gun cotton in the mess piano and blown it up. They had all thought it a great lark and even the flight commander had seemed to enjoy the prank, but perhaps in the cold light of day, he had thought better of it and reported Paul and his fellow officers to the CO. It didn't seem quite so funny now, but at the time, with a few glasses of cognac inside them all, it had appeared a great jape. Moreover, Paul's share of the damage was to be added to his already heavy mess bill.

Thank the Lord, he's stopped, Paul thought as the petty officer finished his typing and placed the document into a folder. 'Shouldn't be long now, sir', the CO's assistant said as he rose from his desk and walked into Wing Commander Samson's office. Paul glanced at the clock behind the desk and noted it was already 10.25. It looked like he was going to miss 'Stand Easy' in the mess and the chance of a cheese roll.

Two minutes later, the petty officer returned. 'The CO will see you now, sir.'

Paul tucked his cap under his left arm and marched smartly into Samson's office before bringing himself stiffly to attention in front of the CO's desk.

'Stand easy, Miller,' Samson responded, before picking up a folder from his desk and looking up at Paul's nervous face. 'I've been reading your flight commander's report on you, Miller.'

Oh God, Paul thought and his stomach heaved. It is about last night and I'm for the high jump.

'It says here that you're shaping up into quite a competent pilot, but you're too inclined to play the fool. Is that so?'

'It's just high spirits, sir. All the young pilots like a good laugh, sir.'

'Yes… I suppose that's true and I'm no kill-joy, but there's a time and a place for a prank and you seem all too ready to be in the thick of any mischief.'

Paul deemed it prudent to remain silent as he listened for his fate.

'Miller, I took you into the Service as a favour to your father. You seemed keen and I saw a spirit in you that I liked. But flying's a serious business and there's going to be a war soon…'

Is there? Paul thought. He vaguely recalled General Edgar saying something similar, but he cast his mind back to the present to listen to Samson.

'…and I'm determined that naval aviation is going to make its mark in it. It could even shorten the war. That means there isn't going to be any place in it for fools and jesters. It's time you grew up and stopped your tomfoolery. Do you understand?'

'Aye, aye, sir,' Paul responded with the typical naval phrase to cover most eventualities.

'You may not have heard, but Mister Baines has decided to take retirement.'

There is a god, Paul thought. He and the other pilots thought the flying instructor too much of a mother hen for teaching young students. He would never fly in anything but perfect weather conditions and was all too 'windy'. But what's that to do with me?

'Naturally, I am seeking a replacement, but in the meantime, it gives me latitude to try out an idea I've had in mind for a few months.'

Paul began to relax as he realised that he wasn't going to get a dressing down after all, but he wondered what the CO was on about.

'If we're going to war, we need to start taking a few more risks in our training. Once the new members of the wing have taken their tickets, I want them to be taught some more adventurous flying, in poor weather as well as good. Do you understand me?'

'Er… not really, sir. I mean, it sounds a good idea.'

'I've seen you fly, Miller… and your flight commander agrees with me. You handle the Avro well. In future, I want you to take the observer's seat and take up a few of the newer pilots. Let them go up into cloud, try some tight turns or steep dives. Shake 'em up a bit. You know the sort of thing. Get them to really fly the machine. Find its limits. Got that?'

Paul was too astonished to reply immediately. 'You mean, you want me to become an instructor, sir?'

Samson smiled for the first time in the interview. 'I suppose I do, Miller. It's time you took some responsibility.'

*****

Paul was now beginning to understand why some of the civilian instructors were 'windy'. It took real courage to teach men to fly. Aviation was hazardous enough without the perils of a nervous student at the stick. And his students had supposedly already learned to fly and even been awarded their tickets! He supposed that he must have been as bad, but it all seemed so long ago.

The next student climbed in to the Avro, his third of the morning. Paul recognised him as Henderson, quite a decent sort, but inclined to be a little too confident in his own abilities. He decided to ginger him up a little on this flight and dent that certainty of his.

'Right ho, Henderson. Just strap yourself in and go through your checks whilst I write up my notes on the last student.' Paul had only been conducting these training flights for a couple of weeks, but he could already see the benefit of them. Once the young pilots had overcome the experience of being scared witless, they became more confident in their aircraft. The flight commander was very pleased and Paul was finding he had a little more respect in the mess. His new duties seemed to be an outward mark of Samson's confidence in him and he was enjoying the kudos. Last night, he had even refrained from the usual mess game of throwing a lieutenant over the bar. My word, he thought. I'm only twenty-two and I'm already beginning to feel old.

Henderson signalled he was ready and Paul instructed him to start the engine. As it fired at the third attempt, Paul again thought it odd to be sitting in the observer's seat rather than in the rear with the controls. He still didn't like the feeling of not being in control. He might have felt better if he had been in a dual-controlled, trainer aircraft, but Samson had been clear that the newly-qualified pilots should broaden their experience on operational machines.

He turned towards Henderson and, over the roar of the engine, shouted, 'Take her up to 2,000 feet and on a course of south-east for Dover.'

Henderson nodded in acknowledgement of the order and waved to the waiting ground crew to remove the chocks, to release the aircraft and he opened the throttle. With a lurch like that of a sprinter at the sound of the starter's pistol, the Avro sped forwards across the grassy airstrip. In Paul's peripheral vision he saw the low, white buildings of the Eastchurch aerodrome pass by to his left. The wash of the propeller blew engine oil onto his goggles that he wiped away with the end of his scarf. Within seconds, the jolting stopped and he could feel the wheels leave the earth and see the ground begin to fall away beneath him. He shaded his eyes and looked up and around to check there were no other aircraft in the immediate vicinity. He had forgotten how restricted the view was above from the front seat with the upper wing lying overhead.

Almost immediately, the engine cut for no explicable reason, but a common enough occurrence not to warrant alarm. It had happened to him twice when he had been a student and the drill was to set the machine into a gentle dive and volplane down to one of the many fields surrounding the aerodrome. A few sheep were about to get a nasty surprise.

Suddenly, Paul sensed danger. Henderson wasn't making for the field directly ahead, but banking to the left and keeping the nose of the Avro above the horizon. Paul took in the situation within half a second and swivelled round to shout at Henderson. 'Don't turn back, you fool! Never, ever turn back,' he screamed, but it was already too late. The aircraft was at a height of only a hundred feet and would lose fifty feet in the turn. The Avro was already at an angle of forty-five degrees and Paul could see her side-slipping towards the ground. He realised Henderson was trying frantically to keep up the nose of the Avro, but Paul knew it to be hopeless. She had stalled and there was nothing more Paul could do but pray.

Chapter 8
July 1914

It was not often that John Miller had the grot to himself. Now a second-year-midshipman, he had been elevated to the exalted six-berth cabin. By rights he should have been about his duties along with his fellow snotties, but he was taking advantage of the fact that this week he was working in the engineering department and was not due on watch in the boiler room until 16.00. He hoped the First Lieutenant would not think to inspect the midshipmen's cabins this afternoon since, instead of studying or writing his journal, John was in his hammock. If truth be told, he needed some sleep.

John looked back on the events of last night with much satisfaction. Perhaps, it would be more accurate to state that he looked back on the events of this *morning* with much relish. Whilst *Warrior* had been moored off the French naval base of Toulon these past two weeks, he had made the acquaintance of the eighteen-year-old daughter of a French engineering commander. He and Rozenn had met at the French Navy's Midsummer Night's Ball. During the subsequent days, he had courted her assiduously and they had moved on from their first tentative kiss and embrace, to an evening of full and passionate kissing the night before. John had even been permitted to feel the outline of her small breasts, but the experience had been less appealing than he had imagined. He had no experience with English girls, but the older midshipmen had told him that continental girls were a little more giving. Certainly, he could not imagine any English girl of his acquaintance kissing him the way Rozenn had. However, even she had objected to him placing his roving hand any higher than the knee. Of course, he had promised to write frequently and call on her when the ship returned to the port later in the year, but he was already imagining the progress he might make with the girls in Brindisi.

His courtship ashore had been long and pleasurable, but he had still managed to catch the last liberty boat back to the ship at 04.00. To his chagrin, however, the First Lieutenant had been on the gangway to witness the return of the last liberty men as the ship was under sailing orders. He had not said a word, but the look had been enough to inform John that the First Lieutenant did not approve of officers returning on board so close to sailing. Nonetheless, after the briefest of sleep, John had presented himself on the quarterdeck, shaved and dressed, but with perhaps less than his usual gaiety, ready for Harbour Stations at 07.30.

Like his fellow midshipmen of the *Warrior*, he regarded the First Lieutenant as bitter and twisted, and overzealous with respect to their training. Lieutenant Commander Collins was certainly a little twisted. Unusually, for a sea-going officer, he walked with the aid of a stick. Two years earlier, he had taken advantage of an admiralty scheme to encourage naval officers to take a flight in an aeroplane. Sadly, the aircraft had landed upside down, killing the young pilot and damaging Collins's spine. It was rumoured in the grot that Collins's future in the RN was under review by the medical hierarchy of the Admiralty and so he was keen to make a good impression on this commission.

John was sure he had only been asleep for a matter of minutes when he was roughly shaken by one of the more junior midshipmen.

'For God's sake, Miller. Show a leg. Rouse yourself.'

In John's dream he had just started to make progress with an Italian *signorina* and rather resented the brute that was shaking him so forcibly. It was only when he was turned out of his hammock that he reluctantly and violently returned to the world of consciousness.

'Miller, you ass. The First Lieutenant has been looking for you everywhere. Thank the Lord he never thought to look for you here. You're to report to him on the bridge immediately.'

John was startled by the news. Was he about to face a dressing down for his carousal ashore last night? He knew he still had to prepare his report on the evolution of Mediterranean mooring, but that was not due with Collins for another week. He wracked his brains for any other explanation, but had the sense to dress quickly whilst he thought.

Seven minutes later, he appeared on the bridge as nonchalantly as he could.

'Sir, you sent for me.'

'About time, too, Miller. I asked to see you half an hour ago. Why weren't you in your part of ship on the quarterdeck or in 'Y' turret?'

'I'm working in the engineering department this week, sir,' John responded smoothly. 'As my next watch is not until the Second Dog, I thought I would make a start on that journal article you asked me for. Do you remember? The one on Mediterranean mooring. It really is clever of the French to save on berthing space by mooring their destroyers stern to, sir.'

'Shut up, Miller. I know very well about the evolution and judging from the time you returned from ashore this morning, I'm surprised you have the energy. However, should your feigned enthusiasm be proved to be true, then I shall expect an article much improved on the usual drivel you force me to read. The Paymaster tells me you speak fluent French. Is that so?'

'Well, hardly fluent, sir, but I get by.' John was enormously relieved he was not in trouble, on this occasion anyhow, and felt he could afford to be modest.

'Do you or do you not speak French, Miller?'

'Er… yes, sir.'

'Right, then. I have just the job for you. If you look over the starboard bridge wing, you will see a fleet of French trawlers. The steamer ahead of them is Greek and her master has reported that he collided with one of the drifters, sending it to the bottom. You are to take one of the boats and visit each of the fishing vessels to establish if any of them has picked up survivors or corpses. Now cut along. The boat's party has been awaiting your pleasure these past ten minutes or more.'

*****

Mercifully, the sea was calm; a continuous vista of blue with no fleck of white horses. John had no difficulty boarding the iron-walled, steam trawler, *Titania*, followed by Seaman Evans and another of the boat's party. Collins had suggested her as John's first call since she was the biggest vessel in the flotilla of fishermen and, perhaps, most likely to have recovered the survivors. As he clambered over the gunwale of the trawler, John was surprised to be greeted by a girl who could not have been much older than sixteen. She motioned him and Evans to follow her to the wheelhouse and introduced them to her father, the skipper of the *Titania*.

Captain Jean-Claude Le Marchand was unusually short and slight of build for a fisherman and John could not imagine him capable of hauling in the heavy trawls. He also spoke with a heavy Corsican accent that challenged John's understanding, notwithstanding his fluent French. After the brief introductions, John explained his presence on board in his best French.

'Captain, my ship is ready to coordinate the search for survivors from the missing fishing vessel, but first we need to know how many men are missing.'

'Lieutenant, I and my men are very grateful for the help from your navy. The *Oberon* was one of our sister ships and I know all the men well. There are eight in all, but I have no wireless set, so cannot say if any have been picked up by my colleagues. But wait, I can see the skipper of the *Orléan* waving. Perhaps, if we approach her, we might gain more news.'

John ordered the coxswain of his boat to stand off and Le Marchand manoeuvred his vessel within hailing range of the *Orléan*. The two captains exchanged words in their native Corsican that John could barely understand. On completion, Le Marchand turned to him.

'My friend says that the next vessel has recovered two bodies from the *Oberon* and suggests you go to speak to her skipper.'

'Very well, captain. I will do that. However, might I suggest we start organising a systematic sweep for survivors? Perhaps you and the *Orléan* could position yourselves in line abreast with my ship, ready to conduct a sweep to the south-east. I'll speak to the other skippers and seek the same cooperation.'

For the rest of the afternoon and long after he should have started his watch in the boiler room, John visited every one of the seven fishermen and organised them in the search of the waters surrounding the last known position of the *Oberon*. He felt like a sheepdog corralling sheep as he harried each skipper to stay in line and respond to the course changes signalled from the halyards of the *Warrior*. It was exhausting work, flitting from one vessel to another, climbing onto their decks and back into his boat. He was exceeding his brief, he knew, in organising the fishermen to help with the search, but it seemed the logical thing to do and he had earlier sent Evans back to the cruiser to explain his intentions. Collins had obviously approved of his initiative as he had sent back Evans with Midshipman Harris to assist him.

John found every one of the fishermen extremely friendly and grateful for his efforts to help them find their shipmates. They referred to him affectionately as *le petit amiral*. They also plied him with generous amounts of cognac and this contributed to his feeling of weariness. So far, the men of the fishing flotilla between them had recovered only the two corpses, but happily two survivors, too.

As John and his little command tucked into a delicious *bouillabaisse* prepared by Maria Le Marchand, the *Titania*'s cook, he observed that despite the absence of a common language, she and Evans seemed to be getting on well together. By chance, Evans was also a member of the quarterdeck party and John had had many opportunities to see him at work. Given that HMS *Warrior* was the first ship for them both and they had joined her on the same day, he felt a bond with Evans and he had never forgotten his help in carrying his sea chest. Nevertheless, the strict hierarchy of a modern cruiser had prevented any form of intimacy between them and this was the first chance they had had to renew that bond. He wondered whether he might enjoy smaller ships, such as destroyers, more than the big ships. On a more macabre note, they had also shared their first experience of seeing a corpse that afternoon. It was an experience that neither was ever likely to forget.

On board the *Gloire* they had seen the body of a young seaman laid out on the fisherman's trawl deck. The young man was about John's own age, perhaps even a year or so younger. He was blond with blue eyes, an unusual colouring for the Mediterranean, and it was the eyes that had so disconcerted John. They had stared wide open, almost as a reflection of the blue sky above. For some reason, he had assumed that the dead died with their eyes shut, much as if going into a deep sleep. In other appearances, the corpse had looked no different from a live person. It was the unblinking, dull eyes that had given away the fate of their owner. It now appeared to John as if the living harboured a pair of lights behind the eyes, but when one died, these lights were turned out. Perhaps conscious of his inner distress, one of the fishermen had gently closed the eyelids of the young man.

He felt better for the meal and had managed to dissuade his hosts from offering him more than one glass of the dark, strong, red wine they were accustomed to consume. As he mopped the last of the soup from his bowl with a chunk of crusty bread, he could hear the fishing vessel being hailed. He looked out through the scuttle for the origin of the noise, but could see little against the bright-red of the setting sun. It was not until he went on deck that he spotted another of the *Warrior*'s boats approaching. In its stern stood a petty officer John did not recognise, but who clearly recognised him from his uniform.

'Sir, we're calling off the search,' the petty officer called. 'You're to report back on board immediately.'

'But there's still nearly an hour of light left, PO.'

'Aye, sir. But we've picked up the skipper of the sunken vessel, as well as another corpse. According to the skipper, the two missing men were in the engine room at the time of the collision and it's nigh on impossible they'd have escaped. The reckoning is that they went down with their boat. Leastways, sir, the light's going anyway and by the time you've been round everyone it'll be past sunset.'

John could see the sense in the decision, but was disappointed not to have the chance to find the two remaining lost men. 'Fair enough, PO. I'll let everyone know. Perhaps you could hang on a couple of minutes and then you could take Midshipman Harris back to the ship. I'll need another half hour yet, so I'll hang on to my boat's crew.'

'No problem, sir. I'll come alongside the starboard quarter.'

It was with genuine emotion that John bade each of the skippers and their crews farewell. On several occasions he was kissed on both cheeks by men with tears of gratitude in their eyes for his part in the navy's operation to rescue three of their number. Every crew deposited a share of their day's catch in the ship's boat and on four occasions he had to stop the fishermen giving the boat's crew a bottle of brandy to take back to their mess. Even so, he was confident some had slipped through his guard, but he did not intend taking the matter further. It had been a long afternoon and evening of work under the heat of the Mediterranean sun and his little crew had performed well. He did not begrudge them and their messmates a little reward.

As he returned on board his ship, the sun was setting and forming a red column from the horizon to a point ahead of the ship's bows. The sea was still calm and, as the seaman hooked the boat onto the falls, he could hear the *chush chush* sound of the *Warrior*'s bows cleaving through the sea, followed by the slapping of gentle waves against the hull. On a less tragic day, he thought, it would have been a beautiful evening to be at sea. He climbed the ladders to the starboard bridge wing and spotted several of his fellow midshipmen with their sextants, notebooks and chronometers, taking a sight of the setting sun and preparing for evening stars. He felt incredibly weary. It had been an exciting day, but the adrenalin from his emotionally-charged body had subsided, he had not had much sleep the night before and it had been a physically tiring day. He also knew he had to be up at 03.30 for the Morning Watch in the boiler room.

On requesting permission to visit the bridge, he was immediately and to his surprise, ushered by the Midshipman of the Watch to speak to the Captain instead of the First Lieutenant. Captain Borrett turned to him from his chair on the starboard side of the bridge.

'Ah, Miller. You're back. All finished then?'

'Yes, sir. Each of the skippers of the fishing vessels has asked me to convey his thanks to you for the ship's part in the search and rescue operation.'

'I'm pleased to hear it. We're all brothers on the sea. What are they doing with the corpses?'

'They've all been transferred to the *Titania*, sir, and she and the entire flotilla are returning to their village. I did offer them the services of the RC padre, sir... if they wanted to conduct a burial at sea, but they preferred it this way, sir.'

'The bishop might have thought that a little presumptuous of you, Miller. But from what I hear, you have had an afternoon of presumption.'

John blanched at the criticism. 'I'm very sorry, sir, if you consider I exceeded my orders, but...'

'Stop, Miller. I'm teasing you and it was very wrong of me. After all, you can hardly tease me back, can you? You've done well, my boy, and when I write home to your father about it, I'm sure he will be very proud of you. You used your initiative and that's a quality to be admired in the Service. Now the Engineer Commander tells me you're working in his department this week. Under the circumstances, he has persuaded the Senior to allow you to forego your Morning Watch so you can get your head down. I'm afraid, after that, it's back to the dull routine of a midshipman's life. But well done.'

Borrett then turned away and called to the Navigating Officer, 'Right, Pilot. Do we have a course yet? It's time we proceeded in accordance with previous orders.'

John recognised he was dismissed and quietly withdrew from the Captain's presence. As he did so, he found himself no longer tired. He basked in pride at what the great man had said. He really hoped Papa would be pleased, too.

Chapter 9

Paul decided he didn't like hospitals. As far as he was aware, it was his first ever visit to one as a patient and there was much about them that he didn't like. For a start, the smell of carbolic soap and floor polish offended his olfactory gland. The noise of his leather-soled shoes on the linoleum floors of the Royal Naval Hospital at Gillingham echoed off the bare, white-washed walls of the 1,000-foot main corridor to annoy his ears. The thread-bare rug of the consulting room and its plain furniture were not pleasing to his eyes, and most annoyingly, he had an itch on his left forearm that he could not scratch due to the cast of Plaster of Paris encasing it. He looked with envy at the pot of freshly-brewed tea on the surgeon's desk before him and realised he was thirsty, too.

The surgeon was a Royal Navy Fleet Surgeon, as denoted by the red cloth interspersing the three gold rings on his reefer jacket, and a specialist in bone fractures. To Paul's impatience, he was spending too much time studying some black sheets of film on which were imprinted the ghostly, fluoroscopic shapes of part of his skeleton.

'Amazing,' the surgeon muttered to himself. 'Absolutely fascinating what these Roentgen machines can show up.'

Paul could contain himself no longer.

'So, when will I be fit to fly again, sir?' It was nearly four weeks since his accident the month before. Tragically, Henderson had not survived the crash, but probably thanks to him releasing his lap strap just before the crash, Paul had been thrown clear of the machine. Mercifully, the aeroplane had not caught fire, but Henderson had broken his skull on the fuselage.

'It's difficult to say, young man. It doesn't look as if your collar bone is fractured as we first thought, but there's still the breaks to your wrist and forearm. The bones are knitting together nicely, though, so… perhaps, another six to eight weeks to be sure.'

'What? Up to eight weeks? It can't be, sir. We may be going to France any day now and my CO needs me.'

'I expect he does, Miller, but more than likely he wants you fit to fly. Even I know you can't fly with one arm. You'll just have to let nature take its course and be patient. Keep your arm in the sling and it'll help things along.'

'But, sir? Eight weeks… surely not? I mean… once my shoulder's healed, I could fly with my arm in this cast… You don't understand what it means, sir. The Service is splitting into squadrons and I don't want to lose my place.'

'Young man, an old saw-bones I might be, but I've been dealing with fractures for nigh on twenty years now. How long have you been a pilot?'

'About a year, sir.'

'Aye, well I'll not presume to tell you how to fly your damned aeroplanes. But listen to me, lad. Whether there's to be a war or no war, you'll not be flying until Mother Nature says you can.'

*****

Petty Officer Durton, coxswain to Admiral Miller, usually loved polishing his officer's Mercedes Simplex Saloon. It was a fine example of German engineering that the admiral had brought back from Berlin in 1908 after his appointment there as His Britannic Majesty's Naval Attaché to the Courts of Berlin, Copenhagen and The Hague. It now lay in the mews garage of Miller's John Nash-designed, neo-classical property in Cumberland Terrace off Regent's Park, a property he had inherited from his father, a *nabob* who had made his money as a ship owner and captain out in India. However, Durton was distracted and vexed by the conversation he had recently overheard in the drawing room.

It wasn't that he was nosey in listening to conversations in the household, he thought, but how else was he to know what was going on and anticipate the admiral's requirements? After all, the admiral was a busy man with an important position at the Admiralty. He couldn't be expected to keep his mind on trivial matters, such as when he had to leave for luncheon or dinner at his club, or be home for some social event his wife had organised. It was all the fault of Master Paul, of course, and he wasn't worth the bother. He might not be the youngest, but definitely the runt of the litter, I reckons, thought Durton. Too much of a prankster and always a worry to the admiral. Typical of him to have joined the highfallutin' Air Service and not gone to sea like a proper officer. And now the mistress was talking of leaving the admiral to go back to Switzerland. And all on account of the young rascal's recent flying accident. He shuddered as he recalled her high words.

'If it hadn't been for you, William, this might never have happened.'

'I fail to see the connection, my dearest. It's not as if…'

'None of your, "my dearest". I'm not in the mood to be patronised. You know very well that but for you, Paul would still be at Cambridge.'

'But, Johanna, that's quite untrue. It was Paul's decision and his alone.' The poor admiral had sounded quite contrite.

'Fiddlesticks, William. You've never denied that you had a chat with Murray Sueter to fix it for Paul to become a Special Entry officer. You should have kept out of it. You'll never be happy until all our sons are in uniform. Praise the Lord that one of our sons had the courage to defy you over that.'

Durton buffed the already gleaming chrome of the headlights and checked his reflection. After adjusting a strand of hair in an attempt to cover his ever-increasing baldness, he moved on to the leather work. The trouble with the mistress, he thought, was that she was a *furriner*. Not that he'd ever served in another household like, but he felt sure a proper English lady would know 'er proper place. Mrs Miller tended to be a bit too fond of airin' her views and far too independent for his liking.

He had not heard the next part of the row as one of the maids had passed and he didn't want the household thinking him one to be eavesdropping – not like some other nosey parkers he could name. But just as he was about to loiter once more outside the drawing room doors, he could not help 'earing the mistress raising her voice and it sort of attracted his attention.

'Don't think I'm going to stand for it any longer. Your interference in our sons' lives is tearing my heart apart. I'm having no more of it, I tell you.'

'But be reasonable, Johanna. All I have ever…'

'Reasonable? You tell me to be reasonable. I've spent too long being reasonable… Watching you turn the boys into an extension of yourself. I'm having no more of it.'

'Where are you going? You can't leave it there without…'

'I'll tell you where I'm going, William. I am going to the morning room to write to my brother, Franz. He's always inviting me to join him at his lodge in Arosa. Since you have driven the boys away from me, there seems little point in taking a *family* holiday in Lancashire. I'm going to spend August with what family I still have left.'

Durton had just had time to step back from the drawing room doors before the mistress had swept past him in a fury. 'Still listening at key holes are you, Durton?'

Now what sort of question was that? Durton reddened as he recalled it. Now a proper lady would never 'ave acted in such a way.

Chapter 10

On the morning of Monday 27 July, rumours abounded throughout the ship. Along with the other ships of the squadron, HMS *Warrior* was riding gently at her anchor in the outer port of Brindisi, rather than at her scheduled berth in one of the inner harbours. All shore leave had been cancelled and the ship still had steam up for sailing. However, the accommodation ladder of the flagship had been lowered and a side party detailed to receive visitors from ashore. The news in Seaman Evans's mess was that the squadron was about to evacuate King Emmanuel and the House of Savoy because the Austro-Hungarian empire blamed Italy for the assassination of the Archduke Ferdinand and was about to declare war on Italy. The senior rates had pointed out to no avail that Italy and Austria were allies as part of the Triple Alliance with Germany. It came as a disappointment to Evans's mess mates when the idle hands instead spotted a lowly Royal Navy captain disembark from a boat and mount the steps of HMS *Defence*'s accommodation ladder.

Captain William Boyle, Britain's naval attaché in Rome, was immediately taken to the cabin of Rear Admiral Troubridge. Some half hour later, a signal broke out on the flagship's yardarm for all captains to repair on board. Naturally, each commanding officer had been expecting the possibility of such a signal and had taken the necessary preparations to ensure they were able to depart their ships within five minutes of the signal being hoisted. Not only was it prudent not to keep an admiral waiting, but each was as anxious as the other to discover the admiral's intentions. News of the assassination in Sarajevo had reached them all before sailing from Toulon, but since then, the squadron had been dispersed and no further news had been received from London.

Several hours later, Captain Borrett returned to the ship and called all the officers together in the *Warrior*'s wardroom. Unfortunately, for John and his fellow midshipmen, the members of the gunroom were not invited, but Collins had promised to debrief them afterwards. It was not until six o'clock that the midshipmen were briefed on the rapidly developing situation on the mainland of Europe. All eyed the First Lieutenant with avid attention.

'Gentlemen, I know to my cost that the more indolent of you have probably never heard of the Austrian-Hungarian empire, let alone

Serbia or Bosnia, so I have brought along a chart to explain to you the geo-political events in central Europe. The more enlightened amongst you will be aware that the Archduke Franz Ferdinand, the heir to the throne, and his wife, were assassinated whilst on a visit to Sarajevo in Serbia shortly before we left Toulon. It has since transpired that the assassin was a Bosnian-Serb and Austria blames the Serbian government for the murder. Whilst we have been cruising the Mediterranean these past three weeks, tempers have been rising between Austria and Serbia, to the point that our government fears war between the two nations is imminent.'

'But, sir, what's this to do with Britain?' one of the midshipmen piped up.

'Harris, bide your time and I will come to that. The problem is that Russia has committed to come to Serbia's aid if attacked and has partially mobilised her army. Germany is backing Austria, and France is allied with Russia. As a consequence, four major European powers may be at war with each other within days. Now even Harris might have observed that Brindisi is part of Italy and that Italy, Austria and Serbia are all neighbours across the Adriatic. Note from the chart, Harris, that the briny-blue yonder forms part of the Adriatic. If Italy takes her part in the Triple Alliance, then we may soon be in a war zone. Even neutral ships can be mistaken for enemy warships if the Italian or Austrian midshipmen's ship recognition is as good as that of you clots. And that's not the end of it.'

'Do you really think we will remain neutral, sir?'

'That's a very bright question, Miller. Surprisingly so, and one that has been exercising the great minds of Whitehall. As the admiral sees matters, in the next few days we could face one of three situations. Austria and Serbia may go to war. This will probably happen and in which case we will be largely unaffected, but may wish to proceed with some caution in the Eastern Adriatic. The second possibility is more complex and assumes that the Triple Alliance goes to war with Serbia, Russia and France. The British Naval Attaché in Rome seems to think that Italy will not join the fray by the way, but that does not lessen the serious consequences of France's commitment to war. With her navy fully committed, it will place more strain on our Mediterranean fleet to cover our interests this side of Suez.'

'If the French do fight, sir, does the admiral think we will stay neutral? After all, we did sign the *Entente Cordiale*.'

'Another good question, Joynson. I'm pleased to see some of you paying attention, but of course the *Entente* is not a formal alliance. According to the attaché's information, the Cabinet is split as to whether we would then go to France's aid against Germany or maintain strict neutrality and broker a peace. His sources suggest that neutrality is still the preferred option. However, he believes the First Sea Lord considers we are morally obliged to support the French. As he sees it, we can hardly stand by whilst the Germans start shelling the French coast right under our noses. Moreover, we do have a formal alliance with Belgium and the Admiralty cannot see how the Germans would attack France except through Belgium. Were such a situation to arise and the King of the Belgians to seek our aid formally, then we might find ourselves committed after all.

'That is the admiral's third hypothesis. It is for all these reasons that the First Sea Lord has ordered all leave to be cancelled amongst the First and Second Home Fleets. For now, the First Fleet will remain in Portland following the summer manoeuvres.'

Collins allowed the gasps of surprise to subside following his bombshell, before dropping another. 'Purely as a contingency, in the event of us joining a war, the Captain has asked me to draw up a list of midshipmen who might be sent back to England to be dispersed amongst the Home Fleets. I will publish this list in due course. For now, the intention is that the squadron will weigh anchor at 06.00 tomorrow, proceed to the south and carry out squadron manoeuvres off Malta until the C-in-C decides otherwise. That will be all, gentlemen. I suggest you start taking the drills a little more seriously in future.'

*****

Admiral Troubridge's squadron did not have long to wait before receiving further orders. The following day, Austria declared war on Serbia. The same evening the Admiralty ordered the Home Fleets to their war stations.

Chapter 11
August 1914

As John entered the gunroom, he noted a huddle around the noticeboard. There seemed a fair amount of excitement, much as when the list of the next *Britannia* cricket First Eleven had been posted. However, he was too tired and hungry to take much notice. He had just finished the morning gunnery watch and needed to grab his breakfast before reporting to his part of ship.

Since leaving Brindisi the week before, Captain Borrett had put the ship on a war footing. That had not just meant additional watch-keeping duties, but as it appeared to John and the other midshipmen, the Captain and Commander were delighting in keeping the entire ship's company out of their pits with regular calls to General Quarters, Collision Stations or Fire Stations. Around this, of course, one was expected to conduct one's part of ship work. John had been put in charge of the picket boat and under the charge of the Gunner, Mister Thistlethwaite. The latter duty was at least more interesting than working on the bridge. The *Warrior*'s fire-control and ammunition supply systems were hopelessly out of date and the new Gunnery Officer had welcomed John's ideas for improvement.

The new Guns was at least a turn-up for the good, John thought. The First Lieutenant, Lieutenant Commander Collins, had landed at Malta the day before, to return to England as being unfit for war service. In his place, Lieutenant Fraser, a Scotsman from Elgin, had been appointed as the 'snotties nurse' or gunroom supervising officer.

Midshipman Cartwright joined him at the breakfast table. 'I say, Miller, you off your scoff or something?' John had foregone his usual breakfast for toast and marmalade only.

'I'm merely too tired to eat, but my stomach craves filling at the same time. You just come off watch, too?'

'Quite right. I'm a bit late because there was a flurry of signals on the bridge that held my attention a while. You'll never guess where we're going now.'

John looked out of the gunroom scuttle and noted the position of the sun relative to the ship's course. 'East I'd say, so not back to England, then?'

Cartwright seemed a bit crestfallen. 'Well… yes, as it happens. But do you know why?'

'Of course not, you fathead. All I know is that one minute we're enjoying a nice cruise around the Med' and the next we're high-tailing it to rendezvous with the C-in-C. I say, Cartwright, we're not at war now are we?' John suddenly felt a surge of excitement course through him.

'Er… no… well, not yet anyhow. The last I heard, nobody's at war with anybody… yet! No, we're on our way back to the Adriatic… on a special mission! What say you to that?' Cartwright tucked into his snorker hurriedly.

'All I can say is that I wish Milne would make up his mind. It's a crying waste of coal and I'm tired of coaling ship.'

Cartwright picked out from his teeth a piece of gristle from his sausage before replying, 'I'm with you there. But you haven't asked what the mission is.' He beamed expectantly.

'Go on then. I can tell you're dying to tell me.'

'We're on the hunt, my boy. We're ordered to seek out a German battlecruiser and her light cruiser escort. The *Goeben*'s the battlecruiser, but I forget the name of her escort.'

'And why is that, dear fellow?' John asked, buttering himself another slice of toast. The wave of tiredness had now washed over him and the sight of Cartwright's rapidly diminishing sausages, bacon, tinned tomatoes and fried egg was making him envious.

'If you spent less time tinkering with rate control mechanisms and more time on the bridge where the action is, you'd know, old man… All right, there's no need to take offence.' Cartwright realised he was in danger of being splattered with marmalade. 'Well this is what I hear, anyway. The *Goeben* is a battlecruiser in name only. She's about the size of one of our battleships – with eleven-inch guns. Admiral Milne is concerned she would pose a huge threat to the French troop convoys from North Africa, should France and Germany go to war. We're being sent to find her and track her. And guess what else?'

John loaded a teaspoon with marmalade and prepared to flick it at the unfortunate Cartwright. Cartwright held up his napkin for protection and added quickly, 'The Admiral has attached two of our own battlecruisers to Troubridge's squadron – the *Indomitable* and *Indefatigable*. What do you make of that?'

John applied the marmalade to his toast. 'That is interesting, Cartwright. If the Admiral has sent two battlecruisers, it suggests he's preparing for trouble. Perhaps Collins was right and we are going to war.' John rose from the table. 'Excuse me, but I need to give that broken rate control clock some attention. We might need it shortly.'

*****

'An urgent signal for you, Herr Admiral.' The senior wireless operator handed the admiral the precious paper for him to read.

The message was highly classified, but the news came as no surprise. Germany had declared war on France. The rest of the text advised the admiral that, as he could not expect to receive any naval help in the Mediterranean, he was free to decide for himself as to his immediate movements. The admiral twirled the end of his dark moustache between his fingers as he considered his options.

The bridge chronometer displayed the time as 18.00, so there were still some hours of daylight remaining. If he maintained this course all the way to the west, then he and his escort could make a dash for Gibraltar and the exit to the Mediterranean. That would mean penetrating the enemy's screen, yet the flagship's boiler troubles would not give him sufficient speed to evade the superior forces. His second option was to head for an allied dockyard and, once the boilers were repaired, to mount an offensive action against the enemy's Mediterranean convoys. He knew that since his flagship was a modern battlecruiser of 23,000 tons, had a speed of nearly twenty-eight knots and with her eleven-inch guns and thicker armour, she was more than a match for the battlecruisers of the enemy. Together with his light cruiser escort, the admiral felt confident he could inflict considerable damage on his foe's convoys. He resolved to maintain his original westward course.

His mind made up, Rear Admiral Wilhelm Souchon, handed the signal to his flag captain. Looking over the starboard bridge wing, he observed *Seiner Majestät Schiffe Breslau* maintaining station a thousand metres astern. 'Signalman,' he ordered. 'Make to *Breslau*, "Germany now at war with France. Proceed in accordance with previous orders to Bône."' As Souchon dictated the message, the men on the bridge cheered spontaneously.

*****

Eight hours later at 02.00, Souchon was awoken by *Kapitän zur See* Richard Ackerman, commanding officer of SMS *Goeben* and hence, Souchon's flag captain.

'I am sorry to disturb you, Admiral, but I have an immediate signal from Admiral von Tirpitz.'

Souchon sat up in his bunk and switched on the electric light above it. 'Very well. What does it say, Ackerman?'

'It says we are to proceed at once to Constantinople, Admiral.'

'But that is ludicrous. When do we arrive off Bône?'

'We will be off the Algerian coast at first light, Admiral. That should be in a little over three hours.'

'It would be a pity to turn back without tasting that moment of fire so ardently desired by us all, would you not say, Ackerman?'

'Like all the men, Admiral, I am keen that the *Goeben* should have the honour of firing the first shots of the war at sea. But Tirpitz's orders are clear, Admiral.'

'Ackerman, you are a good officer and a loyal servant of the Fatherland, but is it not possible that atmospheric conditions in this region may well have interfered with the signal, making it difficult to decode. Tell the *Admiralstab* that the message was garbled and to send it again. I feel certain that we will have completed our operation off Philippeville by the time we have clear instructions. Call me again at dawn.'

*****

'Hallo, Miller. What are you doing up at this ungodly hour? I thought you had the First watch.'

Lieutenant Eric 'Rufus' Fraser unfolded a camping stool and invited John to sit beside him at the forward gun director. It being soon after 06.00, the Mediterranean sun was well above the horizon, but the last of the overnight fog had still not disappeared. The lookouts still wore scarves or mufflers to keep out the chill. Fraser had no need for such garb, relying instead on the fiery-red, bushy beard that had earned him his nickname throughout his naval career.

John noted several drops of moisture beginning to evaporate from the red mat of hair.

'Good morning, sir.' John saluted Fraser smartly. 'Assistant Paymaster Creswell has been taken ill, sir… The Clerk to the Captain's Secretary,' he added quickly in response to Fraser's questioning look.

'Oh, aye. I recall him now. A pimply wee runt of a fellow with the big chin. But you're no surgeon.'

'Er, no, sir. But Creswell collates the confidential signals and I've been detailed to take over his job for the day. A stack of signals came in overnight and I was given a shake to handle them.'

'Hard luck, laddie… Anything interesting among 'em? Hang on one second.' Fraser turned to his assistant. 'Thompson, go fetch the middie a fresh mug of kai, if that widdne be too much trouble. So, Miller, spill the beans. Ye ken speak freely now.'

'It's all quite interesting, actually. It seems the Italians have decided not to honour their obligations to the Triple Alliance and have declared their neutrality.'

'I kenned that, Miller. They announced it before we declared war on Germany yesterday. So, whit's new?'

'Yes, sir, but the latest news is that they are upholding their neutral status by insisting the *Goeben* leaves Messina within twenty-four hours. Moreover, they'll not provide Admiral Souchon with coaling facilities. According to Admiral Milne, that means Souchon must leave Sicily today! The hunt is back on.'

'Now that, laddie, is, indeed, of interest. So, what are our orders then?'

'Milne's expecting Souchon to go north, so he's keeping the battlecruisers with him. He's sent *Gloucester* to watch the eastern end of the strait and if the *Goeben* passes her, we'll be in position to intercept.'

'Aye, well I don't fancy *Gloucester*'s six-inch guns up against the German's eleven-inchers. A pity the Cabinet didnae let the battlecruisers engage them the other day.'

'But, sir!' John exclaimed indignantly. 'That wouldn't have been fair. We hadn't declared war then.'

'No, but if you're going to argue the sensibilities of war, it was hardly fair to hoist a Russian flag at the masthead and then to shell the French at Philippeville and Bône. And if we fail to intercept

Souchon in time, those guns of his will play havoc with the French convoys and hundreds or thousands may yet die for the sake of that legal nicety. Ah, here's Thompson back wi' yer kai.'

John knew from experience to leave the enamel mug of the hot mixture of milk and sweet chocolate to cool before tasting it. Instead, he scanned the horizon to the west in the hope of being the first to see the smoke of the Germans, but the only warships in sight were those of Admiral Troubridge's squadron. He used the silence to muster the courage to raise a question that had irked him for the last couple of days.

'Sir, I was wondering…'

'Go on, laddie. Spit it out, whatever it may be.'

'Well, sir, the list posted on the gunroom noticeboard… of the midshipmen being landed to return to Britain.'

'What of it, Miller?'

'I was just wondering… I was just wondering why my name was not on it, sir?'

'Oh that.' Fraser turned to scan the horizon and then seemed to forget John's presence as he focused on the view of HMS *Black Prince* ahead of *Warrior* in the squadron's formation. John sipped his cocoa quietly. He felt he might have over-stepped the mark with the gunroom supervising officer.

'Are you not happy here, then?' Fraser suddenly asked.

'No, I mean yes. No, I mean, I am happy on board, sir. It's an honour to serve under Captain Borrett, sir. He is a very fine officer and, as a friend of my father, he deserves my loyalty.'

'Aye. I ken what you mean, but that's not answering my question, is it?'

'I suppose not, sir. What I mean is that I'm jealous. The chaps on that list think they might fetch up in a destroyer. Somewhere they might see some real action.'

'They're probably right, laddie. And ye don't think we're likely to see action out here. Come on. You've just read the latest signals. We might be in action tonight, with seven-point-two-inch guns against the equivalent of a battleship. Hardly my recommendation for a quiet life. And if the Austro-Hungarians come into the war on the side of Germany, the Med's going to hot up considerably. What's the real beef, son?'

'Oh, I don't know, sir. I just want to do something important. Perhaps prove myself to my dear Papa. I've a brother in submarines and another in the Air Service. They're bound to be in the thick of it soon. Meanwhile, I'm a snottie in an old cruiser, stuck out of harm's way. It all seems so… mundane.'

Fraser laughed loudly. 'You were born too late, laddie. You fancy yourself as a Mister Midshipman Easy, cutting out French sloops. Weell, who can blame you, but understand me, laddie. Being a naval officer today's not all about swashbuckling courage. You need to master the technology to fight your ship. That includes engineering, fire control systems and torpedoes. By all accounts, Lieutenant Commander Collins thought you a little too fond of carousing ashore to be concentrating on yer journal.'

'So that's why,' John mumbled to himself. Collins had done the dirty on him, he thought. He scraped off a peeling and rusting paint flake from the binocular stand. Fraser interrupted his introspection by laying a hand on his shoulder.

'Listen, laddie. We've all been there. You're young and you like to have fun, but you're under training and that means knuckling down to your studies. And don't look at me in that *murnefull* way. You have some fine qualities that stand you well for the future. I'm impressed with your technical and practical skills. Mister Thistlethwaite speaks highly of your enthusiasm and industry in the gunnery department, but you need to apply those same skills to other parts of ship. In particular, practical seamanship. I've served in destroyers and judging by your journal, it would horrify me to have you as *my* fo'c'sle officer.'

Suddenly, the ship's bugle rang out, sounding the signal, '*Repel Torpedo Attack*'. Without another word, John rushed to his defence station, in charge of 'A' turret, one of the ship's seven-point-two-inch guns. He quickly learned that a look-out on the bridge of the *Black Prince* had sighted what appeared to be a periscope about three miles off in the flat-calm sea. The Officer of the Watch had ordered full speed and John noted that the ship was already up to fourteen knots. It struck him as odd that there should be a submarine in the vicinity. As far as he was aware, the Germans had no submarines in the Med' and the nearest Austrian submarine base was at Pola, far up the Adriatic coast. It didn't matter. All submarines were to be considered hostile unless accompanied by an allied escort. John could not help but think of what his brother Richard might be doing in command of his submarine right now.

He reported his turret closed up and ready for action to Fraser by telephone and was ordered to load with High Explosive, HE. Fraser gave the range from *Warrior* as 8,000 yards. The gun layer made the necessary adjustments to account for the target's position, expected course and speed and those of the *Warrior*. Immediately, John heard the sound of gunfire to starboard. HMS *Black Prince*, to starboard and nearest the enemy submarine, had opened fire. John felt excited. The war was less than two days old and he was in action. He reported the gun loaded and ready to fire.

The ship altered course a little to starboard and Fraser gave him the order, 'Standby to engage with HE at 6,000 yards.' John longed for a drink of water. His mouth and throat had dried up and the temperature in the turret was rising steeply on account of the gun crew's body temperatures and the heat of the sun. John could see that everyone seemed as tense as he was feeling.

He returned his attention to the rate of change. It didn't seem high enough. Perhaps the sub' was stopped in the water. Very soon, the range approached 6,000 yards and he awaited the order to fire. The tension in the turret was giving way to excitement and finally came the order, 'Check, check, check!' followed by Fraser's explanation. The enemy submarine had proved to be a drifting tree with a branch pointed upwards. The captain of the *Black Prince* must be feeling very embarrassed, John thought.

Then the quiet inside 'A' turret was rent by the sound of another explosion. The gun layer had broken wind loudly.

'Go' blimey, I needed that,' he said proudly. 'It's bin buildin' up all watch. Must 'ave bin the beans at last night's scran.'

Chapter 12

It had been good of Samson to come to London to see him, Paul thought. Now Britain was at war, Samson must have a hundred thousand other things to do as he prepared to take his new wing to France. He could have sent for Paul at Eastchurch, but had insisted Paul remain at home on compassionate grounds in support of *Mutti*. He had even tried to visit Pops in hospital, but like Paul, had been refused entry to the ward whilst Pops's life hung in the balance. *Mutti* was there now with Peter.

It seemed unfair that Peter should visit Pops when he could not, but then Peter had been with Pops when some maniac of an Irishman had stabbed him in Green Park the previous Saturday. For some reason, Peter seemed to think the Irishman had wanted to kill him and that Pops had intervened to save his life, but wouldn't be drawn further on the subject. Whatever was behind the attack, it had been fortunate Peter had been on hand. According to *Mutti*, Peter had been able to staunch the bleeding before somebody had flagged down a passing motorist who, by the greatest of fortune, had been a surgeon.

Paul looked across Regent's Park and observed a taxi-cab draw up to the entrance of the house. That must be Samson, now, he thought and he checked the mantelpiece clock. He was twenty-five minutes later than arranged. Sure enough, a naval officer emerged from the motor car, instantly recognisable as Samson by the piratical beard. He looked up to the drawing room and their eyes met. Samson smiled, nodded in recognition and disappeared from view as he approached the front door. Within two minutes, he was shown into the drawing room.

'Sorry I'm late, Miller. I was caught up at the Admiralty.' Samson breezily entered the drawing room and shook Paul's hand firmly and quickly.

'It isn't a problem, sir. I have no other engagements and I know how busy you must be. I'm afraid my mother's at the hospital. She asked to be remembered to you. Please take a seat and I'll order us some tea.'

'Actually, Miller, I don't have time for tea, if you don't mind. I have to return to Eastchurch and have asked the hackney to wait. I suspect the parsimonious clerks will object to the taximeter running on too long.'

'I understand, sir. I had heard you were off to France very soon. I just wish I was going with you. This damned arm is a nuisance.'

'We're not going to France.'

'But, surely…'

'I've just heard. We're being sent to mount patrols off the Humber instead. How is the arm, by the way?'

'Oh… Not too bad. The casts are about ready to come off, but I still have to wear this silly sling. It's a right nuisance. I've taken the PMO's advice and kept the arm exercised, but the shoulder remains a bit stiff, sir. I still reckon I'm fit to fly, though, even it is over the North Sea,' Paul added enthusiastically and with more hope than expectation.

Samson rose and went over to the window to admire the view. 'It seems a pity to go to war in such glorious weather.' Turning back to face Paul, he asked, 'I seem to recall you speak fluent French. Is that so?'

'Indeed, it is, sir. My mother's Swiss and brought us all up to speak French, German and Italian,' Paul replied eagerly.

'German, too. That could be very useful,' Samson muttered to himself. 'Are you fit enough to drive a Rolls-Royce?'

'But I don't have a Rolls-Royce, sir. My father has a Mercedes and won't let me near it.'

'But you can drive?'

'Of course,' Paul lied.

'And you still have a brother at home to see to your mother?'

'Yes, sir.' Paul was wondering where this was taking them. 'My brother, Peter, is at home. He's re-joined the Diplomatic Service and is off to Holland soon, but not for a few weeks. My eldest brother's not too far away either, but at Harwich.'

'He won't be home that often, I'd say. He's the submariner, isn't he?' Without waiting for a response, Samson continued. 'Look, I don't have much time. Would you still like to come to France with me? It wouldn't…'

'Why, of course, sir,' Paul exclaimed.

'Hear me out, Miller. You wouldn't be flying, but you'd still be under my command. I'm not happy with the decision to send us to Killingholme and I've made my case very strongly. I've been to see

Churchill, too, and suggested instead that I take the Eastchurch squadron to Belgium. He seemed to like the idea, so we could receive fresh marching orders anytime. In which case, I'm planning on taking as much transport as I can and forming a new section. My brother, Felix, will see to that, but I need a highly mobile team of officers for support duties. You up for that?'

Paul nodded in agreement and Samson continued, 'This section will comprise a number of touring cars – Rolls-Royces preferably, as they're reliable and have the power for what I have in mind. Your role would be to nip out and about fetching downed pilots. It might even involve some reconnaissance. I've not settled on the details. We could fix them up with a Lewis gun, too, in case of any bother from the enemy. The thing is, I'll need you down in Sheerness by the end of the month, fully kitted and spurred, just in case. Think you could manage that?'

'Without a doubt, sir. I could be ready earlier if need be, sir.'

'No need for that. Sort out your affairs and have your casts removed first. In any case, I don't have the motor cars ready yet. Churchill seems confident he can persuade one of his fellow MPs to rustle up and fund the first batch of vehicles, and then have them driven down to the docks over the next couple of weeks. I'm giving him command of the section with the rank of Squadron Commander in return. I don't know the fellow's name, but ring my assistant at Eastchurch and he'll sort you out with joining instructions. I'd better be off before that taximeter runs off the scale... or whatever they use.'

'Thank you for the opportunity, sir. I'm raring to go. I'll see you out, but just one thing, sir. Do you yet have all the officers you need for this section?'

'No, not really. I've only recently thought of the idea, but Churchill reckons he can provide a healthy dose of volunteers. He's creating temporary commissions in the RNVR by the cart-load. God knows what we'll do with them all. Sorry, but I forgot to ask. How is your father?'

'Still touch and go, I'm afraid. I've not been able to see him, though, sir.'

'Oh. Sorry to hear about that. Well, do pass on my best regards to him when you can. He's a damned fine man.' Samson made to leave, but paused. 'He's a very far-sighted officer, your father. We all owe him much.' With a shrug, Samson dashed into the waiting taxi-cab.

After bidding Samson farewell, Paul immediately removed the sling and danced a jig of joy, to the amusement and shock of the parlour maid. The effort made him wince, but it was nothing. He thought he might call his cousin, Charles, by telephone. Charles was an RNVR Sub Lieutenant and might enjoy an adventure in France, too. But first, he needed to call Catherine.

*****

Paul would never have described himself as·a morning person. He was far too fond of late-night carousing and his pit afterwards. He found the dawn patrols purgatory, but this morning he could see the attraction of the dawn as he walked back from Bedford Square towards Regent's Park. Britain might be at war in Europe, but the streets of London were quiet. The only vehicles on the road were the horse-drawn carts of the dairy men, although he could hear the occasional steam whistle to the east from Saint Pancras station, or it might be King's Cross, he thought. It occurred to him that he should take a short detour to Euston station and buy some flowers for *Mutti*. The flower girls would be there by now, he thought. Already Gower Road was bathed in sunshine. To have the streets to himself on such a fine summer morning was immensely pleasurable. Ah, that word 'pleasure', he thought guiltily.

As he had hoped, Catherine had immediately agreed to meet him in London to wish him luck before his hurried departure to France. They had enjoyed a very convivial evening at a restaurant in Covent Garden whilst he had planned his seduction. She had been ripe for it, too, with both brothers now in France, one with his artillery battery and the other with his RFC squadron, it had not taken much to persuade her that he might be disappearing overseas to meet his maker. Albeit reluctantly, she had agreed to invite him back to her hotel in Bedford Square to offer him some *comfort*. Mind you, it had cost him a sovereign to get past that cross-eyed night porter, but it had been money well spent.

It had not been his first sexual experience, but he had learned well from his tutors, the whores of Sheerness. Dear Sylvia, he reflected. She had been the one to complain that he had handled her like a rugby ball, but gone on to instruct him in the pleasure that a woman can take if her body is handled delicately and in the right places. Paul had remembered his tutelage and taken great care to treat Catherine's body with reverence, such that after a disappointing start, she had yielded to him and taken obvious pleasure from his caresses and massaging. In fact, Paul had found the giving of pleasure more satisfying than the actual sexual act. Catherine had complained that it had hurt and it had only been his animal urges that had committed him to completing his own pleasure. He would need to find a way to make it more pleasurable for Catherine next time.

Then again, he was likely to gain much further instruction on such matters from *les belles mademoiselles* of France. He could not wait to get over there. Best of all, his cousin Charles had expressed an interest in coming, too, if he could get cousin Elizabeth to run the shipyard in his absence. To think, in just two weeks, he and Charles might be in *La Belle France*, drinking cheap wine and gallivanting all over the countryside. Somehow, life couldn't get much better. He resolved to buy *Mutti* the biggest bunch of flowers his last half-sovereign would fetch. He felt sure he could touch her for a loan later.

Chapter 13
September 1914

Already, Paul was learning about the chaos of war. He had reported to Sheerness only to discover that Samson's squadron of transport and stores had left just a few days beforehand without him. Then he had learned with dismay that Samson had been recalled to England and the RNAS support team were due back any day on board HMS *Empress*. Paul had duly reported to Eastchurch to await further orders and discovered from the squadron office that Samson had met with a mysterious and prolonged bout of fog at Dunkirk which was delaying his return. On the fourth, Paul had then been ordered to join the squadron with utmost despatch on the next destroyer run to Dunkirk. Order, counter-order, disorder, Paul had thought.

It was, therefore, with a mixture of relief and joy that he met up with the squadron that evening. He found Samson frightfully bucked from the events of the day. He had just experienced his first fight with his motor cars and was dubbing it 'The Third Battle of Cassel'. Paul learned from his old friend, Flight Lieutenant Sidney Sippe, that Samson and two of his cars had ambushed six German officers in their own car and wounded two of them. Paul had also been introduced to Samson's brothers, Felix and Bill, both of them lieutenants in the RNVR. Felix had brought out his own Mercedes and fitted it with a Maxim machine gun.

A couple of days later, Felix asked Paul to accompany him as interpreter on a visit to the *Forges et Chantiers de France* in the port of Dunkirk. Felix drove them there in his Mercedes.

'So why are we visiting the shipyard, Felix?'

'I want you to tell the frogs that I need to find some armour plate for my car and maybe a couple of lorries.'

'Really? And what are you planning to do with it?'

'It's an idea we've picked up from the Belgians. According to the military attaché, a couple of Belgian aristos have been having great fun harassing the Huns using Minerva cars fitted with armour plate. They call it "*Uhlan* hunting". In typical War Office fashion, the army have poo-pooed the idea, but Charles wants to give it a go. Until we receive more aircraft, he thinks it might keep you young blades in plenty of mischief. I've come up with an idea to fit some plate to our lorries, too, with loop holes for the marines.'

On arrival at the *chantier*, both officers were met by one of the directors of the ship building firm and its English manager. After the usual kisses, glass of wine and pleasantries, Felix got down to business.

The director expressed surprise at Felix's request, but once its purpose was explained, became more helpful. 'Ah, I see. Most ingenious, but I regret we have no armour plating in the yard. All I can offer is boiler plating.'

'I'm not sure that will do, Paul. Explain to him that it needs to withstand bullets.'

'But I can assure you it will,' the Frenchman replied. 'Come. I will show you.'

Thirty minutes later, the French proudly laid on a demonstration of the strength of their boiler plating. Three armed guards assembled in a single rank at a distance of 500 yards from a wall, against which was leaning a huge metal plate. At the command of their corporal, each fired three rounds from their rifles at the metal target. Neither Paul nor Felix were impressed by the French marksmanship as only three rounds had hit the slab of boiler plate, but neither of the three bullets had penetrated the thick metal.

Felix was clearly pleased with the results. 'It's not as good as proper armoured plate and I don't trust it at shorter ranges, but it'll do. Ask the froggy for enough to armour two cars.'

*****

It was not long before 'The Iron Duke', as Felix's Mercedes became known, and the armoured Rolls-Royce faced their first test in battle. At Samson's request, Churchill had sent him 250 Royal Marine reinforcements. He was, also, arranging with Sueter for more cars to be armoured in Britain and transported across to augment the newly-named RNAS Armoured Car Division. It had become clear that Samson's little force was the only outfit capable of combatting the parties of German scouts roaming across northern France near the Belgian border and so the local gendarmes had volunteered to serve under him. The German cavalry, or *Uhlans*, and cycle companies were becoming a particular nuisance to the inhabitants of the villages, robbing them and burning their houses. Samson decided to conduct a sweep between Arras, Amiens and Douai with the intention of clearing out the enemy from the villages.

Samson set out on a 'drive' with a force of four motor cars and twenty-four officers and men, including Paul on a motorcycle. Paul and a Royal Marine who had taken part in the Isle of Man Tourist Trophy races, Corporal Thompson, were sent on ahead as the advanced reconnaissance unit. Just outside the village of Savoy, near Arras, they came across a civilian on a bicycle who flagged them down in an agitated manner.

'Ah, sirs. You are from the British Expeditionary Force, no?'

'Not quite, sir,' Paul replied in his fluent French. 'But how can we help you?'

'It's the *bosches*. There are about twenty in the village with their horses. They're threatening to shoot the mayor if we don't give them money and jewellery. I regret a few are already drunk on cognac and I fear for the young women. Please, gentlemen, we need your help.'

Paul listened carefully and then turned to his marine escort. 'Thompson, take the news to the CO. I'll wait here and keep an eye on the situation. Tell the CO I'll look out for him and meet him with further news.'

As Thompson sped back the way they had come, Paul followed the civilian, pushing his motorcycle to avoid the engine noise alerting the enemy. He hid it carefully in some trees about 400 yards outside the village. The civilian led him into the village and after a short distance, drew up short.

'Not this way, sir. It leads to the square. Come this way.'

The Frenchman took Paul down a side street and into a terraced house. Indicating that Paul should be silent, he led him up the narrow staircase and into a bedroom. Paul immediately recognised that the bedroom offered a view of the square below and he crawled over to the window. Having first removed his cap, he lifted himself up carefully to peer over the sill of the window. Almost directly opposite he could see an *auberge*, outside of which a number of tables had been erected and at which sat a German officer, flanked by an NCO and a bedraggled civilian. Before them, a line of villagers passed, handing over their valuables to be assessed by the NCO and then piled in two large panniers. To Paul's left he could see five young men squatting on the ground under the guard of three soldiers pointing rifles. Another soldier was urinating on the ground in front of them.

The Frenchman joined Paul at the window. 'That is the mayor, sir.' He indicated the seated civilian. 'The brutes beat him publicly with sticks, just like a dog.' He spat contemptuously in the corner. 'Look, there.' He pointed to the left, on the far side of the squatting youths under guard. 'May God strike them down.'

Paul observed that after the villagers had deposited their cash or jewellery, the younger women were then being searched insultingly by two of the soldiers, cheered on by their comrades. Paul was horrified and felt an impulse to shoot them with his revolver. However, common sense dictated that the range was too great and, more importantly, it would alert the German patrol. Instead, he surveyed the square. Off it led a number of side streets, but only two streets were wide enough for a body of horsemen to navigate, or for the armoured cars for that matter; one to the west and the other to the south. Three mounted *Uhlans* were keeping a watch on the street to the south. He memorised the geography and retired silently out of the house.

'Where are they keeping the horses?' he asked the Frenchmen.

'In the stables of the *auberge*, sir. To its rear, on the north side of the square.'

'Thank you. Now make your way to the west side of the square. Stay out of sight from the Germans, but if you see a patrol of the British, help them in any way you can. Got that?'

The Frenchman nodded before scampering away. Paul returned to the position of his hidden motorcycle and waited for reinforcements. He did not have long to wait. Within ten minutes, the naval convoy arrived, Samson at its head in the armoured Rolls-Royce and the Iron Duke at the rear. Paul quickly briefed Samson on his reconnaissance. Samson ordered his brother, Felix, to take the Iron Duke up a side road to the west in the hope of cutting off the *Uhlans*' escape and gestured for the two unprotected motor cars to follow him.

The events of the next few minutes seemed a whirlwind of activity to Paul. The mounted sentries must have heard the approach of the three motor cars and come to investigate. As they turned a corner out of the square, they came face to face with the column. They immediately charged the lead car, but two of them were cut down by the Lewis machine gun. The third galloped back to the square. As

Samson's party entered the square, they came across a scene of panic. A few of the cavalrymen had managed to find horses and were disappearing in all directions, but the majority had been caught by surprise and were still dismounted. As previously agreed with Samson, he, another officer he did not know and two marines jumped out of the vehicles and headed to the stables to cut off the Germans from their mounts.

Paul was the second to reach the stables, after the other officer, but his arrival coincided with a sharp pain in his left shoulder and the almost simultaneous *zip* sound of a pistol shot. Two Germans had either been left behind to guard the horses or had beaten them in the race for the stables. He dived for cover behind a bale of hay, but the other officer calmly shot one of the Germans in the head and was about to shoot the other when he spotted that the German was surrendering. Meanwhile, Paul could hear the two marines outside opening fire with their rifles. Seconds later, he heard two rapid bursts of the Maxim opening up.

'Are you hurt badly, dear chap?' his fellow officer asked. Paul took a moment to take stock of his situation. There was blood on his uniform and a short gash across his upper sleeve. He moved his arm and, apart from the sting of his wound, it moved freely. It dawned on him that he had been shot, but the bullet had literally grazed his arm. He trembled at the thought that a couple of inches further in and he might have taken a wound to his chest.

'Let me have a look at you,' the other officer said and knelt beside him. Paul noted that he had a trace of an Irish accent.

'I'm sorry, but we haven't been introduced. I'm Paul Miller.'

'Just let me apply this shell dressing first and I'll introduce myself in a minute… There, that too tight? No. Right, how d'you do? My name's Annesley, Francis Annesley. Pleased to meet you, Miller. Now are you fit enough to give me a hand with Fritz and Herman here?'

Together, Paul and Annesley examined the wounded *Uhlan*. Despite the bullet to his head, he was still alive, but unconscious. Annesley tossed his colleague a field dressing and indicated to him to attend to the wounded man. Paul examined Annesley unobtrusively. Like him, he was dark-haired, but he parted his hair to the left. He was taller than Paul and was old to be a mere Flight Sub

Lieutenant like Paul. Paul judged him to be about the age of thirty. The name seemed familiar, but he couldn't place it.

'I say, Annesley, that was a bit of pluck… shooting the German like that. I've never shot anybody. And good marksmanship, too.'

'Probably a piece of luck, dear chap. Mind you, I often shoot. Picked up the habit at Eton. It's not my first war either. I fought for the Turks in the Balkans.'

'So that accounts for you having the courage to shoot that fellow. I'm not sure I could have done it.'

'No courage about it. It was him or me. You'd have done the same had you been a yard ahead of me. Anyway, let's not dilly-dally here chatting. We'll leave the marines to keep an eye on these two chaps and see what's happening in the square. It seems rather quiet.'

The square was, indeed, quiet. There was no sign of the Iron Duke, but as well as a bunch of German prisoners under the watchful eye of some marines, Paul could see a couple of corpses strewn about the square. At first glance, he couldn't see any British casualties. Samson seemed pleased with the outcome of the fray, but his mood changed to concern on sighting Paul's dressing.

'Hark, Miller. Are you all right?'

'Absolutely, sir. It really is just a scratch. I was lucky that Annesley's sharp shooting prevented a worse outcome. There's a wounded man and another prisoner back there by the way.'

'I think you mean, Lord Annesley, Miller. Indeed, the Sixth Earl of Annesley. Bravo, Lord Annesley.'

Paul blushed with shame. Now he recalled the name. 'I'm sorry… I do beg your pardon, Lord Annesley. I didn't know.'

'No apology necessary, Miller. Why should you know. In any case, we're all comrades in arms here. Call me what you like.' Annesley turned to Samson. 'What's the count then, sir?'

'Including your man, six prisoners, one of whom wounded, and three dead. The others scattered through the side streets, but I'm hoping Felix will collar them.'

As if on cue, Felix's armoured car rolled into the square with a dejected Felix manning the Maxim. 'Sorry, sir,' he addressed his brother. 'They disappeared into the woods where we couldn't follow. Gave them a burst from the Maxim, but the damned thing jammed.' Felix looked around the square fearfully and then at Paul's wounded arm. 'What's the butcher's bill on our side?'

'None, mercifully, Felix. Except for poor Miller here. We'll have to get the surgeons to attend to that, of course.' Samson smiled at Paul before turning back to Felix. 'It's probably a good thing those beggars got away. They'll no doubt exaggerate our strength and before we know it, the Huns will think there's a large force guarding the approach to the coast. Now I want the prisoners searched. Any loot is to go to the mayor for return to its rightful owners. Any documents are to come to me. Miller, are you up for questioning the prisoners? I want to know where they came from and the disposition of their forces.'

Whilst Paul questioned the prisoners and examined their effects, the captain of the gendarmes arrived with some of his men. After a few words with the mayor, the villagers were galvanised into bringing food and drink to the *auberge* in gratitude to their saviours. However, Paul was in no mood to celebrate with the others. He had found his questioning of the prisoners a dispiriting experience. Their officer and NCOs had managed to escape, and those that had been caught were able to offer little information other than that they were from the 26th Dragoons of Württemberg and their barracks were at Lille. They seemed half-starved, having been on short rations for some time, and had Paul not witnessed their troop's treatment of the village residents earlier, he might have felt sorry for them. Even so, he felt guilty perusing the Germans' personal effects and letters. One of them carried a child's atlas and the map of the whole of France was only three inches square. After reporting his findings to Samson, he was sent to see Staff-Surgeon Wells. Paul liked Wells. He, too, was a qualified pilot and had a more pragmatic approach to aviators' injuries.

'You're not doing too well with that shoulder are you, son?' Wells muttered without the expectation of a reply. 'However, I think you'll live.' He cleaned out the shallow gash on Paul's upper arm with antiseptic, causing Paul to flinch from the stinging. 'Steady, son. There. That wasn't too bad, was it? I'll just dress it now and you'll be right as rain.'

'This isn't going to stop me flying, is it, sir? You said I should be fit by now.'

'Hush yourself. You'll be fine, but I think we'll leave it for a week. Your arm is going to be sore for a while and possibly a bit stiff. We'll immobilise it for a few days, in a sling. That means your motorcycling escapades are on hold, too, for now, but there's nothing to stop you going out in the cars if you've a mind to get yourself killed… Right, we're done there. Off you go and find yourself a grateful *mademoiselle* and some scran. You look quite the wounded hero.'

For once, Paul decided to follow doctor's orders and soon found himself bedded down comfortably in the stables with a pretty wench called Annette.

Chapter 14

The King Edward the Seventh Hospital for Officers had, since its foundation in 1899, become accustomed to the regular patronage of royalty, so the visit by the First Lord of the Admiralty barely raised a murmur amongst the staff or a ripple in the normal, smooth operation of the hospital. Winston Churchill and Admiral William Miller had first met immediately after the Battle of Omdurman, and then again in 1911, when Miller had sought Churchill's help as Home Secretary in a Secret Service Bureau operation against a German spy network. Over the past three years, the two had met frequently.

'Miller, my dear fellow, I am delighted to see you looking so well after your terrible experience at the hands of that treacherous Irishman. I trust you are receiving the best of care?'

'Thank you, sir. I am being extremely well looked after. Indeed, next week I am to be discharged to convalesce at home. Beds may soon be at a premium.'

'I fear you may be right there. Both our army and the French have taken one hell of a beating, but then I believe that even as we speak, the tide may be turning in our favour. I heard only this morning that our counter attack may have been successful. To avoid the French Sixth Army turning his right flank, Kluck has started pulling his army back across the Marne. Good news, what?'

'Indeed, sir. Von Schlieffen will be turning in his grave. Almost his dying words were, "To keep the right wing very, very strong". It is some consolation, at least, for our navy's failure in the Mediterranean.'

'Ah, by that I presume you mean Milne and Troubridge's failure to intercept the *Goeben* and *Breslau*?' Miller nodded. Churchill wrung his hands before continuing.

'Yes, that was a most unfortunate affair. I fear it may have profound consequences. There is to be a Court of Inquiry into the whole show later this month. You will have heard that Germany has presented both ships to the Sultan and Admiral Limpus's naval mission is being expelled from Turkey?' Churchill did not await confirmation or otherwise, but instead rose quickly and walked across to the window. He turned and pounded a fist into the palm of the other hand. 'It won't do, you know… Those two ships are going to cut off the Black Sea to the Russians… And what will that do for their war effort?'

Miller managed to get a word in this time. 'It's not certain, sir, that the Turks will inevitably join with Germany in this war, although I grant, the national fervour is likely to be decidedly anti-British. We did, after all, seize their two Dreadnoughts in build.'

'Thank you for reminding me of that, Miller,' Churchill said icily. 'Well, damn the Turks! I've a good mind to send a flotilla of torpedo boats through the Dardanelles with orders to sink the latest proud additions to the Turkish Navy. General Gallieni in France agrees with me, but Kitchener is proving difficult to persuade.'

'I had heard that Lord Kitchener had joined the Cabinet, sir.'

Churchill didn't appear to hear the comment. 'He seems afraid it'll upset the *Musselmen* the world over,' he muttered as if to himself.

'But how fares Antwerp, sir?' Miller decided it was time to change the subject. He regretted raising it, having seen the agitation of the First Lord.

'What?' Churchill abandoned his inner thoughts. 'Oh, fine. So far, the Belgians are holding out valiantly, but it is a matter that the War Cabinet is monitoring most assiduously.'

'Sir, I am very conscious that as a member of the War Cabinet yourself, you must be very pressed. It is good of you to spare the time to call, sir.'

'Nonsense. After all the sound advice you have so generously offered me these past couple of years and the service you have rendered your country, it is the least I could do. It saddens me to hear that you are forced to retire just when your country faces its greatest challenge. That Irish fellow, O'Malley was it? He has much for which to answer. Of course, he seems to have gotten clean away. I have no doubt he is in Berlin, even now.'

'But it wasn't O'Malley that wielded the knife to bring about my retirement, sir,' Miller responded quietly and grimly.

'But whatever do you mean? I understood the fiend was attempting to slay your son and you were wounded in the affray. Do I have the name wrong?'

'Forgive me, sir. I was speaking figuratively. I've been "yellowed"!'

'Calm yourself, my friend. You'll split your wound open again if you aren't careful. I presume you mean that you are being forcibly superannuated on age, whereas I understood you had been assessed as unfit for further service.'

'Unfit, be damned! I beg your pardon, sir. Thanks to my son Peter's prompt action and some skilled work by the surgeon, my liver is perfectly healed. I just need to gather my strength again. I regret that some of their lordships are using this temporary incapacitation to elbow me out. But it couldn't have come at a worse time.'

'So, I understand. I received a letter from Lord Fisher conveying similar sentiments. I gather your influence with the Foreign Secretary and even the Prime Minister, is rather resented by your superiors. It all seems most unfortunate and I will be more than sorry to see you go, but I'm obliged to say that I cannot be seen to be interfering with individual appointments.'

'But, sir, you must!'

Miller raised himself in his bed and stared fixedly with his deep, dark eyes into Churchill's eyes. As often happened, his interlocutor was transfixed and seemingly quite unable to break eye contact. The effect was almost hypnotic.

'Sir, I will share something with you of which not even the First Sea Lord is aware. A matter that might hold huge sway over the conduct of the war. But first, I must impress on you the imperative to maintain the confidentiality of what you are about to hear. The reasons will become obvious.'

'Very well, admiral. You have my full attention,' Churchill replied meekly.

'Buried in the detail of the Admiralty War Plan was an order to be sent by coded telegram to the GPO cable ship *Alert*, immediately on the outbreak of war. The *Alert* was instructed to proceed to the waters off Emden and to grapple for and sever completely the five cables linking Germany with the western seaboard of Europe and both Africa and the Americas. I understand that the operation was a complete success.'

'Yes, I vaguely recall reading of it, but nobody seemed able to explain its significance.'

'The significance, sir, is that Germany is no longer able to communicate by telegram with its colonies or its fleet abroad except by wireless or cables operated by us.'

'And how does that help us?'

'I was coming to that, sir. For the past year I have been working in absolute secrecy with the heads of Marconi and the Post Office to establish a chain of wireless receivers and operators capable of intercepting German wireless transmissions. I also have an arrangement with the Eastern Telegraph Company to receive copies of all German telegrams.'

'Good gracious. What an audacious project. But are the messages not encoded?'

'Indeed, they are, sir, but we have had a piece of luck. A by-product of my son's adventures out in Persia is that we captured a copy of the *Wilhelmstrasse*'s diplomatic code books. A rather talented member of my staff has verified both that the Germans have not yet changed their cyphers and that, with some effort, we can decrypt their diplomatic telegrams and read the original text.'

'Bless my soul. How absolutely marvellous. Is the Foreign Secretary aware of this?'

'Er no, sir. I regret that when I advised the PUS, it was made clear to me that the diplomats regard this as eavesdropping and, thus, ungentlemanly. They wanted nothing to do with it.'

'How incredibly short-sighted of them, but it is sadly unsurprising. So, are you saying that my department has the power to read all German foreign telegrams?'

'No, sir. I am not. Yes, we have the capability, but we do not have the resource. For obvious reasons, I have shared this information only in part with a very close coterie of people. The intercepts are literally piling up, gathering dust for want of a team of people to process and read them. I have just one officer with the capability for this type of work. Moreover, the Imperial German Navy has its own cyphers and we do not yet have a copy of the key. My staff officer is starting to make headway in breaking a part of the code by reading routine weather reports, but it is painstaking work and any results achieved so far have been achieved weeks after the original transmission.'

'This is all fascinating. The ramifications are stupendous. Such work might afford the opportunity to read the enemy's mind... to anticipate their every move. So how did you plan on taking this project forward?'

'I think you will understand well the need for absolute secrecy, sir. Were the Germans to suspect we could read their messages, then they would not only take more care in their transmissions, such as reducing the power of their transmitter at Nordern, but would change the cryptographic keys. The secret must, accordingly, be made known to only a very small team of people. But we must form a team of specialists with the skills to excel in this kind of work. I had in mind a mixture of bright minds from acadaemia, such as mathematicians and German linguists, as well as officers with operational experience to understand the subject matter. As for leading those teams, I naturally put myself forward to oversee the project, but would deem it necessary to place a civilian in charge of the academics and a naval officer to run the dissemination of the operational information.'

'And no doubt you have some candidates in your sights already?'

'I do, sir. The Director of Naval Education, Sir Alfred Ewing, has a background in underwater cable engineering research and, with the emptying of the naval college of its cadets, I suspect many of his academic staff at Dartmouth might be more gainfully employed. As for the naval officer, in my opinion there is only one man with both the necessary leadership skills and twisted mind for this type of work, Captain Reggie Hall.'

'Now there is a name I do recognise. He has just acquitted himself well in the recent battle in the Heligo Bight. He's in command of the *Queen Mary* is he not? I doubt the First Sea Lord would wish to see him relieved of his command.'

'You are quite right on that score, sir. But I happen to know from his wife that he is in poor health. I am confident that a few discreet enquiries will validate this and the matter would not be as difficult to arrange as it might appear.'

Churchill absorbed all he had just heard in silence for a minute.

'Admiral, I am once again indebted to you. I completely agree that your little project may have the potential to change the course of the war, but I must ask you this, and you must answer me in complete honesty. Are you truly fit to return to the Admiralty… to see the work through?'

'I give you my word, sir. I grant that it will take a few weeks to recover my strength in full, but I can progress matters immediately, nonetheless.'

'Then the matter is settled. I must return to Whitehall to prepare for this afternoon's Cabinet meeting, but rest assured that I will be speaking to the Second Sea Lord this evening to settle your future. Now I must take my leave, but perhaps next week I might call on you at your home to discuss "the project" further. Farewell, stout fellow.'

Paul decided he would enjoy working with Samson's new head of intelligence very much. Father Clancy, as a man of the cloth, was ideally placed to move around the north of France quite freely. Although an Irishman, Clancy had lived in France for much of the past ten years and his church was at Morbecque, the village of Samson's new headquarters. He was a tall man, with thinning grey hair and a long, hooked nose. Although he spoke French like a native, he spoke no German and, thus, Paul and another German speaking officer had been assigned to him. Paul admired the keen intellect behind the piercing blue eyes and the Irishman's wit. His down to earth, man of the world approach had endeared him to the 180 marines and thirty RNAS ratings now camped in the grounds of the *Château Motte au Bois*. Since Churchill's visit a few weeks earlier, Samson was receiving fresh reinforcements via Dunkirk weekly and now had access to eleven cars, three of them shipped over from England with the new Admiralty Pattern armour.

Paul and Clancy toured the grounds of the chateau. 'It's a crying shame to see the old place treated this way... but necessary, of course.' Clancy was referring to the myriad of trenches dug into the estate. 'I'll say one thing, though. That major's a clever fellow. Be careful now.' Clancy drew Paul's attention to a large tree whose trunk had been almost completely sawn through, such that by the tug of a rope, it could be made to fall across the road on which Paul and Clancy were walking. The major was the Royal Marines camp commandant, Major Armstrong.

'So, Paul, what do you think of my idea then?'

'I can see the merits, Padre, but it doesn't seem right to involve boys in a grown-ups war.' Clancy had recruited a team of boy scouts to carry out reconnaissance in return for the loan of a bicycle and payment of one franc a day.

'My reply to that, my son, is that the Germans have no such scruples about killin' babes and children when it suits them. In any case, they should come to no harm if they keep their noses clean. The Germans are hardly likely to start arrestin' wee boys, now.'

'I suppose you're right,' Paul responded unconvincingly. 'I did have another idea, though,' he added more cheerfully. 'The Hun's command structure seems a little loose round here just now and you say the telephones are all working.'

'That's right. It doesn't seem to have occurred to their army to cut or take control of the network.'

'Very well, Padre. Suppose one of us was to ring a village where we know the Germans to be quartered, speak to one of their officers and give them false intelligence of our movements. We could even pretend to be a staff officer and order them to points of our choosing. If it worked, we could play merry hell with them. Ambush them even.'

'Well, I suppose it might work out fine enough. But I'm not sure about the ambush idea. Send them out of your way by all means, but I don't want any part in ambushes. We're all God's creatures, right enough... Is there something wrong, Paul?'

Paul's attention was diverted by the approach of a young, fair-haired RNVR officer. It can't be, he thought. It jolly well is. He began to run towards the oncoming officer. 'Excuse me, Padre. I'll catch up with you later,' he called over his shoulder. The two officers embraced warmly.

'Charles, it really is you? When did you arrive?'

Sub Lieutenant Charles Miller RNVR adjusted his cap before replying to his cousin. 'Hello, Paul. I've just arrived from Dunkirk with a fresh delivery of armoured cars and reinforcements. I travelled in a very strange-looking lorry. Fitted with boiler plates everywhere and a three-pounder gun. It was deuced uncomfortable and slow. I met Edward Grosvenor on arrival, by the way. I didn't know he was here, too.' The two cousins had met Lord Edward Grosvenor, youngest son of the first Duke of Westminster, when shooting on the second Duke's estate at Abbeystead, neighbouring Marton Hall in the Forest of Bowland. William Miller and the Duke were old friends and Lord Edward had recently joined the RNAS.

'But the last I heard, Charles, the Admiralty wouldn't let you come across. They claimed your work running the shipyard was too vital to the war effort.'

'True, but then I approached Uncle William to intercede on my behalf. He's given me a letter for you, by the way. He then had a word with Churchill and here I am. Elizabeth's far more capable of running the yard than me, anyhow. She's the one with the business head. So, what's the set up here?'

'I'll show you round, but you've seen Pops? Was he well? Is he still in hospital?'

'Steady on, Paul. Give a chap a word in edge ways. He's fine and at home. Mind you, he's not fully recovered and not in the best of humour. You won't have heard. He was going to be forcibly retired, but Churchill would hear nothing of it. Demanded he stayed. He's keeping him on close to him in the Admiralty, as some form of advisor, apparently.'

'My word, Charles. That would have stung. Imagine the great Rear Admiral William Miller, VC and CSC, on the retired list and with a war on. Oh,' Paul shuddered. 'It doesn't bear thinking of. Mind you, I wonder which unfortunate had the task of telling him. Can you imagine the eruption?' The two cousins laughed loudly to the amusement and bewilderment of the nearby sentries.

'Come on, Charles, let's begin our tour of inspection.'

*****

Things were hotting up and Paul was delighted to be back flying, even if it was on reconnaissance missions whilst most of the other pilots were engaged on bombing missions over Antwerp. Churchill must have been impressed with Samson's aggressive reconnaissance operations as he had sent over a brigade of marines, placing them and Samson under French command with orders to continue raids on the German invaders and, where possible, deep into Germany itself. Samson was now using either Paul or Sippe to fly ahead of his armoured columns to scout for the enemy. It was on return from one of these reconnaissance missions that Paul discovered that the RNAS force at the chateau had been joined, not just by another squadron of armoured cars under the command of the MP, Josiah Wedgwood, but also, a squadron of the Manchester Hussars. It's starting to get too crowded round here, Paul thought, as he washed and changed after his flight. Sippe interrupted his ablutions.

'Paul, get yourself decent as soon as you can. The CO wants a briefing with all officers in five minutes. No exceptions.'

'Oh, my lord, Pi. I've still got Vaseline all over my face. I've not been back from the airfield two minutes.'

'Sorry, but you'll have to come as you are. Something's up. See you in the mess. I need to grab a few others.' Sippe rushed off leaving Paul to clean his face as best he could and to put on a fresh collar.

*****

Samson looked even more the pirate in Paul's opinion as he waited to start his briefing. There was a mischievous glint in his eyes and he seemed yet more energetic than his usual self. Paul noted that he was not the last to arrive and wondered if he might have spent another minute or two removing the oil from under his chin that was already making a mockery of his fresh collar. When the last officer sidled into the mess, Samson began his briefing.

'Gentlemen, I've just been speaking to Major-General Paris in Dunkirk. He has been sent over with a further two naval brigades and has relieved Brigadier Aston in command of what is now being called, "The Naval Division". He told me that our little outfit here is not just upsetting the Germans, but the British Army, too.'

'How's that, sir?' one of the officers called.

'I think it obvious to all why the Germans are not impressed with our little band. I hear they have even put a price on our heads. Think of that. Many of you are worth more dead than alive. However, it seems that we have now acquired ourselves a new name amongst our own High Command and not just the Army Service Corps.'

Some of the senior rates laughed out loud at the news. The RNAS were short of stores and equipment, and had gained a reputation for pilfering them from any source, including the crew of an unfortunate and previously luxuriously equipped naval airship they had kindly offered to *help*. Now the Army Service Corps had begun to lose trucks as well as tools, they always mounted an armed guard on their depot whenever the RNAS were in the vicinity and called the Armoured Car Division, 'The Motorised Bastards'.

'You may well snigger,' Samson continued, 'but it seems we are now referred to as, "Samson's Circus". The General Staff regard you as ill-disciplined, unkempt and dirty. Our new mode of warfare is not playing the game. Well, I don't care if you are a bunch of wastrels… provided you can fight.'

The men cheered and Paul felt proud to be amongst them. Looking around him, he could see what the army meant. Nobody was dressed completely in official navy uniform. Many of the pilots wore their leather flying coats over a pullover in place of the traditional reefer jacket and some had begun to wear khaki. They looked like a band of brigands or, given Samson's own piratical look, buccaneers even.

'I can tell you this, my merry band of Motor Bandits, we are in for a proper fight shortly and not mere skirmishes with cycle patrols or *Uhlans*. General Paris has orders to reinforce Antwerp and help the Belgians hold it. It will not be lost on even the dullest of pilots I have the misfortune to command…' Samson paused to allow the ribaldry and ragging to cease. 'It will not be lost on any of you, that if we lose the Channel ports, our only alternative is to reinforce the expeditionary force from France's western ports, and that will take up too many escorts we can ill afford to lose.

'Churchill is arranging for thousands of the Royal Fleet Reserve… men for whom there are no ships available… to expand the Naval Division and to be sent as reinforcements. General Paris has rather ingeniously arranged that a portion of his force already in France will be transported to Antwerp on London omnibuses.'

Samson's audience fell about laughing and there were many jokes on the subject before he brought the meeting back to order.

'A fleet of 70 London omnibuses is being shipped over to Dunkirk to arrive this evening. The buses will be manned by volunteer drivers and conductors.'

Again, there was much ribaldry at the expense of any potential female conductors.

'I will, of course, expect my officers and those under their command, to treat the volunteer drivers and conductors, and I mean all, you licentious layabouts…' Samson met the eyes of some of his officers deliberately, 'with complete respect. Our orders are to escort the omnibus convoy to Antwerp with our cars and then to take the fight to the enemy in the hardest way imaginable. I don't care what you look like or by how many names you are called, but I do expect you to bring honour to this unit, the Air Service and to the Royal Navy.' Samson began to raise his voice. 'We do not play by the rules. We play to win. Are we agreed?'

The room erupted in loud cheering. Paul felt a surge of immense pride within him. He and his friends were an élite and he knew that they all felt the same as him. They would follow 'Sammy' anywhere and do it proudly.

Once the brouhaha had died down, Samson continued more quietly.

'I am sending all the remaining aeroplanes to Dunkirk to support the bombing and reconnaissance operations on Antwerp. Sippe, Lord Carbery has had a bad crash and I have had to send him home. You will take your machine to Dunkirk and replace him. Miller, I will need you as a liaison officer, so you will remain with me. As such, we will hand over the *chateau* to the newly-arrived Hussars and all proceed to Dunkirk tomorrow. I expect you to have your men and equipment ready for departure at 07.00. Is that clear?'

There were various questions and then Samson closed the briefing. 'Finally, gentlemen, given that it is our last night here, I suggest we use the evening to show the Hussars some naval hospitality. I do not want any broken bones in the morning, but nor do I wish to hear that the guests have beaten the Motor Bandits in the mess rugger.'

*****

'So, what do you make of the latest addition to Samson's Circus then, Miller?' enquired Captain Ivor Courtney of the Royal Marines Light Infantry and one of the first naval pilots, gesturing to the Hussar officers.

'Quite splendid, I'd say. They make us look positively dowdy.' Unlike the RNAS and Marines officers who were dressed in service dress with a wing collar and bow tie, the Hussars were wearing full mess dress.

'Aye. With all that gold frogging and fur, you'd think them one of the oldest regiments of the British Army. And who would credit they're no more than a yeomanry regiment, too? I hear it said that Kitchener wouldn't let us have a proper cavalry regiment.'

'But, sir. That seems a little mean when one considers the RNAS is barely three months old and half our officers are on RNVR commissions. You're just peeved because you didn't bring your scarlet tunic.'

'True, it's in Dunkirk with the rest of my kit. But that doesn't stop me thinking them a bunch of dandies and not proper soldiers. Probably rich kids, too, who only joined up to impress the local ladies with the uniforms. Bet they'll wet themselves in the face of the enemy.'

'Sir, let's top up our glasses and meet a few of them. I'm sure they're perfectly civil.'

The two officers joined the throng and Paul thought he saw a familiar face. No, it couldn't be. It was over two years since he had seen D'Arcy and he couldn't have aged that much in the time. In any case he was taller and, on closer examination, a captain. However, intrigued, he left Courtney and approached the familiar face and the two hussars with whom he was in conversation.

'Hello, allow me to introduce myself. Welcome to the *Château Motte au Bois* and the élite of the Royal Navy. I'm Paul Miller.'

The two hussar lieutenants introduced themselves and then the captain. 'Captain Ashley Crichton. How d'you do? We're very pleased to meet you chaps. We've heard you've seen a little action with German cyclists.'

'Well, a little more than that. We've seen off a fair few of you lot, too, in the form of the *Uhlans*… I say. Excuse me asking, but you seem familiar. Are you by any chance related to D'Arcy Crichton?'

'Why, I am,' the hussar captain replied cheerfully. 'He's my youngest brother. How come you by his acquaintance, may I ask?'

'My, how interesting. As it happens, my family seat is in Lancashire. Our CO, Samson, is from your neck of the woods, too, so it's a small world. I used to share a passion for motorcycles with your brother… I say, are you all right?'

Paul had noticed that Crichton had suddenly frozen and he put out his hand to catch the glass that Crichton looked in danger of dropping immediately.

'Don't you dare touch me!' Crichton roared and stepped back into three other officers, causing them to spill their drinks and turn towards the scene.

'You, sir, are a damned liar and a cheat. If you were a gentleman, I would call you out.'

'Steady on.' Paul was shocked at the turn of events. 'We've only just met… I can't think what…'

'Be silent, you… bla'guard. The only words I wish to hear from you are those of an apology and to the effect you will repay the twenty pounds wager of which you cheated my brother.' Crichton turned on the spot to leave Paul staring at his back before he was ushered away by a couple of fellow officers. Paul let himself be led away, too. He was too stunned to resist.

Meanwhile, Samson, who had observed the incident, called across to the sergeant in charge of the mess. 'Sergeant, announce dinner quickly. But before you get everyone seated, I want you to change the seating plan and ensure those two officers are seated at opposite ends, but the same side of the table.'

*****

Paul rose at 03.30 and roused Charles, fast asleep in the other bed in the room.

'What's up? It can't be 05.00 already? I only dropped off a few minutes ago.'

'No, Charles. It's a bit earlier, but I need your help with something.' Paul explained his plan.

'Oh, come off it, Paul. We're leaving soon and will like as not never come across the Manchester Hussars again. Let it drop and get some sleep. Let *me* get some sleep, at least.'

'No, Charles. I can't. I've half the squadron avoiding my eye now. No doubt thinking I'm some form of card sharp or swindler. And it made for a completely sullen dinner. We didn't have any mess games. I can't let it go. Come on. Shake a leg.'

'Oh, bother. Very well. I'll do it. They are a bunch of stuffed-shirts, after all.'

Within thirty minutes, the mess piano stool's legs had been almost completely sawn through and every single screw in the piano removed. By the time the cavalry men next played the piano, the RNAS would be far away and somebody was in for an awful surprise, Paul thought with glee.

Chapter 16

Paul could not help but consider the scene before him as comical. Amidst the *boulangeries* and *charcuteries* on the streets of Dunkirk were several London omnibuses advertising such items as Dewar's whisky and Pear's soap. Several of the town's inhabitants were mixing with the Royal Marines to witness the spectacle. Also packing the cobbled streets were the RNAS armoured lorries and a mixture of touring cars, some armoured, some bearing the initials 'RND' and others belonging to French civilians. Amidst the throng of people and marines were the perplexed and worried-looking omnibus drivers and conductors. One or two of them were wearing their uniforms or at least a cap, but the majority were in a very varied attire of plain clothes. One was even wearing a sailor's cap. Several of the RNAS hands and officers were disappointed to note the absence of female conductors. However, despite the apparent chaos, Samson and the marine officers had the convoy ready to leave by 14.00 and Paul was sent ahead by motorcycle with a section of armoured cars to ensure the roads ahead were clear.

Looking back at the rumbling convoy, Paul was pleased to be operating independently of it. The dust could be seen for miles and he imagined it must be very unpleasant for the passengers and drivers alike anywhere other than at the front of the procession. Twenty miles ahead of the convoy, he met up with Father Clancy at Nieuwpoort, to discuss the latest intelligence on the situation at Antwerp. The news was not encouraging.

'I'm afraid, Paul, that if yer 'buses don't get a move on, they might arrive too late. The Belgian forts have begun to fall.'

'What! So quickly? What's gone wrong, Padre?'

'It's those damned siege guns the Germans be havin'. The forts weren't designed to withstand guns of fifteen or sixteen inches. And they're shootin' pretty accurately, too. Can't you do something about those cursed observation balloons?'

'Believe me, Padre, Sammy's doing his best, but we're short of machines, despite the CO's entreaties to London. In any case, no sooner do our boys approach the balloons than they're winched down and the Huns put up a blanket of Archie. My friend, Sippe, regards it as frightfully unhealthy.'

'What do you mean, *Archie*?'

'Sorry, Padre. Our little joke. You know the music hall song, "*Archibald, Certainly Not!*", I presume?'

'Aye, I've heard of it, but I have still to understand yer meaning, my son.'

'Well, the song goes, "*Archibald, certainly not! Get back to work at once, sir, like a shot!*" One of the chaps has taken to singing it whenever he comes across German anti-aircraft fire and we've come to refer to the shell fire as "Archie". We pilots have become rather fond of black humour these days.'

'There's nothin' wrong with that, son. But returnin' to my point. The word's out that the King and his government are evacuatin' Antwerp. The Germans are punchin' a gap in the outer ring of defences to the south and General Paris has gone with his men to Lier to provide reinforcements. The Belgians have already started pullin' out their wounded and heavy equipment by railway, but like as not, they'll be grateful to ye for yer 'buses, too. Now what are you plannin' to do now? Take these reports back to Commander Samson?'

'Actually, no. I'm pressing on to Bruges to organise an overnight stop-over for the convoy. Which reminds me, Padre. According to the CO, the drivers of the omnibuses and their crews haven't eaten since they left England. Could you ask the French to fix them up with some victuals somewhere along the road?'

'That'll be jes fine. Leave it with me. It'll have to be cold, mind. Mebbe jes some bread and sausage.'

'I think they'll eat horse if they have to, Padre. I'll be off then. Cheerio.'

*****

At 03.00 two days later, it was Charles's turn to wake a disgruntled Paul from a heavy sleep. The convoy of omnibuses had been safely delivered the day before and handed over to the marine brigade.

'Hurry up, Paul. We're on the move.'

Paul felt stiff from his few hours of sleep on the floor of the aerodrome hut where he and five other officers were billeted for the night. They had worked late into the previous evening in unloading their train-load of stores. The aircraft that had only just been sent to

Dunkirk, had now arrived in Antwerp. Another case of, order, counter-order, disorder, Paul thought.

'What are we up to this time, Charles?'

'We're to take all the cars and the two lorries to the front line at Lier. The marines need some machine gun support, apparently. We'll discover more when we get there. Now get a move on, you lazy chump.'

On arrival at the Brigade HQ, Paul and Charles were ordered to leave their car behind and to mount a machine gun by one of the bridges over the River Nete. It was still dark and the marine colonel wanted the job done before daylight. Paul was shocked by the scene he encountered. On arrival in Antwerp the night before, he had found the streets thronging with Belgians promenading or shopping in their finery as if the war didn't exist. It reminded him of the ball in Brussels on the eve of Waterloo. He wondered if it was typical of the Belgians and whether it was *sang-froid* or a refusal to acknowledge the truth. On the front line, it was a scene of unimaginable chaos. The streets were empty of civilians and instead, full of rubble, glass and rubbish. Incoming shells seemed to be bursting everywhere and the noise was like nothing Paul had ever encountered. Every now and then, the noise was varied by rapid rifle fire or bursts from machine guns. Charles led the way as he, Paul, their crew of three from the car and a marine messenger crept through the dark streets.

'Just 'old back a little, sirs,' the marine called softly. 'I reckons we're just about there. Beggin' your pardon, sirs, but it might be best if I went ahead now.'

Paul and Charles let the marine pass and followed him down an alley, and to a house on a corner. 'This is where I leave you gen'lemen. If you carry on down the street there, you comes to the river, see.' He pointed in the direction and Paul could see the reflections of shell bursts that marked the otherwise black river. 'The 'uns are directly opposite us on the other side of the river and the bridge is round the corner to your right. If you'll accept my advice, sirs, you'll fetch up in this 'ouse 'ere an' set up the Lewis upstairs. You might want to build yourselves a bit of a barricade, too. Once you start shooting, it might become a bit tasty round here.'

Without waiting for the officers' agreement, the marine saluted smartly, turned about and doubled back the way he had come. However, neither Paul nor Charles saw any reason to ignore the advice and established themselves and the gun in an attic window offering a good field of fire across the bridge opposite. Two of the ratings busied themselves filling pillow cases with earth from the garden. Their gunner, another marine, busied himself sorting out the spare ammunition.

'I say, Boddington,' Charles asked the marine. 'Did any of you bring any tea-making stuff? We might be here hours.'

''Fraid not, sir. I don't 'spect those useless dab-toes down there thought to either, sir. Tell yer where you might find some, though, sir. Look down in front of you.'

Paul and Charles looked out the window into the darkness in bewilderment, but could not see anything that might offer refreshment. They looked at Boddington quizzically.

'Look more carefully, sirs. You see just inside the bank, between the hedgerow. Notice anything different about the way the light catches the ground?'

Paul and Charles stared hard in the direction indicated and then Charles gasped. 'I see what you mean now. Look, Paul... There. Do you see them?'

'See who, Charles? No, wait a minute. I've got it. There's three men down there, in a shallow trench.'

'Six actually, sir. And they're marines. Now I bet you a pound to a piece of shit... beggin' your pardon, sirs... I bet they'll have a stove about them. They'd be ruddy poor marines if they didn't. Now I've some tea on me and there's bound to be a few unbroken cups of some sort in this doss house. Give me half a mo' and I'll get us a fanny of hot water going. I brought plenty of water with me.'

'No, Boddington,' Paul replied. 'I'll go. You're best here with the Lewis, just in case the Huns choose to cross the bridge whilst I'm gone.'

'All right then, sir, but be careful. Keep low and don't pull no surprises on the marines down there. You don't want your head blown orf now, do you?'

Paul went downstairs and to the front of the house, taking care to remain in the shadows. 'I say, chaps,' he called softly. 'We're the Lewis gun party. Up in the window above you. I was just wondering if you could lend us a stove to make a brew.'

'Stay where you are,' a voice called back. 'There's Huns not 60 yards off. Who the hell are you?'

'I'm Flight Sub Lieutenant Miller of the Royal Naval Air Service. There are five of us… including a marine.' Paul heard some quiet chuckling before another voice called back.

'Thank gawd there's one soldier amongst you, then. Whoever heard of sailors with guns. Sounds flaming dangerous to me.' This comment caused a further bout of chuckling, before the first voice replied, 'No offence meant, chum. Course we've got a stove. We're marines aren't we? Just come over slowly and for Christ's sake, keep down.'

Paul crouched and scurried across to the trench in front. He lay down beside it and noted it was only about two feet deep with a single strand of barbed wire on the side of the river. The marines were crammed in it like sardines. All of them had blackened their faces and only the white eyeballs reflected the light of the artillery bursts.

'There you are, sir. And in return, could one of you fill these with hot water and bring 'em back with the stove. We've been here since six last night.'

'No problem. It's awfully decent of you. I'll see what I can do. Thanks.'

Paul took the fanny and empty canteens and began to return to the safety of the house. Suddenly, he noted several chips of brickwork dance out of the wall ahead and sharp reports of rifle fire behind him simultaneously. Instinctively, he threw himself to the ground and lay flat. He turned his head to look behind him, but could see no sign of the enemy. However, he did note that the dawn was breaking. He raised himself on to his hands and knees and began to crawl towards the house, but again shots were fired and this time he swore he could feel a warm whisper of wind only inches from his head. For some peculiar reason, Pops's advice from years back when stalking deer came to mind.

'*Forget the sheep shit. If you don't want the stag to see you, you crawl on your belly.*'

With this advice in mind, and careful to retain hold of the precious stove, fanny and canteens, Paul slithered across the open ground like a snake. Only when he reached the wall of the house, did he rise quickly and run hell-for-leather around the corner. He heard another couple of shots, but none seemed to be close by. Dashed bad shots, he thought.-

Chapter 17

'Wake up, Paul. They're coming.' Paul felt a kick on his foot and woke with a start. He realised he must have dozed off for a couple of minutes after having his share of the tea, thanks to the loan of the marines' stove.

'What's up, Charles?' he responded, now fully alert.

'The Huns are taking up position on the other side of the bridge. Look.'

Paul noted that the light was increasing to his left, but it was still quite dark directly ahead. Even so, he spotted the movements on the other side of the bridge. Various shapes clad in grey were manoeuvring in the shadows. 'What now then, Charles?' he asked.

'I suggest we take our lead from the marines down in the trench. We're here to support them and we'll hold our fire until they open up.'

Paul was surprised by the way Charles seemed to take charge naturally, even though Paul was the senior officer by a small margin. It wasn't as if Charles had had any more infantry training than himself, but Charles had thrown himself into the role with gusto. 'What do you think, Boddington?' he asked the marine next to him.

'Makes sense to me, right enough, sir. If you don't mind me saying, sirs. This is what the marines are trained for.'

'Fair enough then, Charles. We'll hold fire until at least the marines have opened up. But we'll give the Huns a burst if…' Paul's words were interrupted by the sound of rapid rifle fire. It took him a moment to realise it was from the other side of the bridge. Incoming. The rifle fire didn't seem to be specific to any particular target, but some was chipping great chunks of brickwork and plaster from the house in which they were located.

'Keep your heads down, chaps,' Charles responded. 'It's covering fire. Those troops are about to make a rush for the bridge.' He primed the Lewis gun for action. Charles was seated on a milking stool behind a dresser base and several pillow cases full of soil. Paul didn't think it a very safe position. However, he crawled across to obtain a better view of the coming action.

The rifle fire continued and Paul could see the enemy beginning to cross the bridge. He looked down to see the response from the marines in the trench below, but was puzzled not to see any signs of return fire. Now, there seemed to be about twenty Germans on the bridge, being encouraged on by an officer or NCO. It was too dark to tell. The first rank reached almost half way across the bridge, only fifty yards away, and dropped into a kneeling position whilst more of their colleagues began trotting behind to join them. The incoming fire seemed to abate a little, but not before Paul noticed that it was preceded by a mixture of *zip*, *zing* or *phut* noises in their immediate vicinity.

Suddenly, the rifle fire picked up again and Paul saw Germans soldiers dropping to the ground. He looked down and saw muzzle flashes from the marines. They were returning fire at last and seemed to have checked the advance. Some of the Germans now seemed hesitant and others were edging backwards until their officer drew his sword and urged them back again. The marines kept up a continuous fusillade and Paul saw the officer immediately fall to the ground. Good shot, he thought. Within seconds, the Germans began to withdraw, several dragging their wounded comrades behind them. Round one to the marines, he thought, and time to return their stove, canteens and a hot fanny of water.

*****

The second attack began about thirty minutes later. Again, the Germans preceded their advance with covering fire, but this time it was specifically and intensely directed towards the marines' slit trench. In the improved light Paul could see that the marines had very little cover and even he could work out that their position was untenable. This time, the marines opened fire as soon as the Germans offered up a target, but the enemy's withering counter fire was making life difficult for them. Within minutes, the Germans were half way across the bridge and in numbers. Paul was taking his turn in manning the Lewis.

'I reckons they've got far enough, sir,' Marine Boddington suggested. 'Time we gave the boys an 'elpin' 'and, wouldn't you say, sir?'

Paul lined up the gun sights on the leading body of troops, but didn't press the trigger. Something within him froze and a kaleidoscope of different thoughts and images passed quickly through his head. Were he to open fire, he knew the men before him would die. The Germans might be the enemy, but they were fellow human beings and he recalled family holidays to the German Alps and Rhineland. He hadn't joined the navy to kill, but to fly. War was no longer a game. He felt heavy rivulets of sweat stream down the sides of his head and then he was suddenly pushed out of the way by his cousin.

'For Pete's sake, Paul. Get out of the way.' Two seconds later, Charles opened up with the Lewis gun and it was like an invisible scythe as it mowed down the oncoming troops, several of whom seemed to be lifted in the air from the momentum of the 0.303-inch calibre bullets. Just a few bursts caused complete carnage and mayhem. It was enough to stop the attack and the bridge quickly cleared.

'For God's sake, Paul. What was that about?' Charles demanded angrily.

Paul noted that Boddington and the naval ratings suddenly found little tasks to do and avoided eye contact. They must think me a coward, he thought. 'I'm sorry, but... I just funked it... I've never killed a man before,' he added lamely.

'But, Paul. You've been out here two months. Surely, you've dropped bombs on the enemy. It has the same effect you know.' Charles spoke quietly and his anger seemed to have given way to concern for his cousin. 'I suppose dropping bombs seems more impersonal for you pilots.'

'No, Charles. It's not like that.' Paul noted that whilst the marine and ratings seemed to be busy, they were all listening into the officers' conversation. 'I've actually never dropped any bombs for real either. It's all been scouting and recce patrols.'

'All right. I think I understand. But get this into your head, Paul. This is war. It's kill or be killed. You're wearing the King's uniform.'

'I'm sorry, chaps. I won't let you down again.' Paul looked appealingly at the men, but they still seemed too preoccupied with trivial tasks to meet his eye.

'Tell you what you can do, Paul. Boddington, you stay with me. You two, go with Sub Lieutenant Miller and see if there are any wounded marines down there. Take care now. There's bound to be snipers.'

'Good idea, Charles. Right then, chaps. Follow me.' Paul was grateful to Charles for giving him the opportunity to prove he wasn't a coward. He raced down the stairs to the side of the house, followed by the two naval ratings.

'Wait here under cover,' he ordered. Crawling on his belly, he approached the slit trench and called out softly. 'Are you men all right? Any wounded?'

'Corporal Harris here, sir. I've two dead and two walking wounded, but Collins and I ain't scratched. You just stay there, sir. I figure we ought to retire to better cover. It ain't gonna take long for the 'uns to bring up the heavy stuff now. Just give us half a mo'.'

Paul slithered back to the shelter of the house and waited. Perhaps thirty seconds later, four helmeted shapes emerged from the trench, rifles and head first, and began to crawl towards him. Instantly, rifle fire barked from the opposite shore, but the luck of the four marines seemed to hold. One of the marines raised himself to a crouch and started to dash towards the safety of the house. Paul felt a rush of hot air immediately prior to a huge bang. Instinctively, he shut his eyes and hit the ground, but his ears caught the tinkling sound of metal falling against the brickwork. He raised his head and was horrified to see three bloody and mangled corpses, and a marine less a foot in place of the four marines he had last seen only two seconds before. They had been caught by a burst of shrapnel from a heavy gun. However, Paul didn't have the time to be shocked as the first shrapnel shell was followed by another. Without thinking, he rushed across to help the wounded marine and hauled him to the comparative safety of the alley.

Paul whipped off his scarf and bound it tightly around the stump of the marine's injured leg. To Paul's surprise, the marine was not screaming in pain, but eying the vacant space where his foot should have been with puzzlement. 'Are you all right, man?' he asked stupidly. Of course, the marine wasn't all right, you oaf, he thought.

'I'm fine, sir. I was just thinking what my colour sergeant's going to say about me losing half a pair of perfectly good size-nine boots. He'll have my guts for garters, more than likely.'

Together with one of the ratings, Paul managed to carry the wounded and hopping marine into the house. As they mounted the stairs, they could hear the *chat-chat-chat* sound of the Lewis gun firing again amidst the sound of rifle fire and bursting shrapnel.

Paul left the two ratings to use the contents of their first aid bag to improve the dressing of the wounded marine and joined his cousin at the window of the attic. The Lewis gun seemed to be holding back the attack and the German bodies were beginning to pile up on the bridge.

'My, Paul. You're a cool one,' Charles uttered between bursts of fire. 'Leastways, nobody's going to accuse *you* of cowardice. Good job.'

'What do we do now then, Charles? We can't hold them forever. They're bound to switch to HE shortly and pulverise us.'

'Good point and not one I wish to ponder. You're going to have to fall back whilst you can. I'll stay here and keep them occupied whilst I can.'

'Charles, you're mad. At the very best, you'll be captured when the ammo runs out. More than likely you'll be blown to smithereens. Don't be an ass. We'll withdraw together.'

'How far do you think we'd get without covering fire from this little beauty, Paul. We'd be overrun in no time. Particularly with our wounded friend there.'

'Well, leave me here and you go, Charles. I promise not to funk it this time.'

'No joy, Paul. We're short of pilots and you can fly. This is all I know what to do.' Charles broke off to fire another burst from the Lewis gun as another attack unfolded. 'Boddington, pass me another drum.'

'Beggin' yer pardon, gentlemen, but you're in my place. You're right, sir, that someone needs to stay, but this is marine business, not dab-toe stuff. And with respect, sirs, I don't reckon much for your chances with our friend there.' He nodded to the wounded marine and then turned to him. 'What's yer name, mate?'

''iggins. And I think you 'it the nail on the 'ead, mate. I ain't goin' nowhere without my other foot. Anyone got any smokes?'

Paul and one of the ratings produced a packet each. Taking each packet, Marine Higgins replied, 'Well that's sorted then. Marine Boddington and I'll just have a nice little smoke an' keep killin' 'uns whilst you gentlemen withdraw to continue the war another day. You all right with that, chum?'

'Yeah. I reckon it'll take more than a ruddy platoon of Huns to get past two marines. Now you gentlemen be orf and leave us the ammo. We got important business to attend to.'

*****

Paul and Charles managed to withdraw safely from the front line at Lier, but it soon became apparent that the defence of Antwerp was becoming hopeless. At the Marines' brigade HQ they learned that the Germans were crossing the River Nete in force and the marines were withdrawing to the inner forts. There they would be supported by the newly arrived Naval Division with its armoured train and four-point-seven-inch guns. The Royal Marines colonel didn't seem too hopeful about the situation.

'The Belgians are worn out and my men aren't much better. Frankly, they're too old and too few. We've no artillery and that of the Belgians is obsolete. It's just a question of time, despite Mister Churchill's presence,' the colonel explained.

'You mean Churchill is here?' Paul asked.

'That's right. He's taken personal charge of the evacuation and ordered us to hold the line as long as possible to give the Belgian civilians and the bulk of their army time to evacuate and then to cross the Scheldt. Some of the outer forts have already started falling and it's only a matter of time before the Germans bring up their siege guns and start pounding the city.'

'But surely, sir, the arrival of the Naval Division will make a difference?' Charles asked innocently.

'You're Samson's men, I take it… Thought so. Quite honestly, I wouldn't give them a fart's chance in a high wind. They're keen enough all right. But they lack training and, more importantly, equipment. Anyway, Samson's withdrawing. If you can fly, young man,' the colonel indicated Paul, 'you need to make your way to the aerodrome *pronto* and clear out your aircraft and stores to Ostend. The rest of you could take your armoured car to Fort Four… You'll find it at the end of the road to Antwerp from here. I'll be pulling the brigade back there after dusk tonight, so I'll perhaps catch up with you then. Good luck.'

*****

It was almost dusk by the time Paul made it back to the aerodrome. Charles had first diverted to the field hospital with two wounded marines on stretchers. The journey had not been made easier now that the Germans were shelling the road. Paul could see that the eight and twelve-inch shells were being directed by a German kite balloon. He had it in mind to prepare a little surprise for the observer. Everyone in the RNAS was working like a slave to load their stores onto the few armoured cars and lorries available and most of the aircraft had already departed, but Samson had left a couple of Sopwith Tabloids behind in preparation for an attack on the Zeppelin sheds at Dusseldorf and Cologne. However, Paul had a prior use for them.

'PO, I need one of the Tabloid's for an urgent mission. Are they fully armed?' he asked the Petty Officer armourer brusquely.

'Aye, sir. They're armed right enough… and fully fuelled. They're each carryin' a couple of twenty-pounders and fitted with a Lewis gun. Do ye mind me askin', sir, what you intend doin' with one?'

'Not at all, PO. There's a Hun battery that's been annoying me half the day and I intend giving the Royals a little support. I'll take this one. Don't worry, I'll be back within half an hour and bring her back safe and sound.'

Paul jumped into the cockpit without further discussion and left the senior rate to consider his next move. The petty officer was decisive in his response and ordered a couple of riggers to help Paul prepare for take-off. Within five minutes, he was airborne and heading south-east. It was too late in the day to do much about the kite balloon, Paul decided, but a certain artillery battery in Lier was about to pay the price of so many Royal Marine deaths earlier that day. Completely ignoring the rifle fire directed at him from the ground, Paul used the muzzle flashes to locate an artillery battery near the house he had vacated earlier in the day. On his first pass, he dropped the two twenty-pound bombs and was very satisfied with the resultant explosion as the battery's ammunition blew up.

'There, you bastards,' he cried into the wind. 'That's for Boddington and Higgins. May they now rest in peace.'

Chapter 18

'I've a good mind to send you back to blighty, you arse. Do you understand me?'

'Yes, sir,' Paul replied, standing rigidly at attention.

'You knew ruddy well that those Tabloids were earmarked for raids on the Zeppelin sheds. That's a damned sight more important than your personal vendettas.'

'Yes, sir.' Paul knew that Sammy's bark was worse than his bite. He just needed to ride out the storm and say as little as possible.

'Have you seen that machine lately? Riddled with holes. What if one of them had hit your fuel tank? I don't care about the loss of a stupid pilot. I've plenty out here raring for a go at the enemy. But I'm short of aircraft.'

Samson was silent for over a minute. Paul knew the worst was over and he remained at attention, staring fixedly at a spot on the wall over Samson's right shoulder.

'You've put me in a quandary, Miller. And I hate indecision. What am I to do with you?'

'Shoot me, sir?'

Paul noted just a twitch of a smile on Samson's face and knew his arrow had gone home.

'That's probably the most sensible suggestion I've heard you make, Miller. I've a good mind to take you up on it, but that still leaves me with this note.' Samson picked up a torn-off scrap of paper from his make-shift desk.

'Here a colonel of marines asks me to congratulate the daring young pilot who silenced that battery last night. I gather it was an accurate piece of bombing and the absence of that battery at Lier helped the Royal Marines to make their withdrawal last night. You do understand that I can't congratulate you for your stupidity, don't you, Miller? But it also explains why I cannot shoot you or even send you home.' Samson screwed up the piece of paper, threw it into the corner and lit a cigarette.

'So, we'll say no more about it.' Samson sat down and gestured to Paul. 'At ease and listen up.

'Whilst you were up to your tricks last night, I was with General Rawlinson. He's lost communications with General Paris, but wants him to withdraw his marines and the Naval Division. It's all up with

Antwerp now. Rawlinson and the Belgians have settled on making a stand at Ghent to allow the rest of the Belgian Army to withdraw.' Samson picked up another piece of paper from his desk.

'Rawlinson wants me to send an officer with a despatch to Paris. You speak French and I don't need you here. Spencer-Grey and Marix are up for the Zeppelin raids. Look at this.'

Paul looked at the despatch and saw that it included a map. 'This shows the disposition of Four Corps. The general wants Paris to understand it in planning his withdrawal. However, for obvious security reasons, Rawlinson insists it has to be memorised. Were this information to reach the enemy, all Belgium would be lost. If you cannot locate General Paris you give the information to one of his GSOs. Clear?'

'Perfectly clear, sir. Am I to proceed alone, sir?'

'No. Take one of the cars and three others. Your cousin if you like. I'm also sending a troop of those Manchester yeomanry with you as an escort.'

'The Hussars, sir? Is that really necessary? Wouldn't the Lewis gun be more useful than horses, sir?'

'No, Miller. The roads are inevitably going to be crowded with refugees fleeing Antwerp and sometimes a horse will get through where a car cannot. In any case, their colonel tells me that he has some former quarry men in his regiment. They're dab hands at demolitions and will be useful in supporting Paris's withdrawal. Do you ride?'

'No, sir. I'm allergic to horses.'

'Pity, but tough. Now you've fifteen minutes to memorise this despatch and then I want you on your way.'

*****

Somehow Paul had known this would happen as soon as Samson had mentioned his escort. Sure enough, the troop ordered to form his escort was commanded by Captain Crichton. Their reunion had been no friendlier than their last meeting in Morbecque. However, Paul had Charles for company whilst Crichton rode with his troop to the rear.

As Samson had prophesied, the roads were terrible and from Zwijndrecht, on the west side of the Scheldt on the approach roads to

Antwerp, Paul began to give up hope of reaching the city on anything but foot or worse, on four hooves. Women, children, priests, nuns, the sick, the aged and the infirm were all on the roads. Added to the mules, horses and carts, several drovers were attempting to flee the burning city with their cattle, fully expecting the *Uhlans* to be hot on their heels. However, Paul and his escort made the bridge into Antwerp by lunch time and decided to pause to eat before entering the dirt of the city centre.

The air hung heavy with smoke and dust and it smelt no better either. The smells varied from the sweat of the largely unwashed refugees, the rotting of uncollected horse ordure and rubbish in the streets, and the stagnant water of the river that had become a repository of refuse and even dead pets.

They were intrigued to see pass by a Belgian machine gun battery pulled by dog teams. They asked the officer in command for news of General Paris. He had none, but advised that there were reports of some British naval gunners taking over the manning of some of the inner forts near Vremde. The Belgian officer was embarrassed to report that his country's fortress troops were deserting in droves. Paul noted wryly that whilst the officer and his men were dog-tired, their dogs had taken the opportunity of a rest to fight each other.

'Well, what do you know?' Charles interrupted Paul's observation of the dog fight. 'We've company from our old friends.' Charles tugged Paul and drew his attention to two double-decker omnibuses approaching the bridge from the centre of Antwerp. They were the same vehicles the RNAS had escorted just over a week earlier. Paul recognised the leading driver from his naval cap. Both buses were festooned with Red Cross flags and bunting. Paul flagged down the driver.

'Hello. What are you doing here?' he asked of the driver. 'You were supposed to have cleared out days ago.'

'That's right, we did, guv. But then a few of us came back to collect a load of the wounded. We ain't no longer 'bus drivers you know.' The driver pointed proudly to his armband with the initials, 'RNAS' embroidered on it. 'We've volunteered to sign up. Someone in Blighty reckoned civilians couldn't enter a combat zone, so Sammy promptly enrolled us in the navy. 'E's a card ain't he? Had to take a pay cut mind, but ah'd a done it for nuffink.'

Just then they were interrupted by a pretty young nurse whose starched collar and apron seemed out of place in the dusty streets of Antwerp.

'Excuse me, driver. Why have we stopped?'

'Forgive me, miss, but I am to blame,' Paul interrupted. 'We're almost old friends. But I'm seeking information. I'm Flight Sub Lieutenant Paul Miller of the Air Service. I have an urgent message for General Paris and am trying to establish his whereabouts.' Paul was quite struck by the nurse's good looks. She had strawberry-blonde hair fringing her white muslin cap, in stark contrast with her blue-grey cloak, and lively, bright-blue eyes, whose depth of colour set off the fair skin of her face perfectly.

'An aviator? How thrilling. You must be one of Samson's boys.'

'I am that, miss.' Paul was a little lost for words, but recovered. 'May I offer you a piece of chocolate? This Belgian stuff is quite good you know.'

'Why thank you. I'd love some. My name's Sarah Steele, by the way. We're on our way to Ostend.'

'Well. What do we have here then, gentlemen, but a rose amongst thorns.' Crichton had left his men and horses to join the conversation. 'If you're in need of refreshment, lady, allow me to offer you a brandy.' Crichton proffered his stirrup flask.

Sarah wrinkled her slightly snubbed nose, rather prettily in Paul's opinion, and stared hard at Crichton. 'No thank you, sir. I never drink spirits when on duty,' she answered archly and to Paul's satisfaction.

'My, aren't we a prim one?' Crichton replied sourly. 'But not too grand to mix with pirates, I see.' Crichton guffawed loudly and Paul cringed in embarrassment. 'And I see there are more of you.' Two more nurses approached the group. Sarah beckoned them to join the throng.

'Annie, Helena, do come and meet Lieutenant Miller, one of Samson's dashing young pilots.'

'Dashing you say? Huh. They're no more than hooligans. They're not even proper officers.' Crichton interjected.

'And I take it that you are from a proper cavalry regiment, sir, and not one of the yeomanry, sir?' Paul smirked at Sarah's rebuke.

'Tchah! You're a spirited young filly, aren't you? But all fillies can be broken.' Crichton smacked the side of his right boot with his riding crop, menacingly.

'Steady on, Crichton,' Paul intervened. 'You're speaking to a lady. Now, miss. Can you tell me where to find the Naval Divisional HQ?' He ushered Sarah towards the omnibus, on his other side to Crichton. 'I have a map here.' He spread out the map against the vehicle.

'He's moved his headquarters to those of General Deguise, the Belgian general. That's where we collected these wounded men. It's just here… near the lunatic asylum. More or less due East by about ten miles… Not far on the other side of the canal.' Paul was pleased to see that Crichton had lost interest in the conversation and had gone back to his men sulkily.

'My, that is helpful. I am impressed, Miss Steele, by your ability to read a map.'

'Really? And why is that? Because, I'm a woman?' Paul noted Sarah's pale cheeks quickly colour to resemble two tomatoes.

'Er, no… Not at all. There aren't many civilian men that can read a map. That was my point.'

'Oh, sorry. Perhaps I was being a little over sensitive, then. Actually, my brother's in the navy. He's in submarines. We both like walking in the Lake District and that's how I came to learn to read a map, or *chart* in your parlance.' Sarah giggled at the last utterance and Paul noted her pretty white teeth.

'Now that is interesting. I live none too far from the Lake District. Well, not far from Lancaster anyhow. Perhaps we…'

'And I live near Liverpool, miss.' Charles joined the conversation for the first time.

'Sarah, we need to make a move. Need I remind you we have wounded men to evacuate?' one of the other nurses interrupted.

'Quite right, Annie. We do need to move on. I've enjoyed our chat, Lieutenant, and hope I have been of some use.' Sarah held out her gloved hand and Paul was surprised that she shook his firmly. As she boarded the omnibus again, she called out, 'Do come and visit us in Ostend when you're back that way. I'm sure the men would appreciate a visit.'

The driver restarted his vehicle and as he pulled away, Sarah waved goodbye to Paul and Charles. Paul stared after her retreating figure for a few moments before pulling himself together again.

'Come on, Charles. We need to push on.'

One of the armoured car ratings started up the Lanchester and spoke softly to his colleague. 'I'd say the young subby's smitten, mate.'

'Avast there, you insolent devil. I heard that,' Paul retorted with mock outrage. 'But you have to admit, she is an angel.'

*****

If anything, the smell of the decaying city was worse as Paul and his team reached the crossing of the canal in the east of the city. The streets were now full of rubble from the German shell fire and the air carried the stench of rotting flesh. Paul did not care to investigate as to whether it was dead horse, mule or human flesh, but felt sure it was probably a mixture of all three. Worse was the assault on his hearing. Never before had he heard such noise. The German artillery bombardment was now continuous and Paul could see that it was worrying the troop of the Hussars, many of whose horses were becoming very skittish. The Belgian forts were still firing back, but Paul could tell that the rate of return fire was diminishing. To the south and east he could also hear the regular crack of rifle fire. Surely, Paris must withdraw before too long, he thought.

Paul halted the party and checked his map once again. He judged that he was now less than two miles from the Belgian HQ, but given the obstructions in the streets from fallen masonry, he was unlikely to be able to proceed any further except on foot. He jumped out of the car and went up to Crichton and had to shout to make himself heard.

'I think it best you and your men stay here, Crichton. It's likely to be harder from here on in for your horses to pass through the streets and I'll leave the car here, too. I'll carry on, on foot, and meet you back here. I should only be gone a couple of hours.'

'Whatever you say, Miller. But don't be too long about it. I've a good mind to blow the bridges across the canal to slow down the Germans.'

'You can't do that, Crichton. When Paris decides to withdraw, he'll need these bridges.'

'Listen, Miller. I've just about had enough of your high-handed approach. My orders were to escort you as far as I could and I and my men have now done that. Kindly remember that I'm the senior officer here and you are no soldier.'

Crichton turned his horse's head and made to go back to his men, but Paul caught the horse by the bridle. 'But you're also meant…' He immediately felt the pain of a whip across the back of his hand.

'How dare you touch my horse!' Paul let go of the bridle and ducked as Crichton aimed the whip at his head. 'Go to Hell,' Crichton bellowed and Paul was shocked to see the veins of Crichton's temples bulging in anger. Wringing his hand, he returned to the armoured car. He explained his plan to Charles and the two ratings.

'Wait here. I'm going on alone, on foot. I aim to be back in about two hours, but if I'm not back after three, get going and forget me.'

Charles laid a hand on Paul's shoulder. 'I'm coming with you. If nothing else, two might have a better chance of getting through to Div' HQ than one.'

'All right, Charles. I'll not argue. Thanks. But I want you two to keep an eye on the toy soldiers. Their captain's talking about blowing the bridges across the canal. Just make sure he doesn't do it before I've had the chance to get back with General Paris's intentions. Our boys might need the bridges to escape. I don't care if you have to shoot the officers. You understand?'

The two ratings nodded and wished the officers good luck.

*****

It was already dusk by the time Paul and Charles found Paris's headquarters. They were surprised to discover just how small his headquarters staff was; a mere handful of officers. The strain on the general and his fatigue were obvious, but he welcomed the two officers warmly enough and listened avidly to Paul's recitation of the despatch Samson had ordered him to memorise, with only a few questions to clarify detail. A Royal Marines major marked the map before them with the dispositions of the Fourth Corps.

'You say the railway line from Sint Niklaas is running freely?' Paris asked.

'As far as I know, sir,' Paul answered nervously. 'My CO said that the Belgians were organising trains to embark your men there and to take them to Ghent.'

'But I have a signal here from a Colonel Dallas to tell me that the Germans are sitting at Lokeren. If that's the case, they could easily cut the line and outflank us. What do you say, Alfred?'

An artillery lieutenant colonel stepped forward and examined the map carefully. 'I don't think we dare take the chance, sir. Were we to order the division to rendezvous by brigade at Zwijndrecht as planned, sir, we could march to Sint-Gillis-Waas and take the line to Zelzate instead. It's not the most direct route to Ghent, but surer.'

'Very well. I say we stick to the plans we've already issued.' Paris turned back to Paul. 'I've already issued the orders to the brigades to fall back to Zwijndrecht as soon as darkness fell. It's a pity, as I still feel we could hold the inner ring of forts, but the Belgians are deserting in legions and the First Brigade is ill-suited to this defence. I was about to signal the news to the Admiralty when you arrived.'

'Have all the brigades acknowledged the orders to withdraw yet?' Paris had now switched his attention to his staff.

'All except Commodore Henderson's First Brigade of blue-jackets, sir. We can't reach them by wireless and the messenger's not back yet.'

'Damn! They should be withdrawing within the next hour. We've no more messengers available either,' the general muttered.

'Let me go, sir,' Charles piped up.

'I'll go with you,' Paul offered.

'Hold your horses, both of you. Let me think a minute.' Paris studied the map and sucked the end of his pencil for a short while. 'Miller, did you say you came by car?' Paul nodded.

'Very well. This is my plan. I'll accept this young man's offer to take a message to Commodore Henderson. But I want you to return to Four Corps HQ and tell General Rawlinson to prepare to embark the division on the Sint-Gillis-Waas to Zelzate line. Hang on a minute and I'll give you a despatch, but I suggest you head for Burcht, south-west of here. We've rigged up several boats to provide a form of pontoon bridge there as I've ordered the northern bridge to be destroyed. It means leaving your car behind at the bridge, I'm afraid.

'As for you, young man,' the general placed a hand on Charles's shoulder. 'Find the Commodore and tell him to withdraw his battalions of sailors via the Malines Gate and the pontoon bridge. The Portsmouth Battalion of marines will act as his rear guard. He's then to rendezvous as previously discussed at Zwijndrecht. He should find the road from Burcht fairly easy. Colonel Ollivant here can brief you on where to find Henderson. Just give me a minute to confirm the orders in writing.'

*****

Less than an hour later, Paul was back at the bridge where he had left the Lanchester and the Hussars. Except there was no bridge. Nor could he see any sign of the Hussars, their horses or the armoured car and its crew. He checked his watch. It was only 18.00, two and a half hours after he had left his men. He checked his map again. Yes, this was the right place. Then he spotted the detritus floating in the black water beneath him and realised with a jolt that the bridge had been destroyed. Now what do I do, he thought.

It was cold and he didn't fancy swimming across. Besides, it would mean walking for miles to the pontoon bridge in wet clothes and he would still need to find a way to the railway station. The map showed another bridge linking the dikes to the east and west. He decided to try that to the west as it was in the direction he needed to head. A shell burst barely five hundred yards to his right and the ground shuddered beneath him. Instinctively, he ducked before realising that it would have been far too late. His eye caught a large reflection of the light in the canal from the shell explosion. He looked more closely and, to his horror, looked upon the gleaming chrome of the rear fender of the Lanchester, lying partly submerged in the canal. He couldn't understand what it was doing there. There was no sign of a nearby shell burst to have lifted the vehicle into the water. And where were the Hussars and the two sailors from the car? Paul shivered and it was not with the cold.

Chapter 19

Fleet Paymaster Rotter knocked on the admiral's open door and popped his head around it. Rear Admiral William Miller followed the sea-going naval officer's habit of leaving his door open when not engaged in meetings or, at sea, turned in. 'It's good to see you back, sir.'

'Come in, Charles. It's good to be back, even if this is no longer my office. I see the sign painter has already put up the name of Captain Hall and that the Admiralty are reverting to calling the man in my old position, "The Director of Naval Intelligence".'

'You won't be too far away as the First Lord's Naval Assistant, though, sir. And Captain Hall will still report to you.'

'I suppose there is that, but I can't help but feel that the arrangement is only temporary. That's why we need to make an immediate start on the new signals intelligence organisation. Time and tide wait for no man. So, tell me, what's been going on in my absence.'

'I presume you have already heard about Commander Cumming's accident, sir?'

'No. What accident? I haven't been to the SSB yet.'

'Happened at the beginning of the month, sir. Cumming was in France... driving his Rolls Royce. He had his son, Alastair with him. I understand he was a member of the army's new Intelligence Corps. By all accounts, somewhere between Paris and Rouen, they suffered an accident. The car hit a tree and overturned. The next bit's a little sketchy, but the rumour is that Alastair was thrown clear of the car, but 'C' was trapped underneath it. His leg was caught somewhere beneath the knee.'

'It sounds awful. Were either of them badly hurt?'

'I was coming to that, sir. Apparently, 'C' heard his boy cry out, but couldn't free himself to attend to him. So, he took out his penknife and hacked off his leg! The sad thing is that the boy died anyway.'

'Oh, how gruesome. Poor old 'C'. How is he?'

'I can't say, sir. He's still in a BEF hospital, but I had heard he's able to walk with the aid of crutches.'

'What a blow. Now it seems we have two crocks heading our intelligence efforts. I'll make it a priority to call by the SSB as soon as possible. In the meantime, what's happening in your area?'

'There we have had a piece of luck, sir. We've managed to lay our hands on a couple of German Navy signal books.'

'Charles, you astonish me. How on earth did you manage that?'

'Pure luck, sir. We don't actually have the first one yet, but it should be here within weeks. The Royal Australian Navy boarded a German steamer and captured a copy of the German Admiralty's HVB. They've sent it on to us.'

'I'm sorry, Charles. What is an HVB?'

'Sorry, sir. It's the *Handelsverkehrbuch*. The German Naval Staff use it for communications with their merchant ships and the High Seas Fleet.'

'That should make life easier for us. And you say you have another, too.'

'Yes, sir. This time it's the *Signalbuch der Kaiserlichen Marine* or SKB, the signal book of the Imperial German Navy. The Russians engaged a cruiser, the *Magdeburg*, in the Baltic. She ran aground and the captain failed to scuttle her properly. Russian divers found two copies of the signal book and the boarding party another, but they couldn't recover the cypher book. The Russian Naval Attaché handed Mister Churchill a copy only a few days ago. It's been a real stroke of luck, sir.'

'Indeed. And how is Ewing getting along?'

'Well enough, I think, sir.' Rotter seemed a little evasive in his reply so Miller pressed him.

'Has he built up a team yet? Are you clearing the backlog of intercepts? Come on, Charles. With the full command of the English language at your fingertips, "Well enough" hardly suffices as a comprehensive reply.'

'True, sir. The fact is, I'm not party to the picture. Sir Alfred has certainly been busy recruiting German speakers. Indeed, they're bursting out of their office space. But nobody from the DID is allowed entry to the office and they're operating a little too independently in my opinion, sir. From what I understand, they've all been busy with research so far, sir. I have gleaned one thing, though. Sir Alfred has discovered that there's a considerable volume of wireless traffic being generated at a lower frequency to that at

Norddeich. He's managed to set up a facility at Hunstanton in Norfolk to intercept this traffic.'

'Very well, Charles. Thank you for the update. You've given me a few thoughts to ponder before Captain Hall arrives. I'll catch up with Sir Alfred later, but first I'll wander down to the SSB offices. Thank you.'

'Just one more thing, before you go. This is going to sound odd, but an MP called us yesterday expressing concern that a considerable number of enemy messages may be leaving the country through the mail system. A clerk in censorship has told him that only about five percent of the outbound foreign mail is being dealt with. It's clearly not my province, but I was the officer that took the call. It might be worth your consideration, sir.'

'Thank you, Charles. I'll give it some thought.'

Chapter 20

Paul continued to trudge westwards along the canal bank. It started to rain, only softly, but it would be enough to soak him to the skin before long, he thought. It caused him to consider once more the option of swimming across the canal. Both the bridges he had now passed to cross to the south had been destroyed. It had to be the work of those idiot hussars, he thought. But why didn't his men stop the idiocy and why was the armoured car in the canal? Where were his men, too?

He transferred General Paris's despatch to his leather ammunition pouch in an effort to keep it dry. The streets were deserted and lit only by the glow of the great fires that were forming in the city behind him. The next bridge he approached was also in ruins, but as this crossed a narrow inlet from the main canal, he had to turn north to find the next crossing. He froze. Ahead he saw a movement in the shadows. Carefully and slowly, Paul edged to his right to gain the cover of the buildings. By the light of the next artillery burst he saw something to relax him. 'You damned fool, Paul,' he muttered. 'It's only a stray horse.'

Paul approached the horse cautiously in order not to panic it. As he drew closer, he could see that it was tethered. Whilst he was no horseman, he could tell that it was a fine specimen and by its saddle, an army mount. He was just wondering where its owner might be when a voice called out, '*Qui vive?*'

Paul's heart stopped for a second, but at least it was French and not German. He replied quickly in French. 'I'm English. Where are you?' Once Paul's eyes adjusted to the shadows, he saw a slight movement from the corner of two buildings.

'Come here, but keep your hands high.' Paul noted a blue-uniformed Belgian army officer slouched on the ground and pointing a rifle at him.

'Take care with that, sir. I'm a British officer with General Paris's forces.' The Belgian lowered his carbine and Paul saw the sign of relief on the cavalryman's pale face. He also saw the pool of blood in which he lay and the stump of his left leg.

'My word, you're wounded!' Paul rushed forward and looked frantically for some form of dressing to stem the bleeding. In the absence of anything suitable, he undid the strap of his water canteen and tied it above the stump to form a tourniquet. The Belgian groaned with pain.

'How did this happen?'

'Some of your countrymen were destroying the bridges across the canal. I tried to stop them, but I speak no English. I had just dismounted when the explosion took place and a piece of debris sliced off my leg. I'm afraid your colleagues were quite determined on the destruction.'

'Were they by any chance mounted soldiers?'

'They were. British cavalry, but I did not recognise the unit. Are you with them?'

'No. I'm with the Royal Navy. Sub Lieutenant Miller's the name. Those cavalrymen were meant to escort me back to Ghent with an important despatch for the British Fourth Corps.'

'I am Captain Joubert. I'm honoured to meet you. I have seen at first hand the courage of British sailors over the past few days. What a pity you could not have brought some of your field guns with you.' The Belgian groaned with pain. 'Excuse me. My left leg is hurting.' Before Paul could stop him, the Belgian undid the leather strap wrapped around his leg and the blood began to seep out again.

'What are you doing, man? You'll bleed to death. Let me stop that.'

'No, sir. It is already too late for that. I know I have not long left. At least let me die in peace.'

Paul was not trained in first aid, but he recognised, nonetheless, the truth in the captain's words. The Belgian was very pale and he was sweating on his forehead despite the cool evening temperature. 'Can I offer you some water?' Paul proffered his canteen and the Belgian accepted it gratefully. After emptying half its contents, the Belgian asked if Paul had a cigar.

'Sorry, no. But I do have this packet of cigarettes. They're French. Would you like one?'

Joubert merely nodded weakly. Paul lit two cigarettes and placed one between the lips of the Belgian. They both smoked in silence for a minute or two as the cacophony of war continued around them.

'Will you do something for me?' the Belgian asked in a whisper. 'Take this.' Joubert fiddled inside his coat and withdrew his wallet. 'In it you will find a letter from my mother. Write to her and tell her what happened, but tell her it was a German shell and not a British demolition charge. And take my horse.'

'I can't take your horse. I'll gladly write to your mother, but...'

'Please. She is a good horse and I don't want the Germans to have her. In any case, you say you have a despatch for your general.' Joubert appeared to lose consciousness and Paul removed the almost spent cigarette from his lips. The action brought Joubert back to life. 'Please. I beg you. Take Nero to safety. Let her taste fresh grass once more.'

Paul examined the wallet and found difficulty in focussing on account of the tears in his eyes. He found the letter and noted that an address on the outskirts of Bruges was included. He also found a crumpled photograph of what must have been Joubert, resplendent in full uniform and with an arm around a good-looking woman of middle age.

'All right,' he responded. 'I'll take her, but I don't even know how to ride.'

The Belgian took a while before replying. 'She's a good mare. She'll know what to do... May I have another cigarette?'

'Have the packet. I'll light you another.' Paul attempted to light a match, but the box was now wet and he wasted a dozen matches before successfully lighting a fresh cigarette. When he went to place it in Joubert's mouth, he spotted the lifeless eyes staring at him. 'Damn you, Crichton, you coward,' he shouted into the empty street. There was nothing more he could do for Joubert, but follow his dying wishes with respect to his horse and contacting his mother. Gently, Paul removed the Belgian's rifle and placed it in the horse's holster scabbard. Delicately, he removed the ammunition clips from Joubert's pouch and retrieved the strap for his canteen, now slippery with blood. He raised a clenched fist to the sky and called out to the heavens, 'You'll pay for this, Crichton. You and all your cowardly friends.'

*****

Half an hour later, having found the next bridge across the canal intact, Paul arrived at Burcht to discover a scene of orderly chaos. In addition to the several boats tied together to form the pontoon bridge across the Scheldt, a number of boats were ferrying groups of the

Belgian Field Army and Naval Division across. On the other side, Paul could see a battalion of sailors forming up to march away. He assumed that these men must be part of Commodore Henderson's brigade and, thus, Charles must have safely delivered his message. He led Nero across to the queue for the ferries where a small number of Belgian officers with horses were also waiting patiently for their turn to cross. Thankfully, the rain had stopped, but even so he felt chilled to the marrow and even after only half an hour in the saddle, he was grateful to be able to dismount. Not only were the muscles of his thighs and bottom sore, but his eyes were puffed and streaming from the horse's allergens.

In the corner of his eye he saw a Belgian army NCO looking in his direction and talking to two armed sentries. The NCO pushed the sentries in his direction. The soldiers approached him and one asked in French, 'Excuse me, sir. Could you establish your identity, please?' The other watched him suspiciously with his rifle in the port position.

Paul reached into his right breast pocket and produced proof of his identity.

'It says here that you an officer of the British Navy. So why are you dressed as a soldier with the wrong badges of rank and leading what is obviously a Belgian army horse, sir?' the Belgian soldier asked.

'But I am a naval officer. I'm attached to the Naval Division and I'm only wearing khaki because it's more convenient for land warfare.' Paul could tell that neither soldier looked convinced. They all looked across the river to the sailors formed up on the other side and Paul could see that none of the officers wore khaki.

'And the horse, sir?'

Paul began to explain the circumstances of how he came by the horse, but quickly realised it was futile. He cast his eyes around for a fellow naval officer and espied a Royal Marine captain leading his men towards the pontoon bridge. 'Look, ask that officer over there. He can vouch for me.'

The Belgian NCO joined them before sending one of the soldiers off to speak to the marine officer. The soldier asked the marine to come over, but it was clearly done with some reluctance by the marine captain.

'What the bloody hell's going on here?' he exclaimed. 'Can't understand a word of the froggy.'

Paul quickly introduced himself and explained the situation. The captain cottoned on immediately. 'It is fine,' he said slowly and loudly in English. 'This a *pukka* English officer... Friend.' The Belgians looked none the wiser, so Paul translated.

'So why are you not wearing a naval uniform?' the NCO asked. Paul decided it would be better to allow the marine officer to explain, so he translated the question.

'Some of them do. That's all.' Instead of translating the reply, Paul explained that he needed to report to Four Corps urgently and showed him General Paris's despatch. This animated the marine.

'Bloody right, you need to get back. We need those trains to meet us. As it is, we've had to march further than planned. The bloody Belgians have started blowing up the bridges on our line of retreat. Stupid buggers. Just as well you found yourself a horse. But I'd cut cross-country for Beveren if I were you. The roads around Zwijndrecht are reported to be teeming with refugees and the withdrawing army.' The captain turned to the Belgian NCO. '*Il est notre ami. Ami.* You must let my friend pass. *Tres vite. Tres important.*'

The Belgians did not need a translation and the soldiers relaxed. One of them escorted Paul and his horse to the front of the queue for the ferry whilst the others shared a cigarette with the Royal Marines officer.

*****

The first of the battalions arrived at Sint-Gillis-Waas at 07.00 the following morning and immediately boarded the waiting trains. The men were naturally tired after marching over fourteen hours through the night. All were hungry and many very thirsty having carried no water canteens. However, all retained their weapons and many were even carrying boxes of ammunition and trench stores that were to be denied to the enemy.

Paul's journey through the night had not been that much easier. Although he had taken the narrow lanes cross-country, these lanes had still been blocked with the overspill of refugees and troops from the main roads. Some of the battalions had split into companies or even platoons to fight their way through the crowds. Everywhere the verges of the roads were festooned with the detritus of a retreat; abandoned furniture, broken carts and even abandoned motor cars and omnibuses. However, at 03.00, he had arrived at Sint-Gillis-Waas, saddle sore and barely able to walk, from where he telephoned his report through to Commander Samson. He, in turn, had passed on the message to Rawlinson before stationing himself at Zelzate and arranging for hot food and trains to be waiting for the men of the Naval Division on their arrival. By 09.00, only the First Brigade had not entrained for the journey to Zelzate and Paul joined the last of the marines on the train. There he learned that the men he had seen at Burcht had been those of Drake Battalion. The other three battalions, over 1,500 men, including Charles and Commodore Henderson, were still missing. Rumours abounded that the Germans may now have cut off the brigade's escape route and the blue-jackets were doomed.

Chapter 21

Some four hours later, Paul caught up with Samson, sitting with Major Armstrong in the Zelzate station master's office. Paul could not remember when he had last slept, but Samson seemed to be in the same state.

'Good God, man. You look all in. Have you eaten?' Samson might have been tired himself, but he was full of concern for Paul.

'I breakfasted at Sint-Gillis-Waas, thank you, sir.'

'Good. I expect you wouldn't mind a kip, though. I certainly think I could sleep for a full twenty-four hours, given half the chance. What say you, major?'

'I think we would all merit a rest, sir. But it'll have to wait until we retire to Ostend.'

'True. And that's just where you're going now, Miller. You've done well, but save getting the First Brigade home safely, there's not much more we can do for Antwerp now.'

'Is there any news of Commodore Henderson, sir?' Paul asked.

'There is, but it's still a little doubtful. The telephone lines are down, but we did receive a report an hour ago that he and his brigade had reached Saint Gillis-Waas. The men were about to embark on the train.'

'That sounds like good news, sir.' Paul felt relieved that Charles might be safe.

'Except there's a rumour out there that the Germans have already cut the line. Certainly, they're squeezing the escape corridor. I doubt we'll be here more than a couple more hours before we have to retire. The Belgians are already planning to blow the bridges across the canal. As soon as the cloud cover lifts, I'll send out an air reconnaissance patrol to see if we can find out what the ruddy hell the Huns are up to.'

'But if Henderson is cut off, sir, what will he do? Stand and fight to the last man?'

'I hope not. I wouldn't rate his untrained troops against the might of the German army. He hasn't any artillery and his men are likely dead on their feet. No, if he's any sense, he'll nip across the border into neutral Holland.'

'But would that not mean the men would be interned by the Dutch, sir?'

'Perhaps. But better than a POW camp back in Germany. A damned waste of 1,500 men either way. Anyway, that's not your problem. I want you back at Ostend. Father Clancy will need your help. I've made him a lieutenant in the RNAS, by the way. Don't want him shot as a spy if he's caught. Now cut along. The next train's just about ready to leave.'

Paul made to leave and then remembered something. 'Excuse me, sir, but might I request a favour?'

'It depends on what it is. But you've earned one. Go on.'

'Might I trade horse power, sir?'

'Don't play games, Miller. I'm tired and busy. What are you up to?' Samson replied with a scowl.

'Sir, I just need you to look outside for a mere minute. I've brought you something.' Paul immediately headed out the door of the office. Samson and Armstrong had no choice but to follow.

Paul smiled at the look on Samson's face as he saw the Belgian mare Paul had acquired in Antwerp. 'My God, she's a beauty. Where on earth did you find her?' Samson asked with awe.

Paul related the tale of his encounter with Captain Joubert and also his suspicions about the behaviour of Crichton's troop of hussars. The account robbed Samson of his previous delight at seeing the horse.

'Miller, those are serious aspersions you are making and we had better do some fact checking before you relate them to anyone else. I don't like the bit about the car being in the canal. Should my suspicions prove correct, this inter-service rivalry has become decidedly unhealthy. Armstrong, do we know if the driver and gunner made it back? I would be very interested to hear their explanation.'

'I've no idea, sir. All the armoured car men should be in Ostend now, so I'll make enquiries.'

'Yes, please. Right away. Now, Miller. What was this trade you wanted to make?'

'Quite simply, sir. I offer you this gift of one horse-power if you will *lend* me your car and a driver to return to Ostend via Bruges.'

It took a few moments for Samson to work out Paul's meaning. 'You're a cheeky young whelp, Miller. What's wrong with the train?'

Paul explained his wish to call on Joubert's mother and Samson was sympathetic. 'I am happy to spare you the car, Miller, but not the driver. I'm short-handed as it is. In any case why not drive yourself?'

Paul coloured slightly and hesitated before speaking. When he did, he avoided his CO's eyes. 'Because, sir, I can't drive?'

'What do you mean, you can't drive? Why not?'

'I've never seen the need to learn, sir. I have my motorcycle.'

'But hang on a minute. You told me in London that you could drive. I remember asking you. Tell me straight, Miller. Was that a bare-faced lie?'

'Yes, sir. I was just keen to join you out here. I hope you...'

Samson erupted before Paul could finish. 'Unbelievable. An out and out lie. To me, your commanding officer.' Samson turned his back and walked away a few paces before returning. 'Miller, this is no school or university game we're playing out here. It's war and men are dying. The army might think we're a bunch of pirates, but we have discipline, whatever they think. And discipline is founded on trust. You trust me to know what I'm doing and follow my orders. You trust your men and colleagues to do their duty. And I need to know that I can trust you. Do you understand that?'

'Yes, sir.' Paul had never seen Sammy in such a state and began to wonder if he was going to be sent home.

'I can't work with officers I don't trust, Miller. This is your final warning...' Paul saw a ray of hope at the words. 'If you ever lie to me again, Miller, even for the best of reasons, you'll be out of this squadron. Is that clear?'

'Yes, sir.'

'Fine. We'll say no more about it. Take my car. Major Armstrong will find you a driver. Make your visit to Bruges and report to Father Clancy in Ostend. If he's not around, ask Commander Longmore to employ you on reconnaissance duties. But stay out of my way for a few days. Be off with you.'

Paul saluted smartly, turned about and walked away briskly. My, he thought. That was a fizzer, but he'd got away with it.

*****

Following his visit to Madame Joubert in Bruges, Paul returned to Ostend to re-join his squadron, but he had first paid a visit to the hospital. There he had been disappointed to discover that Nurse Steele was off duty and nobody was able to inform him of her whereabouts. After an hour of driving around the city on the off chance of spotting her, Paul returned disappointed to the squadron. The squadron, too, seemed to be suffering a subdued air and he immediately sought out his friend Sippe for news.

'Hello, Pi old chap. Why the sepulchral air amongst the chaps?'

'What ho, Paul. Good to have you back. Some of us were worried our loans might have gone bad. Is Charles with you?'

'Never mind about Charles. I'll fill you in later. Why the long faces in the mess?'

'So, you've clearly not heard. It's Beevor and Lord Annesley. They've been shot down and killed. Our first losses, but I don't expect them to be the last.'

'Are you sure they're dead and not missing. I mean, what happened?'

'They were out on a recce in a new Bristol, along the border. It was misty. You know, the usual filth, and we think they must have become disorientated. Leastways, they came out at low level over the Hun lines at Sint Niklaas and were shot down. To think they both survived the Balkan war, fighting for the Turks, but not when fighting for their own country.'

'I hadn't realised that. I didn't know Beevor, but I liked Annesley. I thought he had pluck. Is there any doubt that they didn't just force land?'

'No doubt about it. Rainey saw it happen.'

'Oh. Thanks for telling me. Did Rainey find out anything more about the position of the Naval Division?'

'I'd heard you'd been playing at soldiers with the Naval Division these past few days. What a mess! As a matter of fact, he did. He saw hundreds of them crossing the border into the Netherlands. By all accounts, it wasn't a pretty sight. They were in disarray and all in. I can't imagine what it must have been like manning the trenches and forts. I'll stick to flying. Anyway, let me treat you to a drink and you can tell me all about your exploits.'

Paul followed Sippe to the mess and over a glass of the local strong, frothy pale beer, he updated him on his recent activities and the loss of Charles.

'I'm sorry to hear about Charles, Paul. He was a good man. I just hope he's learning Dutch now. I can explain your mystery about the Lanchester in the canal, though. Major Armstrong rang through this afternoon. Your two ratings made it back and Longmore interviewed them. It seems your hussar friends cut up rough.'

'They're no friends of mine, Pi.'

'Quite, or so I gather.' Sippe paused to relight his pipe. 'Apparently, soon after you and Charles left, the hussars were keen on lighting a few fireworks. Some of the toy soldiers blew up a couple of bridges, but our boys let them get on with their games. However, when they wanted to blow the bridge where you had left them, things turned nasty.

'As per your orders, the boys put up a show of defiance. Accused them of cowardice and the like. As you can imagine, that sort of language didn't go down too well. Cut home as it were. It got to the point where they positioned the car at the south side of the bridge and threatened to shoot anyone approaching. They say you ordered them to shoot the officers. Is that right?'

'I certainly did, Pi. I didn't trust that Crichton.'

'Rightly so, it seems. The boys should have shot the blighters. Instead... well you wouldn't believe it, Paul.'

'Tell me, you ass, Pi. What happened next?'

'The lads refrained from opening fire and were bundled out of the car and... debagged! Would you credit it? Artillery fire everywhere, the Germans approaching and our brave Lancashire yeomanry are debagging sailors. A bunch of them thought it would be sporting to push the car into the canal, blow up the bridge and leave our lads on the wrong side of the canal, minus their trousers. Fortunately, they soon came upon one of the marine brigades who guided them home safely.'

Paul could believe it, but an anger ignited deep within him. He thought of Captain Joubert and the interview he had had with his mother only a few hours earlier. Then he considered the obstacle Crichton's deeds had created for the escape of the Naval Division. Lastly, he thought of Charles, now either dead, a POW of the Germans or, at best, interned by the Dutch for the duration of the war. Something inside snapped and his anger turned to a desire for revenge.

'Are you all right, old chap? You've gone white as a sheet.' Sippe gripped Paul's left shoulder.

'Sorry, Pi. I'm feeling mad about those cowardly hussars.'

'I'm not surprised. As soon as the word leaked, the whole squadron was all for going over to their barracks and teaching them a lesson. Longmore stopped such talk, of course.'

'Tell me, Pi. Are the Manchester Hussars still billeted at Morbecque?' Sipped nodded. 'Right then. I have an idea and I'd like your help.'

*****

Major Ponsonby surveyed 'A' Squadron of the Manchester Hussars with pride. He rode his horse up and down the ranks of the men under his command at the former RNAS HQ of the *chateau* at Morbecque. He inspected each troop carefully in the company of their troop commander and sergeant. Very smart, he thought with satisfaction. All spick and span. Such a turnout would have done credit to the Sixth Inniskilling Dragoons of his native county Fermanagh. Who said that a yeomanry regiment was inferior to a regular cavalry regiment? Perhaps after this war, a yeomanry regiment might even be offered the opportunity to take its turn with the Household Cavalry. After all, it would spare a regiment for overseas service.

He returned the salute of Captain Crichton as he began his inspection of the last of the troops. What a fine body of men. These were the same men who had served with such distinction under heavy fire from the Germans at Antwerp the day before. Their exploits in demolishing key bridges had done much to slow the German advance and save the Naval Division. It had also boosted the morale of the whole squadron. The Hussars had now been blooded and not found wanting. The colonel had been delighted to hear Crichton's success and hoped it might lead to a transfer to the recently-landed Third Cavalry Division. There they might serve under a proper army chain of command and not this irregular outfit of Samson.

Ponsonby looked up to the sky from whence he could hear the high-pitched drone of two approaching aeroplanes. For a moment, he feared they might form part of a German air attack, but the Squadron Sergeant Major read his thoughts. 'It's all right, sir,' he muttered only within Ponsonby's and Crichton's hearing. 'They're ours. I can make out the roundel on the sides. The Huns carry a cross.'

'Yes, Sergeant Major. Thank you. I can see that.' Ponsonby returned to his inspection.

*****

Paul was flying at only 100 feet and could see clearly the parade of the Manchester Hussars beneath him. He looked behind him and noted that Sippe was tucked in neatly twenty yards astern and off his port side. He exchanged thumbs up signs and banked his machine gently to starboard. Both aircraft lost height in the turn, but that didn't concern either pilot. Paul lined up on the men assembled below and dipped the nose slightly. At fifty feet he levelled out and cleared his gun with a quick burst of fire. Sippe did the same and Paul noted with amusement the astonishment on the men's upturned faces. 'Now I have your attention, gentlemen, we shall begin.' His words were carried away by the wind as he pushed the stick forward and began a shallow dive.

The Manchester Hussars must have had some suspicion of his intentions as a few of the men and their horses began to break ranks. Many of the horses began to act skittishly. Paul could only grin as he aimed for the centre of the parade at a height of only twenty feet. The move caused panic. The horses scattered every which way, some under the control of their riders, others throwing their masters. As he and Sippe flew across what was left of the centre of the parade, the men and horses divided to form an empty corridor, much as corn parts before the wind.

Paul pulled back on the stick sharply and opened up his throttle to gain height rapidly. The violence of the manoeuvre dislodged some of his weapons from his lap and he heard some tinkling before he banked to starboard again, but this time in a much tighter 270-degree turn. Sippe was still there, tucked in off his tail and in perfect formation. This time they crossed the parade ground at a height of fifty feet and began to release their bomb load. Each of them had time to drop their three chamber pots before they had passed over the scene of what had only minutes before been the proud parade of the glorious Manchester Hussars. Now they would be able to boast, too, that they had survived enemy bombing.

Chapter 22
November 1914

John dropped the heavy volume of the *Admiralty Manual of Seamanship* onto his fold-down desk with a loud thump, the noise of which only just masked that of his heavy sigh. He was thoroughly fed up.

'Just what is the navy's fascination with the loading and unloading of horses in warships?' he spoke aloud to nobody in particular. However, it had been enough to rouse Midshipmen Cartwright, a fellow member of the grot, from his slumbers.

'What's that you say, Miller?'

'I'm bored with this journal article on the loading of horses. It seems to be of delightful interest to the Boatswain.'

'You still writing that, old chap? It should have been handed in last week. I'm on with a fascinating account of the increase in efficiency compounding can bring to turbines at low speeds. The Senior's been very helpful in…'

'What are you talking about, you fathead?' John threw his eraser at Cartwright who deftly caught it without breaking stride.

'…with a series of velocity-compounded impulse stages… You know… That thing Curtis invented. That then becomes…'

'Cartwright, shut up! I swear that if you don't shut up, I'm going to kill you.' John picked up his seaman's knife to add credence to the threat.

'What's up, old man? You seem out of sorts.'

'I'm bored. That's what's wrong. Three months the war's been going and we've still to fire a shot in anger.'

'True, but we've come close and we are making a very valuable contribution to the war effort.' Cartwright swung his legs out of his hammock. 'We did, after all, help with the sinking of that Austrian cruiser, the *Zenta*.'

'We were just there. We didn't actually do anything. It was the French that sank her. And before that, we just shadowed those two German ships on their way to Turkey. We could have had them but for the caution of Troubridge.'

'Steady on, Miller. He has just been acquitted at his court martial, after all.'

'Tchah. If he had had more balls, those two ships wouldn't have entered Constantinople and then the Turks wouldn't have joined the war on the side of the Huns. The court martial board should have shot the admiral on his own quarterdeck. They did it to Byng, you know.'

'John, be careful. That's mutinous talk.'

'No, Cartwright. It needs at least two to form a mutiny and at any court martial I will testify that you opposed my views. Tell me. Just what have we actually done out here? If we'd gone back to England with the rest, we might have seen action by now.'

'We did our bit to defend the Nile.'

'Oh, yes. It didn't amount to much, though, did it. It was all boat parties and watching the troops sunbathing and swimming the river.'

'Perhaps this sweep down the African coast with the French will give you the action you crave, old chap. After all, if we do come across the German East Asia Squadron, we'll be up against von Spee's *Scharnhorst* and *Gneisenau*. Golly, look at the time. I'm due on watch in half an hour and tea should be on in the mess. You coming?'

'No. I've got the First and I had better carry on with my journal article. Guns is giving me a bit of grief over it. Say, tell you what, Cartwright, Christopher I mean. How about letting me have a butcher's at your article whilst you're on watch? It'd save me loads of time.'

'Miller, shame on you. Sorry, but no can do. How would copying my article help you learn the subject. It wouldn't be right... What are you doing, Miller?' Cartwright began backing towards the cabin door.

'I've decided, Cartwright, that for the sake of the human race, I really am going to kill you.' John took a step towards Cartwright holding his seaman's knife aloft, but Cartwright was already out of the door.

*****

Despite his love of flying, Paul was already beginning to tire of the daily patrols down the East coast of England from the Royal Naval Air Station at Kenton Lodge, Gosforth, near Newcastle-upon-Tyne. After being sent home by Samson following his affair with the chamber pots and the Manchester Hussars, he was serving a short stint with Number One Naval Aeroplane Squadron, flying Bristol TB.8 bombers. The temporary appointment did at least offer the chance to catch up on some badly overdue sleep and some of his mail had finally caught up with him. There had been piles of it, including four from Catherine, but no news from Richard or John. Like him, he presumed, they were too busy fighting their own war to write these days. However, *Mutti* seemed in better spirits and Pops had written to report his return to the Admiralty following a full recovery from his attack.

The squadron's role was to seek and attack any German ships approaching the North East coast of England. For the first fortnight, the work had been interesting and he had enjoyed flying over such locations as the Farne Isles and Durham. From 1,500 feet or higher, he was usually above the clouds and could see for miles. Frequently, his machine was the only one visible and on a clear day, it was a pleasure to spot the tell-tale wakes of the warships and merchant ships on the North Sea and to select a target. He would then spiral down and imagine dropping one of his bombs on them before circling the would-be victims, giving them a cheery wave and ascending back into the empty skies once more. However, the northern weather had recently taken a turn for the worse and the flying conditions were less pleasant. It now seemed that most days the air station was either enveloped by thick fog or lashed by winter gales. Furthermore, it was cold work, operating in temperatures frequently as low as minus seven degrees centigrade at high altitude. In such conditions, it was often necessary to descend near to sea level just to warm up and prevent a build-up of ice on the wings and struts.

However, unlike the rest of his squadron, Paul had no beef with the lack of action. He had had enough recently. All the airmen envied his experiences serving under Samson in France and Belgium. He, too, had read the reports of his former colleagues' recent success in bombing the Zeppelin sheds at Dusseldorf and the airship base at Cologne. Everyone longed for action of a similar kind, but Paul knew that very shortly he would be facing it again. Whilst the airmen at Kenton Lodge imagined that Paul had been sent to them in disgrace, he had the satisfaction of knowing what had passed between him and Samson at his last carpeting before the great man.

*****

'Idiots! Absolute blithering idiots. As if fighting a real war and making aviation history wasn't challenge enough, you two fatheads have to wage your private war on men of our own side. Take that smirk off your face, Sippe. You should have known better. I've come to expect little better from Miller here.' Samson paced up and down his office in Ostend whilst the two pilots stood to attention before him. The only other witness to the rant was Wing Commander Longmore. Samson stopped in front of Sippe.

'Sippe, I have no doubt this latest caper wasn't your idea, but as the senior officer you should have discouraged it, let alone taken part in it.' Samson moved over to Sippe's right and addressed Paul.

'As for you, Miller. I warned you last time that any more shenanigans, you'd be on the next ship out of here.' Paul's heart sank, but he had been expecting the news and bore no regrets about his actions.

'Instead of fighting the Huns, I'm now forced to deal with the chaos you've both left in your wake. The CO of the Manchester Hussars is the least of my problems. He wants you both court-martialled. I've even had General Byng calling for a report on your actions. Claims you both shot at his men. That can't be true can it?'

'No, sir. We merely cleared our guns, well short of them. Just to put the wind up them. Not that it takes much to put the wind up those cowards, sir,' Sippe replied.

'Cowards you say.' Samson looked across to Longmore who nodded meaningfully. 'Well you might be right there. And I've no reason to doubt the testimony of the two ratings who drove you to the bridge, Miller. Both good, reliable men. I will not have such men treated in this manner.' Paul shot a sideways glance at Sippe, but Sippe appeared not to react.

'I cannot have internecine warfare under my command. Not when there's a real war on. So, I have agreed with General Rawlinson some reorganisation of my command. The colonel of the Hussars will get his way and his whole regiment will come under the command of the Third Cavalry Division. If the Hussars' stories of their gallantry are to be believed, they will be a most useful addition to General Byng's command. As for you two, I'm avoiding the embarrassment of a court martial by sending you home.'

'But, sir!' both Sippe and Paul exclaimed in unison.

'Hear me out. I haven't finished. Sippe, you used to be a test pilot for A.V. Roe, did you not?'

'Aye, sir.'

'And, Miller, I know you've had plenty of experience flying the Avro 504, as well as a little irregular bombing practice.' Paul could see that a faint smile was trying hard to be hidden behind Samson's beard. 'So that solves a problem for me. Commodore Sueter has asked me to provide a team of experienced and daring pilots for a special mission, the details of which are top secret and not known to me. Instead of sending my best pilots, I will oblige the dear commodore by sending him the two of you in the interests of diplomacy, harmony and peace. I do not wish to see either of you for a very long time. Now get out.'

Chapter 23

Paul remembered well his first visit to the A.V. Roe and Company Limited aviation works in Manchester, but this time he was taken to a new site at Newton Heath. There, he was directed to one of the great aircraft hangars to find his new CO, Squadron Commander Shepherd, instantly recognisable by the long, Roman nose, standing with three other RNAS officers and an A.V. Roe employee. The manufacturer's engineer was showing them around an Avro 504, but one that looked very different from those Paul had flown earlier in the year. Paul recognised Squadron Commander Briggs and Sippe, both of whom had been with him in Belgium just a few weeks earlier. He saluted his new CO and reported, 'Flight Sub Lieutenant Miller, from One Squadron, sir.'

The A.V. Roe employee halted his tour and all the party turned towards him. Shepherd returned Paul's salute and approached him with his right arm extended. 'No need for that saluting nonsense in this unit, Miller. I only have me cap on for the ruddy cold. Come and meet some of the rest of the team.'

Briggs cut in, 'Good to see you again, Miller. Just don't go pranging any of these machines.' Paul blushed at the memory of the time his student had crashed an Avro. Briggs was an engineering specialist and took offence when any of his precious aircraft were damaged. 'Not that it was your fault, of course. I'm glad to see you in good health again. You and Sippe went some way to redeeming the honour of the Service with that stunt with the yeomanry. I laughed my socks off when I heard. Pity those pots weren't full. That really would have *pissed off* the buggers.'

'Good morning, Paul,' Sippe added and stood back to allow Shepherd to introduce him to the civilian, one Roy Chadwick, and Flight Lieutenant John Babington.

'Sippe, you can show Miller the modifications. I'm too ruddy cold to hang around here. When you're done, come into the office. The rest of us will meet you there over a mug of tea.'

When the rest of the party had gone, Paul asked Sippe, 'Is everything all right, Pi? The CO seemed a little cool with me.'

'Don't worry, Paul. He just suffers from chilblains and you have to admit, it is rather nippy in here.'

Paul was pleased to see Sippe again. It wasn't just because he was such a good friend. Prior to the war, Sippe had been a pioneer of aviation and the first aviator to fly a hydroaeroplane from the sea. He had also been involved with the successful bombing raids on Dusseldorf and Cologne. Paul felt he was in good company for whatever this mission might entail.

'So why the modifications, Pi?'

'Well spotted, Paul. I'd forgotten you're an expert on the 504. This mission is all very hush-hush, but it's clearly a long-range bombing mission. You'll note the extra fuel tanks in the nose.' The new fuel tanks filled the space for the front cockpit and this had been faired over.

'I'm told that should give us an endurance of eight hours now. If you look down there, you'll see a new rack for carrying four twenty-pound Hale bombs.'

Paul spent a couple of minutes examining the new aircraft. 'What about the covering on the engine, Pi?'

'Ah, well that is interesting. I'm not too sure myself, but I hear it might be to protect it from low air temperatures. Briggs has brought a team of riggers up to tour the machine and I heard them discussing it and the problems of oil at extremely low temperatures. I'm fairly sure Briggs knows more than he's letting on, but even the CO hasn't been told what we're going to be doing. I'd lay a wager we're off to Russia, though… Lord, it is parky. How say you we join the rest for a hot beverage?'

*****

As Catherine left the physician's consulting room, she swept past her mother in the waiting room without uttering a word. She could see Lady Edgar's look of appeal for confirmation of the facts she already knew, but Catherine did not meet her wide and tear-filled eyes. She was determined to maintain her dignity. It was not until she was safely locked in the privacy of the ladies' powder room that she released the floods of tears pent up within her.

'How could I have been so stupid?' she whimpered, beating herself on her forehead with one of her fists. 'The oldest trick in the book and I fell for it.'

For several minutes, she allowed the tears to flow before washing her face and drying her eyes. You might be a silly cow, she thought, looking at her reflection in the mirror, but you've got to deal with it. She adjusted her hair and hat and thought of Paul. What would he be doing now? She had had no word from him since he had left for France. Could it be that he was dead? Would that account for the silence? Or had he really abandoned her? Surely not. He had seemed so sincere. She placed a hand on her stomach and thought of the child that might grow up without a father. If that was the case, then she knew he or she would be more dependent on the love and affection of grandparents and it was only right that Paul's parents should know. Then again, she thought, would they welcome the news of a bastard grandchild? The thought triggered another stream of tears.

'Oh, Paul,' she said aloud. 'I think I could have loved you.' She braced herself against the sink and sobbed once more for another minute. 'Pull yourself together, Catherine,' she said to her reflection. 'You're just as much to blame as him. It's happened, so what are you going to do about it?'

Catherine returned to the toilet and sat on the pan, thinking for a few minutes. She decided that, after all, she would write to Paul's father. Although Paul had described him as strict and even scary, he had at least thought him a decent man. Moreover, Paul's father would have news as to why his son had not been in correspondence. If Paul were dead, the admiral and his wife might even draw comfort from the news of an unborn grandson. Were he to be alive and well, at least Catherine would know where she stood. Once more, she washed and dried her face, ready to face her mother. She was going to need Mummy's support in explaining her situation to Daddy.

*****

Paul felt like a spy as he stood on the quay of Southampton docks staring up at the SS *Manchester Importer*, watching six modified Avro 504s and other spare parts packed in crates being loaded onto the ship. It was dark, but the rain had stopped, leaving puddles on the quay side to reflect the lights of the overhead gantries. Paul imagined this was the sort of place where spies arranged their rendezvous to exchange secret packages or letters. He felt a tingling in his spine up to the nape of his neck. In addition to Shepherd, Briggs, Babington, Sippe and Chapman, the party had been augmented by a team of ten RNAS riggers and fitters, also out of uniform.

'You'd think they were loaded with eggs, the way Babington's fussing over those last six crates, Pi,' Paul remarked quietly.

'So he should, Paul. They contain the engines for our machines on this mission. He told me he had to go to Dunkirk specially to select them.'

'So, what are they?'

'Eighty-horse-power Gnomes as usual, but Babington's made sure these are the most reliable ones. At least that's some consolation. Briggs isn't happy with the airframes.'

'Really? What's wrong with them?'

'According to Chadwick, nothing. But you know what a fuss-pot Briggs is. I'm surprised he can fly with the weight of spare tools and parts he carries around with him. It seems A.V. Roe were struggling to meet the short-notice demand for these beauties and have had to use some parts in the build that didn't pass the usual inspections.'

'Lord! You mean we'll be flying dud machines?'

'Not your problem, old boy. Remember you're just the spare pilot. This mission only calls for four aircraft and the others are merely spares in case of a prang beforehand. In any case, they all handled well enough in the trials at Newton Heath.'

'I suppose, that's so,' Paul admitted grudgingly. 'I wish I knew where we're going, though.'

'Look at those crates for a clue, Paul.' Sippe pointed to the Cyrillic markings painted on the outside. 'I told you we were going to Russia.'

'But if that's the case, why is the ship going to Le Havre and not Scandinavia?'

'We're not supposed to know that, so it might not be true. In any case, we're not going with her, or so I heard. The Pusser has other plans for us, it seems. We'll know soon enough anyway as Dad's just arrived.'

Commodore Murray Sueter had just stepped out of a car a few yards away. He spoke briefly with Shepherd and handed him a large, sealed package. To add to the drama, he was not wearing uniform either. Shepherd gestured to the party to gather round the Director of the Air Department.

'Gentlemen, thank you for your attention. I have just handed your CO sealed orders from the Admiralty with strict instructions that they are not opened until you are at sea. Such is the importance of the mission on which you are about to embark, total secrecy is paramount.' Sueter paused to allow the effect of his words to sink in before continuing.

'You have all been hand-picked for the task and I have every confidence in you. Good luck.'

Sueter shook everyone's hand warmly and stepped back into his car. Shepherd directed them to move to another quay several hundred yards away and halted them alongside a scruffy-looking tramp steamer.

'Gentlemen, welcome to your new home.' Both Sippe and Paul exchanged silent looks of disgust and joined the queue to cross the gangway down to the ship.

Just as the crew members were casting off, they suddenly heard a speeding engine and looked up to the quay side to see a white motor car driven recklessly through the port. When it screeched to a halt, Paul recognised it as the Belgian 1913 FN. In the shadows of the port lighting the only parts of the driver immediately visible were the white cover of his cap and the glow of his cigarette. When he stepped forward, it was apparent to all, that it was an extremely tall RNVR officer, except it was the wrong season for a white cap and the buttons on his reefer jacket were wrong, too. Paul wondered if he was a spy, but as the mystery driver stepped forward, a cigarette in one hand and a heavy parcel wrapped in string under the other arm, Paul noted the gaunt face, monocle and diamond tie pin of Noel Billing, sometimes known as Pemberton-Billing. He had met Billing at Brooklands, that fateful night before he had taken his first flight with Samson. Billing owned a seaplane factory on the Solent and was good friends with Handley-Page.

'What ho!' Billing called across to the astonished party standing on the deck of the tramp steamer. 'Hang on a minute. I've something for you.' He tossed the parcel down to the deck of the ship and, after imitating the flight of a firefly with his cigarette as he disappeared again into the shadows, he returned with an apparently heavier sack. Again, he tossed it nonchalantly onto the deck of the steamer and it landed with a heavy thud and jingle.

'Toodle pip! See you the other side,' he called with a wave and immediately dashed back into his motor car. With a honk of his horn, he drove away at perilous speed.

One of the petty officer riggers was the first to react. He picked up the first parcel and handed it to the CO. This galvanised the tramp steamer's crew into action and they resumed the business of casting off.

'Ruddy rum cove, that, Paul,' Sippe exclaimed. 'What on earth are we up to?'

Chapter 24

Paul gathered with his colleagues in the saloon of the tramp steamer. Only the CO stood. Before him on the dining table lay the mystery parcels that Billing had delivered two hours earlier.

'Well, this is the moment we have all been waiting for, gentlemen. Now we are at sea, I have opened my sealed orders and can now reveal that we are *en route* to Le Havre.'

The audience responded with a groan of disappointment.

'Patience, gentlemen, please.' Shepherd held up one hand to calm them. 'That is only the first stage of our journey. At Le Havre, we will embark with our aircraft and other gear upon a special train, laid on by the French, that will take us all the way across France to the Swiss border. Our destination is a French airship station. There, we will unpack the crates, assemble the aircraft and ready ourselves to carry out a bombing run... on the Zeppelin factory at Friedrichshafen!'

The whole party gasped and began an excited murmur of conversation.

'Gentlemen... Gentlemen, your attention, please.' Shepherd unfolded a map on the table before him. 'Right then. Gather round and listen up. Let's start by telling you where Friedrichshafen is situated. It's in the Alps, on the Swiss-German border, along the shore of Lake Constance, or the *Bodensee* as the Huns prefer to call it. We will be based here, at Belfort.'

'But that must be all of a hundred miles from the target,' Sippe remarked.

'125 miles in actual fact, Sippe, and another 125 miles back. Now you see the reason for the extra fuel tanks. The Germans will think themselves safe that far away. I'm reliably informed you should have enough for eight hours, more than enough for a run of about four and a half hours. Is that so, Chadwick?' Chadwick merely nodded silently.

'However, here's the good news. Navigation will be made simpler by the fact you can run all the way up the Rhine itself until you reach the target zone. Which brings me on to the subject of navigation. You, pilots, have all been selected for your ability and experience in cross-country navigation. It is essential you do not stray across the border of neutral Switzerland. There'll be the deuced to pay if you do. That means you're going to have cut the corner here, north of Basle, and pick up the Rhine again here, to the east.'

Shepherd gave the pilots a few moments to study the map before continuing. 'Now for timing. We need to get the crates unpacked and the aircraft assembled ASAP. That's down to you, Chief, and Mister Chadwick here. Then we need to test-fly them all. I want all the pilots to be completely at home with the new machines. You'll find them quite forgiving and a bit lighter than the usual Avro. But we can't muck about. The French have given us the use of their airfield only until the end of the month.'

'And why is that, sir?' Babington asked.

'No idea. The DAD thinks they had in mind to conduct a similar operation and mebbe they're peeved we've decided to have a shot at it… Now logistics. This little lot might interest you.' Shepherd emptied the sack he had been given by Billing all over the map on the table. Again, there were gasps of astonishment. A pile of bank notes and gold sovereigns greeted them.

'There must be at least five hundred pounds there, gentlemen. Such is the importance the Admiralty places on this mission. For that reason, security is absolutely imperative and all, I mean all, personnel are confined to barracks on arrival at Belfort. We'll all be sleeping in the hangar.' Everyone groaned, but Shepherd ignored them.

'You're not to give a hint of what we're about, even to the frogs, although they'll be lending us a couple of liaison officers. They'll brief us on the local met', etcetera. And that is another reason why the DAD is sending one of his staff to make all the organisational arrangements. You've already met him. The officer who saw us off at Southampton.'

''E was no awfficer, sir,' the chief artificer growled. 'Weren't even properly dressed. Some spy more than likely.'

'I say, sir,' Paul was about to chip in his private knowledge of Billing's identity, but suddenly thought better of it.

'Yes, Miller. What's on your mind?'

Paul thought quickly. 'I was just wondering when we're to meet up with the crates again and how many aircraft will go on the operation?'

'Sensible questions. To be honest, I'm not sure on the former, but we'll find out on arrival in Le Havre. As to the latter, it's four only,

I'm afraid, Miller. There are two spare aircraft and engines and you're the spare pilot. I know that will disappoint you, but I want you just as involved as anybody in the planning. You never know what might happen… Chief, if you and your team need anything, you don't ask the French. Everything goes through the liaison officer, whoever he might be. Got that?'

'Aye, aye, sir,' the Chief responded in a tone suggesting he acknowledged the instruction, but didn't like it.

'That goes for everyone, by the way.' Shepherd looked each officer in the eye meaningfully. 'Fine. Any further questions?'

Nobody said anything. 'In that case, have a good look at the chart and start making a list of questions and requirements for our mysterious liaison officer.'

*****

It had been Billing who had arranged the unloading of the aircraft at Le Havre and had had them loaded on flat bed railway trucks for onward transport to Belfort. He had also taken care to load his 1913 FN, too. Paul had been impressed by Billing's organisational efficiency, but he had noted that he seemed to rub up Shepherd the wrong way. He had refused to discuss any detail of the operation with Shepherd, saying he was answerable to higher authorities and had acted very much as a *prima donna*. Moreover, he had clearly picked up the awe with which the ratings held him and, playing to the gallery, was now acting the part of the dashing spy. Again, Paul wondered if he should tell his CO the true identity of 'the man from Switzerland' as the mechanics had now dubbed him. However, the man seemed a born organiser and had provided everything the riggers and fitters had needed to be able to complete the assembly of the aeroplanes and test-run the engines within forty-eight hours of arrival in Belfort.

Paul taxied his machine back to the hangar and their temporary barracks. The Avro was a beautiful machine and everything Shepherd had promised. Sippe had even dubbed it 'a gentleman's aeroplane'. The other pilots were a fine band of fellows, too, and he couldn't see how such an experienced and capable team could fail. However, they all felt concern as to how the machines would react to the weight of a full tank of fuel and the four Hale bombs. The CO had vetoed the suggestion for a fully-loaded test-run on the grounds that with limited spares available, any possible mishap might write off an aircraft for the mission. This had been accepted after Briggs, the day before, had conducted a taxi trial with a full load and managed to buckle a wheel of the undercarriage and damage the tail skid.

However, fears over the mission aside, the real problem was the accommodation. It was impossible to heat the cold and spacious hangar. It wasn't so bad for the fitters and riggers. They had kitted themselves out with portable heaters around the aircraft on which they were working. Keeping the hangar doors shut at all times for security was an order to which everyone readily adhered.

Paul cut the engine to park his Avro outside the hangar and waited for the great doors to be opened before leaving the shelter of his cockpit for the icy wind. Whilst the ground crew scurried to stow his machine, he imagined how unpopular the open doors would be with the rest of the team as a great blast of air blew flurries of snow into the hangar. The combination of the concrete floor, cavernous roof space and hundreds of gaps through which the easterly winds continually penetrated, meant that the temperature away from the aircraft heaters barely registered above freezing. Briggs had earned himself the nickname of 'Captain Oates' for his habit of going to bed in full flying kit, including sea boots. Less amusingly, everyone had noted the debilitating effect it was having on the CO and a couple of riggers in particular. Briggs had quietly warned Paul that unless the CO's health improved soon, Paul would be on the raid.

*****

The outdoor temperature on the morning of 21 November in Belfort, at minus seven degrees Centigrade, was as cold at ground level as the high altitudes of the north-east of England. There was a strong wind blowing off the nearby Swiss Alps, but this had the advantage of clearing the low cloud and would give extra lift for the take-off of each heavily-laden Avro. The French liaison officers had advised that after all the low cloud of the previous few days, this was probably their best weather window for the raid and, all being well, the returning aircraft would make it back in daylight.

As soon as the great hangar doors opened, Paul felt immediately chilled to the bone by the icy-cold air. It was a bitter morning. Indeed, he had been concerned that the aircraft would not start, but the naval mechanics had already thought about it. Leaving nothing to chance, they had drained the castor oil from all four Avro 504s the night before and lagged the oil tanks in layers of red flannel. Since earlier in the morning, they had been warming the oil and were now in the process of returning it to the aircraft oil tanks ready for a launch at 09.30.

A frisson of excitement passed through Paul and he trembled with the emotion. To the rest of the team it would have looked as if he was shivering. Paul felt sorry for Shepherd, of course, but he could not help feeling pleased by the way events had panned out. Despite the risk to security, Billing had moved the party to a hotel a couple of days previously and purchased another motor car to provide daily transport to the French aerodrome. It had prevented further sickness amongst the RNAS flight, but even so, Shepherd's health had not improved enough to allow him to take part in the mission. As a result, Paul would be flying the fourth Avro. Accordingly, like the other three pilots, he had written a letter labelled, '*Only to be opened in the event of my death*' and left it with Shepherd for his parents should the worst come to the worst. He wondered how Catherine might feel should he not return from the operation. With a pang of guilt, he reflected that he should have written to her by now, but he had never been a great correspondent and there had always been something else going on to offer an excuse for him not to do so.

It was time. All the officers offered the mechanics a helping hand to roll out the four Avros as a means of keeping warm. It really was cold. Paul already thought the marrow of his bones would freeze and it was going to be far colder in the open cockpit at 5,000 feet. That is until we reach the target, he thought ruefully, and he climbed into the cockpit of his Avro.

Thanks to the foresight and careful preparations of the mechanics, all four aircraft engines started first time. Squadron Commander Briggs, as the new leader of the flight, led the procession of aeroplanes to the western side of the airfield. Babington followed ahead of Paul and Sippe brought up the rear. There was a short delay whilst Chadwick and the riggers tested the release mechanism for each of the Hale bombs, but at exactly 09.30, Briggs increased the power of his engine, waved away the ground crew and was the first to take off. When Paul's turn came, he almost found an excuse for pulling out. His stomach was in knots and had sunk somewhere near his groin. Despite the cold, he could feel his face colouring and beads of perspiration on his temples. He hummed to himself to break the tension, but he wasn't sure if it helped. 'Come on, Paul,' he muttered. 'Don't let them see you're afraid.' His gloved fingers shook as he gripped the throttle with one hand to increase power and he waved away the ground crew with the other.

The airfield might have been good enough for launching airships, but it left something to be desired for aeroplanes. The grass was covered with stones and potholes, and Paul worried that the Hales bombs might be jolted clear of the rack on which they hung. Were one to fall, he did not give himself much chance of survival. Then his attention switched to the airspeed indicator. The machine wasn't gaining speed quickly enough and he worried he was running out of airfield due to the increased payload. He glanced to his left and was reassured that he was not as far down the airfield as he thought. The oncoming wind was slowing him down and then, finally, he felt the wheels leave the ground. Immediately, he brought up the nose and began gaining height. Suddenly, all his fears subsided. He was in the air and his fate was sealed.

Chapter 25

The resignation of Prince Louis of Battenburg as First Sea Lord had come as a complete surprise to Admiral Miller. He respected the Prince for his administrative ability and diplomatic skills, but privately, he was pleased by the decision. In his opinion, the Prince was too malleable in Churchill's hands. However, he was not convinced that bringing Fisher back out of retirement at the age of seventy-one was the best decision either. Battenburg had been forced out of office by the Press, purely on account of his German name. How long would it take for them to turn on the House of Saxe-Coburg and Gotha, he wondered.

The frenzied attack on Battenburg seemed to have been started by a newspaper close to Miller's home, *The Northern Messenger*. The paper had launched the attack with the accusation that it was *'a crime against our Empire to trust our secrets of National Defence to any alien-born official'*. The editor had had the backing of Admiral Lord Beresford and it had not been long before other newspapers had followed up the call for Battenburg to resign. How ironic, Miller thought, that Beresford's actions had brought back from retirement his arch foe, Fisher.

Within a fortnight, Fisher had sent for Miller and both admirals were seated comfortably in the high-backed, leather armchairs of the First Sea Lord's office.

'So, Miller, you have surprised me by your resilience. I felt sure that you would be long retired now as a mere captain, but here you are of flag rank. Perhaps the power of your enemies is fading. I thought they had you when you were wounded in August, but like a phoenix from the ashes, you seem to have the power of eternal resurrection.'

'Thank you, Lord Fisher. I merely seek the opportunity to serve my country and presently, there seems much to do.'

'But you cannot be content to remain the assistant to the First Lord, surely?'

'It suits me well enough for the moment, sir. You will have read my brief on the expansion of our signal intelligence department.'

'Yes, I read it with interest. Churchill has high hopes for it. Room 40 OB, as it has been dubbed, along the corridor from here. But it is hardly yielding substantive results.'

'True, sir, but that may be about to change.'

'How so?'

'We have had a piece of luck recently. Actually, a couple of pieces of luck. We had in our hands two of the Imperial German Navy's signal books already. Until recently, this had only allowed us to decode weather reports, as the interesting stuff has been re-coded. However, Fleet Paymaster Rotter, our German specialist, has worked out the key to the re-cyphered messages and we are beginning to see results. Even better, an engagement a few days ago off the Dutch coast has led to us being in possession of what we are calling, "The Miraculous Draught of Fishes".' Unusually, Miller betrayed some emotion by chuckling, but the new First Sea Lord did not understand the joke.

'And what of these fish, Miller,' he asked in an irritated tone.

'I'm sorry, sir. You will recall that Captain Fox and his destroyers sank four German destroyers a few days ago. One of the German destroyer captains was seen to throw overboard what looked to be a lead-lined chest.'

'It would have contained his confidential documents, no doubt. A conscientious action.'

'Indeed, sir, but Captain Hall instructed a couple of trawlers to fish in that area and, to our great delight, one of them dragged up the chest in its nets.'

'By Jove, Miller. That was a piece of luck. And did the chest contain anything of interest?'

'Indeed, it did, sir. Amongst the documents was the *Verkehrsbuch*, the IGN's codebook for its communications with warships and naval attachés.'

'So, are we now able to read all the German cyphers?'

'In theory, but not in practice, sir. The volume of traffic is just too great to read every signal in anything like real time. Ewing is stepping up his recruiting efforts and has widened the net to include mathematicians, sir. I'm expecting a change of tempo within weeks, sir.'

'Excellent. Good work, Miller. Hall's shaping up in his new post, is he?'

'Very much so, sir. He's ideal for this sort of work. I mean it as a compliment when I say he has the right sort of devious mind for intelligence duties.'

'He would have. I knew his father, of course. Tried to have him appointed as Commander of *Inflexible* under me. He went on to be a first rate DNI.'

'That's true, sir.'

'So, with Hall and Ewing in place, and the haul of your precious fishes, it would appear your task is virtually done then, Miller. I'll order some tea before we discuss your next appointment.'

Whilst Fisher rang his bell and followed up by ordering a tray of tea and biscuits, Miller's suspicions were aroused. What did Fisher mean by, 'his next appointment'? He had only been in this current appointment three months. He waited for the steward to depart the office after bringing the tea before giving voice to his thoughts.

'My lord, there is still much to be done in preparing the DID for this war, sir. Interception and decryption of the enemy's signal communications is but one element.'

'Oh? Pray enlighten me. But pour the tea first.'

'Sir, it has come to my notice that very little of this country's mail overseas is being censored.'

'I thought that was the responsibility of the War Office. Some colonel is responsible for it, is that not right?

'Indeed, sir. Colonel Cockerill, the Director of Special Intelligence. But he and I have visited the sorting office at Mount Pleasant and it's chaos there. His staff is lamentably small. I have agreed with him that were I to persuade Mister Churchill to make available to me £1,600, the Admiralty could take on the responsibility. I can tell you that the First Lord has approved the funds.'

'But what has it to do with the Admiralty? Surely it is a Home Office matter. I know Churchill likes to have his fingers in many pies, but as a former Home Secretary, he must realise this, too. I'm surprised you persuaded him to fund the project.'

'But there is method in our madness, sir. After only a week, we have discovered information on how the enemy is placing orders overseas for vital supplies. Many are being shipped in neutral ships or via neutral countries. Such proof of these devious measures will be of inestimable value, both to the Prize Courts being asked to condemn the cargoes, and to our ships in intercepting them.'

'I can see that, I suppose,' Fisher responded grudgingly before standing.

'Notwithstanding, it's time you left all that to Hall. You're no longer the DNI and Churchill has, to my mind… and that of others, I might add… given you unfettered latitude to continue your influence over the DID as you have these past three months. But for him, you would be ashore on half pay now.'

'My lord, I am well aware of the First Lord's patronage and can understand if it has ruffled a few feathers amongst your fellow noble lords…'

'Don't try to soften me up, Miller. Churchill cannot protect you forever and I have agreed with him that you are to be replaced next month. That's surprised you, hasn't it. Cat got your tongue?'

Miller was stunned and sat open-mouthed for a few moments. He recovered and asked quietly, 'Sir, what position do you and Mister Churchill have in mind?'

'Chief of the War Staff. And you'll be promoted to Acting Vice-Admiral. Not bad for someone who was nearly forcibly retired as a Captain.' Fisher beamed with radiance and munificence. 'What do you think of that then?'

Miller took a short while to compose his words. He was even more stunned than before.

'Lord Fisher, I am grateful for the honour you wish to bestow on me, but I am not the right candidate for the position.'

'Right candidate be damned! I'll make that judgement. What's your objection?'

Fisher looked riled and had stamped his foot. Miller realised he would have to tread carefully.

'Sir, I have no objections. I wish merely to register two points that might suggest I would not be the most appropriate officer to fill this appointment. Firstly, I was never a proponent of Mister Churchill's plans to create a Naval Staff. I thought the Intelligence Division had previously fulfilled the duties of the new staff very well. More importantly, given that the administrative and operations functions are married into one, surely it would be better that the Chief of the War Staff had experience of commanding a squadron or division of one of the fleets. My experience as captain of an old cruiser is barely relevant to the post-*Dreadnought* navy.'

'I never thought I would hear you hide your light under a bushel, Miller. Perhaps your lack of senior command will hold against you, but it's too late. As for your scepticism of the relative merits of the

DID and the War Staff, I think that as a former DNI, it makes you well placed to run the new organisation. There… I've hoisted you by your own petard, Miller.' Fisher did a little jig with glee. 'How do you answer that then, Miller?'

'May I assume, sir, that the current DNI will report through me?'

'Of course. It was a mite irregular him reporting to you in your current post anyway.'

'Very well, sir. As you say. I have no choice and it is my duty to serve my country in any way I can.'

'Capital. Now we have that settled, how are your sons? I understand all are in blue.'

'Not quite, sir. My eldest boy is commanding a submarine running out of Harwich…'

'Of course, just won himself the DSO.'

'Quite. My next son is a diplomat in the Netherlands. Another is a pilot in the RNAS, somewhere on the continent.'

'And no doubt covering himself with glory, too. That young chap, Samson, has been giving the Germans hell. I'm glad two of your sons, anyhow, have embraced the new technologies of the day. And what about your youngest?'

'He's in the Med', sir, with George Borrett. Although I see they're due back next month to join the Grand Fleet on blockade work.'

'Yes, Borrett is to get a battleship, the *Monarch*. And has your youngest son any specialisation?'

'Not yet, sir. He's still a snottie, although from his letters home he seems to have an interest in gunnery.'

'A noble specialisation, but I suspect it will be the torpedo that has more impact on this war.'

'It had not escaped my notice, sir, that you became a torpedo specialist. Now, if you will excuse me, my lord, I must prepare to hand over to my successor.'

'Certainly, certainly. But before you go. I and the good lady are having a bit of a shindig at home to celebrate Saint Andrew's Day. You up for coming?'

Miller was well aware that Fisher needed little excuse for a little dancing. 'I will first check our social diary with Johanna, but if we are free, we would be delighted to attend, Lord Fisher.'

Paul levelled out at 5,000 feet, but could see no sign of the acting CO or Babington. This concerned him since he needed them for navigation on the first section of the flight. The French had insisted that no maps be carried in any cockpit for fear that in the event one of the aircraft was to crash, they did not want the Germans to know that the flight had taken off from a French airfield. Paul banked to starboard and looked down to see Sippe taking off, five minutes after he had. He decided it would be prudent to wait for Sippe instead of trying to overhaul the two leading airmen, so he put the Avro into a lazy starboard 360-degree turn. As he had expected, the combination of low air temperature and an 80-knot wind chill was freezing and Paul wondered how he would survive another four hours of this.

Slowly, Sippe caught up with him and, after an exchange of waves, Paul signalled that Sippe should take the lead. Paul tucked in behind and about fifty feet above Sippe's machine and they headed east. Forty minutes later, they spotted the Rhine ahead and turned south to follow it on the French side of the border. Soon afterwards, they recognised the sight of Basle ahead. It was time to turn to port to try to avoid entering Swiss airspace and hope to pick up the Rhine again on its east-west course. They were about to enter German airspace and Paul wished they were still flying as a formation of four. Suddenly, he saw Sippe waggle his wings to draw his attention. Drawing nearer on Sippe's port side he saw him point ahead and to the right. In the distance he could see two dark specks in the air. Both were south of Basle and in Swiss airspace so Paul relaxed a little. It was unlikely to be a pair of Huns. More likely a pair of Frenchmen who had strayed into Swiss airspace. However, it would be worth being ready and he signalled to Sippe that he was going to test his Lewis gun.

After firing a one second burst, he was happy that his gun was functioning correctly and Sippe followed suit before altering course to the south-east. Paul resumed his station slightly astern and above him. It soon became clear that the unidentified machines now edging ahead, were travelling in the same direction and Paul wondered if they might be those of Briggs and Babington. Sippe clearly had the same idea as he increased speed to close the range. Paul concentrated on his instruments and discovered that he no longer felt quite so cold. Perhaps it was adrenaline kicking in, he thought. The cloud lay low beneath him and Sippe, but to his right in the distance he could still see the snow-covered slopes and peaks of the Alps poking through the thick white blanket of cloud.

The wind now had more of a southerly aspect and Paul thought the drift might help them pass clear of Switzerland, but without a map he could not be sure. He concentrated hard on looking for enemy aircraft and at the same time trying to pick out a view of the Rhine beneath the gaps in the clouds below. There it was, right ahead. Sippe signalled to indicate that he had seen it, too. Paul had often been content to be alone in the skies with just the throb of his engine for company, but today he was glad of Sippe's company.

Soon after altering course to follow the Rhine to the east, the cloud dispersed and they had their first clear view of the mighty river below and the steep mountains either side. It was beautiful countryside and he could not help but think back with fondness over the many happy walking holidays he had enjoyed with his family in both Switzerland and Germany before the war. It was hard to credit that he was now intent on delivering death and destruction to the German people of Friedrichshafen on the beautiful holiday resort of Lake Constance. He had even stayed in the Hotel Kurgarten where Count Ferdinand von Zeppelin had designed his first airship. The world had gone mad. Somewhere in Germany he had relatives. At least Switzerland had maintained her neutrality or else he might have been bombing his Swiss cousins. It was not healthy to dwell too deeply on such matters, he decided. It was time to focus on his mission, the destruction of the massive construction sheds, workshops and floating dock for launching the airships, and the hydrogen producing plants.

Slowly, Paul and Sippe gained ground on the leading aircraft and were able to identify them as Avros. They must have ignored the instruction to stay outside Swiss airspace and taken the easier option for navigation by following the Rhine all the way, Paul thought. I don't jolly well blame them. Soon, however, he lost sight of the aircraft as they entered cloud. Ten minutes later, he and Sippe, too, entered cloud and Paul lost sight of his partner. Not long now, he thought, before the two lead machines are over the target. Then it dawned on him suddenly, that by the time he and Sippe approached the target, the Germans would be fully alerted to the attack. He felt as if a massive hand had immediately gripped his guts tightly.

'Come on, Paul,' he said out loud. 'You've got to see this through.' He pushed the stick forward and took his machine beneath the cloud to a height of 3,500 feet, and only just in time. The great river had turned to the north towards Schaffhausen and Paul had inadvertently crossed in to Switzerland. He banked to port and crossed to the west side of the river. As if from nowhere, he spotted his colleagues. Sippe was a mile to port and Babington had dropped back to about two miles astern and to starboard. He caught a brief glimpse of Briggs well ahead, but quickly lost him.

Sippe now took the lead as the flight of three Avros turned to starboard onto the approach for the lake, visible about ten miles ahead. Babington seemed to be having engine trouble and was dropping further behind. Suddenly, Paul saw Briggs again and simultaneously, so must have the Germans. They immediately opened up with an intense barrage of anti-aircraft fire. The noise was terrific and Paul felt another jolt of fear. The sky ahead was beginning to fill with the black puffs of smoke of the bursting shrapnel from the anti-aircraft shells. The leading Avro was still short of the target when it was suddenly lifted several feet vertically, but it carried on. Sippe signalled to Paul to follow him down. Paul put his aircraft into a steep dive and only when they were mere feet from crashing did Sippe pull out to settle at an altitude of ten feet above the water. Paul assumed that Sippe's reckoning was that they might avoid detection this way. He was mad.

By now they were over the lake and they followed its northern shore. Paul had no time to look out for Babington or to check his watch for the time. He was too occupied weaving his machine in 'S' bends to distract any gunners that might have spotted them and in keeping his toes out of the water below. Within seconds, or so it seemed, they were only five miles from the target and Sippe increased height ready for his bombing run. With so much fuel already expended, Paul noticed the improved performance in gaining height. They quickly reached 1,000 feet from where Paul could once again observe the battle ahead. To his horror, he saw another burst of shrapnel burst close to Briggs's port wingtip and the aircraft flip on its side. The pilot righted his machine initially, but very soon it began trailing a thick plume of black smoke and losing height in a slow spin to port. Mercifully, it had not caught fire.

Sippe had levelled out at 1,200 feet to begin his run, but Paul decided to gain more height still before he commenced his run. At the same time, he spotted one of the hydrogen-producing plants and altered course towards it. As he did so, he could see the shrapnel bursts ahead of him in his path and getting closer. He eased back the stick to gain yet more height and confuse the gunners below. Levelling out again at 2,500 feet, his attention was diverted by a huge explosion and fireball below. The bombs of one of the pilots had hit the large airship shed and the Zeppelin inside had caught fire. An Avro sped beneath him at low level across the lake pursued by a trail of anti-aircraft fire. He thought it might be Sippe, but he was not sure.

Ignoring the mayhem around him, he pushed the stick forward and put his machine into a steep dive, lined up on the hydrogen plant. His Avro gained speed rapidly and the wires of the wing struts whistled loudly above the noise of the rushing air meeting them. The airspeed indicator needle passed 100 knots, but Paul ignored it and focused instead on the target rising rapidly to meet him. The wings of his aircraft started to shake and he in turn trembled in excitement. It was like descending one of the steep sides of a Lancashire valley at full speed on his motorcycle. It was totally exhilarating and he loved it. He prayed silently that his wings would not fall off and, as he approached 1,000 feet, he released two of his bombs.

By now, the aircraft was in a near vertical dive and, after counting to two, Paul eased back on the stick gently to arrest the steep descent. As the nose slowly rose, he felt the aeroplane buffeted by a huge explosion below and he was momentarily blinded by a flash of vivid reds and oranges. His bombs had struck home and the subsequent ignition of the hydrogen had caused a massive fireball. He noted his altitude had only been about 300 feet when the explosion occurred and that had been a bit too close for comfort. However, the force of the explosion seemed to have stunned the anti-aircraft gunners into inaction as he was troubled no further by their fire.

He looked around for another target and spotted an Avro on the ground. It was Briggs. He had managed to land his machine, but Paul was livid to see that a group of townsfolk had dragged him clear of the cockpit and were giving him a swift beating. Paul immediately turned his Avro on its wingtip and made a tight turn to port. He prayed that his controls were still functioning, but all seemed well. He quickly lined up on the crowd surrounding the grounded Avro and dived down to fifty feet at maximum speed. His blood was up and he was determined to punish Briggs's assailants. Let's see how they like a little hot lead, he thought, and he reached for his Lewis gun. In the corner of his left eye he could see a squad of soldiers running towards the scene and he immediately changed his plan. Let the Germans be the ones to bayonet Belgian babies and murder civilians, he thought, and he adjusted his height to run in at the crowd of civilians at twenty feet. Those with the faster reactions immediately scattered and the rest dropped to the ground. As Paul pulled back on the stick, he saw Briggs wave to him. He appeared to have taken a wound to his head. Still gaining height, he looked over his left shoulder to see that the German soldiers were pushing away the brave citizens of Friedrichshafen and taking Briggs prisoner.

Another puff of evil and acrid black smoke above him indicated that his priority must now be self-preservation and he turned to the north to escape the anti-aircraft fire. To his right, he spotted another Avro making an approach on the target with the sun behind him. Paul thought that a good idea as he hoped it might put off the aim of the gunners below, so he turned east before beginning his next run. He picked out the floating airship shed at Manzell as his next target, but decided on the more conventional altitude of 1,000 feet for this run. He flew over the parade ground of a barracks from which a platoon of soldiers was directing its rifle fire at him, but he realised it was no threat. It was the anti-aircraft shells that bothered him. With the wind now behind him, he was flying at a speed of eighty knots and so he played a game with the gunners, alternately closing his throttle to slow his machine to about fifty knots and then opening it fully to achieve eighty knots, all in an attempt to confuse the gunners.

His luck held and he took satisfaction from the sight of the hydrogen plant on fire and further explosions as the surrounding hydrogen tanks were caught up in the blaze. The Zeppelin shed came into view and he dropped two hundred feet quickly, both to confuse the gunners and to increase the accuracy of his bombing. He ignored the noise of the shrapnel exploding around him and imagined this was a standard practice run. Just as he was on the point of releasing the bombs, his aeroplane shook violently and he felt a sharp pain in his right bicep. He had been caught by a burst of machine gun fire through the floor of his aircraft and a splinter of his cockpit now pierced his leather coat. Phew, that was close, he thought, as he pulled at the toggle to release his third bomb, but nothing happened. He tried again without success before releasing the fourth bomb successfully and simultaneously climbing. Looking back, he could see that the two second delay had been vital in ensuring that his bomb exploded beside the Zeppelin dock and not in it. Worse, a fat, juicy Zeppelin sat unscathed inside the dock ready for launching.

He passed out of range of the anti-aircraft fire and looked around for the other two Avros. He caught sight of one, also flying west, but could see no sign of the other. He joined up with the other pilot and realised it was Sippe again. He, too, had a Hale bomb hanging from its rack. They both went up to 6,000 feet and followed the Rhine once more, this time westwards. Paul checked his watch and noted it was 12.30. He had quite lost track of the last hour and a huge feeling of relief engulfed him. He had survived. However, any euphoria he might have felt was quickly replaced by one of hunger. He had breakfasted several hours earlier and now his stomach was rumbling. If Sippe wanted to cut the corner across Switzerland back to France, that was fine by him. It would be at least 14.00 before they would be back for lunch.

Chapter 27
December 1914

Paul removed the post and daily newspapers from the breakfast tray and attacked his two soft-boiled eggs. After three months at war, breakfast in bed was a luxury with which he would never tire and dear *Mutti* was very happy to indulge him. After buttering his toast and applying a thick layer of marmalade, he turned his attention to the post and newspapers. The newly-delivered letter was addressed in a hand he knew well. Excitedly, he slit open the envelope.

It was from Charles and he was safe. He reported that after finding Commodore Henderson, he had joined with his brigade to make the withdrawal from Antwerp. According to Charles, the blue-jackets had been worn out and not up to the long march to Sint Gillis-Waas, and had lost formation. Even so, they had made it to the station and had already entrained before Henderson had heard reports that the Germans had cut the line and his line of retreat. Rather than surrender his brigade to the Huns or waste his men in a futile and one-sided battle, he had elected to cross the border into the Netherlands. Most of the brigade had then been interned by the Dutch, including the Commodore, but Charles and a small number of other officers and men had evaded the Dutch, and sneaked along the border before crossing back into Belgium. Charles had then elected to join the rest of the Naval Division permanently.

Paul was delighted by the news. He, also, thought Charles would be very suitable as a Naval Division officer. He had shown more wit than he when it had come to infantry tactics.

Now in an extremely buoyant mood, Paul considered rising. It was already 09.20 and it was extremely lazy of him still to be in bed, but he had nothing planned for the day. Actually, that was not true. The evening before, Pops had asked to see him at 12.30. He would be coming home for luncheon and would like to see Paul first. All week Paul had seen little of Pops as he had been working late at the Admiralty, but he had noted that his parents didn't seem as close as usual. Paul wondered what this latest summons could entail.

He was still in debt, but other than with his tailor, not too badly and Mister Gieve was hardly likely to bother Pops with it. 'Hang it, Paul,' he said to himself. 'Why are you still afraid of Pops?' He reflected on his past three months of action. Pops should be proud of his behaviour. It was even possible that Shepherd might have recommended him for a medal after the Friedrichshafen raid. Perhaps, then his elder brothers might cease looking down on him. It was more than just their extra height. Paul was very conscious of his height of only five feet nine inches compared with his tall brothers and father, but he was at least an inch taller than John. But what had his other brothers done in this war? Well, Richard had sunk the *Hela* and won the DSO, so he allowed that to count, but it was time he and his fellow regular officers started taking the RNVR seriously. Mind you, even the regular RNAS officers still looked down on him and the other Special Entry officers. If he could win a medal, that would make them all change their tune. And there was Peter safely tucked up in the embassy in the Netherlands. Why didn't Pops put pressure on him to join up. John, at least, was in uniform, but no doubt drinking gin for Britain in the Med'. No, he was finished with being put down by his elder brothers and this time he was not going to allow Pops to bully him. He would hear him out, but stand up to him. Words might be said, but too bad, although he still depended on Pops for his allowance.

His mood now slightly soured, he pushed away the breakfast tray, reached for his dressing gown and swung his legs out of bed. After removing the breakfast tray to a safe place, he picked up Catherine's letters and returned to his bed. It was time he dropped her a line in reply to her many letters over the past several weeks. She would understand his delay, he felt sure. After all, there was a war on. Better still, he might go to see her. He still had a further week's leave. He licked his lips and grinned wolfishly as he contemplated a tumble in a barn somewhere on her father's estate, beyond prying eyes. Then again, he thought. Was that wise? Catherine's later letters had seemed to contain a note of desperation to see him. He wondered if she might be a little possessive and too serious about their relationship. He was too busy enjoying himself to be tied down in a relationship and a visit might encourage her further. He would have to give it some thought before acting.

Paul cast aside Catherine's letters and picked up the newspapers. It was the first Saturday of his leave in Cumberland Terrace and having time to read the newspapers in a leisurely fashion was also a new-found pleasure. Actually, Paul didn't normally pay much attention to the newspapers, but he did enjoy reading about the raid on the Zeppelin sheds at Friedrichshafen. *The Times* ran extensive coverage of the Battle of Ypres and Paul was pleased to note that the Allies had contained the German advance. It meant that the navy could still supply the BEF through Dunkirk, Ostend having fallen so quickly after Antwerp. He wondered what had happened to Sarah. He had neither seen nor heard from her since that day in Antwerp. Perhaps Pops would have some means of tracing her. His appointment at the Admiralty seemed to keep him well-informed on most matters.

However, *The Times* had nothing new to report on the raid in this morning's edition, so he turned his attention to *The Northern Messenger*. Although originally a Manchester newspaper, and still a source of regional news, it was now widely popular nationwide. The front page brought him up with a jolt.

At the bottom right corner was a photograph of Crichton. His attention gripped, Paul read the main article accompanying the photograph and could not believe what he was reading. He was tempted to throw the newspaper across the room in anger, but a masochistic fascination drew him back to the piece by, 'A Special Correspondent at the Front'.

'Fie,' he cried. 'Where was he? Paris?' He knew there had been no newspaper correspondents in Belgium covering the Siege of Antwerp or Samson's operations. The headline read, *'Navy irregulars to be honoured at the expense of our brave soldiers'*. The piece suggested that the Lancashire Hussars had fought a valiant rear-guard action in Antwerp to save the Naval Division, but Samson was ignoring it to favour his own officers in his recommendations for decorations. To Paul's certain knowledge, the reporter had stitched together a whole series of blatant lies. Certain phrases made him incandescent with rage.

'We understand that Captain Crichton and a troop of Lancashire Hussars forced their way through the enemy lines to deliver an urgent despatch to General Paris. This heroic action in itself was a major factor in the saving of the inexperienced, poorly-trained and ill-equipped sailors of the Naval Division, but the gallant Captain Crichton and his men, under heavy fire from German artillery and machine guns, then risked their lives further by destroying key bridges to delay the enemy's advance, thereby ensuring the safe

withdrawal of the naval brigades who had been hastily despatched to defend Antwerp in the place of regular soldiers.'

Worse, the article went on to make unwarranted criticism of Samson's command. *'We understand that the brave Lancashire cavalrymen were at the time under the operational command of a naval aviator, Acting Wing Commander Samson. Our readers might wonder why a naval aviator was directing ground operations more relevant to the command of a professional soldier. It has been reported that Samson heads a group of naval irregulars who have taken it upon themselves to roam the Belgian and northern French countryside in their expensive motor cars in pursuit of German bicyclists. A War Office source had this to say, "Samson's irregulars have earned themselves the soubriquet of motorised bandits. They are ill-disciplined, scruffy and experts at thieving War Office stores sent to supply the professional army."'*

Somebody at the War Office has got it in for Sammy, Paul thought.

'It could be asked why naval airmen are being employed at the Front when the army has its own Royal Flying Corps. However, another source confirms that many of Samson's officers are not aviators, but wealthy gentlemen who have earned their commissions solely by donating their expensive motor cars for Samson's use. A well-placed and reliable Admiralty source…'

'Probably some junior clerk with an axe to grind or in return for a back-hander,' Paul muttered between gritted teeth. How was it these people could add two and two together and make it a plausible five?

'…has confirmed that Commander Samson has forwarded a batch of recommendations to reward his own men's gallantry, but none for those men of our very own Lancashire Hussars. We cannot but ask ourselves if Commander Samson is guilty of bias or is hoping that a string of gallantry awards will give legitimacy to his own irregular operations, or provide a smokescreen for the unsuccessful campaign to defend Antwerp by forces who should have been employed more appropriately at sea.'

Paul wondered why he was punishing himself by reading the scandalous article again. It was complete codswallop and hadn't even deserved a first reading. Even so, it was after reading the final paragraph again that Paul connected the piece with Crichton's father, Lord Sedburn, the proprietor of the newspaper.

'We call upon the people of Lancashire to join our campaign to see justice for the brave men of our own Hussars. Why should gallant officers such as Captain Crichton not be decorated instead of wealthy gentlemen joy-riders who had neither the place nor the experience to be at the Front? Sign our petition. Contact your MP. Let the voice of Lancashire be heard.'

It was too much. This time Paul did throw the newspaper across the bedroom in a fit of temper. His morning was ruined.

*****

Paul surveyed his father carefully to detect any trace of his mood. He seemed tense and Paul could see crow's feet had appeared around his eyes. More strikingly, Pops's full head of dark hair had turned grey. Paul had never enquired as to what his father did at the Admiralty, but he assumed the war was causing him some strain at work. He also noted the additional ring on his sleeves to denote his new rank of vice-admiral. Some things had not changed. His father's enormous height and his straight-backed, shoulders-high bearing for a start. Moreover, Pops still wore the old-fashioned wing collar. Surely nobody else wore them these days?

Whilst Pops paced the room, Paul was relieved to be seated. When Pops was about to deliver his familiar dressing-downs, one remained standing. Paul thought it was done to maximise the psychological advantage of the difference in their height. However, he wished Pops would sit down, too. His pacing was making Paul feel agitated.

'I bumped into Murray Sueter this week, Paul.' At last, Paul thought, the great man speaks. 'We discussed that raid of yours on Friedrichshafen. I gather it didn't cause as much damage as we had hoped, but no fault of the airmen involved.' Paul wondered if the last words were added as an afterthought.

'No, on balance, it was a great success. You and your colleagues have shown what can be done with airpower and the psychological impact on the Germans will have been immense, too. Already I've read reports that the Germans are moving their factories further into Germany to avoid being caught out again. You did well, Paul.'

My, praise indeed, Paul thought. Perhaps all this is about is Pops wanting to tell me at last, in his own roundabout way, that he's proud of me.

'Did the Commodore have any news of Briggs?' Paul asked.

'Ah, yes. He did. We've heard courtesy of the Dutch and Swiss that he was taken prisoner and badly wounded. He received a bullet in the head, but the Germans report that their surgeons operated on him successfully and he is recovering well. I pity the poor fellow, incarcerated in a Prisoner of War camp for the rest of the war. Better than being dead, though.'

'It is good news of a sort, Pops, I mean, Father.' Paul noted the shot of reproval in his father's eyes.

'Your mother and I are very pleased you returned safely. I'm being indiscreet, of course, but Murray mentioned that your CO has put you up for a decoration. I presume you knew that, though?'

'Shepherd did offer a hint, Father, before he sent me on leave.'

'By all accounts, you did well under Samson, too. I'm sorry we've not had much chance to talk since your return. Your mother tells me you've another week of your leave left. Are you planning on spending it here? Naturally, you're welcome,' Miller added swiftly.

'I'm not sure yet, Father. I might stay in town and take in a few shows. Why do you ask?'

'I wondered if you might be paying a visit to the Fens of Cambridgeshire.'

Paul's guard was immediately up and he could feel the hairs on the back of his neck rise with it. Was this a loaded question? He hadn't mentioned Catherine to his mother, even.

'Cambridgeshire, Father? You mean to the university? My days there seem a long way off now, Father.'

'No. I was thinking more of Langford Hall. I understand you have a friend there.'

Paul gave a start. How did Pops know about that? He eyed his father with a mixture of incredulity and suspicion. He saw Pops pick up an envelope from his desk and remove a letter from inside.

'Paul, I'm not going to beat about the bush. I know of your friendship with Catherine Edgar. She wrote to me worried sick about you. Since you have failed to respond to her letters, she had no idea as to whether you were alive or dead. Hence, she wrote to me.'

Paul was too shocked to speak and his father filled the silence.

'The girl obviously thinks something of you and is concerned, so I've written back to her. I've explained the vagaries of the postal service in wartime and that you've been preoccupied of late. More importantly, I've told her you are alive and well.'

Paul was impressed by and thankful for Pops's tact. 'Thank you, Father. I'm truly grateful. I have been a little busy for correspondence since I left for France.'

'But could you not have telephoned the girl? You found the time to call your mother from Manchester and Kenton Lodge.'

'Yes, Father. That's true. I should have thought of it,' Paul replied sheepishly.

'So just what is the state of play between you and Miss Edgar?'

Paul was startled by the question. It was not like Pops to enquire into his romantic liaisons. *Mutti* yes, but Pops had never shown that much interest in him. There was something odd in this line of questioning.

'She's just someone I've been seeing a little this year, Father. Just a friend. You know, a companion at the theatre now and then. Why do you ask?'

'Because this letter suggests the relationship is more intimate than that. Indeed, she reports she is expecting your child.'

The news was like an artillery shell exploding nearby. Paul was completely stunned. His father gave him time to absorb the news. A thousand thoughts flashed through his brain at the impact of the news. Oh, my God! What do I do now? What would Catherine expect of him? He would have to go to see her now, but what of her father? So that's why she seemed so needy in her last couple of letters. She must have suspected, but why didn't she say? His father interrupted these thoughts.

'I'm sorry it was I who had to break the news to you, Paul. Had the girl known you were alive, she would no doubt have told you herself. I presume there is a basis for the allegation?'

Paul thought the term, 'allegation' an odd word to apply, but nodded silently.

'I know it's a delicate question, but can you be sure that the child is yours?'

'Father!' Paul stood in outrage. 'Catherine's not that sort of girl.'

'You may mean that, but she's still found herself in a deuced awkward spot. And you know what this means, Paul, don't you?'

Paul returned to his seat and nodded. 'Yes, Father. You expect me to marry her.'

'No, Paul. It is not what I expect that matters. It is your duty that counts. Think on it.'

Paul did think about it. He imagined life married to Catherine in Cambridgeshire. There was no doubt that he was fond of her. She was fun and spirited, but the thought of life stuck in the Fens struck him as dull. And there was still a war on. Could he take that responsibility? Would he be expected to leave the RNAS afterwards? Then he thought of Sarah and her smile as she waved him goodbye in Antwerp. He was only twenty-two and not ready to be tied down for life. He made up his mind, but knew that the next few minutes would be worse than Antwerp.

'I will telephone Catherine immediately after luncheon, Father, and arrange to go down to see her.' Paul saw his father relax in his chair. 'Then I shall tell her and her parents that I will not marry her!'

'What?' Miller leapt to his feet. 'You can't do that. You'll break the girl's heart and how will she fend for herself? And who's going to take her on afterwards with a bastard child? I told you to think carefully, Paul.' Miller stared into Paul's eyes and Paul began to feel their hypnotic effect. He broke the eye contact and stood to confront his father, notwithstanding the seven-inch disadvantage in height.

'No, Father. I will not marry Catherine. I don't love her and it would not be right. I will explain that.'

'Sit down, Paul, and listen.' Miller sat down and Paul resumed his seat a little reluctantly.

'Paul, love is a strange thing. For some, it comes naturally and for others, it comes with time. I was fortunate that I loved your mother from the start. That love grew even stronger when Richard was born. You and Catherine are going to share a child. A child that will be her flesh and blood and one that will carry your genes. What can there be as a bond that is stronger? Surely, love can grow from that bond.'

Paul saw his father's face soften but the gaze was as intense as ever. He imagined himself a father. He would bring up his son differently. His son would have no need to fear him. Could he be happy with Catherine? He stopped dreaming. No. He would stand by his decision and live with the consequences, much as Catherine would have to.

'I'm sorry, Father. My mind is made up and you shall not dissuade me,' he responded defiantly.

'Very well then, Paul. If your mind is made up, I shall not seek to change it.' This was rare news to Paul. 'But I hope in time, you will come to a different decision. There remains to discuss the upkeep of the child.'

'I don't think you have need to worry on that score, Father. The Edgars are not poor.'

'How dare you take such a cavalier attitude to your responsibilities, Paul!' Miller shot to his feet and it was the first time he had shouted in the exchange so far. Miller lowered his voice to a steely growl. 'Whether or not you choose to marry the mother, you will take some responsibility for the child. I have given the matter much thought. With immediate effect, I will be halving your allowance and allocating the other half to Miss Edgar. I will then match it, that is double it, from my own pocket. Start getting used to relying on your naval pay in future. Do you understand?'

The words hurt Paul deeply. A halving of his allowance would curb his lifestyle considerably and he half wondered if he had made the right decision. But he had stood up to Pops and there was no going back now. He might even survive the encounter. He stood to make his leave.

'Yes, Father. I understand and it is only fair. Indeed, it is more than fair and very honourable of you.'

'And you still intend going to see Miss Edgar and her parents to convey your decision? You realise that if her father is of my mind, he'll probably take a horse whip to you?'

'Possibly, Father, but there I do know my duty. I will telephone immediately after luncheon.'

'Very well. I will grant that you have courage, my son. Now let us repair to the dining room for that luncheon.'

Chapter 28
February 1915

'Gentlemen, ho!' called the Intelligence Officer.

The Commanding Officer of One Squadron, Dover, entered the briefing room breezily whilst his men stood to attention.

'Please be seated, gentlemen,' Squadron Commander Courtenay ordered. 'Today's mission will be focused on Belgium... And specifically, on Ostend, Zeebrugge and Bruges. It is to be one of the largest raids the Royal Naval Air Service has been privileged to mount and, as such, we are to be joined by several other units from all along the South East coast. However, before the detailed briefing commences, for the benefit of some of the newer members of the squadron... and possibly certain illiterate dilettante who derive their news purely from the pages of *Sporting Life*... No, 'C' Flight, I was not directing my remarks solely at you, but if the cap fits, wear it.'

The members of both 'A' and 'B' Flights jostled and jeered Paul's flight. Having only recently shipped his second stripe, Paul was the junior flight commander in the squadron and his flight was nicknamed, 'The Crèche'.

'Gentlemen... and members of 'C' Flight, of course, we should all be proud that the Royal Naval Air Service has quickly achieved an outstanding reputation.'

'Hear, hear,' several members of the squadron called. Courtenay continued.

'The Royal Flying Corps remains committed to missions of reconnaissance and artillery spotting on the Front. We all know the BE2 is not capable of much else. Thanks to the First Lord's insistence that the navy is not wedded to the Royal Aircraft Factory for the procurement of our aircraft, we are blessed with aircraft suitable for a wider application of air power. Whilst we remain responsible for Home Defence, the DAD is switching the focus of the RNAS to what he calls, "strategic bombing". That means our focus will move away from tactical support to the army. Instead, we will intensify our longer-range bombing missions to hamper the enemy's efforts to bring up reinforcements and materiel to the front line. This will include railway depots, ammunition dumps and fuel depots.'

'But what of the Zeppelins?' somebody asked. 'Are we going to relinquish our support to the Fleet, sir?'

'Why not?' somebody else called out. 'Deuced waste of time anyway. In the five years it takes our scouts to reach the Zeppelin's altitude, Captain Otto has had his lunch and then merely orders an increase in altitude to drink his coffee in peace. We can't get at them and they're laughing at us.'

'Gentlemen, order,' 'A' Flight's commander called.

'Thank you. To answer your questions, no, we will not give up on the Zeppelins, but we are going to take a different approach,' Courtenay responded.

Both Zeppelins and submarines were posing a significant threat to naval operations. The latter prevented the navy from using its capital ships to impose a close blockade of the German High Seas Fleet. Furthermore, until the construction of anti-submarine nets and defences at Scapa Flow was complete, the navy's own Grand Fleet was at risk in its home port. The Zeppelins were posing problems in many other ways. Zeppelins deployed from the airship base at Borkum, one of the Frisian Islands, were able to detect mines off the German coast, newly-laid by RN minelayers as a blockade measure. German minesweepers were then able to clear the mine fields as quickly as they were laid. The Zeppelins were also used to shadow the Fleet and report back its position and manoeuvres. Of more concern to the Government, was the Zeppelin's capability to undertake bombing missions over English towns and cities.

'Until we have the technology to intercept the Zeppelins and submarines on operations, we will hit their bases. The Christmas Day raid on Cuxhaven has demonstrated the capability of naval aeroplanes launched from ships to hit the enemy's home territory, although low cloud and mist prevented the bombing of the Zeppelin sheds... this time.' Courtenay pointed to the wall chart of the German coastline and indicated the site of the damaged harbour.

'From now on, we have the means to intercept the Zeppelins on their return to their bases, by which time they will be low on fuel and their crews tired. Increasingly, gentlemen, you will find yourselves tasked to bomb more Zeppelin sheds and factories.

'And that brings me to today's mission. The RNAS will be bombing the submarine berths at Zeebrugge, German military installations in the Bruges area and, last by no means least, the railway station and marshalling yards of Ostend. The latter target, gentlemen, is designated to us. Now pay attention to the Intelligence Officer's briefing.'

*****

Paul admitted to himself that he was enjoying the war, although that was not something he could admit to his parents. He was probably the junior and youngest flight commander in the RNAS, but his experience in action and the newly-gazetted 'Mention in Despatches', for his activities in Belgium and the raid on Friedrichshafen, had gained him the respect both of the young officers in his new flight and the rest of the squadron. In the main, he thought them a splendid bunch of fellows and he enjoyed the camaraderie of squadron life.

He had been disappointed not to win the DSO after the raid on Friedrichshafen, but that award had rightly gone to Sippe. Even so, it meant Richard still had the edge over him following the award of his DSO for the sinking of the *Hela*. Neither of them had been granted leave to join *Mutti* for Christmas, so he imagined that with John in the Med' and Peter swanning about in Holland, she would have experienced a lonely and miserable day. Another aviator had told him that Richard's submarine had somehow been involved with rescuing one of the Cuxhaven raid crews, but the details had been a little scant.

Paul levelled out his Avro 504 at 6,000 feet and headed across the Channel. He prayed that he would cross the expanse of water without engine trouble since, at 05.30, it was still dark and the weather below was cold and overcast. Were he or any of the squadron to ditch at this hour, the destroyers might struggle to find them. However, his Avro was becoming considered a lucky aircraft. Whilst the squadron had lost several pilots of late, no harm had befallen anyone flying the Avro. As he crossed himself, he noted wryly how he had become more religious after Belgium. *Mutti* was a devout Catholic and since Charterhouse, he had rarely taken Mass except in her company to please her. Like a growing number of his brother officers, he was now firming up his belief in God.

Flying further east, he saw the beginning of the dawn light and, with the improving light, a line of four destroyers spaced out at intervals across the Channel in positions to pick up pilots who ran into difficulties. The Avro was one of the faster aeroplanes, so Paul had taken off later than the rest of his squadron. It looked as if nobody had been forced to ditch. A flash of movement to his right caught his eye. It was a curtain of white spray from a submarine off the French coast, opening its main vents for diving. Paul recognised it as an E-class boat. Might it be Richard's, he wondered.

Paul took the end of his scarf to wipe his steamed-up goggles. It was now light enough to pick out the white crests of the waves below. He always reflected on how odd it was that these white lines appeared stationary from the air and yet were, of course, continually in motion. It was, also, odd to see both the coast of England behind him and that of France ahead at the same time. Behind him, English farmers would be up to tend their stock, the civilian population largely unaffected by war. Ahead, there would be several French and Belgian farmers left with no stock to attend, such were the ravages of the greatest war in history. As a pilot now based in England, Paul seemed constantly to slip from one world to the other. He felt a pang of sympathy for the army in the trenches of France and Belgium, and Charles, of course. They were completely immersed in this war for twenty-four hours a day.

Four miles short of Calais he banked to port to follow the coast in a north-easterly direction. He waved to the pilot of a slower seaplane on a similar course, but between him and the coast. The cloud base over France was lower, so he descended to 4,000 feet. Now safely over the Channel, his next worry was the Hun Archie. As well as shrapnel, the Huns had taken to firing a form of flare that could set fire to the fabric of an aeroplane. Mind you, he didn't much like the look of the weather ahead either.

The cloud ahead was thickening and taking on a dark and stormy colour. The CO had instructed all pilots to land at Dunkirk if they encountered problems with the weather or cloud. For a moment, Paul thought about taking up this option, but he noted that the seaplane pilot was continuing. The squadron would not find its newest flight commander wanting whilst others were prepared to take the risk. Once more, he looked astern and was pleased to see the other three machines of his flight loosely formed on either side of his tail. He waved to them encouragingly, but only the nearest two pilots responded.

As he and his flight flew abreast of Nieuwpoort, he spotted several flashes from the ground and the tell-tale signs of anti-aircraft fire – puffs of black smoke. They reminded him of a puffball mushroom exploding. The Huns were clearly putting up a good show. Unfortunately, the clouds were becoming thicker and lower, too. Paul knew that German gunners could calculate the height of the cloud base accurately and so it would be easy to judge the height of British aircraft silhouetted against the cloud base. He had no choice other than to lose height, but he signalled to his flight to edge further out to sea. Soon, it became apparent that this might not have been a wise choice.

Although now two miles further off the coast and at the extreme range of the anti-aircraft fire, the clouds further offshore were darker and lower. It started to rain heavily and the clouds were taking on a very stormy hue. Paul had no wish to enter the storm clouds, but nor did he wish to come within range of the German guns. He was reminded of the dilemma of the ancient mariners who had to choose their course between Scylla and Charybdis. Briefly, he pondered the alternative of returning to Dunkirk. He now had the fate of his flight to consider, but what if the rest of the squadron were to have won through? The Crèche would never live it down. Moreover, as a decorated officer, more would be expected of him.

Reluctantly, Paul banked to starboard and headed closer in to the coast, but not before signalling to his flight to spread out a little. It concerned him that he could only see two machines behind him. Was Hurley still with them or was it just the poor visibility?

The German gunners opened up again and Paul constantly manoeuvred his machine to different heights and adjusted his throttle to alter his speed in an effort to put off the gunners' aim. They were now beginning to find his range and height. A green flash exploded with a *whoosh* just beyond his starboard upper wing tip. It was one of the new flares and as it hung in the air, Paul could see why they were being called flaming onions. A loud bang astern followed. Looking back, Paul perceived three puffs of shrapnel bursts perfectly placed to have straddled his position just a few seconds before. It was enough to stiffen his resolve.

Banking his aircraft to port and losing as much height as he dared, Paul entered the cover of the storm clouds. The aeroplane was immediately buffeted by the turbulence of the air and the temperature dropped markedly. He was dismayed to have lost sight of his whole flight. It would have to be every man for himself now and he worried about Hurley, an inexperienced navigator.

When he judged that he was about seven miles out from the coast, he turned back onto a course to parallel the coast to Ostend. By now the turbulence was quite violent and he discovered that he was in a snow cloud. His aircraft was being bounced about like a rubber ball and gaining or losing 200 feet of altitude within seconds. He descended to 1,500 feet, but suddenly, he felt scared. He seemed sure that he was flying straight and level, but the altimeter was still turning slowly anti clockwise, suggesting that he was losing height slowly. The compass indicated he was turning to port and the air speed indicator showed that he was losing speed. Something was wrong with his instruments.

Paul tried to work out what could have caused this phenomenon and then a feeling of dread gripped his stomach. It then squeezed it very hard, indeed. He must be going into a spin with little more than a thousand feet to spare and yet his body was telling him that this was normal. He vaguely remembered an experienced flying instructor warning him at Eastchurch that this was why clouds could be a killer. You could be flying upside down and not realise it. One of the staff-surgeons had suggested it might be something to do with the ears, but nobody knew. He had to trust his instruments. Instantly, Paul's training kicked in and he applied corrections to the rudder and ailerons to counter the spin. He then arrested his descent and levelled out at 900 feet by his altimeter. No sooner had he done this than the compass started spinning madly. With an erratic compass, he was hopelessly lost in cloud. He should have diverted to Dunkirk. The Crèche might then be alive.

The next few minutes were some of the worst of his life. He felt not just scared, but very lonely. He had no idea of his course and could only pray that his altimeter was correct. Gingerly, he let his height fall to 500 feet in the hope that he would see the ground or sea beneath him. Even then, although he managed to minimise the turbulence and sudden variations in altitude within the clouds, he still found himself flying blind. He did not dare fly lower in case he found himself flying into an obstruction on land, the ground itself or even the sea. At least it had stopped snowing, hailing and raining.

This unhappy situation continued for about ten minutes in all and during which his only company was the sound of his Gnome engine and his propeller throbbing through the cloud vapours. In this grey world Paul imagined he had departed the land of the living and was now the Flying Dutchman of the air, doomed to fly alone and blind for eternity. He reached out to grab the strands of cloud around him, but naturally, they had no substance. He thought of his parents, his brothers, his grandmother and Catherine. Was he doomed never to see them again? He looked back with regret and shame at his last meeting with Catherine, on his leave before Christmas.

She had taken his refusal to marry her calmly and told him that she had not expected it of him. It was enough for her to know that he was alive. In fact, she'd been quite a brick. Catherine had only asked that he write to her from time to time and take an interest in the child after he or she were born. Lady Edgar had not been happy at that and had suggested he never made contact again. She had insisted that Catherine only needed her family's support and had spurned his father's offer of financial assistance – 'guilt money' she had called it. It had been a difficult meeting and, fortunately, the general had been absent at the War Office. Even so, Catherine had kissed him fondly goodbye and he had been tempted to take her in his arms and to kiss her passionately, despite the presence of her frosty and disapproving mother. Instead, he had shaken her firm hand formally. He had been a cad, even by his own standards.

Was her kiss on parting to be the last he was destined to receive? The fear in his stomach gave way to a yearning in his heart. This war was proving that life really was too short. There seemed to be no future, just the present, and life must, thus, be lived in the here and now. A quotation from Tennyson's *'In Memoriam'* sprang to mind, *''Tis better to have loved and lost than never to have loved at all.'*

He suddenly felt the need to pray aloud to God to spare him. 'Lord, if you would spare my life today, I in return, would spare another man's life. Please, God, grant me just this one request and I will not waste it.' He would ask Catherine to marry him, too.

Strangely, having fixed on this course of action, he felt calm and less in peril. The word 'peril' brought to mind the words of the Naval Hymn and he found himself singing them aloud to the clouds.

'Eternal Father, strong to save,
Whose arm hath bound the restless wave,

Who bidd'st the mighty ocean deep,
Its own appointed limits keep,
Oh, hear us when we cry to Thee,
For those in peril on the sea.'

He sang the last line with gusto. The hymn was a comfort and he felt curiously happy once more. Everything was going to work out.

Suddenly, his prayers were answered. He saw a break in the clouds beneath him. Although only fleeting, the glimpse through the cloud had been enough to reveal that he was flying low over the sea. A warm glow flowed through his body and Paul wondered if this was God's love. His pious brother Richard would be jealous. Magically, his compass righted itself again and he noted that his course was north. Although he was lost, Paul knew that this was the one course he should not follow. He had plenty of fuel and if he turned west, he would eventually cross the English coast, but it would mean abandoning his mission.

Gently, he banked the Avro to starboard to complete a 180 degree turn and settle on a new course of south. He figured that he had a chance of picking up either the French or the Belgian coast this way. Ten minutes later, he was proved correct when he observed the coast through the thinning cloud. It was still too cloudy to pick out any landmarks, but he suspected it was Belgium.

The visibility was still poor as Paul crossed the coast and headed inland looking for any navigation marks that could identify his position. He continued his heading of south and at an altitude of 500 feet. Soon afterwards, he sighted a railway line running east-west and, with relief, he was able to identify his position. He had crossed the coast between Zeebrugge and Ostend. This was the Bruges railway line to Ostend. He had completely overshot his target area. Executing a tight turn to starboard, he set a south-westerly course to intercept the railway line and follow it into Ostend. Mercifully, he had not been spotted as there was no anti-aircraft fire. Perhaps the gunners were not expecting an attack from this quarter or maybe they thought the cloud would have prevented the possibility of attack from the air. Either way, Paul was determined to profit from the Huns' error.

Three minutes later, the sky erupted with smoke and explosions, but Paul no longer cared. God had heard his plea for help and accepted his bargain. He would now not die and so he pressed home his attack at low level without any shred of fear or distraction. Making allowance for his speed over the ground, of which he had much experience in the Avro, he released his bombs just short of his target of Ostend railway station. To his delight, he spotted a loaded train just leaving the station. He had clearly caught the Huns by surprise. At this heigh, he could not miss and, immediately after releasing his bombs, he banked his aircraft sharply to starboard, almost standing it on its wingtips. He heard the sound of a loud explosion behind him, but was too busy heading out to sea and gaining height rapidly to look back at the extent of the damage to his target. He knew he had hit the target and he felt pleased with himself.

He headed out to sea and gained height promptly, but still beneath the cloud base. When he judged he was far enough out to sea to be out of range of the enemy Archie, he banked the aeroplane to port to return to France. As he did so, the aircraft lurched violently and he heard a tremendous bang astern. The Avro's nose dropped suddenly and the aircraft started losing height rapidly. He wrestled with the controls, but struggled to arrest the steep dive. The altimeter needle was spinning smartly anti-clockwise and Paul knew he didn't have much height.

Looking behind him, he was horrified by the sight. Half his dépannage had been blown away and worse, his fuselage was on fire. Now flying over the sea at over 100 knots, with little control of the aircraft, the fire was quickly spreading towards him. He was going to die after all, but he silently prayed to God that it would be the sudden death of the aeroplane breaking up as it hit the sea and not the slow, torture of burning alive once the flames reached the cockpit. His last thought was that God could be cruel after all.

Chapter 29

This was a call that Commodore Murray Sueter, the Director of the Air Department, had already put off too long. As the DAD, it was not his usual responsibility to contact the next-of-kin of RNAS casualties. Thankfully, that was the job of the squadron commanders as there had already been too many losses. However, this was personal. It involved an esteemed colleague and friend.

As Sueter waited for the other party to come to the telephone, he silently rehearsed what he planned to say. He knew his friend well enough to know that a brisk and direct approach was the best course.

'Hello, Sue. How nice to hear from you. Is this a social call? I trust you and Elinor are keeping well.'

As always, Sueter was impressed by Admiral Miller's capacity to recall the smallest detail. Although Sueter had once worked with Miller in the Intelligence Department, had since met him several times during his tenure in the Admiralty's Ordnance Department, and more recently during his appointment as DAD, as far as he could recall, Miller had only met his wife on one occasion, at a garden party at Buckingham Palace. Sueter racked his brains to recall the name of Mrs Miller, but without success and then he realised he risked being diverted from his carefully rehearsed speech.

'Hello, William. We are both well, thank you. Although Elinor frequently complains that she doesn't see enough of me during this wretched war. I'm sure your good lady feels the same about you, so I will not keep you. I'm afraid I'm ringing you on business. I have some news for you. Are you quite alone?'

Miller took some moments to reply, but when he did, his voice had lost its breezy tone and he spoke quietly. 'No, I'm with Johanna. Just give me a minute to shut the doors off the hall and fetch a chair.'

*****

Miller knew it had to be bad news and felt his stomach drop. The fact that Sue was ringing meant it concerned Paul. He fetched a chair to the telephone table, but did not pick up the ear piece immediately. As a seasoned and experienced officer, he knew the risks all four of his sons were facing in this war. The odds of all of them coming through unscathed were slim. He wiped away a tear in his left eye and braced himself for what was to come. It would be better if he stood, he thought.

'Hello, Sue. Tell me straight. It's Paul isn't it?' Please let him be a prisoner-of-war, he thought.

'I'm afraid so, William. He was shot down yesterday... over enemy lines... and has been posted missing. A telegram has been drafted to this effect, but I stopped it being sent. I'm sorry I couldn't leave here to call round with the news in person.'

'I quite understand,' Miller spoke very softly. 'Missing' at least offered some hope, he thought. He now fought hard to keep his emotions in check. 'Is he presumed dead or is there some hope?'

'I can't say too much over the telephone, William, for reasons you will understand. Drop by the office tomorrow and I will give you all the detail I have. But I fear you may have to prepare for the worst, old friend.'

Miller didn't trust his legs not to buckle, so he sat down reluctantly. 'I have to tell Johanna, Sue. I need to know the worst. You know that, Sue.'

'I do know you well enough to understand that, William, but we cannot be certain. I can tell you that Paul was leading a flight on a bombing raid. They separated in the cloud, but one of his flight saw Paul's machine hit by anti-aircraft fire and plunge into the ground. He and another pilot then risked their lives to fly over the crash site. There wasn't much left, I'm afraid, and no sign of Paul being thrown clear.'

'What do you mean, there wasn't much left?' Miller's voice was no longer soft, but had an edge to it. 'Tell me warts 'n' all, Sue. As my friend.'

Miller could hear Sueter breathing on the line, but he didn't speak for half a minute. 'All right, William. You're an old friend and I'll be honest. I didn't want to tell you this, and for God's sake don't tell his mother. Paul's aircraft was engulfed in flames when it hit the ground and it exploded on impact. He would have been killed instantly.'

A shudder passed through Miller and he struggled to remain aware of his surroundings as he let drop the ear piece. His mind was filled with the horror of the scene in which he imagined his son wrestling with the controls of his aircraft whilst trying to hold back the flames.

'Please, God,' he said softly, 'Let him have hit the ground before the flames claimed him.'

He felt the vibrations of the telephone ear piece and heard the squawks from it. He had forgotten that Sue was still on the line. He replaced it by his ear.

'... all right. William, answer me. For ...'

'It's all right, Sue. I'm still here,' he responded in almost a whisper.

'Thank goodness. You had me worried. Look, we'll find time to meet tomorrow. We'll know more from the Red Cross within a few weeks. Just look after Johanna. I'll ask Elinor to call by with our condolences sometime. Is there anything more I can do for you?'

Miller suddenly felt devoid of energy and speaking was too much of an effort, but he willed himself to reply. 'No. We'll be fine. Thank you for calling, Sue. I appreciate it must have been difficult. Now I must face Johanna.'

He didn't wait for a reply before hanging up the ear piece. He sat quietly in the hall for several minutes, the only sound being the ticking of the large grandfather clock in the corner.

Throughout his long career, he had faced death many times and seen men die, but this affected him so much more deeply. He remembered Paul as a small boy and his foolish antics, always looking for approval. Tears began to flow down his face, misting his eyes. How could he not be here now? One doesn't expect to lose a child. Had he shown him enough love? When he thought about it, he could only remember being hard on Paul, but that was because he didn't want him going off the rails with his pranks. Paul was a decent lad who just needed some guidance. But had Paul died knowing that his father loved him? He would never know now. Again, he imagined Paul's last few moments of life.

Paul had told him of the pilot's fear of fire. He had heard stories of pilots jumping to certain death to avoid death by fire. Whilst the Americans had conducted trials of parachutes from moving aircraft, they were still too heavy for military use. Paul had said that was why some pilots carried a loaded revolver to use in favour of a long, slow and agonising death. Was that how Paul would have chosen to die? By his own hand? Such thoughts overwhelmed him and he began to sob quietly.

He had often known fear and the effect it had on his stomach. He had often likened it to a rat gnawing at his intestines and he had always overcome it by some form of action. This time it was different. He felt as if his stomach was slowly filling with molten lead and this lead was now spreading into his whole blood stream. Movement seemed to involve too much effort to merit its attempt. His brain was slowing up and he was overcome by weariness. He felt on the edge of oblivion and he thought that if he just let go, he would fall and be released from the spreading pain. The temptation to give way was too much. Then, much as some instinct in the drowning man causes him to kick for the surface, Miller's sub conscious stirred him to consider the practicalities of the situation. He had to break the news to Johanna, but spare her the full story and support her in her grief. She was important now.

He stirred himself to move. Slowly, he stood and headed for the cloakroom. He washed himself and examined his face in the mirror. The man looking back at him looked old and tired. Rings were beginning to form beneath his dull eyes. 'Pull yourself together, Miller,' he ordered the reflection. 'Into action again, my boy.'

The resolve to act braced him, releasing him from his temporary lethargy and paralysis. With a straight back and shoulders high, he crossed the hall to the drawing room, passing Durton on the way. He merely nodded to Durton to acknowledge his presence before entering the drawing room and closing the double doors behind him. Johanna was seated at her desk, clearing her correspondence.

'Who was that, dear?' She looked up and asked him. 'You were gone a while.'

'Come and sit with me on the sofa, Johanna dear, and I'll tell you all about it.'

Moments later, Durton's blood ran cold as he heard a loud and anguished animal howl emanate from the drawing room of 19 Cumberland Terrace.

*****

John couldn't help feel that events were conspiring to keep him out of the war. Few would have been more pleased than he at the news that HMS *Warrior* was to return to Britain to join the Grand Fleet. The excitement of hunting for Admiral von Spee's East Asia

Squadron had turned to disappointment when the ship's company had learned that Vice Admiral Sturdee's force had annihilated the German squadron and wreaked revenge for the defeat at the Battle of the Coronel. However, they had all expected action as part of the Grand Fleet, only to find themselves excluded from the recent Battle of Dogger Bank. To pour salt in the wound, having spent weeks of inactivity protecting the Suez Canal the previous autumn, the Turks were now mounting an offensive on the area and a combined force of British and French ships were forcing a passage through the Dardanelles. We should have stayed in the Med', he thought as he slammed down the gunroom copy of the latest edition of *The Times*.

'What's up, old man? You seem browned off,' Midshipman Cartwright asked.

'Of course, I'm browned off, you ass. I'm bored. Bored, bored, bored, bored and bored.'

'Bored? But you've your Fleet Board next month. Shouldn't you be busy preparing for that?'

'That's not what I mean. Of course, I've plenty to do, but I want to see some action. What's the point of being in a war if you don't see the enemy, Cartwright?'

'I suspect many in the army wouldn't agree with you, dear chap. They're taking some fearful casualties.'

'And so's the navy, thanks to those infernal mines. At least the troops have a chance to fire back. The most excitement I've had this year so far was on rounds during the Middle this morning.'

'Really, Miller. Do tell what happened,' Cartwright's moon face beamed expectantly.

'Came across four stokers playing cards outside the chronometer room. Had to run 'em in.'

'Gosh, Miller. That was a bit harsh. Putting them in the rattle. They were off watch.'

'Had no choice. I was with the marine corporal. Anyway, they should have had their heads down instead of gambling. Whatever, my mind is made up. I'm going to ask for an appointment to a destroyer as soon as I ship my first stripe. Guns has said he'll support me. And if that doesn't work, I might even join you and apply for submarines.'

'My, that's a bit drastic isn't it? You'd have to bone up on your engineering.'

'I don't care. Just provided I see some action.'

The man was roused to semi-consciousness once again by the noise. It was a slow, grinding noise that he had heard many times and had always seemed to presage good things. He was sure he had heard the same noise a long time ago in a different life, but his brain was too tired to focus his memory on its source. He opened his eyes, but was still unable to see anything. All he could see was that there was now light where often he had been completely shrouded in darkness. He did not know where he was, nor from where he had come. He was not in pain, but thought that this had not always been so. Of late, he had started to become aware that he possessed a body, but one over which he had no control and from which he felt detached. He felt as if wrapped in cotton wool, but knew that once the voices came, he would be moved and feel more sensation in his body. His brain was still muddled and not capable of much conscious thought, but it was a comfortable feeling. Overall, he felt at peace and very comfortable. However, he welcomed the regular coming of the voices. It broke up the mixed routine of sleep and semi-consciousness in complete silence.

As he knew he would, he heard the arrival of the voices. He could not tell what they were saying as the noise was muffled, but it was a gentle sound. He knew that the next stage would be sensation on his body and finally within him. He waited like a baby for it all to begin.

*****

Doctor Gustave Schotsmans surveyed his patient with great care as he and his assistant, Nurse Marie-Pierre de Trooz, gently rotated their patient to change the dressings. The burns were healing very nicely and Schotsmans decided he could start to reduce the dosage of morphine. The airman was extremely lucky to have survived. As with so many airmen, he had the advantages of youth and fitness to help him respond positively to the trauma, and his thick flying gear had spared him the worst of the flames. However, what had really saved his life was the sea. The fishermen who had rescued the young airman had reported that they had seen him leap from his burning aeroplane with his clothes ablaze, from a height of about 100 feet.

By a stroke of fortune, he had landed in the sea rather than on the shore or land. Even so, the fall should have killed him or he should have drowned, but miraculously, apart from the burns, he had only suffered a nasty bump on the head, presumably as he left the aeroplane, and a broken collar bone and severe bruising to his lower back on impact with the sea. It was not clear how he had avoided drowning, particularly given the weight of his flying clothing.

More amazing was that the immersion in salt water seemed to have had a recuperative effect on his burns. This was of immense scientific interest to the Belgian doctor and he was resolved to follow up this discovery. In the meantime, for the past ten days, he and his attractive assistant had skilfully avoided the German patrols to visit this farmhouse cellar twice a day to tend their patient. As well as administering morphine for the pain and shock, they had been carefully applying salt-water-soaked dressings to the areas of burnt flesh. Schotsmans was extremely pleased with the results and decided it was time to remove the bandage covering the entirety of the patient's head except for his mouth and nose.

Schotsmans watched with interest as his young nurse tended to their foreign patient. She was still extremely attractive, despite her sad face, a result of losing her brother in the defence of Antwerp. She would be a fine catch for somebody one day. Sadly, that was unlikely to be the case with this young airman.

Marie-Pierre rolled over her patient and bathed his buttocks and genitals. Schotsmans winced when he saw again the scars of the burns on the airman's back and upper right arm. At least the black and purple bruising to his waist was turning to a mixture of greens and yellows. The doctor regarded the rest of the young man's naked body. He was slim, too slim in his view, but of a muscular physique. He might once have had a handsome face and head, but was now likely to have been badly disfigured by the burns on the right side. Even so, he could not help but notice that Marie-Pierre seemed fond of the foreigner. She was much gentler with him than he had seen her with other patients… and there was a look in her. After seven months of war, they had both seen dozens of terribly injured soldiers; Belgian, French and even German. Often, despite their horrific wounds, they had borne their suffering with quiet dignity. It was odd how many of them, of whatever nationality, had died with their mother's name on their lips. Schotsmans had seen first-hand how the twenty-one-year-old nurse had treated them all with a maternal fondness, but this was a different expression. When she was not conscious of being watched, she seemed to gaze at the airman tenderly and Schotsmans had even seen her smile again. He hoped his assistant was not becoming too attached to her patient. As soon as he was well enough, they had to send the Englishman on. It was too dangerous for him and them to hide him for too long. In any case, with her looks, Marie-Pierre could have the pick of any young Belgian man she chose.

Marie-Pierre turned her patient back onto his side. The airman seemed to stir and become slightly agitated. She reached for the teapot and applied the spout to the only gap in the bandages. Only once the injured man had finished drinking did she allow the doctor to commence removing the bandages and dressings to the head.

*****

Paul was still in a dream. He was in a sack from which he could not escape, being rolled about by he knew not what. It was not unpleasant, but he needed to breathe, to see and to hear. This denial of his senses stressed him, but soon afterwards, he always felt a wave of pleasure move through his body to return him to the cloud on which he lay before his dream ended. Today's dream was a little different. He could hear again. It took his brain a little time to register that the noise was that of two soft voices. He opened his eyes again in the expectation of seeing again, but still he couldn't see. This frightened him. Why could he not see? He tried to move, but he must still be tied in the sack. He cried out at the darkness and for the first time his cries were heeded. He felt a pleasant stroking of his head and a calming noise. He couldn't understand the words, but the voice sounded like *Mutti*. He relaxed at the thought and felt his dream ending, but the gentle sensation on his face continued and suddenly, there was light. Cautiously, he opened first one eye and then the next. The image before him was blurred and alternated between light and shade. He tried hard to focus, but the shadow reappeared and he felt his eyes being pulled about. He heard the voices again and followed their direction with his eyes. His sight was blurred, but he could make out two dark shapes, although no detail.

The simple movement was enough to tire him and he allowed himself to drift back to his dreams.

*****

Over the next few days, Paul started to become much more aware of his surroundings. He still felt very tired and dreamy, but his eyes were now able to focus and he felt pain in his right shoulder, face and back. This pain was uncomfortable, but bearable. He became more conscious of his body and tried to move his head and limbs. His arms were bound, but moving his legs did not pose much difficulty, except that he lay on his side and unable to turn onto his back. Twice a day, he would be turned on to his other side by a pretty nurse whose name he did not yet know. He had tried to ask, but his lips were too painful for speech. The nurse was petite, with long brown hair tied behind her head and fixed in place with a chignon. Although pretty, he considered her looks spoiled by the angular nose that seemed a little large in proportion to the rest of her face.

Gradually, his faculties were returning and he recognised the language the nurse and the doctor were speaking. It sounded like German and he understood some of it. He realised that his carers must be Flemings and speaking their local form of Dutch. The doctor was a tall, slim man in his fifties with a full head of white hair and a beard and moustache to match. He had once used English to ask Paul if he was British, but had since made no further attempt to communicate with him directly.

From his alternate positions, Paul worked out that he was in a cellar of some sort. Partial daylight filtered through above him, presumably at ground level. He judged that the yard outside must be cobbled as he now often heard sounds of a horse and cart above him. His bed was a straw palliasse laid on an old table, to one side of which had been nailed a board lined with another palliasse to stop him turning onto his back.

As the days wore on, he saw the doctor less frequently, but still the nurse visited twice daily. He began to look forward to her visits and not just to break up his monotonous, lonely routine. Now that the doctor was no longer injecting him with obvious pain killers, his body had become more accustomed to pain and touch. The nurse had very soft hands and sometimes when his dressings dried out and stuck to his wounds, she somehow managed to remove them in a way that seemed almost sensual. Indeed, on one occasion he had been extremely embarrassed as he lay naked on his side. As she had leaned across his body to apply a fresh dressing to his back, the pressure of her small and tightly bound breasts against him and the caressing of her hands had produced an erection from him. Unfortunately, this had been witnessed by a slovenly-looking girl who was increasingly visiting the cellar to assist with his nursing. The girl had giggled at his aroused state and this had humiliated him. He decided he did not like her. Within a few days, he liked her even less.

The girl was a fair-haired, buxom and chubby girl of about eighteen. Her round face was quite pretty, but the effect was marred by her dishevelled appearance and long, dirty hair. Paul had become aware to his shame that through being bed bound, he was soiling himself. It was the girl's job to help with the changing of his bedding and often to wash his nether regions. He was becoming acutely aware that not only did she have rough hands, but they seemed to be slyly lingering unnecessarily over his buttocks and between his thighs. Despite the moral discomfort, the physical sensations were sexually arousing and the effect seemed to be gratifying to the girl. Paul could not bear the helplessness and determined to do something about the situation. Despite the difficulties of manoeuvring his face and lips, he addressed the doctor on his next call.

'*Herr Doktor, sprechen sie Englisch oder Französiche*?' The effort to speak caused blood to run down one side of his face, but Schotsmans replied in good French.

'Do not speak, my friend. It is too early.'

Even so, Paul persisted. 'Doctor, might you provide me a chamber pot… or even a bucket?'

Schotsmans nodded in understanding. 'I am sorry, friend. It would do you no good. You are still far too weak to stand, but let's see what I can do.' He looked around the cellar and then grunted with satisfaction. He returned with some empty wine bottles and proceeded to unbind Paul's arms. 'Now you must promise me to stay in bed, but these might offer you some relief. As for the needs of your bowels, there is little I can do for the moment. But I may be able to lay my hands on a commode. You might soon be fit enough for the girls to lift you on and off it. You must be patient.'

Even this concession was still humiliating for Paul, but he knew he had no choice. He was as helpless as a baby.

'Now, if you will promise not to speak, I will tell you a little of your situation. Just reply to my questions with a nod or shake of your head. Is that understood?' Paul nodded in reply.

'I assume you are English? Thank you. We had no way of knowing. All your clothing had been burnt away. You are very lucky to be alive. Had you not jumped from your aircraft, you would undoubtedly have perished in the crash. As it was, you landed in the sea and two fishermen were near enough to see you fall and rescue you quickly. No. You must refrain from speaking.' Paul had tried to frame a question.

'You have been here for three weeks. The family who are harbouring you are taking great risks, but the Spaaks are a good family. They had two sons in the army. One was killed at Sint Niklaas and the other taken prisoner by the Germans. They see that offering you shelter as repaying the *Bosches* for the loss of their sons. When the Germans didn't find your remains in your burnt-out machine, they searched the countryside for you and threatened death to anybody offering you shelter. The local patrols were quite active for the first two weeks, but I think the Germans have resigned themselves to the fact that you are either dead or have escaped. Even so, we must all remain cautious.'

The doctor applied a cup of weak broth to Paul's lips and seemed pleased to see him able to swallow it without choking.

'Now we must try to restore your strength so that we can send you home and spare the risk to the Spaaks.' Paul noted that Schotsmans did not refer to the risks that he and the nurse were, also, facing in treating him. He assumed that the other girl must be a daughter of the family offering him shelter.

'I am a little concerned about your eyes. Your goggles spared them from the flames, but you have scarring to your right eye, nonetheless. How many fingers am I holding up? One? Two? Three? Mmm. Clearly, there is some blurring there. As for the rest of you, your burns are healing nicely, although there will be some scarring, I'm afraid. The important thing is you rest and build up your strength. I'm Doctor Schotsmans, by the way, and my nurse is Marie-Pierre. She keeps me well informed of your progress.'

Chapter 31

Paul eased himself off the commode and staggered across to the chair positioned half way across the cellar towards the steps. Each day he was determined to move the chair further away until he could make the steps in one attempt. He knew his health had improved over the past three weeks, but felt no better for it. No longer bed-bound, he could at least attend to his body's natural functions on his own. But that did not spare him the humiliation of having Paula taking away his soil and urine in the chamber pot, or washing him. Conversation between them was difficult as she spoke very little French, but Marie-Pierre, who spoke the language fluently, had confirmed his suspicion that she was the eldest daughter of the Spaaks.

Paul didn't mind the pain from his burns. The doctor had reported that his collar bone had healed perfectly and that fresh skin was now starting to grow over some of the burnt flesh. His sight had returned to normal, but he had lost some hearing in his right ear from the damage caused by the burns. His frustration stemmed from his weakness and boredom. At least it was no longer an effort or painful to speak and he had enjoyed the daily opportunities to converse with Marie-Pierre. He wondered why he had ever thought her nose too big for her face. It seemed perfect now. Through her, he learned of the increasing food shortages for not just the Belgians, but the Germans, too, since the recent imposition of a blockade by the Royal Navy.

The news had made him even more anxious to escape Belgium, not just to remove the danger to her, Schotsmans and the Spaak family, but to see *Mutti*. It made him sad to picture her receiving the telegram to inform her of his death. Or had he been posted as missing. He had to build up his fitness again. Despite the chronic food shortages, the Spaaks were doing their best to feed him, but he needed exercise, too, to rebuild his wasted muscles. Again, he heard the grinding noise of the stone slab affording access to the cellar being opened. His heart leapt at the thought it might be Marie-Pierre.

*****

One evening, perhaps two weeks later, Paul had lost track of the days, he was on the point of falling asleep when his attention was caught by a noise from the cellar steps. It had been Schotsmans's idea to leave the cellar entrance open in the evening. As well as offering welcome ventilation, it gave Paul the opportunity to take exercise by repeatedly climbing up the cellar steps and around the kitchen above. However, he was under strict instructions never to leave the kitchen. Schotsmans had impressed on Paul that there was not just danger from the Germans. The fewer people aware of his existence on the farm, the better. A casual and innocent remark about coming across a stranger at the farm would be dangerous. Too many of his countrymen were ingratiating themselves with the Germans in return for food and there were informers everywhere. Whilst Paul would only face internment, those who had aided and abetted in his shelter would face the firing squad or prison at best.

On hearing the noise, Paul was instantly fully alert, his first fear being that his hiding place had been discovered by the Huns. Panic gripped him when he saw the light of a lantern descending the steps. It was only Paula. An amusing image of Paula as 'The Lady of the Lamp' entered his head. Since he had been able to stand, there had been less call for Paula to attend to his intimate needs, but she still washed him and lately had given him his first shave for months. On the last but one occasion she had washed him, she had slyly aroused him with her ministrations with the cloth to his loins. With a squeal of pleasure, she had then gone on to relieve him of months of sexual frustration. Paul blushed at the memory. He had enjoyed the experience, but had also been unaccountably shamed by it. It had made him feel cheap.

Even so, his antipathy towards Paula had lessened. She had smartened herself up a little, was always anxious to please and had even learnt some French so that they could exchange a few words of polite conversation. However, there was no reason why she should be calling on him at this late hour. He watched her warily as she crossed the cellar towards his bed. Quietly, she called out to him in French.

'English. Are you still awake?' Paul noted the use of the familiar address of '*tu*'.

'Yes. What do you want?' He used the more formal '*vous*'.

'It is such a warm night, I thought you might like a cool cup of cider. One of the hands found some hidden from the *Bosches*.'

It was indeed a warm spring evening and Paul guardedly accepted the proffered cup whilst Paula poured them each a measure from the stone pitcher she was carrying. She sat down on his bed next to him. He suddenly felt nervous that underneath the bed sheet he was completely naked. For a few minutes, neither of them spoke and, as they drank their cider in silence, Paul began to relax. Perhaps Paula was genuinely being kind to share with him this cider. The last of the beer and wine had been consumed weeks ago.

Once they finished the cup of cider, Paula offered him another. Paul politely refused. It was strong stuff and he knew that, in his weakened state, he would not have the head for much. The action seemed to offend Paula.

'Why do you not like me? Did I not help you when you needed it most? Did I not clean up your filthy puss, piss and shit for you? You treated me like a filthy peasant when you were the filthy one. What have I done wrong?'

'I'm sorry Paula. Of course, I like you and I am, indeed, most grateful for all you have done for me. I don't know what I would have done without you.'

He felt ashamed that he had clearly let his early feelings for her show too obviously. Moreover, her words made him feel guilty. He took her hand gently.

'Thank you for all you have done. I know what risks you and your parents are taking for me. I'll gladly take a second cup of cider. It was kind of you to bring it.'

Paula's sullenness changed instantly to a glow of pride and she poured another cup of cider for him only. However, instead of passing it back to him, she leant over and pressed it to his lips.

'I'm glad you like me. You are such a brave English soldier. I would do anything for you.' As she said this, she took his hand and held it to her bosom. Since she was dressed only in a thin, cotton nightshirt, Paul could feel the contour of her ample left breast and the stiffening of the nipple. He hadn't had a woman since his early days in France and the touch pleased him. Moving his fingers slightly, he took further pleasure in the obvious enlargement of the nipple pointing up under the nightshirt. Paula responded by putting down his cup and, in one swift movement, removed the night shirt over her head to reveal her completely naked body. Paul viewed her large breasts with complete astonishment. When Paula leaned forward to remove his bed sheet, her breasts swung gently from side to side. They were so much bigger than those of Catherine or any of the tarts he had previously bedded. Much as the rabbit is mesmerised by the cobra, he was so fascinated by the size of the breasts before him that he was not immediately aware of Paula's gentle caresses of his stomach and inner thighs. She smiled, placed her right nipple in his mouth and began to take her pleasure.

*****

Captain William Hall used Vice-Admiral Miller's absence to help himself to more sugar for his coffee. He was known in the Admiralty as 'Blinker' for his need regularly to lubricate his piercing blue eyes on account of a dry-eye medical condition. Although aged forty-four, he had already been a captain for nine years on account of his early rapid promotion. His bald pate and the remains of his curly grey hair suggested he would be older. Ill health and his predecessor's intervention had led to his command of the *Queen Mary* being curtailed so that he might take up the position of DNI.

'Sorry about that, Reggie. Churchill wanted to see me urgently for a minute.' Miller had returned to his office. He poured himself a fresh cup of coffee. 'On my way back, Hope wanted to show me the latest dispositions of the German U-boats. There seem to be rather too many of them now they've shifted their base to Ostend. I'm very impressed with Hope's plot, though. You and Room 40 are producing some good results.'

'Thank you, sir. Although I'm afraid that Ewing and I are not seeing eye to eye, sir.'

'Again? I had hoped that you had put your difficulties aside.'

'Never mind that, sir. I think you have your own difficulties.' Hall nodded in the direction of the newspaper folded beneath the coffee table. 'Have you read the *Northern Messenger* yet, sir.'

'I have, although I'm surprised you read it. It tends to focus on matters in the north of England.'

'I make it my daily business to read all the newspapers. Forgive me, sir.' Hall picked up the newspaper and opened its pages. 'This latest attack on the Admiralty and you in particular is absolutely scandalous. Indeed, it's libellous.' Hall scanned the offending article again, chuntering with disapproval as he did so.

'The World's greatest ever Navy is being humiliated – Crisis at the Admiralty – Heads should roll.

Yet again the Royal Navy has suffered a humiliating defeat and this time, not at the hands of the powerful German High Seas Fleet, but by puny Turkey. Last week, we learned that the might of the Mediterranean Fleet was crippled by the loss of no less than two battleships and the damage of another to cheap mines laid by the Turks. Such a loss is the greatest incurred by the Royal Navy since the glorious Battle of Trafalgar, but on this occasion, there was no glorious victory to justify such heavy loss of life. Instead, the Royal Navy is no nearer to forcing a passage through the Dardanelles Strait to knock Turkey out of the War.

On behalf of our readers and the nation at large, we ask why the Royal Navy commanders did not order the sweeping of the area for mines? Why is it that the minesweepers deployed to the theatre are manned by civilians and not brave Jolly Tars?

This humiliation has occurred barely two months since our mighty navy failed to win a decisive and overwhelming victory over an inferior force at the Battle of the Dogger Bank last January. Despite superiority in numbers, Beatty's battle squadron suffered heavy damage to his flagship, the Lion *and to the destroyer, the* Meteor, *in return for what? Merely the sinking of the* Blücher. *At least, on this occasion, the Royal Navy was in place to prevent the Imperial German Navy bombarding the coast of England. Our readers will recall with sadness, the terrible deaths and injuries sustained by innocent northerners in Scarborough, Hartlepool and Whitby when the most powerful navy ever built was still in harbour whilst the dastardly Hun was bombarding our coast with impunity.*

We have no doubt that our brave sailors share our frustration at the Admiralty's apparent ineptness to marshal its forces, either to bring the German High Seas Fleet to a decisive battle or to destroy the coastal fortifications of little Turkey. Whilst our brave lads face the perils of the enemy shells and mines, their noble lordships wring their hands in dismay.

We have heard rumours of discord between the First Sea Lord, Lord "Jacky" Fisher and the First Lord of the Admiralty, Mr. Winston Churchill. It is said that Fisher does not support the

Dardanelles adventure. Whilst these two great beasts exchange fiery salvoes of paper, the War Staff is run by Vice-Admiral William Miller, an officer who has never commanded anything more than an elderly cruiser. Moreover, an officer of foreign blood married to a German. Perhaps his loyalties are being tested. Like those retired admirals who questioned his fitness for the appointment, we can only ask if he is fit to remain in post.

To our noble Sea Lords and admirals of the Admiralty, we place you on notice that this country will not support such incidences of incompetence. Our navy has been funded from the taxes of hard-working northerners. It is manned by men from our cities, towns and villages. Such men have fire in their bellies and the will to win this war, but our lions can no longer be led by donkeys. It is time that heads should roll.'

'Do you intend to sue, sir?' Hall threw the newspaper onto the desk in disgust. 'That bit about your "foreign blood" and Johanna being German is a disgrace.'

'No, Reggie. It would merely draw attention to issues further and some would say that there's no smoke without fire. My mother is Persian and my wife is Swiss, but a German speaker. In any case, the feature raises some valid points. De Roebeck should have ordered that area of water swept. At least Keyes has manned the minesweepers with the survivors from the sunken ships.'

'I heard that the civilians wouldn't conduct operations under fire. Is that right, sir?'

'I'm afraid so. I suppose one cannot blame them. It's a shame we cannot refute some of the allegations, though. Had it not been for your intercepts, Beatty would never have been in position to intercept the scouting squadrons at Dogger Bank. It was, indeed, my own inexperience that caused the delay in the information being passed on to the Fleet commanders.'

Hall drank some of his coffee before resuming the conversation. 'I was wondering, sir, if it's not impertinent. Have you ever crossed swords with the newspaper's proprietor? It's not the first time you've come under fire personally from his rag.'

'No. At least not as I'm aware. I don't live too far from Manchester so I might have come across him at some function or other, but I don't recall it.' Miller had, in fact given the fact much thought and had wondered if he was being paranoid.

'Anyway, changing the subject, it's a shame our little project with the Turks didn't come off.'

'Do you mean the attempted bribe?'

'Yes. I've just been discussing it with Churchill. He wanted to know why the Cabinet was not aware of it.'

'I do think, sir, that your plan to offer three to four million pounds to Turkey to withdraw from the war, to remove their mines and hand us the *Goeben*, might have commanded the interest of the Cabinet, sir.' Hall smiled broadly.

'Couldn't trust any of 'em to keep their mouths shut.' Both men laughed. 'Anyway, how were we to know that Constantinople had been promised to the Russians?'

'How did the First Lord take the news, sir? Did he threaten to clap you in irons?'

'No, he merely frowned and went on to discuss the German U-boat campaign. Probably as well it wasn't still McKenna in his place, hey?'

'Too true. But for you I might have been facing a two-year prison term.'

The Home Secretary had discovered the NID's operation to intercept foreign-bound mail and threatened Hall with prosecution for interference with the King's mail. Miller had discreetly brought the matter to the Prime Minister and the threat had been quietly dropped.

'Be that as it may, it's concerning Germany's new policy of sinking neutral shipping that I asked to see you, Reggie. The Americans aren't happy about it and Churchill thinks this may be an opportunity to persuade them to join the war on our side.'

'I thought he might. How can I help? I've already drafted a few ideas to feed the newspapers with stories of American casualties, but the Germans haven't yet given me the opportunity to execute the plans.'

'It will take more than the occasional sinking of a US-flagged neutral to bring them into the war and the Germans are relying on the fact. To that end, we need to know more of their activities in the US. Uncover any nefarious activities against the interests of the US government... subversion and breaches of their neutrality, that sort of thing.'

'I understand. Is there anywhere you'd like me to start, sir?'

'Yes. Contact your naval attaché in Washington and ask him to find a chap called Voska. I don't know his full name or whereabouts, but he was expelled from Bohemia for political agitation. His immigration records will be held by the US authorities. He'll be just the man to recruit other Austro-Hungarian dissidents to penetrate the German and Austrian consulates and embassies… even German companies such as Hamburg Amerika. It would be handy to know of any plans to ship goods via neutral ships or countries.'

'I understand perfectly. I'll send a cable to Captain Gaunt today. Anything else, sir?'

'No. That will be all for now. Thank you for giving up your valuable time.'

'Not at all, sir. Is Johanna well, sir? I heard about the loss of one of your sons.'

'I believe so, William. Thank you for asking. In actual fact, I haven't seen her for many weeks. After Paul was shot down, she decided to return to her family in Switzerland for an extended holiday. You'll understand I've been too busy here to give her much company and she's taken Paul's loss quite hard. Indeed, other than a letter to advise me of her safe arrival, I haven't heard from her.' Miller wondered if he ever would. Johanna had barely spoken to him after he had given her the news of Paul. She seemed to blame him for Paul's death.

'I'm very sorry to hear that, sir. Please pass her my best regards when you next write.' Miller could tell that Hall was embarrassed by his earlier question. He knew that the shrewd head of the NID would have deduced accurately the difficulties in the Millers' marital affairs.

Again, Paula shrieked her animal-like noises as she was finally spent of pleasure. She flung herself on top of Paul and lay still. Paul felt revulsion at their recent intercourse. It wasn't just that he found Paula unattractive. She smelt of the farmyard and her unshaved armpits reeked of sweat. What had begun as an affair of lust after several months without sex, was now a torment to him. Except during the week of her curse, she had crept down to the cellar on most nights to share his make-shift bed. On each occasion, she had literally thrust herself upon him. Sexual intercourse with a woman had never been this easy and he was tired of the experience. It made him feel… well dirty. Used even, like a gigolo.

He wanted to feel that sense of longing for a woman again. Somebody who might not be attainable and needed wooing. He thought of Catherine and tried to picture her face. After so many months, it was difficult and he had lost her photograph in the flames of his flying clothing. But for his imminent departure for France and his forceful persuasion, he doubted she would have accepted his advances. Then she might not be expecting his child. Might it have been born yet? He made a mental calculation and realised that there should be another month to go before the due date. He had been wrong to refuse to marry her and he recalled his pledge to God on the fateful day he had been shot down. Well, God had let him live and he must in turn keep his bargain. He would marry Catherine if he could escape to England.

He felt an urgent need to pass water and eased himself off the bed from beneath Paula. Paula began snoring. As he made use of the chamber pot, Paula turned onto her left side with her back to him. He glanced over to the bed at Paula's lank, greasy hair and fat buttocks and felt disgust. She was no *Venus of Urbino* and no more would he lie with her.

*****

Schotsmans appeared pleased with Paul's progress. At his request, Paul went through the series of callisthenics he had been prescribed to follow.

'Not bad, young man. The muscle wastage appears to have disappeared, although I still consider you've lost too much weight.'

'You would probably be able to say the same of most of the Belgian population, doctor.'

'True. I'd say it was time we found a way to send you back to England.'

Paul brightened at the thought. He felt as a caged animal. 'Really? When?'

'Hold fast, young man. We must balance the risks of you staying here versus those of allowing you to leave the farm. With those burns on your face and your relative youth, you would immediately arouse the suspicions of any German patrol that you had seen military service. Moreover, your confinement here has not allowed you to build up any physical stamina.'

'Well, I can't be too far from the coast, can I? Surely, if you could just find a way to let me reach the shore, I could persuade a fishing boat to take me out to sea. There's bound to be a destroyer hanging around not too far from the coast.'

'It sounds easy, doesn't it? Don't you think the Germans have thought about that, too? They have barbed wire and patrols with dogs along the beaches. The fishermen, also, report increasing activity by patrol boats along the coast now the Germans are moving their submarines to Ostend and Zeebrugge. I think our best option is to try to get you to the border with Holland. Once you cross the border, you can try to find a way back to England.'

'But would I not be interned by the Dutch?'

'There is that risk, but not if you had the right papers and they thought you a refugee. I have heard that thousands of Belgians have escaped that way.'

'Let's do that then. Can you provide me the right papers, doctor?'

'I fear no, but worry not. I may have a way. I have heard there is an English nurse working at Sint Gillis who I believe is helping wounded English and Belgian soldiers to escape. If this is true, she will know what to do. I will make enquiries.'

'But where is Sint Gillis, doctor?'

'In Brussels.'

'But that's miles from here. You said yourself that I'm not strong enough. How would I make it to Brussels?'

'I didn't say you would, my friend. I am a doctor and not a member of the Resistance. We need to seek the help of those more experienced in these affairs. Have patience. We have lasted this far, haven't we?'

Paul nodded glumly and sat down. 'You're right, doctor. It's not that I'm not grateful for everything you, Marie-Pierre and the Spaaks have done. It's just the sooner I am back in England, the sooner you are all at less risk and the sooner I can get back to fighting the war.'

'I understand that, young man. But we must allow matters to run their course. I will contact Nurse Cavell at once. In the meantime, you must work on your stamina. I think we might risk allowing you access to the kitchen above from now on, but only after dark. You could take your supper with the Spaaks. Try and learn some Dutch from them, and climb up and down the stairs repeatedly to build up your stamina. A week of that will make a tremendous difference.'

'Thank you, doctor. I will do as you advise. It will make a refreshing change to have some company for dinner.'

'Farewell, my friend. I will visit again next week… or sooner if I have any positive news,' he added in response to Paul's crestfallen look.

*****

It was five days before Schotsmans returned. In the meantime, Paul had had a fearful row with Paula after spurning her advances one evening. He had never seen such a fury in a woman. She had completely lost control of herself. He barely remembered the details, it had happened so quickly, but he shuddered at the memory of the screaming, the throwing of pots, the smashing of bottles, the wailing and the frenzied attack on him with a pair of shears. He had truly feared for his life and had it not been for the intervention of Paula's parents, woken by the noise, he suspected he might not have had the strength to hold her back much longer. Since then, he had rarely seen the girl and on those few occasions, he had been startled by her looks of malevolence towards him. Indeed, despite the warmth of the April evenings, he now ensured the stone slab between the kitchen and the cellar was in place before going to sleep. He feared a surprise attack at night.

Schotsmans had arrived after dark and decided it was safe enough to meet Paul in the kitchen instead of the cellar. He lay before him on the table, a map of Belgium.

'I have news, Paul, but it is not what we had hoped. The Germans are no fools and know that many Belgians have fled across the Dutch border to aid the Allies in their fight against the Germans. Indeed, I was shocked to hear that not thousands, but many hundreds of thousands of my countrymen have already escaped. No doubt, many of them were soldiers who had been lying low for several months since the occupation. As a result, the *Bosches* have not just increased their patrols of the border, but begun constructing an electric fence along the border. It is to be up to three metres in height and carry 2,000 volts. We call it the *Dodendraad*. I don't know how to translate that into French.'

'It sounds like *Totendraht* in German, so that would translate as the Wire of Death. It would be an enormous undertaking. Surely it cannot run the whole length of the border?'

'I believe it will. Look at the map. It will run from here on the coast, along to the Scheldt and eventually all the way down to Aix-la-Chapelle, about 200 kilometres in all. Already posters have been erected to say that anyone approaching the fence within 100 metres, further away in some cases, without due cause, will be shot without trial.' Schotsmans looked dejected.

'But surely, doctor, there must be gaps somewhere.'

'Perhaps. But let me tell you my other news. It is not all bad. I have made contact with the English nurse, although I discovered she is in fact the director of the nursing school. She is a brave woman. The risks she is taking… Monumental. She has a wonderful network of sympathisers working for her. Miss Cavell has offered to provide you shelter in one of her safe houses in Brussels.'

'But doctor, I would have to travel across half the country to reach Brussels,' Paul interrupted.

'Exactly, dear friend. My thoughts precisely. You are safe here with the Spaaks for the moment and the border is much closer. But we still need papers and Miss Cavell has promised to obtain some for you. Moving you is not going to be easy. Your disfigurement and youth would immediately arouse suspicion amongst any German sentry or patrol. Moreover, young man, the German Secret Police takes a great interest in anyone travelling more than fifty kilometres from the address registered on their identity card. But, do not look so depressed, my friend, one of Miss Cavell's assistants has had an idea. I told you we would be right to consult experts in this business.' Schotsmans rummaged in his medical bag and pulled out a folded piece of paper.

'Look at this. It is a poster the Germans have put up calling for volunteer workers in Germany. Their conscription has left their factories short of labour. As this poster shows, they are calling for volunteers to report to Brussels and Antwerp where they will be recruited and put on trains to Germany. You, my friend, have volunteered to return to Germany to the aid of the Fatherland!'

'I'm sorry, doctor. You've gone one stage too far. What do you mean, I am returning to Germany?'

'The necessary papers are being prepared for you to become Charles Moller. Your father was German and your mother Belgian. You are a mechanic who suffered burns during a factory fire and these exempted you from conscription into Belgian military service. You have lived in Ostend all your life. All clear so far?'

'Absolutely. It's an ingenious idea. I speak German so...'

'*Hallo*, Paula.' Schotsmans rose to greet her as she entered the kitchen and he addressed her in Dutch. Paul recognised the words for 'private consultation', but no more.

Paula stared at the map on the table and replied in a sentence that included the word 'water'. She poured hot water from the stove into a metal container that Paul assumed was for warming her bed and withdrew after glancing again at the map.

'A word of warning, young man. The fewer people who know about this plan, the better. I don't want you discussing it with the Spaaks even.'

'Understood. So how do I cross the border?'

'I will arrange to take you to Blankenberge, here. It's the port where the fishermen who fished you out of the sea live. I haven't told you before, but we are here, near De Haan. It's only a few kilometres to the harbour. There, a guide will take you to the border at Sluis.'

'I have two questions, doctor. Firstly, why not let me take a fishing boat out to sea from this harbour? It's too small for military use, so I cannot imagine it would be heavily guarded. And what happens at Sluis? Is the fence there not electrified?'

'To answer your first question, I told you before that the Germans are no fools. They carefully monitor who goes in and out of the harbour. The fishermen have to book out their trips to sea and report back on their return. Were they to go missing, their families would suffer. Moreover, some boats are ordered to take a German guard. Such a course of action carries too many risks.'

'Lord, the Huns are being efficient. So, what about the wire at Sluis, then?'

'Your papers will show that you are travelling to Antwerp, but Sluis is not far from the route you would follow. There the fence is only one and a half metres high. The Germans haven't finished the construction work. Your guide will see you across the fence. Then you are on your own. Clear?'

'I think so. But if the fence is live, how do I get over without being fried?'

'I cannot say. All I know is that there are ways. Some of the Resistance have found a way and regularly cross with messages for your intelligence service.'

Paul was not thrilled by the idea, but realised he had to trust the Belgians. 'All right. When do I obtain the correct papers and when do I leave?'

'I cannot answer either question. All I know is that the documents are produced by somebody outside Brussels. It would not do for me to know too much if you understand. You will leave when I am told the guide will be ready to take you. In the meantime, I will find you some better clothes, including some stout boots. What size are your feet?'

'Forty-four.'

Schotsmans was clearly surprised by the readiness of the answer and asked suspiciously, 'I understood the English used a different measurement for footwear.'

'They do, doctor,' Paul answered quickly. 'But my mother's Swiss and I regularly had boots made for me out there.'

'Ah, that explains your proficiency in German.'

'Doctor… You didn't think I was a German spy, did you?'

'No. Your burning aircraft erased any possible suspicion on that score, but it would not surprise me if the Germans didn't think of planting spies on innocent, patriotic Belgians. Rest easy, my friend. I and the Spaaks are in too deep now. We would not have risked our lives this far if we had not trusted you. Farewell, my friend. I will send Marie-Pierre with the new clothes and boots.'

Paul's heart leapt at the news.

Chapter 33

Four days later, Marie-Pierre brought Paul the forged papers, some Dutch currency for his journey and the best clothes and boots Schotsmans had been able to find. Before leaving, she checked his wounds one last time. Notwithstanding her intimate knowledge of his body, he felt awkward dropping his trousers to allow her to examine his buttocks and lower back.

'You will always carry the scars on your upper back, Paul, but the rest of you looks good.' Paul wondered how he should take that. As he began to do up his belt and tuck in his shirt, she stroked the right-hand side of his head. As always, it felt like a tender caress and his heart melted.

'It's a shame,' she continued, 'that the fire has spoiled your good looks, but I'm sure the young English ladies will not mind. Has your hearing improved?'

'A little, but it is not as good as that in my left ear.' Marie-Pierre moved her fingers lightly over the stump of his right ear. It sent a tremor of pleasure through his whole body.

'I suspect the young English ladies will not mind a few scars so much once this war is over. I have seen so many brave young soldiers with far worse injuries and I fear those left unscathed will be the very few.'

Paul realised that she was still stroking his ear and, without thinking, he took hold of her wrist to hold her hand there.

'Marie-Pierre, I owe you my life. I am well aware that without your nursing and the skills of the good doctor, I would have died long ago.' He gazed into her brown eyes. 'I will never forget you.'

He leant forward on impulse and kissed her fully on the lips. Marie-Pierre did not seem to object, so he took her in his arms and kissed her more passionately, but this time she broke away.

'No, Paul. Now is not the moment. Perhaps, when this dreadful war is over, you will return and we might meet again. For now, let us part as friends.'

She leaned upwards, kissed him softly on both cheeks and caressed the scarred side of his face one last time before switching to Dutch. 'Oh, hallo, Paula. I didn't hear you come down.'

*****

'Thank you, miss, you have been very helpful.' Lieutenant Scheer thanked his informer in fluent Dutch and politely showed her to the entrance of the German Army's local *Kommandantur* in the former mayor's office of De Haan.

'Would you like me to have one of my men drive you home?' The woman shook her head and left the building hurriedly. 'No, miss,' he called after her quietly, 'You either don't want us to know where you live or for others to know you have been to see the German Secret Police.' He watched her retreat down the street whilst he stubbed out his cigarette with his shoe. The woman never turned around and, once she had disappeared from sight, Scheer walked briskly back to his office. As he passed down the corridor, he reverted to German to call to his sergeant in the office next door.

'Jakobs, ring through to Ostend. I want twelve armed men here as quickly as they can get here. Then meet me in my office.'

Scheer picked up the map of the local area from his desk and examined the roads around the farm he had been discussing with his last visitor. He made a few notes before his assistant joined him.

'Something is up, Lieutenant? And no doubt related to that filthy slut you have just been entertaining, I would wager.'

'Quite so, Jakobs. However, she has her uses. You recall the British aeroplane that was shot down ten or so weeks ago. The one in which we could find no remains.'

'Ah, now you mention it, sir, yes… I do recall it. There was a report that he jumped out over the sea, but we never recovered the body. Surely, he didn't survive?'

'He did, Jakobs,' Scheer replied gleefully, rubbing his hands. 'And now I know where he is.'

'But surely nobody has been foolish enough to shelter him? They know full well the punishment… and the Mayor will forfeit his deposit with us.'

'And this time it is not just ignorant peasants with twisted ideas of patriotism, Jakobs. The airman was wounded and has been treated by a local nurse and doctor. Study this area of the map. I need to wash my hands after touching that filthy trollop.'

*****

Two days after saying goodbye to Marie-Pierre, Paul was dressed in his new clothes and saying farewell to Mister and Mrs Spaaks. There was no sign of Paula. Indeed, he hadn't seen her for two days. He checked the clock in the kitchen yet again. Schotsmans was not just late, but very late and Paul was anxious to be underway as soon as possible.

After an hour, he wondered if something might be wrong. Might the doctor have suffered an accident, he wondered. Or had he attracted suspicion and been arrested by the Germans? A vice squeezed his heart at the thought. Were Schotsmans to be arrested, then the Germans would surely find this farm and then what? And what about Marie-Pierre? His heart sank with the thought. Come on doctor. Where are you?

Ten minutes later, Mister Spaaks suddenly bade him to return to the cellar. Then Paul heard it. The noise of a vehicle engine approaching the farm. Was this the doctor or could it be a German patrol come to arrest them all? Paul did as he was told and waited on the cellar steps.

Two minutes later, he was relieved to hear the cheerful greetings of the Spaaks addressed to the doctor and he returned to the kitchen. Schotsmans rushed up to him.

'I'm sorry I'm late, Paul. I couldn't help it. One of my patients died of a heart attack. When I arrived, there was nothing I could do, but it all took time and I couldn't refuse to go. You must have been suffering all sorts of ugly thoughts.' Schotsmans gripped Paul's shoulder in a tender manner. 'I see you're dressed and ready, anyway. Do you have your coat?'

'Yes, doctor, I'll fetch it right away.'

Within a minute, Paul was wearing the peaked hat he had been given and carrying the six-buttoned, double-breasted navy-blue pea jacket. He embraced the Spaaks, bid them an emotional farewell with renewed promises to contact them after the war, and followed Schotsmans to his car, a dirty and mud-splashed, yellow, two-seater.

'Jump in, Paul,' Schotsmans called. 'It's only ten kilometres, but I want to be back before curfew.'

'It's a very compact vehicle you have here, doctor. Is it Belgian?'

'No, it's French… A Zebra. It has two cylinders rather than four, but only cost me 3,000 francs. It suits me well enough for my rounds… I think we'll keep the roof up. It might make you less conspicuous.'

*****

Just under an hour later, Paul entered a small bar on the outskirts of Blankenberge as instructed by Schotsmans. The doctor did not accompany him. He had explained that he was not to see or be seen by the guide for security reasons, but that Paul was to order a coffee and a packet of Gitanes cigarettes. When he was given the cigarettes, he was to appear to change his mind and ask for Gauloises cigarettes instead.

Paul approached the bar and ordered the coffee and cigarettes in French. He looked at the other customers in the bar. It was still late afternoon and trade was slack. Paul was relieved to see no soldiers at any of the tables, but he had been warned that the Secret Police did not wear uniform.

The barman brought him a small cup of black coffee, but no sugar. Paul made no comment. He knew that foodstuffs were in short supply, but he did ask to change the cigarettes. The barman took back the cigarettes and looked at the burns on his face carefully, before withdrawing to the room behind the bar. A minute later, he offered Paul a packet of Gauloises and a note with one word written on it, '*Toiletten*'.

Paul thanked the barman and slipped the piece of paper back to him discreetly before tasting his coffee. It tasted awful, but he drank it in a leisurely fashion, surveying the scene around him. Nobody seemed to be taking any interest in him. He noted the sign for the toilets in the corner, finished his coffee, pocketed the cigarettes and paid his bill, remembering to leave a tip, a custom he had learned in Switzerland.

He was on the point of entering the men's toilet when he felt a prod in the back and a voice whispered to him in French, 'Don't look back. Let me pass and follow me.'

Paul did as he was bid and followed the man out of the bar across the street. His guide was dressed in an old and tattered overcoat with his cap pulled low on his head. He appeared to be even shorter than Paul. With his heart pounding, Paul followed his guide, twenty yards behind. He wore no uniform and carried no military identity. If this was a trap, he knew he would be shot as a spy.

Chapter 34

At last Jacques allowed Paul to rest. Paul's leg muscles and feet hurt after just two hours of walking. He didn't know where he was, but that they were skirting south of Zeebrugge instead of passing through it. Jacques had insisted on travelling at night and that meant they were breaking the curfew.

Paul didn't know his guide's full name or even if he was really called Jacques. All he had said was that he was an electrician in the port and he had a brother who farmed along the border. Fortunately, he spoke quite good French and had proudly told Paul that he was a regular *passeur* in the *tuyau* set up jointly by the Belgian Resistance and British Military Intelligence organisations. Despite his short stature and wiry frame, he was very fit and had been frustrated by Paul's relatively slow pace. Paul regretted he had not had the chance to break in his new boots and his lack of stamina after over two months of isolation in the farmhouse cellar of the Spaaks.

He munched his bread and sausage gratefully. 'How much further, Jacques?' he asked.

'That depends. It depends on how many patrols the Germans have on the roads. Normally, I would say, perhaps, fifteen kilometres. We should have you over the border before daylight. I can then rest up with my brother before I return in daylight.'

'And what happens when we reach the border? How do we get across the fence?'

'Only you will cross the fence, my friend. We will be met by someone on the other side and they will make the preparations to allow you to cross. Don't worry. We have done this before, many times. They will usually give me a package to pass on to our network... papers, cash, I'm never sure... and you will be met by an officer from British Intelligence. Now come. We must keep moving.'

'Just a minute, Jacques.' Paul adjusted the laces on one of his boots. He felt sure he was forming a blister on his heel, but he had no choice but to continue anyway.

Very soon, Jacques signalled for Paul to lie low. He crept forward whilst Paul waited in the bushes. There was a half moon and when the clouds passed over, it seemed incredibly light and Paul felt vulnerable in his semi-exposed position. He knew they must be near a road as he could hear occasional traffic. This would be the main road to Bruges, he surmised. Jacques suddenly appeared beside him.

'Damn. The Germans are busy tonight for some reason. There is a check point about two hundred metres to the north and I have just seen two cyclists pass by. Thank the Lord for the cloud. We can cross if we are careful. Follow me and watch what I do. No noise.'

Paul followed Jacques, crawling on his belly and intensely conscious of every rustle and snapping twig. When he arrived at the verge of the road, he could see the shaded light of the checkpoint and the fireflies of at least three cigarettes in the darkness.

'Take off your boots and tie them round your neck, like this,' Jacques whispered.

It was a relief to remove his boots and Paul waited for the next cloud to obscure the moon.

'Right. We go in a minute. Stay low. Ready?'

Paul nodded and prepared to rush across the road. Just as he was setting off in pursuit of Jacques, the guide turned back and pushed him roughly into the verge.

'Listen,' Jacques urged.

With the hearing in his right ear impaired, it took a moment for Paul to hear the noise of two approaching bicycles coming around the bend. Both carried lamps on the front and would easily have picked up the two crouched figures crossing the road but for the sharp hearing of Jacques. Paul didn't dare to move back into the bushes for more cover, but lay as flat as he could and prayed for the best. Would the cloud now clear to allow the moon to illuminate their position? He waited with dread to find out.

Seconds later, he could see the two soldiers, each with a rifle slung over his shoulder. One was portly and Paul could now hear him complaining to his colleague about the number of kilometres he would have to ride this shift. As they approached the positions of the men lying on the grass verge, the cloud passed by to reveal the full light of the moon. The cyclists were now so close that Paul could smell distinctly the mixture of sweat and garlic sausage. He held his breath and buried his face into the cool grass. Mercifully, his left ear picked up the sounds of the bicyclists moving further north and he felt safe to breathe again.

However, he did not have time to dwell on their close shave as without waiting for the moon to be obscured by another cloud,

Jacques partly lifted him by the collar of his coat and told him to cross immediately. Both men sprinted and quickly gained the safety of the bushes on the other side of the road where they were able to replace their boots. About a hundred metres across the next field, Jacques called a halt to allow them to catch their breath.

'Why didn't you wait for another cloud, Jacques?'

'I hoped that the light of the bicyclists' lamps would prevent anyone seeing our shadows behind and I didn't want to risk staying there any longer. I cannot think why the *Bosches* are so active tonight. I wonder if they have downed another airman. Leastways, we must be more careful. We still have another road to cross.'

*****

Lieutenant Scheer and his men were waiting for Schotsmans when he returned to his surgery. Scheer was seated in the doctor's chair, pointing a pistol at Marie-Pierre sitting on the other side of the desk. Before Schotsmans could react, he felt strong arms grip him from behind and shove him onto the vacant chair beside Marie-Pierre.

'So, doctor,' Scheer addressed Schotsmans in fluent Dutch, 'Where have you been just now?'

Schotsmans turned to look at Marie-Pierre, but two hands grasped him firmly by the side of his head and turned his gaze towards the officer before him. He knew he had to think quickly and, whilst he could not reveal the truth, he deemed it best to stick to a story that had a semblance of truth.

'I have been attending to a patient… near Wenduine, on the coast.'

'Really, doctor? You seem to have been a long time on your visit.'

'Yes, I was. I am sorry, I don't know your rank.'

'I am *Leutnant* Scheer of the German Military Police. Now that is clear, perhaps you would continue to explain your movements this afternoon.'

'Certainly, Lieutenant. My patient died, unfortunately… a heart attack. There was nothing I could do except comfort the widow, sign the death certificate and arrange for the undertaker to call. But it all took some time, I'm afraid.'

Scheer removed his glasses and began polishing them. The activity took two minutes before he spoke again. Schotsmans could feel his heart pounding and hoped his nervousness was not showing. He didn't like the look of this Scheer fellow and wondered what Marie-Pierre might have said already. He still didn't know why he was being questioned.

Having apparently satisfied himself that his spectacles were clean, Scheer continued.

'I already know you and the nurse here have been treating an English airman. The Spaaks are now in custody.' Scheer paused and Schotsmans was stunned by his words. How did Scheer know this? Had somebody informed? Surely Marie-Pierre would have said nothing.

'I thought the news might surprise you, doctor. So where is the airman now?'

'Airman? I don't know what you...' Schotsmans reeled from two blows to the side of his head on the signal of Scheer.

'Let's not make this difficult, doctor. I have much respect for the medical profession, but you in turn must respect mine. I have been a policeman all my life and I know when somebody is lying to me. Now, you can answer my questions here, in a civilised manner. Alternatively, I will have you and the nurse taken to my headquarters for interrogation.' Scheer looked menacingly at Marie-Pierre.

'It would be a pity to spoil this young lady's lovely looks, would it not?' He nodded to somebody behind Schotsmans who immediately gripped Marie-Pierre's hair from behind. 'Now tell me, doctor. I just want to know two facts. Where is the airman? And who else has helped him? Think carefully before you answer, doctor. The Spaaks have confessed already and I have a witness as to your involvement.'

Schotsmans wondered if the German was bluffing. He and the Spaaks had been careful to remove all traces of the Englishman's stay. But who could be this witness? Perhaps it was somebody merely reporting a suspicion and the Lieutenant had no real evidence. It might prove painful, but he decided to play the innocent and hope that Marie-Pierre would follow his lead.

'I know the Spaaks. They are patients of mine and good people. But I know nothing about any airman.'

Scheer stood up. 'I am sorry to hear that, doctor. You are making life very difficult for me and for yourself, but you leave me no choice. I don't envy you the next couple of hours.'

Scheer clicked his fingers and both Schotsmans and Marie-Pierre were dragged to their feet by powerful guards. Scheer put on his hat and left the room without saying another word.

*****

'Take off your clothes.'

Marie-Pierre looked at the plain-clothes policeman seated in front of her with incredulity. She was in a bare cell and three uniformed soldiers were looking on.

'I beg your pardon,' she exclaimed.

'I said take off your clothes. Strip!' the policeman barked in good Dutch.

Marie-Pierre realised she had no choice and began to undress. The policeman examined each article of clothing as she removed it and cast them aside on completion of his inspection. She stopped when she was down to her underclothes. The policeman looked up.

'Continue. Everything.'

'But, sir,' Marie-Pierre protested. Suddenly, the chemise was ripped off her back violently.

'I said strip. Either you do it or one of my men will do it. Hurry.'

With huge reluctance, Marie-Pierre removed the remains of her torn chemise and crouched as she dropped her drawers. She felt humiliated and covered her breasts with one arm and her groin with the other hand. The policeman completed his examination of her underclothes and looked up at her wolfishly.

'Hands high,' he ordered. Marie-Pierre began to cry.

'Please, sir. No,' she whimpered. One of the soldiers immediately gripped her arms and held them above her head.

'Now, that's better,' the policeman said quietly. 'Very nice. For a Belgian, you have a nice body.' Marie Pierre's flesh crawled as the policeman ran one of his fingers slowly over her tiny breasts and slim buttocks.

'Fritz, Wolfgang, would either of you fancy a turn with her. She might have small tits, but I don't think it would bother you, hey?'

Marie-Pierre heard the men laugh and she cringed with fear. Surely, they were not going to rape her? This horrible man had spoken in Dutch so that she might hear the threat.

'So, you are Marie-Pierre de Trooz. A nurse from De Haan.' The policeman nodded to the soldier behind her and he let go of her arms. Marie-Pierre immediately tried to hide her nakedness again, but the policeman shook his head.

'No, de Trooz. I prefer you the way you were. So much more inviting. Put your hands by your side!' He leered at her embarrassment.

Marie-Pierre did as she was ordered. Tears continued to pour down her cheeks. She began to feel the need to urinate with fear, but tried not to think of it. It would be even more humiliating were she to wet herself in front of this evil man. No, she would face this. So what if she was naked? She had seen plenty of naked men in the course of her nursing. Come on. Just imagine this as a physical examination. Above all, don't let the bastards have the satisfaction of seeing your humiliation. She stood to attention and pushed her small breasts forward. The policeman spotted her new stance.

'So, de Trooz. You have some spirit after all. Very good. Let us make this easier for everyone. I have finished with your clothes and you can have them back as soon as you have answered my questions. I don't need to know much. I have heard the story from other sources. I know you have been treating a wounded English flyer at the farm of the Spaaks for nearly three months. I know he was badly burned and that he is no longer there. I just want to know where he is or where he is heading. What name is he travelling under and who else has helped him. So, in your own words, miss.'

The policeman smiled in a friendly manner and it was not lost on Marie-Pierre that he had addressed her as 'Miss' for the first time. She wondered herself where Paul was now. Doctor Schotsmans had made all the arrangements for his move himself. But she did know the name on his identity papers and that Doctor Schotsmans had been to Brussels to arrange their production. If she could keep that information secret, was there any point in withholding everything else? This policeman obviously knew most of it anyway. It must have been Paula who had given them away, but why? Marie-Pierre had never liked Paula, but surely even she would not inform against her own parents.

'I'm waiting.' The policeman interrupted her thoughts.

She thought again of Paul and his farewell kiss. No, she resolved. She would tell this policeman nothing more than he obviously knew already. Paul had to be given the chance to escape. To bring revenge on these monsters. That would be her contribution to freeing Belgium.

'Very well, sir. I admit that I did care for an injured airman, but I don't know where he is now.'

Chapter 35

Like Scheer, Jakobs was a reservist and had been a policeman before the war. Both were of German ethnicity and had had to maintain their membership of the German army reserves as a secret. However, whereas he had lived in Antwerp all his life, Scheer was from Brussels and had been living in Germany for two years prior to the war. He didn't like Scheer. He was too much of a zealot and Jakobs was a little afraid of him. He was feeling especially nervous since he had some news that he knew his superior was not going to like.

'So, what progress have you made in the last few hours, Jakobs?' Scheer asked him from the other side of his desk.

'We may have a lead, sir. Schotsmans's car is a distinctive colour and the local *gendarme* spotted it heading north this afternoon.'

'But does that not tie in with what the good doctor says himself? Wait, I have it here.' Scheer opened a folder and found the report for which he was searching.

'Yes. He said he was visiting a patient in Wenduine. The widow of his patient backs up his story.' Scheer laid the file on his desk.

'Yes, sir. But the call was in the morning and this report is of the vehicle going north late in the afternoon... and with a male passenger!' Jakobs added triumphantly.

Scheer expressed no surprise. 'Ah. And what does the doctor say of this?'

'He is being less than fully cooperative... despite your more persuasive methods, sir.'

'I detect that you don't approve of my methods, Jakobs. This is not a time to be squeamish. We are at war and must use extreme measures, if necessary, to exterminate this resistance movement. We have too few troops to spare to police the population otherwise.'

'I understand that, sir.' Jakobs responded noncommittally.

'Perhaps I ought to interrogate him myself.' Scheer rose from his chair.

Jakobs held up his arm. 'I would wait a while, sir. He is unconscious and our own doctor is unable to rouse him. I fear the men were a little too enthusiastic in their work.'

'I see. We must revise our methods and training a little, I think. What about the girl? Has she said much?'

'Indeed, she has, sir. But not much more than we knew already. She confirms the story from the peasants about him being brought to the farm by two fishermen and that …'

'Those fishermen… They are in custody, I hope,' Scheer cut in.

'Yes, sir. And they took little persuasion to tell us all they knew. But returning to the girl's story. She claims not to have seen the airman for two days. She admits to nursing him, providing him with clothing and new identity documents, but she is adamant that she never looked at the documents or knew of Schotsmans's escape plan.'

'Do you believe her? Have you employed all of the more persuasive tools you seem to disapprove of?'

'The beatings? No, sir. We have not harmed her. The men had an antipathy to beating a woman… But I did employ another method, sir and… yes, I think I believe her. The peasants confirmed that she hasn't been near the farmhouse for two, that is now three days, sir.' Jakobs noted from the clock behind Scheer that it had passed midnight.

'I will speak to those men, Jakobs. You must all learn that women of the Resistance are just as dangerous as soldiers. They must not be treated leniently.'

'Would that rule apply to children, sir?'

'Why not, Jakobs? If children are old enough to fight us, they are old enough to suffer the consequences.'

Jakobs shuddered at the reply, but his superior did not seem to notice. This is not why I became a policeman, he thought.

'So, Jakobs, we have six people in custody plus the testimony of the peasant girl and yet we are no nearer to finding the airman. Given the time he has now had and the report of Schotsmans heading north, he's probably close to the Dutch border by now.'

'Forgive me for asking, sir, but why is it important to capture this airman? After all, hundreds of French, Belgian and no doubt British soldiers have already crossed the border.'

Scheer slammed the table with his fist, startling Jakobs. 'That is precisely the point. Already hundreds of enemy soldiers have escaped to fight another day against the Fatherland. That outflow must be stopped and they would not have been successful without help. The Resistance must be providing them with organised shelter, documents, guides, food and goodness knows what else. Both

Schotsmans and this flyer are key to us discovering the source of this illegal aid. Surely, you understand that, Jakobs?'

'Of course, sir, and that is why I have asked for more patrols on the approaches to the Dutch border. But before he lost consciousness, Schotsmans did reveal something that might be of use. The men were experimenting with the use of electricity on his genitals and it seemed to cause him enormous pain.' Again, Jakobs shuddered, this time at the memory of the gruesome methods his men had applied to the doctor. This time Scheer did notice his emotion.

'So, Jakobs. Perhaps these new methods of persuasion do have some validity. What did he reveal?'

'Quite frankly, sir, I would not treat a dog this badly… And the man's a doctor, too. Yes, sir, I know there is a war on,' Jakobs paled before the glare his superior had just given him. 'We found in his coat a ticket stub for a rail journey to Brussels this week and questioned him about it. As you suspected, sir, he was receiving help from the Resistance…'

Scheer punched his left hand with the fist of his right. 'I knew it. What did he have to say?' Jakobs imagined Scheer was slavering like a dog before feeding. He was leaning forward across his desk expectantly.

'He claimed to have visited a Doctor Carel in one of the hospitals in Brussels. This colleague provided the forged documentation for the evading airman. I've already rung the department in Brussels to trace this doctor.'

'Excellent, Jakobs. Good work. I assume you pressed the prisoner for the name of this hospital?'

'I tried, sir, but the doctor will not be talking further.'

'Why not? You said he was merely unconscious, not dead. We must try again.'

'I'm afraid the men are inexperienced in your new methods, sir. Whilst a further shock was being applied, the doctor managed to spit out his gag and bite off his tongue. That's when he lost consciousness, sir.'

'Idiots!' Scheer exploded.

*****

Paul didn't know how he had done it, but after eight punishing hours of walking through the darkness of the Belgian countryside, he was now sheltered behind a hen cabin just a few hundred yards from the Dutch border. Both his feet were blistered and he felt he couldn't take another step, but his freedom was in sight – only that sight was of the menacing electric fence. Although lit at periodic intervals, the ground opposite him and Jacques was in shadow. The Germans had compensated by patrolling the fence with sentries on foot.

'Take off your boots,' Jacques ordered again. Paul was too tired to argue. He would be glad to leave them behind and never see them again. He began tying them around his neck, but Jacques stopped him. 'No. Put them down. You will not need them the other side. They will be of more use to us.'

When Paul was ready, Jacques continued his instructions. 'We wait for the next sentry to pass. Once he has gone by, we have four minutes to cross that open ground and for you to cross the fence before the next sentry approaches. There's no need to crawl, but keep low as you run.'

'But how are we to cope with the fence, Jacques?'

'Don't worry about that. It will be taken care of. Remember, we are experts. Just follow the instructions you are given. I will not wait for you to cross as I have to get back here before the arrival of the next sentry. Wait. Where is your coat?'

'It's here. I just took it off to run across the field.'

'No, my friend. You must wear it. It's essential.'

Paul was puzzled, but again was too tired to debate the issue. Jacques opened one of the egg boxes of the cabin and, after a little rummaging, pulled out an electric flashlight. He checked his watch and then switched the flashlight on and off quickly, twice. In the distance Paul could see the signal repeated by some unknown observer.

'Now. We go. Hurry, but be careful.' Jacques immediately set off across the field and Paul followed almost in his footsteps. It took them less than a minute to reach the fence and Paul was very careful not to touch it. Suddenly, two packages were thrown from the darkness on the other side and landed nearby. Jacques stuffed one into the front of his coat and passed the other to Paul.

'Here, put these on.' The package comprised a pair of rubber gloves and rubber-soled gym shoes. Whilst he reshod his feet and donned the gloves, a man appeared from across the other side of the fence wearing huge rubber gloves. He held up what looked to be a wire and fastened each end out of Paul's sight, before lowering a rubber mat over the lower two strands of wire.

'Throw him your coat and identity documents. Then climb over. There should be no electricity running through this section of the fence, but the rubber mat is a precaution. Good luck, my friend.' Jacques shook Paul's hand warmly, waved to his fellow *passeur* and loped back to the cover of the hen hut.

Paul hesitated to make the crossing. It had not escaped his attention that neither of the professional *passeurs* had attempted the crossing themselves. He didn't know what 2,000 volts felt like, but was certain it was not good for him.

The guide on the other side of the fence gesticulated wildly. '*Kommen. Kom snel.*'

Paul realised that he had to move quickly. The sentry would be passing by again soon and these men were risking their lives for him. He thought of Schotsmans and Marie-Pierre. He had to trust their associates. Slowly, he wriggled across the mat whilst the guide held up the strand above him. Was it his imagination, he thought, or was the mat throbbing? It didn't do to dwell on such matters. The fact was that he was not frying. Carefully, he passed over to the other side and stood up. He was free, on neutral soil, three months after being shot down.

The Dutchman disconnected his wire and removed the mat and his gloves. He gave Paul a pair of shoes and gestured to him to return the gym shoes and gloves. Just as Paul did so, he pulled out a pair of sheep shears and Paul feared for his life once again. Was this an elaborate trick by the Germans to murder him in a neutral country? However, he need not have feared, although the Dutchman's next act was almost as alarming. He used the shears to snip two buttons off the pea jacket.

'What the devil are you doing? he cried.

The Dutchman merely smiled in response, handed Paul back the pea jacket and pocketed the buttons. Perhaps he keeps the buttons as trophies, Paul wondered. But why all the rigmarole about the jacket?

The guide led him about fifty yards from the fence into the shadows of Holland and Paul saw the outline of a dark car parked in the lane. A tall man stepped out of the car and came towards him.

This must be the military intelligence officer, Paul thought. As he closed to within a few yards of the man, something stirred in his mind. The man wore a suit and no hat. There was something vaguely familiar about him. Paul's suspicions were confirmed when the officer exclaimed, 'Good God! It can't be. Is that you, Paul?'

It was Peter and the two brothers embraced each other warmly.

*****

The Mayor of De Haan watched with pity as the prisoners were brought into the town square. First out of the lorry were two fishermen from Blankenberge. The mayor didn't know them, but had read their names in the German proclamations announcing this morning's event. He was relieved to see that neither man seemed to have been cruelly treated and both walked across the square without hindrance. The same could be said of the next two prisoners, Mister and Mrs Spaak. Poor Spaak, the mayor thought. He had often shared a drink with him in the café and Spaaks had helped with the mayor's latest election campaign.

The assembled crowd gasped as the pretty and very popular district nurse was led out from the lorry. She was dishevelled, but showed no sign of any injuries. Could the rumours of German cruelty towards and torture of prisoners be untrue, the mayor thought? He noticed that Miss de Trooz had a far-away look and she walked defiantly across to the group of other prisoners. There was then a delay as the final prisoner was brought out of the lorry.

Again, there was a gasp from the crowd, a murmur and then a sullen silence. The mayor noticed that several members of the crowd were wearing small sprigs of ivy on their outer clothing. Doctor Schotsmans was carried off the back of the lorry. Whilst the other prisoners had walked unaided, Schotsmans was supported by two soldiers. His once full-head of grey hair was now patchy and matted with blood and filth. His eyes were black and puffed up such that he must have had difficulty seeing and a vivid-red trail of blood could be observed beneath his mouth and all over his collarless shirt front. He bore the appearance of a broken doll, unaware of events around him. The escort led him to a stake, recently erected on the edge of the square, and bound him to it. Before they had finished, the doctor began to slide to the ground and it took another soldier to bind his legs to the stake whilst the others held him up.

A German officer then addressed the crowd in German, pausing occasionally for his words to be translated into Dutch and French.

'The following have been tried by a court martial convened by the local military commander of the Marine Area. Jost Maes, Daneel Peters, Gustave Schotsmans, Hugo Spaak, Louise Spaak and Marie-Pierre de Trooz. They have all been found guilty of the crimes of harbouring and assisting the escape of an enemy of Germany, contrary to German Military Law. The sentence for the crimes is… death.'

The mayor heard a loud scream and commotion to his left in the crowd. It was coming from Paula Spaak. She was on her knees sobbing, screaming and rending her clothing. He found it hard that she could be this affected. After all, there were rumours that it was she who had denounced her parents to the Germans. She would be dealt with soon and made to face her own trial, but by her peers.

The German officer continued. 'The sentence is to be carried out by firing squad immediately.'

The junior officer in charge of the firing squad saluted him, turned about and marched across the front of the twelve soldiers standing in front of the prisoners. None of the prisoners other than Doctor Schotsmans was bound and the mayor saw Hugo Spaak support his wife as she crumpled and burst into tears. The village priest blessed them in Latin and those prisoners who could, along with most of the crowd, crossed themselves. Meanwhile, the junior officer called the firing squad to attention. The mayor wanted to look away, but knew that he would be punished for doing so. He and his colleagues on the council were all under orders to witness the execution.

The German soldiers took aim with their rifles and just before the order to fire was given, Marie-Pierre shouted loudly and defiantly, *'Lang leve het koninkrijk van België'*.

Seconds later, only she and Louise Spaaks remained standing. The German officers were furious. Clearly, each member of the firing squad had chosen the male prisoners as their targets. A snigger ran through the crowd as the junior German officer, in a fury, ordered his men to reload. It resembled a scene from a pantomime. Some of the crowd began to sing the Belgian National Anthem. The singing drowned out the orders to the firing squad, but thirty seconds later the mayor heard the rifle fire and saw Marie-Pierre de Trooz and Louise Spaak fall to the ground, their chests stained with the blood from several bullet holes. The crowd fell silent again as the German officer took out his pistol and began shooting each of the prisoners through the head at point-blank range.

Chapter 36

Catherine was bored with pregnancy. When she had heard of Paul's probable death, she had been glad of the baby. She would always have a part of him and she had looked forward to the company of a child. Now, she wanted it over. It wasn't just the discomfort and the disfiguration of her once slim body. In recent weeks, her feet, ankles and hands had swollen grotesquely. It was Mummy's fussing and insistence she couldn't do anything that riled her most. 'Are you sure you should be riding in your condition, Catherine?' and 'Be careful on the stairs, dear.' Ughh, it was so frustrating, she thought.

She picked up the latest letter from Admiral Miller. He had been absolutely charming and, despite the pressures of work at the Admiralty, had even called on her parents one weekend to make their acquaintance. Daddy had told her of the admiral's generous offer to make a financial provision for the child. Catherine felt sure that he would make a wonderful grandfather. If only Paul were alive to see it.

Her eyes misted up as she recalled their last meeting. Of course, she had hoped he would marry her, but she couldn't let him know that. Indeed, she respected him more for his decision, something that neither of her parents would ever understand. He had been honest and said that he wasn't ready to – or sure he could – change his lifestyle for the responsibilities of married life. Moreover, whilst he was fond of her, he wasn't convinced that he loved her and it would be bad for them to be tied to each other in such circumstances. That had hurt her. She would never have let him lie with her had she not loved him. But then, there had been no point having a scene. Her two elder brothers would have laughed at the thought of her playing the tearful, wronged woman. She was fortunate to have plenty of help on hand and felt confident she could raise the child on her own. Even so, Paul's look of relief had driven a knife through her heart when she had told him.

She felt the baby kick and that pleased her. He or she had not been quite as active lately. At first, she had been convinced it would be a boy and a rugger player at that. Now she wasn't quite so sure. She would mention it to the doctor the next time he called. Oh, to think that in four weeks' time, she would be rid of this lump and free to be more active. Mind you, she thought, then I'll just be a *milch* cow.

*****

On the road from Sluis to Terneuzen, Paul had the chance to catch up with Peter. They had not seen each other since soon after the war had started.

'I cannot wait to send a telegram to Papa and *Mutti*, Paul. We all thought you dead.'

'So, what were they told, Peter? Did somebody see me go down?'

'Yes. I gather one of your squadron saw you go down with flames and assumed the worst. You were posted as "Missing – Presumed Killed". Of course, we all had some hope for a month or so that you might be laid up somewhere or even a POW, but those hopes faded ages ago.'

'How awful for *Mutti*,' Paul said quietly and sorrowfully.

'It was rough on Papa, too, you know.'

'Really? I would have thought his feelings would have been good riddance to bad rubbish.'

Peter slowed the car slightly and looked at his brother strangely. 'You don't really think that do you, Paul?' he asked softly. 'I mean Papa might be a stiff old thing, but I know he cares. He's just… so Victorian in his feelings. You know, stiff upper lip and "Long Live the Empire".'

'I know. You're probably right, of course. I just wish he wouldn't try to keep me on the straight and narrow so much. Just… well, leave me to plough my own furrow.'

Peter chuckled. 'I think that an unfortunate way of putting things.'

'What d'you mean?' Paul snapped.

'I'm sorry, Paul. I shouldn't have laughed. But Papa… Oh, he'll be mortified that I let it slip.'

'Let what slip?' Paul asked angrily.

'I'm sorry, Paul. When he thought you were dead, he tried to comfort *Mutti*. She took the news awfully badly, you know. He told her that she was to become a grandmother to try to soften the blow. And then he wrote to me to say I would become an uncle. I'm afraid we all know about you and Catherine.'

'Damn and blast him. That was my business.'

'I know, Paul. But remember, we all thought you dead. I'll be honest. I rather liked the idea that some part of you would live on in the child. Think about it from Papa's perspective.'

Neither brother spoke for a while, but eventually Paul broke the silence. 'I'm sorry for being so touchy. But since all my secrets have been laid bare, let me tell you another, but promise not to tell *Mutti*. I want to tell her myself. No, don't interrupt. Hear my news first. When I get home, I'm going to ask Catherine to marry me. What do you think of that?'

'I think it the least you could do. I had presumed that you had already done so, but the war intervened.'

'Well, I hadn't as a matter of fact. But I'm going to now. Actually, I'm a reformed character, Peter. I'm even looking forward to going to Mass again, with or without *Mutti*.'

'Golly!' was Peter's only reply for a moment, but he then added, 'I'm afraid you won't find *Mutti* at home when you return. She's taken a long holiday back in Switzerland and Papa's not sure when or even *if* she's coming back.'

'What? But why? Surely Pops has that wrong.'

'I'm not so sure. She wrote to me from Switzerland and suggested the same thing. In a roundabout way she blames Papa for your death… I mean you going missing.'

'But that's ridiculous. It was Archie that shot me down and not Pops.'

'I'll explain it later. We're nearly at Terneuzen now and I need to discuss how we get you home. I'll put you up in a hotel and stay a couple of days. Then I have to be back in Rotterdam. By the way, your documents are on the back seat.'

'I was wondering about that. What was the rigmarole about throwing over my coat and documents before I could cross? And then the cutting off two of my buttons?'

'Ah, you noticed that, did you?'

'Of course, I ruddy did. It was all a bit cloak and dagger.'

'Maybe so, Paul, but I'm afraid we had to factor in that sometimes our precautions for the fence don't work and accidents occur.'

'You mean somebody fries on the wires?' He laughed at his unintended poetry, black as it was.

'Regrettably, it has happened. Then we don't want to leave forged documents on the corpse for the Germans to find.'

'But what about the coat and the charade with the buttons, Peter?'

'Mmm. The buttons contain messages written on tissue paper by the Belgian Resistance.'

'You mean that had I been caught on my way to the border, I might have been arrested and shot as a spy instead of being treated as a POW?'

'That was nothing to do with me, Paul. The Resistance have to resort to all sorts of means to get messages… and people, across the border.'

'That reminds me, Peter. The guide said I would be met by an officer from Military Intelligence. My word. I had no idea. All this time I've been envying you a cushy life as a diplomat in Amsterdam, and it turns out you've been a spy!'

'No. Goodness me. Not at all. My life's far more mundane that that. I'm responsible for passport control and am now based at the consulate in Rotterdam. As I speak both French and German, I'm often the one sent down to the border to meet refugees. I suppose, because I ask them a few questions, the guide mistakenly assumed I'm an intelligence officer. Heaven forfend, Paul. Whilst you and Richard have been risking your necks for God and country, I really have been leading the cushy life of a diplomat. I really wish I could do more for the war effort, but the Diplomatic Service is very strict about staying out of espionage. I can see that I've disappointed you.'

'I am disappointed, Peter. I suddenly saw you in a new light. So how do I get home?'

'Good question. I can't take you on to Rotterdam as I daren't take the risk of you crossing back into Belgium. I'm protected by my diplomatic status. Instead, we'll fix you a berth on a ship leaving Terneuzen for England. Keep your identity papers. I'll check them out for you. As far as the Dutch authorities are concerned, you will be just another Belgian refugee escaping to England. We don't want you interned, do we?'

Paul wondered if Peter was being entirely straight with him.

*****

'Whatever is the matter, dear?' Lady Edgar asked of her daughter solicitously. 'You're sweating profusely.'

'I don't know, Mummy. I just don't feel very well. Perhaps I've caught a chill.'

'It wouldn't surprise me if you have. I warned you not to go out walking too much. You'll have tired yourself out and lowered your resistance to infection. I know it's May, dear, but you can still catch a chill. Now if you'd just listen…'

Lady Edgar's advice was interrupted by a scream of pain from her daughter. She was writhing and holding the lower part of her swollen stomach.

'My goodness, Catherine. Is it the baby? Is it coming? Quick. Let me put a cloth down. If your waters break, I don't want a mess on the cushions.' Lady Edgar made to leave the room to fetch a cloth or towel, but was brought back by a howl of anguish.

'Mummy! Call the doctor.' Catherine screamed in pain again.

Lady Edgar rushed over to her daughter and took hold of her hands. 'Don't fret, darling. It's natural.' Her attention was then drawn in horror to a reddish fluid beginning to streak down the inside of Catherine's legs. Some might have thought Lady Edgar foolish, but she had given birth to three children. Her concern for her daughter overcame any thoughts of sparing the cushions. She helped Catherine into a lying position on the sofa and screamed at the top of her voice for somebody to call the doctor.

Chapter 37

Paul laid down his pen and read through his letter again before blotting it and laying aside the single sheet of paper. It had taken a week to find a berth in a ship bound for Britain. The German's policy of using submarines to sink neutral shipping suspected of carrying supplies to Britain had deterred many ships' captains and their owners from running the risk, and especially after the sinking of the *Lusitania* earlier in the month. Under huge pressure from the Germans, the Dutch, in particular, were no longer willing to run the risk of putting into British ports. Nonetheless, at last he was bound for home. The *Hird*, a Norwegian tramp steamer, was proceeding north-west at eight knots on her way to the Tyne with a cargo of starch from the factories of Terneuzen, before picking up a cargo of coal for her home port in Norway.

On Peter's advice, Paul maintained his identity as a Belgian refugee and mixed little with the crew or the handful of other refugees embarked. Peter had been concerned lest the ship might have to turn back for Holland or be intercepted by the Germans. Since saying farewell to Peter, Paul had dwelled often on their conversation about his relationship with Pops and that between their parents. It hardly seemed credible that there should be any strains in their parents' marriage. They had always struck him as very close and affectionate, with many common interests such as music and walking. Even more incredible was Peter's suggestion that, by joining the RNAS, Paul might have contributed to any strained relations. That at least was something he might put right with his letter.

Indeed, he felt that there were many things he needed to put right. He had started by attending Mass daily in Terneuzen. He had not forgotten his prayer to God three months previously, over Ostend. God had kept his side of the bargain after all, by sparing his life. He, in turn, would marry Catherine and spare another man's life when he next had the chance. But there was more. His caddish behaviour towards Catherine was just one element of his life of which he would not be proud were his day of reckoning to come. He didn't share Pops's values and he most certainly was not going to *kow tow* to him in future. After all, he was nearly twenty-three and had fought for and been decorated by his country. But, perhaps, he had given poor old Pops too much cause to keep him on the straight and narrow, as he had put it to Peter. He meant what he had said to Peter. He was a reformed character. He would be a good husband to Catherine and father to their child. He might take a little more care to survive this war, too.

He picked up the letter again and signed it after reading it one last time.

'My darling Mutti,

I know that Peter will have sent you a telegram to inform you that I am alive and well, although I am not the most handsome brute through a little scarring. Forgive the brevity of this letter, but you know how poor I am as a correspondent.

I am on my way back to England and will be asking Catherine to marry me at the first opportunity. I am confident she will accept me, although I wouldn't blame her for rejecting me. I've hardly treated her fairly. Anyway, I would very much like you to return home to attend the wedding. I want to manage it as quickly as I can. Please send a telegram home (in London) to say you will come.

I, also, plan on having a serious conversation with Pops. I am well aware that I have been a disappointment to him, but he will have no cause to fault me now. My time in the clouds has brought me closer to God and I am now a very much reformed character. On the subject of Pops, I hope you don't harbour a mistaken belief that he encouraged me to join the RNAS. Very much the opposite. He wouldn't give his consent until I gained my Aero ticket. However, that is not a decision I regret. I love flying and the Service is filled with some really splendid chaps. We all hate this war, but think we are best placed to bring about its end more speedily.

Anyway, I am reaching the end of this paper and remember you telling me that one should not write on the reverse, so I will close now. I love you very much and will pray for your safe (and speedy) return home.'

Feeling satisfied that he might have struck the right tone, he placed the letter in an envelope and sealed it. He had just done so when he heard a commotion outside. Having nothing else to do, he went to investigate.

A couple of the seamen were gesticulating wildly and Paul followed the direction of their gaze. He was just in time to see the sea disturbed and the dark and sinister shape of a submarine surfacing about 600 yards off the starboard beam. Although he had never seen one before, he immediately recognised it as being a German U-boat from the newspaper photographs. He watched it with fascinated horror. There was something unnerving about such a powerful weapon of war appearing out of nowhere, having been hidden beneath the waves. It was so... well, sneaky almost. Even before the U-boat had finished surfacing, an officer appeared on the bridge and seconds later, sailors poured out from the front of the fin to man the gun mounted on the casing.

Paul looked up at the bridge for any sign that the Norwegian captain intended heaving to. Far from it, he must have ordered an increase in speed as Paul could see a puff of soot appear from the funnel and feel simultaneously the rumble of the engine increasing speed. A member of the crew was busy bending a fresh Norwegian flag onto a halyard.

Before he had even had the time to look back towards the U-boat, he heard the bang of its gun fire a single round. Within seconds, Paul could hear and feel the ship's engine stop. The captain then appeared and gave an order Paul could not understand to the crew standing beside him. Looking to starboard again, he could see that the German officer was manoeuvring the submarine closer to the *Hird*. Then he thought he saw something else. He looked again, carefully avoiding attention to himself. Yes, his airman's eye had picked up a speck above the horizon. It could be a bird, he thought, but if it was further away, then might it be something else, he wondered hopefully.

In response to the captain's order, the seamen began to lower the boats on the ship's falls. At the same time, the Germans were busy pulling up a small rubber boat from the fore hatch of the submarine. The south-westerly wind was pushing the *Hird* closer to the U-boat, too, such that the water between them was now only two hundred yards. One of the German sailors was preparing a heaving line to throw across to the *Hird,* once the two vessels drifted closer to each other.

Paul looked above the horizon to the north again and his heart leaped. The speck in the sky was now taking form and it wasn't a bird. Please don't let the Germans see it, he prayed. He couldn't believe his luck. Even at this distance, he could recognise the distinctive shape of the aeroplane he had last flown the previous year, the Bristol TB.8. It might even be manned by a couple of his former colleagues at Kenton Lodge. The Germans were too busy with the arrangements for boarding the *Hird* and had so far failed to spot it. However, that suddenly changed.

The lookout on the bridge resumed his watch and shouted the alarm. Immediately, a klaxon sounded and the captain of the U-boat ordered the opening of the main vents. Spouts of air plumed upwards like those from the blow hole of a surfacing whale. The fore hatch was already underwater as the submarine began to submerge and the casing crew disappeared smartly through the fin, abandoning the rubber boat. Last to disappear was the officer on the bridge, only three seconds before the fin, also, disappeared beneath the waves. It was all over in, perhaps, twenty seconds, but by now the distinctive four-wheeled undercarriage of the TB.8 was clearly visible and the Norwegian crew had spotted it, too. They began waving excitedly to the approaching aircraft, but were interrupted by another order from the captain. Paul felt the engine vibrate once again through the deck and the *Hird* picked up speed whilst the crew raised the boats dangling over the side.

The Bristol bomber was too late to catch the submarine on the surface, but even so, the pilot banked the aircraft to starboard onto the course the U-boat had been taking when it had dived. Immediately afterwards, the observer began releasing his payload of twelve ten-pound bombs, straddling the water ahead of the U-boat's last known position. As each bomb exploded, it sent up great columns of water. With his payload released, the pilot circled the aircraft overhead, awaiting signs of the success or failure of his attack. Paul joined the crew in waving and saw both airmen wave back.

After ten minutes, Paul and the crew were equally disappointed not to see the U-boat re-surface or any wreckage appear. It seemed that the U-boat had made a lucky escape. The crew of the bomber must have come to the same conclusion as they passed over the *Hird* one final time, waved and headed back to the north. It was all a little of an anti-climax, but Paul suspected the U-boat might stay deep for a long while yet and in that time the Norwegian captain was wasting no effort to take his ship closer to South Shields.

Another flash appeared on the horizon, followed by the dull boom of yet another explosion. Catherine had read H.G. Wells's *War of the Worlds* and believed she was seeing an enactment of Wells's imagination before her eyes. To the north-east of her position in Regent's Park, probably somewhere over Stoke Newington, she could see the huge, long shape of the Zeppelins coming closer and dropping yet more bombs. More menacing, due to their invisibility, two other Zeppelins were wreaking destruction over to the east. Every now and then, she could hear the drone of the engines, but otherwise the harbingers of destruction seemed silent as they pressed on leaving a trail of fire.

'They're dropping incendiary bombs, Catherine,' her husband informed her. 'Each of those monsters can carry about one and a half tonnes of bombs,' he added.

Catherine clung closer to his arm and shivered. 'It's so awful. They seem unstoppable.'

'We do seem unprepared, my darling. We've too few guns and searchlights, but they can be stopped. Any minute now the sky will be buzzing with aircraft from Eastchurch. It's a pity we didn't pick them up crossing the coast.'

'Have you ever shot down one of those monsters, Paul?' Catherine stroked the wings on his left sleeve.

''Fraid not. It's much easier to hit them on the ground. But give me a chance… As soon as I'm back in Belgium that is.'

'Oh, Paul, I do wish you didn't have to go back. Not after what happened when you were last there.'

Paul turned Catherine to face him and kissed her softly on the head. 'You know I must go. Your brothers understand that, too. Somebody has to take on the Hun.'

They both turned back to watch the flames over the east of London. There were dozens of them. Catherine thought how lucky she was to live in Cambridgeshire. The Germans were targeting the east coast and London with their frightful shelling and bombing. Had it not been more convenient for both her father and Paul's father for the wedding to take place in London, owing to their commitments at the Admiralty and War Office respectively, then she might never have witnessed this spectacle. Somehow, she had seen the war as something happening across the Channel, but now it had touched her personally.

Losing Paul's son had been awful for her, but Paul's telegram from Newcastle had bucked her no end. It had been almost as great a surprise when he had called on his way to London to ask her to marry him. After all, without the baby, there had been no need. But he had told her about how his time in Belgium had given him the time for reflection and a change of heart. He had also told her of the miserable time the brave Belgians were having at the hands of those beastly Germans. His imminent return overseas had made it necessary to arrange a much quieter wedding than she or her mother would have liked, and in a registry office no less! However, neither she nor Paul were prepared to wait. Sadly, neither of her brothers had been able to attend, but at least Paul's mother had returned from Switzerland in time. She glanced up at the right side of his face, illuminated by the glow of the fires to the east. The scars were still pretty horrid, but after three weeks, she was becoming used to them.

'Did I tell you, Paul, how good your father was to me whilst you were away?'

'Yes, dear. Many times. He might be a bit of a stick-in-the-mud, but he knows how to do the right thing. I'll give him that.' Paul took her hand and kissed it.

'Maybe you should try to be more like him.'

Paul laughed. 'Hardly. He's a relic in his own age group. No, I'm glad we're on better terms, but we're never going to be alike. He seemed to get on well with your father, though.'

'He did. I'm not sure I can say the same about our mothers, though. There seemed to be a stiff politeness between them, but no warmth.'

'Well, if it comes to that, Catherine, your mother doesn't seem to have quite taken to me. Mind you, I can hardly blame her after the way I treated you.'

'Don't worry. She's thawing. I heard her showing off to her great friend, Agatha, that you were quite the hero in the Naval Armoured Car Division.'

'I'm sorry, Catherine, but I fail to see the significance.'

'If you recall, her friend's nephew is Mister Cherry Apsley-Garrard, the polar explorer.'

'I do… and?'

'Well, it seems that he's joined the Armoured Car Division, too, so you're suddenly *de rigeur*. All you have to do to butter up Mummy now is to tell a few tales of your experiences last year. Their repetition will keep her and Agatha entertained for hours. It's a pity you've never flown across the Antarctic. You'd instantly be the hero.'

'I see,' Paul murmured quietly. 'At least your father seems much more relaxed about me.'

'I think Daddy has always liked you… ever since that day we first met when you dropped in on us.'

'Yes, I did *drop in* on you, as it were. But for my misfortune with my engine, I might never have met you, Catherine Miller. To think, only yesterday you were plain Catherine Edgar.'

'Hey. Less of the plain, thank you. I might still be a bit roly-poly, but…' Paul pulled her towards him and kissed her.

'No. There's nothing plain about you. And you'll soon lose that weight once you're back riding.'

'I will. I'll be sure to be slim again for you on your next leave. Then we can have a proper wedding night.' She nibbled the remains of Paul's right ear gently.

Paul squeezed her waist tightly. 'I shall look forward to it, but we can't hurry that. Remember what the doctor said.'

'I know, but I'll soon be well again. And in any case, I don't want to give you any excuses to seek out the Belgian *mademoiselles*. Come on. Let's go back to your parents. It suddenly seems ghoulish to be standing out here watching the East End burn.'

If you enjoyed *The Wings of the Wind,* please share your thoughts on Amazon and/or Goodreads by leaving a review.

For the next instalment of the *For Those in Peril* series, read *Where the Baltic Ice is Thin.*

Follow Shaun Lewis on Twitter @shaunlewis1805
On Facebook @shaunlewis-theauthor
Website www.shaunlewis-theauthor.com

Author's Note

In this novel, my plot has been less constrained by the timeline of historical events. Even so, I have stuck to Ian Fleming's maxim that, *'Everything I write has a precedent in truth'*. I could have based my plot on the many heroic adventures of the legendary Air Commodore Charles Samson, whose real experiences on their own would make a fascinating book. However, it suited me better to place my flawed hero, Paul Miller, elsewhere in mid-1915, so that he is positioned to relate the tale of other RNAS courageous exploits in a subsequent novel.

The parts of the novel describing the historic events on board the *Hibernia* and at Brooklands are based on fact. Similarly, the descriptions of service in armoured cars in France and Belgium, and the Royal Naval Division's rear guard action at Antwerp in late 1914, are closely aligned with the actual history, although I have played around with dates by a few days here and there. Even though difficult to find, Samson's autobiography, *Fights and Flights* is fascinating reading. More easily available is John Oliver's *Samson and the Dunkirk Circus*. The actions of the fictional Manchester Hussars are not related to those of the Oxfordshire Yeomanry who actually served under Samson.

My portrayal of the raid on Friedrichshafen is largely accurate, but obviously, there was no Paul Miller on the raid. Shepherd did, indeed, fall ill, but the replacement pilot damaged his aircraft on take-off and was not able to participate in the operation. The tale of Paul's escape from Belgium is purely fictional, but is inspired by real events. The Belgian population was extremely badly treated by the German invaders and several thousand courageous civilians helped the allies in many ways, not just in repatriating allied soldiers and airmen to safety, but in providing vital intelligence. Edith Cavell's contribution to the war effort is already well known, but it is worth researching *La Dame Blanche* for more information on the courageous work done by the Belgian civilian population. The enormously long electric fence was built to hamper this resistance work.

As for John Miller's adventures, I have based some on my own naval experiences and abstracted the theme of the tedium of life as a midshipman in a cruiser from Alexander Scrimgeour's diaries. The hunt for the *Goeben* is very well covered in Barbara Tuchman's *The Guns of August*.

I will now leave Paul to rest awhile. My next novel, *Where the Baltic Ice is Thin*, continues the story of his elder brother Richard, this time in command of his submarine flotilla in Russia.

About the Author

Shaun Lewis was born in Rutland and educated in Shropshire and Scotland before joining the Royal Navy at Britannia Royal Naval College, Dartmouth. In a career lasting twenty years, he served in surface ships and submarines, as well in appointments as a Chinese Mandarin interpreter and intelligence. He now lives in Lancashire with his wife, Hilary, and enjoys walking, fly fishing and cricket. He is the author of four other naval thrillers.

www.ingramcontent.com/pod-product-compliance
Lightning Source LLC
Chambersburg PA
CBHW071131200626
46817CB00018B/2665